MOUSE HUNTER

Jon Traer, M.D.

Published by Jon Traer, M.D.
2383 Julienton Drive, N.E.
Townsend, GA 31331-5021
USA

www.jontraer.com

Publisher's Note:
Mouse Hunter is a work of fiction. Characters, places, and incidents
mentioned are the product of the author's imagination, or are used fictitiously.
Any resemblance to persons living or dead, or to businesses, establishments
and locales is entirely coincidental. U.S. federal entities mentioned in this book actually
exist; however, their actions and interactions as portrayed here should be considered fiction.
The medical information regarding hantavirus infections in humans is partially accurate,
but should not be construed as medical fact or advice for the treatment and prevention of such
infections in humans.

Cover Design:
Front and back cover designs are by the author. Electron microscopic image of the
hantavirus (background of front cover) is from public domain files produced by the
Center for Disease Control and Prevention in Atlanta, Georgia. Biohazard symbol and mouse
photos are from public domain files available on the Internet.

ISBN-13: 978-1463723118
ISBN-10: 1463723113

Pagination by
Darien Printing & Graphics
Darien, Georgia
USA

Printed by CreateSpace
Charleston South Carolina
USA

Available at www.jontraer.com

Also by Jon Traer, M.D.

Going to the Gradies

Beyond the Gradies

Beyond Beyond

ACKNOWLEDGMENTS

We do not create terrorism by fighting the terrorists.
We invite terrorism by ignoring them. –George W. Bush, 2005

A simple quote can reflect a mindset I personally find worth acknowledging. It is this certain way of thinking about terrorism that has encouraged me to write this short novel about bioterrorism.

Admittedly, I find myself disappointed when I don't see this mindset in some of our elected political leaders. On the other hand, I'm inspired when I see this mindset embodied by many of our ordinary citizens, especially ones who elect to get personally involved in our antiterrorism efforts when presented with a chance to do so. Fortunately, I clearly see this mindset in our military and federal law enforcement professionals. I see it at facilities dedicated to the training of these brave men and women who have chosen not to *invite* terrorism by *ignoring* terrorism; instead they have dedicated themselves to fighting it. All too often, while fighting terror, they make the ultimate sacrifice: their lives. Words alone cannot reflect my gratitude for their diligence in doing a job that must be done; it must be done if civilization in America is to survive as we know it today.

Though *Mouse Hunter* will be the fourth novel I've published, I realize I am a little-known amateur hobby writer. I still need assistance, especially when it comes to converting a manuscript into a finished product. I thank Wendy Johnson at Darien Printing & Graphics for her pagination and getting things ready for print. To Ron Fleury, Dr. Daniel Good, Gene Wesolowski, and Jerry Cummings, many thanks for suggestions and the hours of proofreading. To Miguel A. Cruz-Lopez, many thanks for help with the Spanish language elements in this book. Any residual typographical and grammatical errors are my own. To Kaye, my hazel-eyed sweetheart and wife: Many thanks for keeping the honey-do list short and under control during the time it took me to write *Mouse Hunter*.

AUTHOR'S NOTE

The fictional account of the particular attempted bioterrorism attack depicted in this novel has not yet happened; however, as a physician, I feel it is within the realm of scientific possibilities. To realize that a potential bioterrorist has many different organisms that could be used to inflict terror and death, one needs only to recall the "anthrax letters" of 2001.

This novel is not about a microorganism that is as well-known as anthrax; it is about the Sin Nombre virus, a Spanish name meaning "without name." Among today's doctors, this virus is more commonly known as "hantavirus." That virus *naturally* exists here in the U.S. One of its more common natural hosts in the wild is the white-footed deer mouse pictured on the back cover of this book. Except for parts of the Southeast, that mouse is found throughout most of United States east of the Rocky Mountains.

In May,1993, the Center for Disease Control and Prevention (CDC) in Atlanta, recorded an outbreak of a previously unknown pulmonary illness in the Southwestern United States. A cluster of cases soon followed in an area shared by Arizona, New Mexico, Colorado and Utah. That area is commonly known as "The Four Corners." The first known victim was a young physically fit Navajo man suffering from shortness of breath. He was rushed to a hospital in New Mexico and died very rapidly. Unfortunately, a number of other fatal cases soon followed. Initially, this "new" illness left physicians and researchers baffled. They soon discovered evidence of hantavirus in tissues of the human victims. Additional research indicated an identical virus could frequently be found in the tissues of the otherwise healthy population of local white-footed deer mice. Thus, the mouse-to-man transmission was soon established.

Humans infected with certain strains of hantavirus develop what is called hantavirus pulmonary syndrome, or HPS for short. This illness causes a severe lung failure that is fatal in approximately half the patients who acquire it. HPS causes human lungs to fill with fluid and rapidly lose the ability to extract oxygen from the air breathed in by the patient. Some have likened it to "drowning with your head above water." While the natural occurrence of HPS is still relatively rare in the United States, *there is no treatment except for supportive care* in a hospital setting.

For readers living in the Southeastern United States, there is less concern they will acquire a hantavirus infection from their *natural* environment. But what if a bioterrorist should decide to transport hantavirus to your area, and then intentionally distribute it in a way that would expose you to it? Should you be frightened? Should you run if you trap (or see) a cute little gray-brown mouse with white feet and belly? You bet you should! And report it to the CDC's Special Pathogens Branch in Atlanta. Why? Your local environment might contain mice carrying hantavirus, and you could have been exposed to it. You don't need to panic and develop an abnormal fear of mice; you don't need to become a "musophobe," as such persons are called by our psychiatric brethren. Just be observant, report your observations to the proper authorities, and try to avoid breathing air in mouse-infested surroundings, especially dusty ones.

At the time of this writing, ongoing research is being aimed at developing a vaccine that will offer humans long-term (possibly lifetime) immunity against HPS. If/when that vaccine is developed and administered to a given population, the bioterrorists' arsenal will have lost yet another weapon among the many microorganisms they could have chosen to inflict terror and death. Additional research is being done to find an effective antiviral drug to be administered to the unfortunate few already infected with hantavirus. Hopefully, these advances will change the grim outlook associated with this rare disease.

PROLOGUE

Early July, 2001: A retired surgeon and his wife, a nurse, were now in their fourth year of "living a lie." Together, they lived it every single day of those four years. In their make-believe world they often felt like Gypsies as they roamed the United States in their 1997 Fleetwood Discovery motorhome. For the last two weeks their RV had been parked at the Gallup RV Park in New Mexico, just off historic U.S. Route 66, perhaps better known today as I-40. July's triple-digit midday temperatures held the park's visitors to a minimum at that time of year. The couple cared less. That meant fewer people they'd have to lie to about their true identity.

In most RV parks and campgrounds the retired medical couple invariably ran into other retirees with interesting and diverse backgrounds. Some were people they would have liked to befriend, or at least get to know well enough to engage in honest conversations in a social setting. But they had truthful conversations with virtually no one. There was, however, *one exception:* They spoke truthfully to their assigned member of the U.S. Marshals Service, the federal entity that had originally encouraged them to voluntarily agree to live the lie their whole existence had now become. Once each week they were required to use a secure satellite phone, or "satphone," one that had been issued to them by the U.S. Marshals Service. They used that phone to truthfully report their exact location, the status of their health, and give their personal assessment of any "potential threats" they encountered.

It had now been four long years since they had entered WITSEC, a federal witness protection program. They'd served as noncriminal witnesses for federal prosecutors, and had been required to use their real names during the trial; therefore, their true identity was known not only to those actually on trial, but it was also known to those criminals' accomplices who'd escaped prosecution. Retribution was feared. As valuable witnesses, they had been carefully escorted to and from court sessions by various U.S. Marshals Service officers. Between court dates, they had been sequestered in a government-owned safe house in Richmond Hill, Georgia. Two U.S. Marshals, their so-called "house marshals," had actually lived in-house with them 24/7 at the safe house.

The actual trial had taken place at the federal courthouse in Brunswick, Georgia, about an hour's drive south of their Richmond Hill safe house. Following the conclusion of a long but successful prosecution of the drug smugglers, the couple had reluctantly agreed to having their identity changed. Upon leaving the safe house, they immediately entered the "freedom" of the WITSEC program for continued post-trial protection. Their testimony had indeed been invaluable, and provided eyewitness accounts and photographic evidence regarding a portion of the drug-smuggling operation, one that had occurred in very close proximity to their former retirement home at Dunham Point in McIntosh County, Georgia.

The retired couple had loved their McIntosh retirement home, but their fear of criminal retaliation overpowered any sense of safety and comfort if they continued to live there following the trial. Initially, the couple harbored great fear of reprisal from the main criminal elements being prosecuted: members of Mexico's Sinaloa Cartel. In addition, they feared two McIntosh County Sheriff's Deputies, who, to a lesser extent, had been involved in the drug smuggling scheme. Prompted mostly by fear for their personal safety, they sold their retirement home, voluntarily entered WITSEC, and they'd since lived in their *only* home, a 37-foot diesel-powered Fleetwood Discovery RV. They knew the WITSEC program would not allow them to leave the Continental U.S. Neither would it allow them to travel within the U.S. to visit and communicate with family members, not even old trusted friends. They could not disclose the fact that their true names had been legally changed. They could not reveal that WITSEC had provided them with multiple documents to prove the "identity lie" they now lived. Despite the beauty of the America Southwest—and most of the rest of the country they had traveled—they now struggled with one major emotion. It was no longer fear of being harmed by criminals; it was *boredom.*

In the RV's efficient galley, Kristin (her WITSEC name) had quickly prepared their breakfast. Over their scrambled eggs, bacon, toast, OJ, and coffee, Kristin sighed, looked down, and began fidgeting with the napkin in her lap.

"What's wrong, honey?" her husband asked, seeking an explanation for her odd behavior.

"I'm getting bored out of my mind, Little Man," she shot back, fighting tears, and using her favorite pet name for him. "Bored! So bored I think it's getting to me mentally! I feel like a social hermit. Every time we try to make friends, we lose them because we're so inhibited in what we can tell them."

They both stood so they could embrace over the RV's narrow dinette table. "Me too, honey," he replied. "I think this 37-footer has started shrinking about an inch each day."

"Well, let's just tell them we want *out* of their damned WITSEC program! We were told our being in the program was *voluntary*. I'm tired of telling lies to nice people. I'm tired of being 'Kristin,' and want my old name back. I want my hair to be blond and long again. I'm sick and tired of using Clairol to keep it red. I want to see my family again. I want you to call me 'Anne' again, especially when we make love. I want to be Mrs. Anne Telfair again. I want you to be my 'Mark' again. I want to—"

"Quit living the lie!" he finished for her, as they stepped away from the dinette to the RV's aisle, where they enjoyed the consolation full-body contact had always provided when they hugged. Anne dried her eyes with a napkin snatched from the dinette, then gave him a long deep kiss.

Before speaking, he loosened his embrace, then held her at arm's length, and peered into her beautiful hazel eyes. "No matter what, remember I love you. Even with short red hair. And when you let it grow out I'll love you still, even if it'll mostly be gray."

"Promise, Little Man?"

"You bet. And we're supposed to report to the Marshals Service tomorrow morning, even though I know damn well that GPS they put on the roof of our RV tells them exactly where we are."

"When you call them on the satphone tomorrow, will you inquire about the procedure for getting us *out* of WITSEC?"

"Yes. I'm beginning to feel exactly the way you do. Bored. And I don't want a good-looking woman that's taller than I am pissed off at me! I don't want you to beat me up!"

"Little Man, I'd never intentionally harm you physically ... though I think we've tried to screw each other to death a time or two!"

"No complaints from me. Glad we've still got the 'horny gene' we both must have been born with," he replied. They began laughing while retreating to the RV's bedroom for a quickie beneath its mirrored ceiling. The customary nap that followed their lovemaking was interrupted by someone outside frantically pounding on their RV's door.

1

The pounding continued. Mark jumped out of bed, quickly donned knee-length shorts, sans his Jockey shorts, then quickly pulled a T-shirt over his head as he slid his feet into flip-flops, and quickly paddled up the aisle to their RV's door. In passing the galley he quickly removed the little .38 Smith & Wesson they kept in their silverware drawer and slid it into the cargo pocket of his baggy shorts.

The urgent knocking on the door continued. Mark cautiously opened the door, just a crack at first, having no idea what awaited him on the other side.

"Thank goodness you are home! I hate to disturb you this way, but I knew you were home because you're plugged in and your AC is running!" the man blurted. His speech was accented English, though easily understood.

Mark found himself briefly speechless as he studied the short olive-skinned man in his early 50s. The stranger wore shorts similar to his own, but he also had on sand-colored boots that came to his knees, appearing to be snake leggings of some sort. His safari-style khaki shirt was sweat stained in spots, otherwise clean. Though clean-shaven and beardless, his long gray hair was pulled back in a ponytail that protruded beneath the brim of his tan pith helmet. Dark sunglasses made it impossible to evaluate his eyes. In his right hand, the stranger held a dusty white cloth sack of some sort.

"Uh … what can I do for you?" Mark asked, still cautiously observing the "strangeness" of the stranger. The man quickly removed his sunglasses, but his eyes remained dark pools of mystery, revealing nothing. "What can I do for you?" Mark again asked.

The strange man attempted a smile, then said, "Well, actually I'm a biologist, one who's in a bit of a bind at the moment. I'm down on Pad 128, and my AC isn't working. I think I've got a blown 50-amp buss fuse in my Winnebago's panel. Earlier today I checked, and the RV park store doesn't have any more of them left in stock. You wouldn't happen to have a spare, would you? I'll be glad to pay you generously."

Mark paused, pretending to be thinking about any spare fuses he might have. He was positive he had several in his small tool box, but his next words were a little slow in coming: "What's your name, and what have you got in that sack that looks like a pillowcase? It looks to me like there's something moving inside it."

"Oh that! Let me explain. My name is Dr. Al Abbas. I'm a virologist, a Ph.D., and currently work at the University of Arizona in Tucson. This is indeed a pillowcase I'm holding, and inside it I have a number of white-footed deer mice I've trapped during the cool night. They are very sensitive to high temperatures, and it looks like I'm going to be unable to keep them cool enough to survive the trip back to my lab in Tucson ... unless I can get the AC in my RV to work. It's already well over 100 degrees inside my camper now. Please help me, if you can."

Mark glanced at the table beneath the awning extending from the top edge of his RV's roof. A large round thermometer resting on a table beneath the awning indicated it was already 103 degrees in the shade. It was only 9:15. Mark finally spoke. "Let me go inside first, to be sure my wife is dressed. Then we'll step inside my RV to keep your mice cool. Then I'll check my toolbox for that fuse you need."

Mark briefly stuck his head inside the RV's door to alert his wife to the fact they were going to have a visitor. She quickly dressed and moments later opened the RV's door to signal she was now acceptably clothed for "company." Mark and Dr. Abbas stepped inside the Fleetwood Discovery to be greeted by delightfully cool 68-degree air.

"Oh, thank you so very much for your kindness! Especially the coolness inside your impressive motorhome. I'm sure my mice will appreciate the reduction in temperature, even if they don't realize what an exquisite RV you have here," Dr. Abbas replied, resting the squirming pillowcase on the aisle floor next to the dinette. "I'm sorry but I didn't catch your name ... nor that of this very beautiful woman here," the stranger said, then seemed to fix his penetrating gaze on Anne's anatomy in a sexual way.

"My name is 'Jon,' and this is my wife, 'Mary Kristin,'" Mark replied, using their WITSEC names, not wishing to disclose any additional details about themselves.

"So, do you think you have that fuse I need?" Dr. Abbas asked.

Anne remained silent, but kept a watchful eye on the thing (or things) squirming inside the pillowcase; its open end was secured only by a single black plastic zip tie. Mark retrieved his toolbox from a closet. He quickly located the needed 50-amp fuse. He had three of them, and handed one to Dr. Abbas who expressed gratitude, then quickly retrieved his wallet to extract a crisp 20-dollar bill. Mark shook his head, held his palm outward, then said, "I need no payment. Just install it and get your camper cooled down."

"You need to know I'm not much of an electrician ... nor a mechanic. Could you possibly give me a hand?"

Mark nodded an affirmative about helping him replace the fuse.

Anne finally spoke. "Dr. Abbas, are you sure you don't have snakes in that pillowcase? I notice you are wearing things to protect your legs from snakebites."

"Mary Kristin, you are not only very beautiful, but very observant. What I have inside this pillowcase are mice. I am indeed wearing snake leggings, sometimes called 'chaps.' You see, New Mexico has over 30 species of rattlesnakes. Unfortunately, the white-footed deer mice I trap here are one of the rattler's main sources of food. Almost invariably, I'll see at least one rattlesnake when I check my Havahart traps on the cool ground in the early morning hours. I do that before the mice return to their deep burrows, which protect them from the heat of the day ... and before it gets hot enough for the rattlers to become really active."

"Honey," Mark said, "keep an eye on things here. I'm going to walk down to Pad 128 with Dr. Abbas and we'll install the fuse."

Mark and Dr. Abbas were out the door before Anne could muster the few angry words of objection she had in mind. The 50-yard walk to 128 took only a few minutes. The Winnebago's door and windows were open. It was an older model, perhaps from the late 70s Mark guessed.

When they went to the electrical panel, it was already open, and its main 50-amp fuse was missing. "That's the bad one I took out," Abbas explained, pointing to the floor. Mark saw a 50-amp fuse resting on the carpet beneath the panel. It had an opaque ceramic body, making it impossible to tell if was blown just by looking at it. Without Dr. Abbas having noticed, Mark picked it up and pocketed the "bad" fuse, then immediately stepped outside the Winnebago to verify the RV's power cord had been disconnected from the electrical box provided by the RV park. He returned to the camper and inserted the fuse he'd brought from his own toolbox. "Should be OK now, Dr. Abbas," Mark said, then instructed the Winnebago owner to reconnect his RV to the park's power box. A moment later, Mark heard the hum of the roof-top AC unit, and he began feeling cool air coming from the interior vents. *Maybe his mice will now be fine,* Mark thought.

When Mark stepped outside, Dr. Abbas was in the shade of an umbrella stuck through a hole in the center of a small circular table. He calmly sat in an aluminum folding chair while removing his snake leggings. "I can't thank you enough, Jon," Abbas said, then again offered to pay for the fuse. Mark again refused.

With Dr. Abbas in tow, Mark rapidly walked back to Pad 122 where his Fleetwood was parked. He found the door locked, a precaution he'd encouraged Anne to practice when he was not present in the camper. He then knocked on the side of the camper beneath a window. Anne's face soon appeared at the window, to verify if was Mark and Dr. Abbas. She opened the door to allow Dr. Abbas to retrieve his mice or "whatever" he had concealed inside the sack. Without words, the doctor immediately departed, slowly walking back to his Winnebago, squirming sack in hand.

From the expression on Anne's face, Mark knew his spouse was displeased with him. "Little Man, we need to talk. Like right NOW!" she loudly exclaimed.

"About what?" he replied, hoping his face was expressing the innocence he was trying to project.

"About your leaving me *alone* in this camper with a sack full of *live* God knows what! And with no gun! I checked the silverware drawer. It's gone! Or have you decided—without telling me—to keep it somewhere else."

Sheepishly, without words, Mark removed the pistol from the pocket of his shorts and placed it back in the silverware drawer. From another pocket he removed the "blown" Winnebago's fuse, and placed it on a counter in the galley.

Anne continued: "Well at least you had enough sense to carry our gun with you when you just walked off with a complete stranger. A weirdo stranger, if you ask me. Did you see the way he looked at me?"

"Anne, perhaps I didn't exercise the best judgment. We did not slip up and give Dr. Abbas our real first names, and I never mentioned our real last names either. Those short shorts and halter top you're wearing invite stares from men. But I certainly didn't like the way he looked at you either!"

Anne seemed a little calmer now, but far from being her usual calm self. "Little Man, what's that thing you just put on the counter?"

"It's the fuse that was blown. Just a different brand name than the ones I have for our camper. Electrically, it's identical to the ones we use."

"You sure it's blown?"

"Well not positive, Anne. When I replaced it with one from my own toolbox, his Winnebago's AC started working fine."

"Can you check it? To be sure it's really blown, and that this was not just some ruse to get you to leave me alone in our camper with the things he had in that sack?"

This whole thing is getting to her ... this WITSEC stuff ... the boredom. She is losing it, and becoming overtly paranoid, Mark thought. "If it'll make you feel any better, I'll get my multimeter from my toolbox and check it. I'll do that right now," he said, hoping that would give him some more "thinking time" about how to deal with his loved one, whom he feared was going off the deep end.

Five minutes later, Mark was shaking his head as Anne looked on. "The meter says there is no loss of continuity across this Winnebago's fuse."

"Meaning ...?" she asked.

"This fuse is good," Mark responded, a surprised look on his face. "I tell you what, Anne, I need to do another test. A test under load."

"Like how?"

"Like remove the 50-amp buss fuse from our own RV's panel, and substitute this one from the Winnebago. Then see if it'll function with the load of our AC running."

It took only minutes to start the "under load" test Mark had begun 15 minutes ago. *The AC in the Fleetwood functioned flawlessly!*

Anne gave Mark one of her "I told you so" looks, and went to a closet to retrieve a handheld vacuum cleaner.

2

Instead of immediately confronting Mark about the incident again, Anne busied herself using a cordless Black & Decker Dustbuster to vacuum the spot on their RV's carpet where Dr. Abbas had rested his cloth sack. While the men were busy changing the fuse in the Winnebago, she had observed a lot of rambunctious movement and had heard occasional "squeaking" noises inside the sack. As a precaution, she had a black iron skillet at the ready to smack any creature that might penetrate the thin cloth. Movement within the sack had apparently caused some dust to sift through the cloth. Whatever the dust was, it was quite fine, off-whitish in color, and looked like someone had randomly sprinkled a small amount of flour on their RV's burgundy carpet at the spot where the sack had rested. Nonetheless, the Dustbuster was quickly removing it.

Mostly to collect his thoughts, Mark had elected to take a long shower while Anne—a stickler for their RV's cleanliness—was busy with her Dustbuster. The shower's soothing water allowed his thoughts to come freely, but they were mostly questions: *Is Dr. Al Abbas really a Ph.D. biologist at the University of Arizona? Why would a biologist need wild mice, especially since all university biological labs have access to stocks of many strains of standard white mice that could be ordered from a large number of commercial breeders? Is my Anne really going off the deep end? What can I do to help her prevent it? How difficult is it going to be to get us out of WITSEC? If I move our RV now, where should we go? Is there any possibility of us ever getting a permanent real home again, one that doesn't have wheels?*

"Shit," he muttered aloud as he stepped out of the shower. He then noticed Anne standing there with a bath towel extended to him at arm's length. At least she was smiling. Without words, he accepted it and began to dry his nude body.

"Mark, I'm sorry I got so upset earlier today. I mean about us getting out of WITSEC … about how bored I've become, and about you taking our gun when you left me alone in the RV after that Dr. Abbas showed up."

"No apology needed, honey. I now feel the same way you do about WITSEC. I wonder what became of the other witnesses that were with us in the Richmond Hill safe house? That Dr. Roberson, the biologist … and Oscar, the old black waterman? I think Oscar was 83 when we left the safe house. He could even be dead by now. Dr. Roberson must be in his 50s by now. Heck, I'll be 60 next month, and you'll be 54!"

"Well, we're both Leos … so 'happy birthday' a little ahead of time. But Mark, tomorrow you're still gonna call about the possibility of getting us out of WITSEC, aren't you? That's the only birthday present I want."

"Yes, I'll bring that up when I call. I think we should at least explore that as an option."

* * *

To relieve boredom, the couple decided to take a walk about 30 minutes before sunset. Mark noted the heat of the day was fading fast as he and Anne began their arm-in-arm stroll. "That's where Dr. Abbas had his old Winnebago parked this morning," Mark commented, as they passed Pad 128. "Wonder if he's now on his way to Tucson with his mice?"

"Little Man, I could care less, as long as the darn things are not in *our* camper!"

"Wonder how far Tucson is from Gallup?" Mark asked. "Gotta be over 250 miles … maybe five or six hour's drive time," Mark guessed.

"Why don't we walk up to the convenience center for the park? We can see if they have a registry that might show exactly when that so-called Dr. Abbas checked out. I'm sorry, but that guy still gives me the creeps, and I don't really know why. He never looked me in the eye, just kept staring at my cleavage! And my crotch! I want to be sure he *really* left the park," Anne said.

Mark could not help but think: *She does have nice cleavage, and even I can't resist looking! But her paranoia is still there. Best we confront that head on.* "Sure, honey. We can do that," Mark replied. "It's only a short walk."

Arriving at the park's convenience center a few minutes later, Mark approached the handsome young male attendant on duty and spoke: "I realize this may be a strange request, but may we look at your registration book and see who's on Pad 128?"

"Sir, you don't want to file a complaint, do you?" the young attendant asked, a look of concern on his face.

"Oh, no! Nothing like that," Mark assured. "I just met the fella this morning, and helped him with a little electrical problem in his camper. Said he was a biologist and didn't know much about electrical things."

"What kind of electrical problem?" the clerk asked, possibly concerned about a potential fire hazard in the park.

"Well, at first he thought he had a blown 50-amp fuse in his camper's panel. Turned out it was OK. He told me you guys were out of fuses here in the store, so I gave him one of my spares," Mark explained.

"I don't understand that!" the attendant replied. "I haven't had a single request for a fuse of any size today. Besides, I've got plenty of the 50-amp jobs in stock."

Anne looked at Mark. She then cast her eyes to the park's registration book. Conspicuously, it rested on the end of the counter. *Better check it ... to keep Anne satisfied,* Mark thought. He quickly leafed through the large book, and located a sub-registry for Pad 128. Dr. Al Abbas had signed in two days ago, and signed out at noon today. Upon arrival he'd indicated his camper was a 27-foot 1978 Winnebago, and carried an Oshawa, Ontario license tag, NKK-008. No permanent address, forwarding address, or contact information was in the spaces provided. *Strange,* Mark thought.

"May I ask why you're so interested in the fellow who checked out of 128 today?" the curious young clerk asked.

"I can't quite put my finger on it," Mark replied. "The fellow said he was trapping white-footed deer mice for some 'lab studies' at the University of Arizona."

"Well I certainly hope that's not the case!" the clerk replied. "It's illegal. I majored in biology in college. Not all the white-footed mice are endangered, but the specific subspecies we have here at this RV park are definitely on the endangered species list! Our local mice have been tested, and the ones we have here don't carry any known diseases. They just serve as food for our rattlesnakes and a few hawks. Believe me, I know what I'm talking about. As I said, my college major was biology, but I'm now in graduate school at UA in Tucson, and working on my doctorate in molecular biology. I'm just working in this RV park for the summer trying to put together a little extra money for my fall semester expenses. I've never heard of a Dr. Abbas being on the faculty there, but then there are certainly a lot of professors I haven't met yet."

"Thanks for the information" Mark said, extending his hand to the nice-looking young man. My name is Jon, and this is my wife Mary Kristin," Mark said, using their WITSEC names.

The tall buzz-cut blond blue-eyed youngster also extended his hand. "I'm Bradley Buck, but my friends call me 'BB' or 'Brad.' I know you've been with us a couple of weeks now, but I don't think I was on duty the day you checked in at the park. I'm sorry I can't control the temperature here, but otherwise I hope you guys are enjoying your stay here at Gallup."

* * *

Mark and Anne soon left the convenience center. They'd purchased a couple of cold Cokes, and began walking slowly back to their RV parked on Pad 122.

Anne took a sip of her Coke, cleared her throat and spoke. "Honey, I know you think I'm a little paranoid. Well, maybe more than just a little. But you've gotta admit some of this does not add up. About that Dr. Abbas, I mean."

"Well, maybe so. Just remember the name Bradley Buck, and that Ontario tag number … uh, KKK-008 wasn't it?"

"No, Little Man. It was 'NKK' … not 'KKK.' But at least you got the numbers right!"

"Anne, I wish I had *your* memory. That's one reason I'd never cheat on you. You'd catch me for sure!"

She gave him a playful slap, then a kiss on the cheek. "You know I'm all the woman you can handle, and I'll see to it you don't have to go looking elsewhere! And even at 60 you're still all the man I'll ever need."

They both smiled, briefly kissed again, and resumed their stroll and talk.

Mark continued: "It does seem odd that Dr. Abbas would be driving an RV with a Canadian license plate … but I guess he could have borrowed it from a friend."

"Maybe so," Anne replied.

"I think there's an Internet connection at our pad. I guess we could connect our laptop, get online, and check the University of Arizona's website. Just see if we can find a Dr. Al Abbas listed among the professors there."

Anne smiled. "Is my paranoia rubbing off on you?"

"For the moment I'd prefer to call it *curiosity.*"

As soon as they arrived at their RV, Mark entered and quickly returned with their recently purchased laptop computer. He placed it on the table beneath their camper's awning, and soon made the necessary connection to the park's provided outlet. Now dark, it was a pleasant 72 degrees beneath the camper's awning. In no time they were comfortably surfing the net. They soon located UA's website and discovered the university had an extensive posting on the web. There was even a second campus south of Tucson located at Sierra Vista, a few miles from the Mexican border. Mark, with Anne still looking on, soon learned their biology department was quite large and had numerous subdivisions. The very last subdivision they searched was known as UA's "Department of Molecular and Cellular Biology." Apparently there was no "Dr. Abbas" listed anywhere, on *either* of UA's campuses.

Anne finally spoke. "Still think I'm paranoid?"

Mark didn't answer her question but looked at his watch: 9:00. "Let's walk back to the convenience center and see if that young man is still there."

"You talking about Bradley Buck?" Anne asked.

"Yeah. Maybe we haven't looked in the right place on their website. Let's see if young Bradley can help us old folks out."

"Good idea, Little Man. These kids today know more about computers than you and I will ever learn in our remaining lifetime."

Five minutes later, laptop in hand, Mark and Anne entered the convenience center. No other customers were there. They approached the counter to find Brad talking on his cell phone. "Gotta go, sweetie. Gotta customer. Love you, too. I'll call you tomorrow about this same time." Bradley blushed. "I'm sorry, but you folks caught me talking to my girlfriend in Tucson. She's also in grad school at UA and working on her doctorate. We're both at the 'dissertation stage' in the Ph.D. process. She's doing microbiology, mainly virology. Anyway, nice to see you two again … Jon and Mary Kristin, wasn't it? Can I help you with something?"

Mark explained: "Maybe so, and sorry to interrupt your call, Brad. All we need is some information. Using our computer we've tried to find a Dr. Al Abbas on the University of Arizona's list of profs, but we can't find him."

"Which UA departments did you look under?" Brad asked.

"Biology subdivisions. Every last one of them, I think. Ended up looking at molecular and cellular biology last," Mark explained.

"Wow! That's where I am now. Molecular and cellular," Brad replied. "For a fact, I'm positive there is no 'Dr. Abbas' in *that* division.

Can't say for sure about the others, though. Mind if I use your laptop for a minute? I've got an Internet connection behind this counter. Let me give it a try."

Mark carefully placed his laptop on the counter and Bradley made the connection. In no time the kid was tapping keys and had pulled up a current alphabetical list of *all* UA professors, ones working at either the Tucson or Sierra Vista campus. No Dr. Abbas was found on either list. "Hmm," Brad said. "Let me call my girlfriend again. Maybe she knows of a Dr. Abbas in the Microbiology Division."

Mark and Anne stood silently by while Brad flipped out his cell and punched a single button. Obviously he had his girlfriend on his speed-dial list. "Hi, it's me again. I know I promised to call you tomorrow, but could you answer a quick question for me?" Brad paused and went to the registration book to check the spelling of the professor's name. "Cindy, do you recall ever hearing of a Dr. Al Abbas in the Micro Division? That's A-l, then a space, not a hyphen, then A-b-b-a-s," Brad said spelling it out for her. "He might have a doctorate tacked on to the end, like Ph.D."

There was a pause while Brad listened a few moments to his girlfriend's reply. "Three years ago? You sure?" Another pause. "That's odd!" The expression on Brad's face told Mark and Anne one thing— Bradley was truly surprised. His intense sky-blue eyes couldn't have been opened more widely. "Honey, I'll explain more when I get there this weekend. Can't wait to see you. Love ya. Bye." Brad took a deep breath and slowly exhaled while staring at Mark and Anne. Brad fell silent for a moment.

Anne finally spoke. "Well …?"

Brad took another long breath before talking. "At one time there was a professor by that name there in UA's Microbiology Department. He was there just as my girlfriend was finishing up her college at UA. As I said earlier, she's now in graduate school, too. She says about three years ago, a Dr. Al Abbas had mysteriously disappeared from campus after apparently kidnapping a graduate student coed. It seems he then fled with her to another state where he reportedly raped her. The coed somehow escaped and returned to campus, but she subsequently dropped out of school. Cindy also said a lot of high-tech lab equipment and Level 4 biocontainment cultures had apparently disappeared along with Dr. Al Abbas. She said the kidnapped coed had been his primary assistant in the virology lab. She also told me it was rumored the FBI and CIA were somehow interested in Dr. Abbas, but the whole matter had gotten quickly hushed. That's all she remembers about it. At that time I was in a different division, and I never heard anything about the event at all!"

3

After their visit with Bradley, Mark and Anne retrieved their laptop and slowly walked back to their RV. Anne was the first to speak. "Little Man, you still think I'm paranoid, don't you?"

"I'm not sure anymore, Anne. But we certainly have a lot of unanswered questions about Dr. Abbas. From my earlier conversation with him he implied he was presently an *active* professor at the University of Arizona in Tucson, and indicated he had a lab there. But now I'm not so sure that's true, at least not at the present time. The Canadian plates on his RV might have some benign explanation, but that still leaves me with questions in my mind. Also the 'blown fuse' that really wasn't 'blown' is troubling to me."

"How about the lie Abbas told us? Doesn't that bother you, Mark?" Anne asked.

"Which one?"

"The one about the convenience center not even having the fuse in stock. I don't think Bradley was telling a lie when he said no one had even inquired about a fuse today."

"Perhaps you're right, Anne. But last time we started questioning things that didn't make complete sense, what happened to us?" Mark asked.

"We ended up getting so intrigued, we found ourselves involved in trying to solve a drug-smuggling mystery ... then ended leaving our coastal Georgia retirement home, and wound up in this darn WITSEC program! Mark, you're still gonna report to our marshal in the morning, aren't you?"

"Sure! Remind me to put our satphone on charge tonight when we get back to the camper."

* * *

The couple fixed themselves double martinis soon after returning to their RV. Mark put their satphone on its charger, while Anne microwaved a TV dinner. Mark toyed with the idea of again using their laptop to see what else they could find about Dr. Al Abbas on a Google search. Anne quashed the idea. "Little Man, we need food and sleep. Let's just eat, and set our alarm for 7:00 a.m. I've got a sneaky feeling our boredom is about to end."

They had slept soundly when the alarm faithfully signaled at seven. Anne put on coffee, while Mark prepared to make his required satphone call to Clinton Salizar, their designated "contact U.S. Marshal." For the last six months Clinton, a.k.a. "Clint," had been the assigned marshal that monitored their whereabouts. Neither Anne nor Mark had ever laid eyes on the man, but surmised he was a younger marshal who had gotten stuck with the menial task of keeping up with those in the government's WITSEC program.

Promptly at 7:00, Mark punched numbers into his satphone. It was answered on the first ring: "Good morning, Jon. I hope all is well with you and Kristin. I've currently got you at latitude 35.5087, longitude 108.4373. That puts you guys still at that Gallup RV Park in New Mexico. How's the weather there?"

"Hotter'n hell," Mark laughed. "But it really gets cool at night. Beautiful area, otherwise. And Clint, I hope you've got more than the usual five minutes you allow for this call."

"I've gotta tight schedule this morning, but if we run over a little I'll still be OK time wise. Whatcha need?" Clint asked.

"First of all," Mark began, "the boredom of being in WITSEC is getting to both of us, especially Kristin. What is the procedure for us getting *out* of the program?"

Clint paused for several moments, apparently thinking. "Jon, you and Mary Kristin have a pretty thick file with the Service. I'd have to review it at length and figure out exactly which legal procedures we'd need. In addition, there'll be a slew of new identity docs you guys should have. Are you two absolutely positive you want out? It could take a month or two to get it done. I don't need to remind you that you two are close to the Mexican border, and it was mainly that Mexican drug cartel the Service felt was most likely to recognize and harm you. Why don't you guys move closer to the center of the U.S. before we undo anything?"

"We can certainly do that, Clint. Any suggestions?" Mark asked.

"I don't know, maybe Utah, Colorado, Wyoming … somewhere farther from the Mexican border. I personally wasn't too happy about you guys going to Gallup in the first place, but I got overruled by my boss. Have you guys seen many Mexicans in Gallup?"

"Virtually none," Mark responded. "At least not anywhere near the

RV park. We've previously been in Wyoming RV parks a time or two, and they were nice. Days are usually much cooler, there. From here, it would take us a couple of days to get to central Wyoming where it's flat. The Rocky Mountains are not the most fun drive in a 37-foot RV!"

"I can only imagine," Marshal Clinton Salizar replied. "Let me get the ball rolling by doing some research in your Service File. I'll expect a call from you at 0700 three days from now. That OK?"

"Sure. I'll call even if we're on the road by then. And I've got something else I want to mention before we get off this secure phone. Yesterday, Mary Kristin and I ran into a strange man, a Dr. Al Abbas. Met him right here at the Gallup RV park."

"You think he may be a threat?"

"Don't know," Mark honestly responded. "But there are a number of things about that particular man that just don't add up."

"Such as?" Salizar asked.

Mark next gave the marshal their observations about things that didn't fit. He included the apparent lie about the blown fuse, the Winnebago's Canadian tag number, and the Dr.'s apparent trapping of mice that were on the endangered species list. Mark next mentioned they could not validate his claim of being a current professor at the University of Arizona, not even after thoroughly searching UA's website. Because the marshal interrupted him a time or two to clarify spelling and numbers, Mark assumed Salizar was taking notes.

"Very interesting!" Clint replied. "I'll put some guys on it, and let you know what we find when we talk next. I personally hope you'll be in Wyoming by then. And by the way, Wyoming's Hispanic population is nil. And you guys still have no health issues, right?"

Mark laughed, then said, "Only boredom, perhaps a touch of paranoia, and maybe a little depression. I think we can handle those on our own."

Salizar, too, laughed on his end, then said, "Remember 0700, in three days."

The phone then went silent, letting Mark know Salizar had hung up. *Probably already jabbering to some other poor soul trapped in WITSEC,* Mark thought.

Anne had been at Mark's side during the entire satphone conversation. She insisted Mark recount the whole of Salizar's message, especially the part about getting them out of WITSEC.

"Well, what did he say about getting us out?" Anne immediately asked.

"He said he has to review our WITSEC files, and we're to contact him in three days. Might take a month or two to do all the legal stuff and get us new identity documents. He also suggested we move farther away from the Mexican border, but I don't think it had anything to do with Dr. Abbas. He seemed more concerned about our proximity to Mexico, which makes us closer to elements of the Sinaloa Cartel," Mark explained.

"What did Salizar say about that oddball … that Dr. Abbas?" Anne asked. "I heard you give him the details about the things we thought were strange."

"His only comments were *'Very interesting,'* and that he'd 'put some guys on it.' That's all he had to say."

"So, Little Man, you think we should move?"

"I'm sure that would please Salizar. If we follow his suggestion— like kiss his ass a little—maybe the Marshals Service will be a little more cooperative about getting us out of WITSEC."

* * *

Mark and Anne spent most of the remainder of the day preparing to put their RV back on the road again. They'd agreed on Wyoming as a destination that would please not only themselves, but hopefully Marshal Salizar as well.

Using their laptop, Anne did the "map work," plotting a course that would avoid the worst of the mountains, ones she knew Mark hated because he couldn't use cruise control and the RV's fuel efficiency dropped off to a measly four or five miles per gallon.

Mark emptied their septic holding tank, took on a full tank of fresh water, checked propane levels, changed oil and filters for their diesel engine and diesel generator, checked radiator coolant levels, even checked all tire pressures, including the two rarely used bicycles strapped to the rear of their RV.

As the day cooled near sunset, the couple decided to walk to the convenience center at the Gallup RV Park. Both Mark and Anne smiled when they saw Bradley Buck behind the store's counter talking on his cell. Brad put his thumb over the mouthpiece, and said, "Girlfriend, again. Be with you guys in a sec."

Mark and Anne chuckled, then moved to another area of the store to allow Bradley a little privacy. Anne whispered, "You remember how it was before we were married and were separated … and you were in the Air Force up there in Michigan, and I was still stuck in Atlanta?"

"Honey," Mark whispered back, "if we ever get separated again, I think I'd still call you every day." His heartfelt words obviously pleased her. She squeezed his hand and gave him a quick peck on the cheek.

Bradley terminated his call with another "love ya," then turned his attention to Mark and Anne. "Good to see you, Jon. You too, Mary Kristin. What can I do for you?"

Mark answered, "Brad, we just wanted to stop by and let you know we'll be pulling out early in the morning."

"Heat getting to ya?" Brad asked.

"Well that and boredom," Mark replied. "And I need to pay you for a dumping fee, and get paid up on anything else I might owe the park."

"It's $2.50 for the dump, and if you pull out before 10:00 a.m. tomorrow, you won't get charged for an additional day. You've prepaid the daily fee through today. You don't owe anything else."

While handing Mark the change from a five-dollar bill, Bradley said, "Darn! I almost forgot. That Dr. Abbas came by here about one o'clock today and gave me an envelope. He said to give it to the customers who had their RV on Pad 122. He even wrote 'For Jon and Kristin, Pad 122' on the outside." Bradley opened the cash register again, retrieved a sealed white envelope and handed it to Mark.

"Thanks," Mark said as he accepted it, and stuffed it into a hip pocket of his jeans. "What was he driving when he came by? That older Winnebago?"

"Didn't see a vehicle. Just walked up, as far as I could tell," Bradley explained.

"Did he say anything else?" Anne piped in.

"He indicated it was just some money he owed you two. That's all," Brad replied.

Mark and Anne stared at each a brief moment before Mark spoke: "Very interesting, Brad. Did he do anything else while he was here in the store?"

"Well, I was with another customer, but I noticed he went to our registration book and wrote something down on a separate piece of paper."

"Brad, mind if the wife and I look and see if he left any forwarding information?" Mark asked. "When we looked at the book yesterday we noticed he left those spaces blank." When they looked again, Abbas had recorded no new information; the space for "forwarding information" still remained totally blank. *I bet he got the tag number for our RV, and probably wrote down our full WITSEC names,* Mark thought, now wondering if Anne's paranoia was contagious.

"Be my guest. Check the book all you want. The park owners certainly don't consider the information in there confidential," Brad said, as he slid the large black book directly in front of Mark. "We don't allow customers to put their e-mail addresses in it, but phone numbers and physical addresses are OK. In fact, the cops occasionally look at it when they're looking for somebody. You guys aren't retired cops, are you?"

"No. We're retired medical folks. I did surgery, the wife surgical nursing. We're just interested in Dr. Abbas, mainly because our encounter with him seemed so weird."

"Weird is right!" Bradley said, then laughed. "But then a lot of the profs are that way."

The convenience center remained free of other customers. Mark, Anne, and Bradley soon entered a three-way conversation. They both liked Bradley, and wished they could have been more truthful with him about their own past. Anne had discreetly nudged Mark when he'd earlier admitted he was a "surgeon," and she a "nurse." She'd given him one of her "quit giving details" looks, and rightfully so; they were, after all, still in WITSEC.

They learned Brad's girlfriend, Cynthia Loveman, or "Cindy," was an excellent student currently beginning her dissertation for her Ph.D. in microbiology. Brad was also beginning his own dissertation in molecular biology. They both hoped to marry after grad school, then enter the arena of medical research with some large pharmaceutical company. "Maybe we'll find one interested in drug and vaccine development that will hire us, and leave us well-fixed financially," Brad had explained.

Before their half-hour conversation was finally over, Bradley had given Mark and Anne his cell phone number and the address of the apartment he shared with Cindy near the UA campus in Tucson. Brad had seemed a little surprised—shocked actually—when Mark and Anne indicated they had no cell phone ... but there was no way they could admit they instead had a secure satphone, one issued to them by the U.S. Marshals Service. Nonetheless, they all agreed to stay in touch. Bradley gave them an open invitation to visit if they happened to be in the Tucson area. "Remember, we've got an extra bedroom in our apartment," Brad had said, as Mark and Anne left the convenience center.

Now slowly walking back to their RV that was "ready to roll" early the next morning, Anne silently began shedding tears.

"Honey, what's wrong now?" Mark asked. "We'll be leaving here in

18

a few hours."

"It's just the same old shit, Little Man!" Anne blurted. "You meet some fine folks, and you can't even engage them socially ... can't get to know them better. I'll bet Brad and Cindy are a very interesting couple, ones we'd like to have an honest adult professional conversation with. But what do we do? We give them first names that really aren't ours, and virtually nothing else!"

Could Anne be menopausal? Is that complicating her feelings of paranoia? Am I going to need some professional help for her? Mark's mind questioned.

Without words, Anne suddenly brushed tears from her eyes, turned, and wrapped her arms around him. She then kissed him, oblivious to another couple walking in the street. "Sorry I lost it, Little Man. I'll get it together, especially if you give me what I need in bed tonight ... before we get on the road in the morning."

4

Considering their ages, their "session" that evening was long and intense. Both were still catching their breath when Anne finally managed to speak. "Little man, I think I must be a closet voyeur."

"*Closet voyeur?*" Mark asked.

"Yeah! You know, a Peeping Tom. I never felt that way until we got this darn RV with a mirrored ceiling in our bedroom. I feel kinda kinky when I want a little light left on."

"I don't think that's necessarily 'kinky,' Anne," Mark replied. "Neither of us are exactly ashamed of our bodies, making love or not."

"But I have a confession," Anne admitted. "When I'm on the bottom, I like to watch your butt muscles contract while we're doing it. And for a 60-year-old you've still got very sexy buns!"

"Ditto your buns, on all counts … when *you're* on the top. So I guess that makes me a 'closet voyeur,' too."

They both managed a laugh, that soon faded. In five minutes they both were sound asleep.

* * *

Neither awoke during the night. When the alarm buzzed at six the next morning, both felt rested and refreshed. They'd already mutually agreed they'd leave no "forwarding information" at the convenience center when they left Gallup. They showered quickly at the RV park's community shower to conserve their own on-board water supply. A quick breakfast of cold cereal was all either wanted and they were on the road by seven, heading east on I-40 to Albuquerque.

Having arrived in Albuquerque by late morning, they picked up I-25 North, and almost made it to the Colorado line by day's end. After spending a "free night" at an I-25 rest stop, the next full day of travel placed them in Cheyenne, Wyoming, well north of the Colorado State line. Mark was quite pleased with Anne's "navigation," and her selection of excellent secondary roads that allowed them to bypass congested interstate roads through Denver.

Now using a Cheyenne Wal-Mart parking lot for the night, they ventured out of their RV to do a little shopping, but soon returned. Putting their groceries away, Anne commented, "You're supposed to call Salizar at seven tomorrow, aren't you?"

"I haven't forgotten, honey. Have you picked out an RV park for us in Wyoming yet?"

"Sure have. It's one we've never stayed in before. It's in Lander, Wyoming. Almost in the middle of the state. That should keep Marshal Salizar happy!"

"Screw Salizar!" Mark exclaimed. "What about us? We'll be the ones staying there. And we don't know for how long. What facilities do they have?"

"After I checked which roads we'd use, I also used our laptop to check their RV parks. The 'Sleeping Bear RV Park' is actually on the edge of Lander. They've got gravel pull-through pads, 50-amp electrical, water and individual septic connections ... plus *Internet* at each pad! And they've got plenty of shade trees—a big difference from hot-as-hell Gallup!"

"OK, OK! Just asking," Mark replied, a little tired after 12 hours of driving. "Do we need reservations?"

"No. Before leaving Gallup, I made them online using their website. Indefinite stay, beginning tomorrow. I made the required deposit using the credit card the Marshals Service gave us. It went right through. No problem!"

"You continue to amaze me, Anne."

* * *

Their night in Cheyenne in the Wal-Mart parking lot was not a romantic one. Both were exhausted. The sound of their alarm clock at 6:00 a.m. reminded them where they were. Neither felt ready to be awake yet. The soothing muted hum of the RV's diesel generator had kept their AC running through the night, and had tempted them to hit the alarm's snooze button. *Can't do that ... need to call Salizar at seven,* Mark remembered, as he dragged himself out of bed and checked the satphone they kept in the front of their RV. *Probably doesn't need it, but I'll put it on charge anyway,* Mark thought. He then turned his interest to his most urgent need: coffee.

After coffee and breakfast, both felt alert enough to have an intelligent phone conversation. Per usual, Marshal Salizar answered his phone on the first ring.

"Morning, Jon. You're exactly on time, 0700. I've got you at latitude 41.1577, longitude 104.8069, so that puts you in Cheyenne, Wyoming. You're currently not moving. Assuming my satellite info is correct, I see you're parked in a large parking lot, which should be at a Super Wal-Mart on the south side of Cheyenne. That correct?"

What a freaking anal nerd! Mark thought. "Yeah, that all fits. Kristin is with me, and we both feel fine. So how about getting to our question about getting out of WITSEC? You said you had to research our files. Remember? And what about that Dr. Abbas I told you about last time?"

There was a long pause on Salizar's end. At first, Mark thought it was the usual transmission-reception delay characteristic of satellite phones. "You still there?" Mark finally asked.

"Still here," Salizar said. "Just being sure your file contains signed nondisclosure agreements, and it does. Even though you two are in WITSEC, what I'm about to tell you is still covered by those NDAs signed when you two were made privy to a lot of DEA's information about that drug-smuggling operation down there in Georgia."

"We understand the NDAs are still binding. So what about our questions?" Mark asked, a little impatience edging into his voice.

Salizar began, this time with an answer: "Getting you two out of WITSEC will not be very complicated, at least not in your specific case. It's even less complicated if you two elected to change your names back to the original legal names you two had before you entered the program. Your file indicates 'Dr. Marcus Milton Telfair, M.D.' is your original, and Kristin's was 'Mrs. Anne Hunt Telfair, R.N.' Is that correct?"

"Yes. And it's nice to hear someone speak our real names. When can you get started?" Mark asked.

"Immediately. Might take about a month to six weeks to finish everything. We'll probably still need to have a face-to-face meeting with you guys to sign some papers, especially the petition to the court to change your names again. Plus I'll need to give you your new identity and other legal documents. But let me give you this warning: For now, *don't* under any circumstances use any name other than your WITSEC names. Don't do that until it's final, and you two have the supporting documents in hand to prove it. So, for right now, you're still Mr. Jon Wayne Traer, and your wife is Mrs. Mary Kristin Traer. Is that clear?"

Control freak! Mark thought, but didn't dare say it. "Yeah, that's clear."

"Now," Salizar began, "I need to appeal to your and Kristin's sense of loyalty to your country … to the *security* of our country. It seems the Dr. Al Abbas you two stumbled upon back in Gallup has been intensely hunted by the FBI for the last several years. He is a Muslim, a suspected kidnapper and rapist, and they think he could be a potential bioterrorist. He was under surveillance by the FBI while he was teaching at the University of Arizona in Tucson. After allegedly kidnapping, then raping a coed there, he disappeared into thin air. Unfortunately, he took some potentially lethal viral cultures with him when he vanished. He's a real Ph.D., a microbiologist with a special interest in virology. They know he trained at the University of Al-Madinah Al-Munawarah, an Islamic educational institution functioning on a world basis under the auspices of Saudi Arabia."

"Wow!" Mark said. "We really know how to stumble into trouble, don't we?"

"After reading your Service file, I'd say you two *definitely* have a knack for that!"

"What about that old Winnebago with the Canadian plates?"

"It was stolen in Canada, but the FBI thinks he has since changed the plates. That camper is now at some RV park in Arizona, and currently bearing Arizona plates," Salizar replied. "Abbas was apparently out in the field when agents first found it. They found the door unlocked and searched it. They feel sure it's the one you mentioned. The Canadian plates—with the numbers you previously gave me—were found inside the vehicle … along with a minilab full of live mice in cages and a lot of laboratory equipment. Fortunately, the FBI was able to stick a GPS unit on the camper without getting caught."

"So you'll be able to track him now, won't you?" Mark asked.

"The U.S. Marshals Service won't be doing the tracking. It'll be the FBI. All I'm asking is that if you see Abbas again in any park, give me a call immediately. In fact, I want you to call me on your satphone *daily* at 0700, weekends included. Understood?"

"OK by me," Mark reluctantly replied, though thinking: *control, control, control!* "Well, this sure ends our boredom, Salizar. Anything else?" Mark asked.

"Yes, a thought just struck me. You don't happen to have anything that might have his fingerprints on it, do you?"

"*His* fingerprints? You mean Dr. Abbas?"

"Yes. Like something he might have handled, before you guys left

Gallup."

"Let me think a minute," Mark said, then paused. "Well, the guy did leave a sealed envelope at the convenience center in Gallup. It was subsequently handed to me by the attendant there, and I stuffed it into a pocket of some jeans I was wearing that day. I think it's just a few bucks he felt he owed me."

"Great!" Salizar exclaimed. "If you haven't already rehandled or opened it, by all means *don't!*"

"To tell the truth, I'd forgotten all about it. I think it's still in the pocket of those jeans that are now in our dirty clothes basket," Mark explained.

"Can you check that right now?" Salizar asked. "Just to be sure it's still there? But *don't* touch it!"

"Sure. Just hold on for a second," Mark replied.

Anne wore a quizzical look while Mark quickly went to check their dirty clothes. Seconds later he returned to the phone. "Salizar, it's still there, in the hip pocket of my jeans. It's folded in half. I didn't touch it again, just looked. It's probably nothing more than a note or a small amount of paper money he felt he owed me. But why is that envelope so important?"

"It's like this: The FBI lifted prints during their brief visit to the Winnebago they found in Arizona. Unfortunately, his prints are not on *any* record the FBI can find anywhere. And it seems everything had been meticulously wiped clean at his lab in Tucson before he disappeared from there several years ago. The FBI thinks his disappearance from the UA campus was planned well in advance. The coed that states she was raped did have semen in her vagina. That means they have the DNA of the alleged rapist. You may not realize this, but when you lick an envelope to seal it, you leave a little of your body's own cells and salivary protein behind. Plus it's frequently possible to get clean prints from the *interior* of the envelope, especially from inside the flap before it was sealed."

"What do you want me to do with that envelope in the meantime?" Mark asked.

"Just keep it in the jeans where you've got it now. When you get to your next RV camp, give me a call. I'll arrange for somebody from the FBI to pick it up from you. You'll probably have to sign some chain-of-custody documents. Be sure to use your WITSEC names when you sign them. They're the only names the FBI will have for you two. If the forensic lab finds the envelope contains money, you'll be reimbursed with new money. If it contains a note, you'll be given a 'clean' typewritten transcription, and the FBI will retain the original. Is that OK?"

"That's fine with me," Mark replied.

Hearing only one side of the conversation, but apparently anticipating the need for further information, Anne hurriedly wrote the name of the RV park she'd chosen. She handed her note to Mark, who read the park's name to Salizar: "Our intended destination for today is the 'Sleeping Bear RV Park and Campground.' It's near Lander, Wyoming. I'll call you when we get there. Anything else?"

"Yes. Do you have a computer that's connected to the Internet?"

"Not while we're traveling," Mark answered, "but we can connect as soon as we get situated at the RV park in Lander. Why is that important?"

"I would like to have current photographs of both of you guys … your appearance may have changed since the photos we have in your WITSEC files," Salizar explained.

"Well, we're obviously four years older now. Instead of long blond hair, Mary Kristin now has short dark red hair, and I have a full short beard that is salt and pepper. No mustache. Otherwise we're unchanged. I'm assuming you want me to e-mail you our current photos. Is that it?" Mark asked.

"Yes," Salizar answered. "And I'll e-mail you file photos of the two FBI agents who will be meeting you at that 'Sleeping Bear' place. As it stands right now, their names will be Niccolo Drago, and Luigi Lorenzo." After Mark clarified the spelling, he wrote the names down. Salizar continued: "The pictures I'll be e-mailing to you will be the same ones Drago and Lorenzo have in their FBI credentials. Don't give that envelope to them unless you're completely satisfied they are who they say they are."

"I'll give you a call when we get there and we're connected to the Internet. Anything else?"

"No," Salizar replied.

Mark hung up the satphone, and turned to Anne to answer the "thousand questions" he knew were stored in her inquisitive mind. Following a half-hour conversation, she knew exactly what Mark knew. Her bottom lines had been, "I'll look forward to us getting out of WITSEC … but I don't feel boredom anymore," and "I don't believe I've ever met a real agent with the FBI before … but those names you wrote down—that 'Drago' and 'Lorenzo'—sound like Italian Mafia names to me!"

She's still got a little paranoia going ... but she's not nearly as bad as Marshal Clinton Salizar, Mark thought.

5

The drive to the Sleeping Bear RV Park and Campground had taken a little over eight hours. The only stop made along the way had been to top off their diesel tank about 50 miles before they'd arrived. Early on they had learned diesel prices were far cheaper on the open road at truck stops, as opposed to diesel sold at or near RV parks. Anne had done some of the driving when they were on open flat lands, and Mark actually felt half-rested when they rolled into Sleeping Bear.

They drove directly to the park's convenience center to register. There had been no glitches in the online registration process Anne had used. They quickly signed in as "Mr. and Mrs. Jon Traer," and were assigned to Pad 16. "Can't miss it," the elderly man at the registration desk had said. "It's on the very east end of the second row."

As soon as they were situated on their assigned spot they made electrical, septic, water, and Internet connections, then leveled their camper with the RV's built-in hydraulic leveling jacks. Mark made the promised satphone call to Marshal Salizar. The line was busy. He tried again at 4:30 p.m., and again at 5:00. Still busy. Finally, a few minutes after six, Salizar answered. He immediately apologized. "Sorry if you couldn't connect. Even these sophisticated secure phones the Service uses don't have a 'call waiting' function like the civvy cell phones. I've had nonstop calls from the FBI. Several different agents have called, but Agents Drago and Lorenzo are now working in central Wyoming. The Bureau says they will definitely be the ones to meet with you and Kristin at Sleeping Bear. Their ETA at Sleeping Bear will be about 2030 today, so don't move your camper unless it's essential. I'll need your e-mail address to send you their pictures, and you can use 'reply to sender' to send me current photos of you and Kristin. I trust you guys have a digital camera and know how to attach images to an e-mail."

"Salizar, it is the year 2001. We may be getting old but we are not complete techno-idiots," Mark added, a touch of sarcasm now in his voice.

"Well, be sure you don't put any text or name labels on the images!" Salizar shot back.

Mark exhaled audibly, then reluctantly gave Salizar their e-mail address, feeling that this was just one more invasion of the modicum of privacy they still had left while in WITSEC.

"How'll you know what to tell them about our location?" Mark asked.

Salizar quickly explained: "Simple ... unless that GPS on the roof of your RV craps out. You are now at latitude 42.8265, longitude 108.7186. Your RV is parked at the east end of a row between two shade trees. On satellite I can still see most of the top of your rig. From your WITSEC file, I've described your 'departing vehicle' as a 1997 bronze and white 37-foot Fleetwood Discovery motorhome, with Georgia tag RMK 1208. Has that changed? Anything I need to add?"

I'm just glad you can't see what Anne and I do in bed on the inside, Mark thought, his disdain for WITSEC swelling in his mind. "Nothing significant has changed, Salizar. But for your information there are now two bicycles secured with lockable cables to the rear of our RV." Mark mentioned that trivial point hoping to piss off Salizar a bit and let him know he still didn't know everything, despite the state-of-the-art GPS and the satellite imagery he had at his command.

* * *

Now 7:00 p.m., and knowing the arrival of the FBI could be eminent, the couple quickly made their current 'mug shots' as Salizar had requested. Mark uploaded them to their laptop, and had them ready to attach to the marshal's e-mail when it arrived. Over microwave dinners, they discussed their current situation:

"Assuming Salizar's ETA for the FBI is correct, they could be here as early as 8:30," Mark commented.

Anne sighed. "Well, we've certainly kissed Salizar's ass by complying with every single little request he has ever made. I still think I want out of WITSEC. But I have some lingering reservations."

"*Reservations?*" Mark questioned.

"Yeah. I've been thinking."

"About what?" Mark asked , taking the last bite of his Stouffer's microwaved tuna-noodle casserole.

"We don't know where things are going with this Dr. Abbas, the Ph.D. microbiologist fellow the FBI seem so interested in."

"But we haven't really gotten ourselves involved in that ... like we did with the evidence we supplied against the Sinaloa Cartel. We know Sinaloa has collapsed on the East Coast, or so the newspapers said after the trial in Georgia. Neither of us is interested in going to Mexico where that cartel is still active," Mark explained.

"Little Man, that envelope from Abbas—the one we're supposed to give the FBI—could be considered 'evidence,' don't you think?" Anne asked.

"Well, technically. I guess. Anne, are you now doing a one-eighty about us getting out of WITSEC?"

"I wouldn't go that far. Maybe we should get Salizar to continue to *prepare* to get us out of WITSEC … but not actually do it until we see what happens with Dr. Abbas."

* * *

They didn't hear any vehicle drive up, but a knocking on their camper door was unmistakable. Mark peered out to see a late model black Ford Crown Vic parked in the lane in front of their camper. He quickly pocketed his little .38 before opening the door. *They won't notice it in these baggy shorts*, he thought. Dusk approaching, Mark flipped on an exterior light by the camper's door. He cautiously opened it. Two men, each clean-cut and dressed in dark suits stood there. One stood well over six feet; the other was shorter and about Mark's height of five-six. The taller of the two immediately identified himself: "FBI. I'm Agent Niccolo Drago. My friends call me Nic, and my partner here is Agent Luigi Lorenzo." Both men presented credentials. Mark studied both carefully. Department of Investigation, FBI, a gold shield, and photos that matched their faces were apparent. "We're here to speak with a Mr. Jon Traer."

Anne, as usual, was two steps ahead checking e-mail. She already had their laptop on, its screen facing only her. She studied the agents' facial images Marshal Salizar had attached to his promised e-mail. "They match, Jon," were her only words.

"I'm Jon Traer. Please step inside," Mark said. "That's my wife, Kristin, sitting at the dinette table with the laptop computer."

The couple exchanged handshakes with the two men, and Mark directed the agents to have a seat on the RV's sofa. "Mr. Traer, I hate to ask you this question, but is anyone else presently inside this RV?" Agent Drago asked.

"No. Just me and Kristin," Mark answered truthfully.

"Would you mind *slowly* removing the gun from the pocket of your shorts? Outline looks like a little S&W .38 snub to me," Drago said, and slowly but casually slid his right hand beneath his suit's jacket.

Mark blushed horribly. *So much for my attempt at stealth,* Mark thought, as he very slowly removed the little pistol and placed it back in their silverware drawer.

"Thanks. That's better. Mind if I look around your camper?" Agent Drago asked. "Nice ride you got here. This really is impressive!"

"Thanks. Look all you like. Just help yourself," Mark replied.

Drago made a quick search of the RV while the other agent, Lorenzo, remained with Mark and Anne. "Clear," was Drago's only comment to his partner as he returned from the rear of the camper and resumed sitting on the sofa.

"We really appreciate your cooperation with us. The U.S. Marshals Service is the one who gave us this current heads-up. They were supposed to e-mail us your current photos, but something got screwed up with the wireless stuff in our car ... or maybe it's because we are out in the middle of nowhere. But our GPS works fine. That's how we came right to the spot where you're parked. Anyway, we're here to pick up what may be some evidence that will give us a breakthrough in a five-year-old case the Bureau is still working. The Marshals Service has indicated that you have in your possession a sealed envelope that was given to you by a person who calls himself Dr. Al Abbas. Is that correct?"

Mark and Anne stared at one another for moment. Agent Drago finally cleared his throat, apparently to remind Mark to answer the question.

"That's not entirely true. It was given to me secondhand," Mark replied.

"*Secondhand?*" Drago asked, seeking clarification. "By whom?"

"A young man who was a clerk at the convenience center. I'm talking about the convenience center at the Gallup RV Park back in New Mexico."

Oh God! Here we go again ... getting ourselves and others involved, Mark thought.

Drago took in a deep breath. He exhaled, then asked, "And what would that young man's name be?"

Mark again paused. *I wonder how serious an offense it would be to lie to the FBI?* Mark's mind questioned. He then stared at Anne. Her face was neutral, but her eyes said *tell the truth.* And he did.

"Agent Drago, the young man that gave me that envelope is named Bradley Buck. I think he's just an innocent graduate student doing summer work to help with his expenses at the University of Arizona. He told me the envelope had been given to him directly by a Dr. Abbas the day before we left the RV park in Gallup."

The two FBI agents smiled, yet said nothing. During Drago's questioning, his partner, Agent Lorenzo, had been making constant notes in a small black book he'd earlier removed from his suit's jacket. Upon completion of the 40-minute interview, Agent Drago again thanked them, and sent Lorenzo back to their car to get some "CoCs," subsequently explained to be chain-of-custody documents.

Agent Lorenzo quickly returned with an attaché in hand. He removed multiple documents and evidence containers. Mark directed them to their "dirty clothes" basket. After sorting through some of Anne's enticing lingerie, Agent Lorenzo finally located Mark's jeans. He used tweezers to carefully remove the envelope from the Levi's left hip pocket, then slid it into an awaiting Ziploc "evidence bag." Mark noted the bag bore a label with day, date, time, Mark's full WITSEC name, and the name of the FBI agents as well. Mark had initialed or signed multiple labels and documents before the agents finally left. In parting Agent Drago had simply said, "Thanks. If we need to get in touch with you again, it will be through the U.S. Marshals Service."

After the agents' Crown Vic silently pulled away, Mark and Anne screamed "SHIT!" in unison.

Anne yelled, "Here we go again! They've now got stuff—evidence stuff—with *your* name and signature and initials on it ... and it's *still* your legal name! I can see you having to go back to court! I can see us being caught in WITSEC forever. Let's just have a couple of martinis and make love. Tomorrow we'll decide how we're gonna get out of this mess."

* * *

Back on the highway, their Crown Vic running a little over the legal limit, Agents Lorenzo and Drago were having a little "adult conversation" before entering a professional discussion about the evidence they had just acquired.

"Say, Drago? You notice the melons on that Kristin Traer chick?"

"I'll say! She's stacked like a brick shithouse in a ten-acre field. I know she's a little older, but I'd sure like to try that one on for size. When I checked out their bedroom in the very back of the camper, the whole freaking ceiling is mirrored!"

"No shit! So, what do you think she sees in that little short guy

31

she's married to?" Lorenzo asked.

"Beats me, Lorenzo. Maybe he's built like you. You do know what all the ladies call you behind your back, don't you?"

"No. Never entered my mind. What do they call me?"

"'The Italian Stallion,' you short big-dicked little fucker!"

"I can't help it. It's just the way God made me!" Lorenzo exclaimed.

"Oh whatta 'handicap!' You've now got my deepest sympathy," Drago said, then burst out laughing.

6

Agents Lorenzo and Drago had driven almost 100 miles on tortuous secondary roads. Finally they located an isolated greasy spoon just outside Laramie, Wyoming. They stopped there and were eating fairly decent barbeque sandwiches. Unfortunately, they were still in the middle of nowhere, and both were fatigued and dreading the remaining drive down to the Denver Field Office in Colorado.

"Looks to me like Wyoming should at least have a freaking Regional Field Office. But they don't!" Drago complained. "Wonder if we could get the Bureau to send someone up from Denver to meet us halfway?"

"No way," Lorenzo replied. "That would mean adding another link to the chain of custody. That would be their excuse not to do that. Looks like we just happened to be working in the right place in Wyoming at the wrong time. That's why they sent our butts to pick up that evidence on Abbas. We were probably the closest agents 'not productively engaged,' as our boss would say. I'll bet that's why they sent us."

"Well, I sure hope we get a decent break in the Abbas case. Otherwise, I'm gonna be thoroughly pissed," Drago replied, expressing his true feelings.

Wishing they could have chased their barbecue with ice-cold beers, instead of black coffee, they got back on the road, eventually heading south on I-25 to Denver. Driving in shifts, the agents finally rolled into Denver's Field Office around 2:00 a.m.

"They don't pay us enough to do this kinda shit!" Lorenzo loudly grumbled at the Regional Field Office Agent who'd politely received them ... but had promptly directed them to *another* location within the City of Denver.

With calm professionalism the Field Office Agent replied: "Look, I'm really sorry, and I know you guys are beat after working almost 24 straight ... but the rules say your evidence *must* go to a lab that meets all the FBI's quality assurance guidelines for laboratories performing forensic analysis on chemical and biological evidence. The good news is that an approved lab we use for that type testing is open 24/7, and it's only about five blocks from here … and there won't be any traffic at this hour."

Both Lorenzo and Drago blushed, then apologized to the Field Office Agent for their language and attitudes. They quickly delivered the evidence to the FBI-approved lab and had repeated another chain of custody in less than 30 minutes.

Exhausted, but satisfied they'd done everything "by the book," Lorenzo and Drago mutually declared themselves "off duty." Each inhaled several double scotches at a nearby tavern, then crashed into beds at the nearest flea-bag motel.

* * *

At Wyoming's Sleeping Bear RV park, the piercing beep of their satphone awakened him. It was 7:30. *Oh shit!,* Mark thought, as he checked his wristwatch and remembered they were now supposed to call U.S. Marshal Salizar *every* day at 0700. On the ninth or tenth beep, Mark finally answered it.

"I thought we had agreed for you to report promptly at 0700 *every day!*" Salizar began without preliminaries.

"We had. But Kristin and I stayed up a little late last night … and both drank more martinis than we should have. Plus, I have nothing to report other than the transfer of the evidence to the FBI went exactly as planned. Other than nursing a hangover, we both feel fine. Any progress on getting us removed from WITSEC?"

"I'm making progress on getting you two out," Salizar answered. "I should have everything in order a little sooner than I'd planned. I think we will be ready for a face-to-face meeting in about three weeks. Are you guys planning on moving anytime soon?" Salizar asked.

"Haven't decided yet," Mark truthfully replied, but wouldn't have told Salizar until the very last minute even if they'd already decided on their next move. *I like playing the passive-aggressive game with this control-freak,* Mark thought.

"Well, you guys let me know when you decide to move your RV. I can track you anyway, you know. I just want to be sure you won't encounter Abbas again without being forewarned. You need to realize the FBI is pretty stingy with the information they give me about their tracking of Dr. Abbas. In fact, at the moment, I have no idea where he is. The FBI says it's nothing personal, it's just a 'need to know' thing,"

Salizar replied, a tone of resentment toward the Bureau now in his voice.

* * *

Hearing Mark talking on the satphone, Anne finally stirred in bed. Near the end of Mark's conversation with Salizar, she got out of bed and went directly to the bathroom, then to the fridge and drank about half a quart of V-8 juice. "Hope this will make my head feel a little better," she replied. "You want some juice, Little Man? I'm going to take a couple of Tylenol, too. You want some?"

"Yeah, thanks. Some of both. And I think we're getting too old to drink like we did last night … but our lovemaking wasn't half bad, was it?"

Anne grinned. "No complaints in that department. We've both still got that part down pat! But what did Salizar have to say this time?"

"He sounded upset that we didn't call him *exactly* at 7:00 a.m. today. I think he was pissed he had to 'lower himself' to initiate the satphone call to us. He again reminded me *we're* now supposed to call *him* every day. Reading between the lines, I think Salizar also resents the FBI's being skimpy with the information they give him." Mark then filled her in on the rest of the conversation he'd had with Salizar.

Without comment, Anne put some coffee on to perk, brought Mark a tall glass of V-8 juice and two Tylenol, then she sat down at their dinette facing him. "You know I've about had it with Salizar. We're sucking up to him … to someone we've never seen. And we're doing it simply because we know he can expedite getting us out of the program. And now, it's like he wants to tighten his control over our lives, not loosen it. That seems strange if we're gonna get out of WITSEC soon. And our kissing his ass just to stay on his good side is getting to me. This business about the FBI communicating with us *only* through the U.S. Marshals Service that is tracking us, and then the FBI *independently* tracking Abbas but apparently not sharing their information with the Marshals Service—well, this just does not make any sense to me! Especially if they are truly serious about trying to avoid us having another encounter with Dr. Abbas."

"Agreed," Mark said. "It's like the left hand doesn't know what the right is doing, and vice versa. And I don't know why, but thoughts of Dr. Abbas still give me the creeps. I think the FBI knows a lot more about him than they are willing to tell us, or the Marshals Service. I especially didn't like the way Abbas looked at you, Anne. Like when he came inside our camper, bearing a sack filled with 'wiggling things' and took off his sunglasses, then stared at you. His beady little eyes are such a dark brown his pupils are almost impossible to see ... but I could still tell he was staring at you. Remember what that Bradley Buck's girlfriend said ... about Abbas kidnapping and raping a coed graduate student?"

"Mark, I think you're now the one getting a little paranoid. But I also think it's time we move on, and leave Sleeping Bear."

"I think you're right, Anne. But where to go?" Mark asked.

"I'd vote for going back to Arizona. Maybe Tucson, to visit Bradley Buck and his girlfriend. I'd like to find out anything we can about this mysterious Dr. Abbas. The girlfriend may be able to give us some more information. It doesn't look like we'll learn anything new from the Marshals Service," Anne summarized.

Mark thought a moment. "I think we should consider getting us a civilian cell phone, or perhaps use some regular phone to contact Bradley Buck. We know the Marshals Service satphone we have won't work to contact his civilian cell. Anyway, we've already involved Bradley by being honest and giving his name to the FBI. And Brad gave us his cell number before we left Gallup, remember?"

"Yes, he did. And I wrote it down," Anne replied. "And I think it's only fair that we continue to be honest, and tell Bradley exactly what we've done. If Abbas is ever caught, and goes to trial, my guess is that it'll probably be a federal charge. At least the kidnapping part would be. I don't know if trapping endangered species of mice is a big deal, but the federal folks could probably make it one if they wanted to. No matter what, I think everybody involved in the chain of custody of that envelope will be subpoenaed to testify."

* * *

After three days of travel Mark and Anne found themselves located about 60 miles northwest of Tucson, Arizona. Using a payphone at a rest stop near Casa Grande, Arizona, they called the cell number for Bradley Buck. A feminine voice answered, and Mark replied:

"Hi, I'm Jon Traer. I met Bradley Buck in Gallup, New Mexico, and he gave me this number. I'm sorry if I got it wrong and disturbed you."

"I'm Cindy Loveman, Brad's girlfriend. You've got the right number. It is Brad's cell, but he's sleeping right now here in our apartment. He drove most of the night to get here, then crashed into bed. He's now through working at the RV park for the summer.

Anyway, I answered his phone for him. Do you want me to wake him up? Any message you want me to give him?"

"Don't wake him up. Just tell him Jon and Kristin Traer called. We'll call back later when he's awake. What would be a convenient time?"

"Just call back in about three hours. He's currently in the process of writing his dissertation for his doctorate. I'm sure he'll be awake by then and should be here working on that. I'll let him know you called. Bye, now," Cindy said, in a soft feminine voice as she clicked off.

Anne had been standing next to Mark as he spoke at the payphone. "Well …?"

"Apparently Brad and his girlfriend are both at their apartment. His girlfriend answered because he's asleep. She said he's through working at the RV park for the summer, and said to call back in about three hours," Mark explained.

"Why don't we just stay parked right here at this rest stop. We could fix us an early supper, maybe ride our bikes for some exercise. That should give old Salizar something to ponder with his fancy GPS and satellite stuff!"

"I like the way you think, Anne. Salizar sure wasn't happy when he checked in with us at seven this morning. I told him we'd be in the 'Tucson area' for a bit. He wanted to know exactly *why* we'd be there, and again reminded me we'd be close to the Mexican border, and therefore closer to the Sinaloa Cartel's territory. I lied, and told him we'd just be 'sightseeing in Tucson.' I mentioned the Pima Air and Space Museum, along with the Red Rocks of Sedona … and the Kitt Peak Observatory."

"Mark, we've already seen all that stuff!"

"Yeah, we have. But that was *before* Marshal Clinton Salizar became our 'Contact Marshal' … our overly protective 'keeper.' Anyway, I promised him we would not actually venture into Mexico. Reluctantly, he seemed satisfied but reminded me WITSEC could not protect us if we ever crossed the U.S. border … and that such a crossing could be grounds for our 'mandatory expulsion' from WITSEC."

Anne smiled. "At least we know one surefire way of getting us out of WITSEC—just break their damn rules!"

"And that leaves us with exactly what?" Mark asked. "No valid identity documents! No title or registration documents for our vehicle. No vehicle insurance cards. No valid Social Security cards, not even birth and marriage certificates. No valid driver's licenses, no credit card. No way to access our retirement funds and bank accounts, and no health insurance. And no subsistence funds that WITSEC electronically places into our bank account each month!"

Anne sighed. "Looks like we're going to have to undo the WITSEC thing their way … or we're really screwed."

7

After a light supper prepared in their RV at the rest stop, then an hour's worth of bike riding, Mark again used the pay phone to call Bradley Buck. This time Brad answered the phone:

"Hi, Jon! Cindy said you'd called earlier. Glad you didn't forget my invitation to hang with us for a bit. Where are you located now?"

"We're at a rest stop on I-10. We're about 60 miles from Tucson's city limits."

"I assume you're still driving your motorhome, right?" Brad asked.

"Yes. Is parking it going to be a problem?"

"At the apartment parking it will definitely be a problem. Parking RVs is prohibited at our apartment. But I think I've got a way to get around that. Give me the phone number you're calling from, and I'll get right back to you," Brad said, then clicked off.

"Parking our RV is a problem," Mark explained to Anne, who stood by.

* * *

Five minutes later, the payphone rang at the rest stop. It was Brad. "Problem solved, Jon. I've got a friend who's in the aviation business, and he's currently in the process of retiring and selling his company's assets. He's already sold most of his planes, which were crop dusters. He has several aircraft hangars that are empty, and said you'd be welcome to use that space to house your RV. He said he's eventually going to sell the hangars, too, but that's several months away."

"Brad, that's almost too perfect. How much is the rent?"

"It's free. The owner's name is Cal Camarada. He's a multimillionaire, and money is the least of his concerns. He's also a longtime friend of Cindy's dad."

"Can't beat that price!" Mark exclaimed. "But how do we meet?"

"The airfield is only a 20-minute drive for me. It'll probably be better if you meet me there. I'll be driving a dark blue VW convertible with a tan top."

Brad gave Mark directions from the 1-10 rest stop to the airfield. While Mark drove there, Anne packed a small overnight bag with their "essentials," including their digital camera, travel alarm, satphone and its charger, and their little .38 revolver. A little over an hour later they entered a large gate that had an arched sign overhead: "Camarada Aviation, Inc." Brad was already there, waiting, smiling.

"Well, that went smoothly," Brad said extending his hand first to Mark then Anne. "I told Cindy to stay at the apartment … didn't know how much luggage you'd have, and you can see what I'm driving. Not a lot of extra room, and it's our only vehicle."

After Mark backed the 37-foot RV into a giant metal hangar shaped like a Quonset hut, he did a quick walk-through to be sure everything in the RV that was supposed to be "on" was left "on," and things that were supposed to be "off" were indeed "off." Brad helped him slide the hanger's metal doors closed, then locked it with the large padlock Bradley had thoughtfully brought from his apartment. "Here's the key," Brad said, handing it to Mark. "I've got another spare key at home. Ready to ride to our apartment?"

"You're the driver, Brad. But are you sure this is a convenient time for us to visit?" Mark asked.

"Cindy and I both are busy writing our dissertations, but we've found we are more productive when we periodically take a complete break from our writing. I'm at a good temporary stopping place on my paper, and so is she on hers. Cindy did part-time work in the university book store this summer, and as you already know, I've done some work at the Gallup RV Park in New Mexico. We've both put enough away to cover this fall's expenses. In fact, if you guys hadn't showed up here, we were both planning a three-day vacation just to look at local attractions we've not yet had time to visit in Tucson. Perhaps you guys could join us in some local sightseeing?"

"We don't want to intrude," Anne said, realizing she'd said virtually nothing during the first ten minutes of their ride in Brad's car.

"You won't be," Bradley assured her, as he now wheeled the VW bug like a pro through the increasingly complex maze of Tucson's streets. "Well, here it is!" he finally exclaimed as he pulled into a marked parking place at the Loft Apartments on East 6th Street. "It's nothing fancy, but what we can afford … and it's only a short walk to campus. And I hope Cindy has had enough time get our spare bedroom ready for company!"

Nothing fancy? Anne thought the minute she entered. Hardwood floors. Nine-foot ceilings. Modern chrome and leather furniture.

Granite countertops. Multiple ceiling fans. Ceiling-to-floor windows afforded a beautiful vista of an army of saguaro cacti standing like soldiers with arms raised in surrender to the setting sun.

A small late-20s woman suddenly appeared and introduced herself. "Hi! I'm Cindy, Brad's girlfriend," said the petite platinum blond who stood all of five-two. She wore her hair in a ponytail. A black silk-like formfitting two-piece jogging outfit offered full arm and leg coverage, yet left little to the imagination. *Perfect figure for a small woman,* Mark immediately thought.

Per WITSEC protocol, Mark immediately introduced himself as "Jon Traer." "And this is my wife, 'Mary Kristin,'" he added, using Anne's WITSEC name.

"Make yourself at home," Cindy said with a smooth soft-spoken Midwesterner's accent. "Could I get you guys a cold beer or some iced tea?"

"Beer for me," Brad replied. "I'm now on vacation!"

"Beer for me, too," Mark replied.

"Same here," Anne said.

"And I'll have iced tea," Cindy said. "It's not that I don't like booze. I guess it's just that I'm so small, and have such a small blood volume, it always goes right to my head … and I do really stupid things! I learned that in college. I'm just not cut out to be a drinker, but I have no problem with those who choose to consume."

The foursome had settled on stools surrounding a large granite-topped island in the middle of the kitchen area. The guys were now on their third beers, Anne on her second. Cindy still nursed her large glass of iced tea.

The young couple eagerly began sharing their current studies at the University of Arizona.

"Hantaviruses are the subject of my current research. More specifically, my work relates to the hantavirus known as Sin Nombre virus, which in Spanish means 'without name.' I usually just call it 'hanta,' but what I'm referring to is Sin Nombre. That particular strain of hanta causes a rare but severe lung failure in those who get infected by it," Cindy eagerly explained, her intense blue eyes now seeming to glow with excitement. "Brad mentioned that you guys are medical folks. Jon, you're a retired surgeon, and Kristin you're a nurse, right?"

Mark and Anne stared briefly at one another, each wondering how much of their true past they should reveal. Mark finally spoke. "Yes that's correct, Cindy. I think we did mention that to Brad while he was working at the RV park in New Mexico." Mark paused, then said,

"Cindy, they don't teach us surgeons and surgical nurses much about the hantavirus. While studying microbiology in med school, I do remember reading about it. But I don't recall it being a problem in *this* country. To my knowledge, I've never seen an actual case of someone infected with that virus."

"That's not surprising," Cindy said, giving her ponytail a sexy flip with her head. "It's not exactly a common illness here in the U.S. In fact, between 1993 and 2000, only 205 cases were reported to the Center for Disease Control in Atlanta. I think there are probably thousands of cases that go undiagnosed, making the disease grossly underreported. Many American doctors are not even aware of it at all, or at least don't consider it in their differential diagnosis for someone with a severe acute lung failure. Hanta carries at least a 50 percent mortality rate, and currently there is no specific treatment. The antibiotics and antiviral drugs they've tried to date have been totally ineffective. Currently, hospitalization and supportive care on a ventilator is the *only* chance a patient has for survival. The strain of hanta in this country causes what is called hantavirus pulmonary syndrome, or HPS for short. Other strains of hanta in other countries, Korea for example, produce a hemorrhagic fever and kidney damage. But my dissertation is limited to HPS. It was first officially recognized to be here in the U.S. in 1993. There was a tightly clustered outbreak of a highly fatal viral lung infection at the Four Corners region of the U.S. You know, where Utah, Colorado, New Mexico, and Arizona all meet. I was a freshman in college at the time that outbreak happened, and I think that's what initially stirred my interest in hanta."

"Cindy, does the CDC have much data on hantavirus?" Mark asked.

"Not really. And the bulk of what they have is from my very own original epidemiological research I did while in college. I placed my work in their big bureaucratic hands over three years ago. Not a single word of thanks! But hopefully the CDC now realizes hantavirus is not contagious, person-to-person. I think I've proved that to them. At least for the American Southwest, the disease is carried by the white-footed deer mouse. The mice themselves don't get sick from it, they just carry it. You have to acquire the virus by *inhaling* aerosols contaminated by an infected rodent's urine and feces. The disease has also followed bites by infected mice, or the consumption of food contaminated with infected rodent urine, droppings, or saliva. But acquiring hanta that way is extremely rare. I'm hoping my graduate dissertation will point them in a direction of educating the general public and physicians about how to take steps to avoid inhaling the virus in the first place! Other work I'm doing, I hope, will ultimately lead to development of a vaccine. Brad's research in molecular and cellular biology will complement my work regarding vaccines. A hantavirus vaccine is coming ... it's just a question of when!"

Anne's face reddened, but she said nothing as she popped out in a cold sweat. She could feel the short hair on the back of her neck standing up. *If that Dr. Abbas had mice in our camper, have Mark and I been exposed to hanta?* her mind questioned.

8

"Kristin," Cindy asked, "do you feel OK? You look very red-faced to me."

"I think I'm just having a hot flash. I'm 54, and it's about time for that kinda thing. Just wait young lady, your day is coming," Anne said jokingly, then looked at Mark. "I think I'll just step outside for a moment until it passes."

Brad and Cindy wore quizzical expressions, but allowed their guests to step outside alone. "Brad and I will stay inside and start preparations for our meal. I hope tacos are OK," Cindy explained.

"That would be fine. We both love 'em!" Mark said, and followed Anne outside to a small walled patio where it was several degrees cooler than inside the apartment. Anne's color slowly began returning to normal.

"Anne, are you really having a hot flash?"

"Don't know, Little Man. I could be having a reaction to a thought I just had."

"A thought?"

"Yeah. About Dr. Abbas ... and that sack filled with mice he brought inside our camper!"

"Anne, maybe you're letting your imagination run wild. I think you are letting that information Cindy gave us about inhaling the hantavirus influence your objective thinking. If Abbas is indeed a virologist, do you think he would be crazy enough to carry the damn things around with him?"

"No, I guess he wouldn't," Anne said, now feeling better again. "But before we leave Brad and Cindy's company, I want to pick their brains about Abbas."

* * *

Over a long and fairly authentic Mexican meal, Mark and Anne learned infinite details about their hosts' backgrounds. Where they were born and raised, where they went to high school and college,

44

details of how they met in graduate school at the University of Arizona, and even details about their parents and other family members. Cindy had revealed one detail about her dad that immediately caught Mark and Anne's attention: "My dad is with the FBI. He's a senior agent working out of their Denver Field Office. Something to do with bioterrorism," she'd said.

It was Bradley who first realized their lengthy mealtime discussion had been very one-sided. "Well, it looks like Cindy and I have dominated the whole conversation. We haven't given you guys a chance to tell us details about yourselves."

For a full 30 seconds, Anne and Mark stared at one another. Their hosts sensed the silence was awkward, and Cindy finally said, "We don't mean to pry into your private life."

With a hint of tears in her eyes, Anne said, "Cindy, Jon and I are living under very unusual circumstances. It's been that way for four long years. We hope those circumstances will soon end, and we can resume a normal life where we can be completely honest with the fine folks we meet."

"Can I venture a guess?" Cindy asked.

Mark and Anne said nothing, just nodded a "yes."

"You two wouldn't happen to be in some federal protection program, would you? My dad has told me about them, and says they can be absolutely devastating to those who are trapped in them."

Mark and Anne blushed horribly. Cindy spoke: "I trust Jon is not joining you in your hot flashes! But I'll accept your mutual blushes as an affirmative answer. I won't pry anymore, just tell us what you're comfortable with. I can assure you anything you tell us will stay right here. Growing up in an FBI family you quickly learn to keep your mouth shut. If it makes you feel any better, Brad's dad is with the CIA. He knows how to keep his mouth shut, too."

That was all the excuse Mark and Anne needed to "unload" four year's worth of pent up frustration that was presently morphing into hostility toward WITSEC. They spent the next two hours explaining the circumstances that led to them being trapped in the program. They explained their original names had been Dr. Mark Telfair, M.D., and Kristin's had been Mrs. Anne Hunt Telfair, R.N.; WITSEC had legally changed their names to Mr. Jon Wayne Traer, and Mrs. Mary Kristin Traer respectively.

As a gesture of comfort, Cindy tenderly placed her small hand on Anne's arm. "I'm sure it's been a pain to *always* remember to use your WITSEC names. As I understand the process from my dad, you two will have supporting documents for your WITSEC names only. If we're within earshot of others while you two are here, Brad and I will simply use 'Jon' and 'Kristin,' and not make any mention of the fact you're a retired doctor and nurse. I know that when Brad and I finally earn our Ph.Ds., we certainly plan to have that fact tacked on so it will become part of our legal names."

Mark entered the conversation. "You're right, Cindy. We both worked so hard to earn our professional titles, and we feel cheated when it's not part of our legal names anymore. How can we find out more about Dr. Abbas? He told me he was a Ph.D., which may or may not be true. I'm not even sure the name he gave us is his true name. We could find no listing under that name on UA's website. Neither could Brad."

"It's like this," Cindy began, "I've already told Brad all I remember about Abbas and his strange disappearance from campus during my first year at UA. I also told him about the viral cultures and lab equipment that apparently 'went missing,' too. If my dad's in the right mood, I may be able to get him to do a little poking around. He'll probably know a lot more than he's ever told me. As 'Jon' and 'Kristin' would you two like to meet my dad? I can tell you right now he won't tell you anything over the phone."

"That would be great!" Anne said. "The U.S. Marshal who monitors our movements in WITSEC is named Clinton Salizar. We talk with him using a secure satellite phone the Service issued to us when we first entered the program. In fact, we've got to call him at 7:00 a.m. tomorrow, to report our current location. We've never met Salizar personally, but he's headquartered in Atlanta, we think. Neither of us is very happy with him. He's very controlling, and won't give us any significant information about Abbas. Salizar did arrange for us to briefly interface with the FBI at an RV park back in Lander, Wyoming. We gave two FBI men a sealed envelope that Abbas had first given to Brad, who then gave it to us the following day. I'm afraid we may have unintentionally involved Brad, by telling the agents Brad was the one who passed the envelope to us at the RV park. We have no idea what was actually inside it, nor do we know what the FBI's tests on that envelope have revealed."

"As I said earlier, I'm on vacation," Brad announced. "I don't care if you gave my name to the FBI. I have nothing to hide. In fact, I'd be glad to drive you guys up to Denver to meet Cindy's dad. I need to get to know my future father-in-law a little better anyway."

Cindy smiled. "If we left early in the morning, we could be in

Denver early tomorrow evening."

"I may have an even better idea," Brad said, as he picked up Cindy and swung her around like a toy doll, then gently put her down. "I'm gonna call your dad's friend, Cal Camarada. I think he still has his personal plane."

Carrying his cell phone, Brad stepped into their bedroom for privacy. Five minutes later, he returned, smiling. "Well it sure pays to know friends of Cindy's dad! I just talked with Cal Camarada, the guy who is lending us the hanger to house your RV."

"And ...?" Cindy asked Brad.

"Cal has a personal plane, a twin, a 'Cessna 310 Navajo C.' He said he'd be delighted to fly the four of us up to Denver. He said all he has to do is check aviation weather, file a flight plan, and barring anything unusual, we could leave in the morning and be there well before noon. He said unless he calls back in the next few minutes, we should plan to meet him at his airfield at 8:00 in the morning."

"I don't have any problems with that," Mark said. "But I'll have to get up early enough to call Marshal Salizar at 7:00 to report our location."

"No problem," Brad said. We'll set a clock in time for you guys to make your check-in call to the Marshals Service, then eat breakfast, and still have time to make it to Camarada's airfield by 8:00."

"Can I ask a question?" Anne asked Brad.

"Sure," he replied.

"Exactly what kind of pilot is he, this Camarada fellow?" Anne asked, a little uneasy about small planes.

"Very experienced," Brad assured. "He's flown military jets while in the Air Force. He flew corporate jets after he left the military. Even flew crop dusters for awhile, and taught others to fly them. I know he still has an active instructor's license, and has volunteered to teach *me* to fly ... once I get this graduate school stuff behind me."

* * *

Exactly at 7:00 a.m. the next morning, Arizona time, Mark called Marshal Salizar using the satphone:

"Thanks for calling on time," Salizar replied. "But you've got a problem."

"Problem?" Mark asked.

"Yeah. I can't locate you with my GPS. Therefore, I can't locate you on our satellite imaging system. I don't understand what's wrong!"

Salizar exclaimed. "My GPS is working fine on tracking my other WITSEC folks. But I get no reading from the one we mounted on the roof of your camper."

Too fucking bad! Mark thought before speaking: "Just try *trusting* us for once, Salizar. We are definitely in Tucson, Arizona. We're gonna do a little sightseeing, that's all. We've detected no potential threats here, and have no health issues. End of story."

"Well, get the GPS on your RV fixed," Salizar demanded. "We gave you a credit card for just such contingencies. So use it!"

"I'll deal with it ASAP," Mark said, knowing full well the reason Salizar could not get a GPS reading was because they had their RV totally enclosed inside a metal hangar building.

*   *   *

The foursome arrived at Camarada Aviation's field at 7:45 a.m. Mark noted a late-model black Porsche Boxster convertible parked next to the open hangar. Cal already had his plane out on the hangar's concrete apron, and was in the process of doing his external preflight inspection. Cal projected total confidence as he went down a list he'd earlier removed from his flight bag. His trim six-foot frame, piercing blue eyes, deep tan, snow-white hair and neat little white mustache made their own statement.

Cal seemed so focused he didn't even acknowledge their arrival until he'd completed his preflight. "We're ready to roll," Cal finally said, sticking his right thumb in the air, then extending his hand individually to his passengers. "Weather's fine, but if you get airsick and puke in my plane, that'll put you on my shit list! I've got barf bags aboard, but you shouldn't need them."

The pilot wasted no time assisting his passengers as they boarded and buckled in. Cal pulled the wheel chocks, stowed them inside the plane, then boarded himself and slipped on his headset and wire-framed aviation glasses with amber lenses. He started the engines, studied his instruments a moment, then taxied to the end of the runway. After a run-up and scanning instruments, he released the Piper 310's brakes and they quickly accelerated down the runway. Anne had been tightly gripping Mark's hand across the narrow aisle, but relaxed when she saw they were in the air. "Never felt us leave the ground! I've never been in a plane this small before, only LifeFlight helicopters," she said.

"That's the way it's supposed to be," Mark replied with a smile.

"Good weather. Good pilot. Good plane."

When they reached their cruising altitude, Cal passed out individual headsets to his passengers, and indicated where to plug them in. "Can everyone hear me OK?" His passengers nodded an affirmative choosing not to speak over the harmonic drone of the Cessna's twin engines. "We'll be flying Visual Flight Rules, or VFR. Our altitude will vary, but we'll average about 12,500. Our cruising airspeed is 185 knots. Our ETA for the Walden-Jackson County Airport in Colorado is 11:47 local. The airfield there is a little over 8,000 feet above sea level. Temperature on the ground there is 62 degrees. I've got some extra jackets in the luggage bay, should any of you guys find it too cool when we deplane. Any questions?" There were none. "Good. Relax and enjoy. I may point out some landmarks as we fly over them."

Cal was silent most of the trip, but those aboard could hear him occasionally jabbering on the radio. About an hour before their planned arrival at Walden-Jackson, Cal was apparently talking to someone at or near the field. "Our courtesy car is already there? And the keys are in it?" he asked, seeking confirmation. "OK, good. ETA is still 11:47," he said signing off.

He then spoke to his passengers. "For a short while, I'm going to descend to 2,500. Just chew or yawn if your ears are bugging you. I want to take a closer look at Four Corners. I recently read they've put some kind of monument there … and I want to see if it's large enough to be a valid nav aid when flying VFR."

Cal banked the Cessna and spiraled down to 2,500 keeping a sharp eye out for what he hoped to find. "'Monument,' my ass!" Cal muttered. "All they've got is a concrete slab on the ground with a tiny marker in the middle of it. Bet it's just a Geodetic Survey marker. But they've got at least 100 Airstreams and RVs parked around it. Now that's hard to miss!" Cal exclaimed, laughed, then slowly climbed back to 12,500. He then penciled some notes on his aviation chart.

In another 30 minutes, Cal started slowly descending through a cloudless sky, this time flying in a straight line. "We're about 15 minutes out. Everybody buckled?"

"Yes," his passengers said in unison. The passengers now had their heads tilted toward the aisle, peering through the Cessna's windscreen, waiting for the airfield to magically appear.

"November 1 2 2 Alfa Zulu on final for Walden-Jackson, runway 4, coming from 035 magnetic, 045 true, altitude 1,100." There was no response, but Cal hadn't expected one at the small uncontrolled field.

He was happy enough to see the field at least had a functioning windsock, and that there were no deer or antelope on the runway.

Anne again gripped Mark's hand across the aisle as Cal made a textbook landing. She released his hand only after the engines stopped.

9

At the remote field, Cal quickly secured his plane with chocks and tie-downs. Everyone accepted their pilot's kind offer of jackets. Mark estimated the air temperature to be in the low 60s, upper 50s at best. They piled into an old Suburban (their "courtesy car"), and Cal drove about ten miles before finally giving up on getting the vehicle's heater to work. Otherwise, the vehicle functioned fine. Following Cindy's driving instructions through portions of the Boulder Mountain Park, an hour's drive placed them at Louis Loveman's farmhouse on the northern outskirts of Boulder, Colorado.

Before anyone got out of the Suburban, Cindy gave a brief explanation: "My dad's name is Louis, and he'll be around here somewhere since it's a weekend. This is where I grew up as an only child. Everything still looks the same, and Dad actively participates in farming the place, mostly hay and corn. I haven't been back here since Mom died a little over three years ago. She died from a glioma, a type of brain cancer. Dad insisted that she be buried here near one of her favorite fishing ponds. It was really terrible at the end, but she wanted to die at home. I'm sure the place still harbors both bad and fond memories for my dad, but he prefers to live here alone with his dog. Weekdays, he commutes by car to the FBI Field Office in Denver. Since the farm is actually situated north of Boulder, it's a 50-mile drive to work. I've tried talking him into getting a condo in Denver for his workweek there, then stay at the farm on weekends. But my dad is ..."

"I gather he's rather stubborn, right?" Anne asked.

"You got it! Stubborn as some of those darn goats he once tried to raise!" Cindy exclaimed, pulling her hands back inside the sleeves of the too-large jacket she was wearing. "But I love him anyway, and I can't wait to see him!"

As soon as Cindy stepped out of the Suburban, a 100-pound German shepherd ceased his barking and charged to Cindy. The dog almost knocked her down in the process. "Samson, down boy! I love you too, but take it a little easy, will ya!" Cindy said, as she lovingly

51

rubbed the face of the shepherd, who now stood on his hind legs, with both paws resting on her shoulders.

Mark heard a shrill whistle as a hulk of a man stepped through the front door of the rambling ranch-styled brick home. Appearing to be well over six feet, with broad shoulders and thick neck, only his snow-white hair and a distinct limp gave any hint of his age. The man yelled, "Samson, down! Sit! Stay!" The dog immediately complied.

Cindy ran to her dad, who scooped his "little girl" up in his massive arms, and for a tender moment held her like an infant. "Cin, the older you get the more you look like your mom!" He kissed her on the forehead before gently placing her back on the ground next to Samson. The dog had not budged an inch since the sit-stay command from Louis Loveman. Mark got the immediate feeling that Louis Loveman was accustomed to being in charge and obeyed, no matter what the situation.

Cal approached Louis with his hand extended. Louis immediately responded, "Thanks for getting my little girl here in one piece, you crazy old flyboy. And thanks for the heads-up on her arrival. Sneaky little daughter didn't even tell me she was coming!"

"It's a Saturday, Dad. I knew you'd be here ... and I wanted to surprise you!" Cindy replied.

"Well, you did! And it's nice you brought Bradley with you. He better take good care of you when he takes over," Louis said.

"Not to worry, sir," Bradley said, smiling and stepping forward to shake hands with a man he'd met only once before. Unfortunately, their first and only prior meeting had been at the funeral for Cindy's mom.

"And who are these other folks with you?" Loveman asked, pointing to Anne and Mark.

"They are some new friends. They are staying with us at our apartment in Tucson," Bradley explained.

Cindy did the introductions. "Daddy, this is Jon Traer, and his wife Mary Kristin. They have a problem. I thought you might be able to help them out. They are the main reason we made this trip ... so they could meet you in person."

After shaking their hands, Louis replied, "Help them out? In what capacity?"

"As an agent with the FBI," Cindy replied.

"No promises, Cin. But I will promise to listen. Let's step inside where it's a little warmer, and you can take off that damn jacket that's ten sizes too big!"

* * *

Despite Louis Loveman's gruff box-like exterior, Mark and Anne both instantly liked him. He had bushy jet-black eyebrows, a full head of hair, yet every hair on his scalp was white as snow. Despite an intimidating appearance, it was obvious that a big tender heart lurked beneath his exterior, especially if the situation had anything to do with his daughter, Cindy.

Now sitting in a comfortable and very masculine study inside the home, it took a solid hour of conversation for Mark and Anne to explain their situation to Loveman.

Louis had requested that he interview 'Jon' and 'Kristin' alone, in the privacy of his study. The couple first revealed their original names, and openly admitted Mark was a retired surgeon, Anne a retired nurse. They started at the beginning, explaining how they'd helped gather evidence that led to a big drug bust down in McIntosh County, Georgia. That had led to them becoming federal witnesses against the Sinaloa Cartel, which, in turn, had led to them being placed in a federal witness protection program, one called WITSEC."

"I'm quite familiar with the program. It is managed by the Department of Justice through the U.S. Marshals Service. Correct?" Louis asked.

Mark and Anne nodded an affirmative, then explained how they now felt like Gypsies living in a 37-foot motorhome. They told Louis how they'd recently encountered a Dr. Al Abbas at an RV park in Gallup, New Mexico. They stated Abbas had indicated to them he was trapping mice of a specific species, yet stated no reason why he wanted those particular mice for a lab he claimed he had at the University of Arizona in Tucson. Mark explained how they had tried to verify Abbas was a professor at UA, but couldn't. They explained how the strange Dr. Abbas had left the RV park, but the next day he'd apparently returned briefly to leave them a sealed envelope at the New Mexico RV park's convenience center. Bradley, who was then doing summer work at the RV park's convenience center, had passed the envelope to Mark and Anne, who subsequently moved on the next day heading to another RV park located in Lander, Wyoming. They'd been carrying the envelope with them, still unopened. They had informed the Marshals Service about the "oddness" of Abbas and had mentioned the envelope that had been passed to them. Their monitoring marshal, Clinton Salizar, had subsequently arranged for them to give that unopened envelope to two FBI agents who drove to the RV park in Wyoming to personally pick it up.

They explained how they were growing dissatisfied with Clinton Salizar, who now insisted on monitoring their whereabouts on a *daily* basis. Mark explained: "He treats us just like children. We have to call him daily at 0700 on satphone. At first he gave us a few tidbits of information about Abbas, then clammed up." Mark noted the mention of Al Abbas seemed to have perked up Louis Loveman. Louis suddenly began taking notes, writing them on a yellow legal pad while seated at his study's leather-topped desk.

At the end of an hour, Mark finally said, "That's all we know, sir. We don't know if this Dr. Abbas is for real, of if he poses any real threat to us."

Loveman quickly replied. "Abbas is for real. He's the principal subject of an ongoing FBI investigation that's now several years old for the Bureau. Before I tell you more, let me first remind you that you've probably signed nondisclosure agreements while you were gathering evidence for the drug bust down in Georgia. Those agreements apply to *all* federal law enforcement information you have been given, irrespective of the particular branch that gave it to you."

"Yes, we both signed 'NDAs,' as they called them. I understand the agreement extends across federal agency lines. My wife does, too," Mark said.

"OK," Loveman said. "Here it is in a nutshell: Dr. Al Abbas is a very real person. He's a brilliant virologist to boot. He was born in Saudi Arabia and carries a Saudi passport. He is a Ph.D. who trained in Saudi Arabia, then came to the U.S. on a work visa that allowed him to teach microbiology at the University of Arizona. As you probably know, that's where my daughter is now working on her doctorate. Bradley, her boyfriend, is also there working on his. We now have solid evidence Abbas raped a grad school coed at UA several years ago after mysteriously disappearing from the campus. Our lab in Denver was able to retrieve his DNA from cells he left behind when he sealed the envelope he'd left for you guys at that RV park in Gallup. That DNA matches DNA from semen found inside a coed that claims she was kidnapped, transported across a state line, and repeatedly raped by Abbas. We also now have fairly good prints from his right hand, plus several partials from his left. That information was all obtained from inside the envelope's flap. But DNA and prints are our aces in the hole, so to speak. We don't want to bring him in on kidnapping and rape charges, at least not just yet. We now know he is working with al-Qaeda, and is a member of a militant Islamic cell. Before we nail him, we want to get the bigger picture of why he's here in the U.S., then try to learn who his accomplices are."

"What else was in the envelope?" Mark asked.

"A non-counterfeit 20-dollar bill, and a note that said 'Thanks.' The note was signed with the initials 'AA.' That's all, except for some dust that is going to be subjected to electron microscopy and other studies."

"Do you have any idea where Abbas is presently located?" Anne asked, voicing her major concern. "That man stared at me in a scary sexual way when he was inside our camper at Gallup."

"Did he make any overt overtures of a sexual kind?" Loveman asked.

"No," Anne admitted. "It's just the way he stared at me, my breasts and crotch. I felt like he was trying to undress me with his dark scary eyes."

"I think you can relax," Louis said. "But don't let your guard down. Abbas is currently in Gainesville, Georgia," Loveman replied. "He's living there in a motel, and had abandoned an old stolen Winnebago in Alabama. That RV has been taken to Atlanta for forensic evaluation, but it's been wiped so clean we don't expect to find much.

"Apparently Abbas has just purchased a defunct 150-acre chicken farm in Gainesville, Georgia. The three buildings on the farm are quite sizable, each about 100 feet long and 50 feet wide. We are quite curious as to exactly what he plans to do with them. We do know he has not yet applied for any of the state and federal permits required to operate a commercial egg or poultry production facility."

"Thank you, sir," Mark said. At least we have some information that tells us we're not likely to encounter Abbas again. Do you have any suggestions for us?"

"Yes, several," Louis replied. "First, try a little harder to work with your U.S. Marshal. He's probably a younger overzealous marshal, one who's enjoying the control he has over your lives. Second, don't get out of WITSEC just yet. Just keep your identity as it is for now. Third, I want both of you two to consider being unofficial FBI informants. To that end, I'll give you a secure satphone programmed for a frequency that's different from the one you've received from the U.S. Marshals Service. You can use it to securely contact me at any time. Also, I'll contact the Department of Justice. I think I can get them to direct your Marshal Saliziar to back off this stupid daily check-in crap he insists upon. I can keep you current as to where Abbas is located. Unless you personally hear otherwise from me, don't go anywhere near Abbas."

"*FBI informant?*" Mark asked.

"Yes," Loveman replied. "'Informant' is not as well defined in the Bureau's regs as it should be. The rules we have about it are often not strictly followed, but it's still a valuable law enforcement tool. Here in the privacy of this room, I'll be first to admit our so-called 'informant status' has been abused over the years. It's been abused by the Bureau. It's also been abused by our criminal and noncriminal informers alike. If I put you in that status, it could cut through some red tape should I need to quickly tell you something ... or if you need to tell the Bureau something. It allows me to issue to you a special secure phone. And we never had this conversation here in my study today. OK?"

"Sure," Mark replied. "But what if the others that came with us ask questions?"

"I don't care if you tell Cal, Cindy, or Bradley what we've discussed. They know how to keep their mouths shut. I'd trust those folks with my life. I insisted on interviewing you two privately only because I had absolutely no idea what you two wanted to discuss."

"Thanks for listening to us," Mark said. "The rules you gave us about confidentiality seem simple enough, and we'll follow them."

"Good. Consider it done," Louis said, as he reached across his desk to again shake hands with Mark and Anne. He then opened a desk drawer, withdrew a satphone, and handed it to Mark. "It's charged and ready to use. Does the satphone you received from the Marshals Service look identical to the one I just handed you?"

"Looks identical," Mark replied.

"Good. Here's the manual and charger that go with it," Louis said, as he removed those items from another desk drawer. "My direct 15-digit number is written inside the front cover of the satphone manual. I suggest you both commit that number to memory. Get Cal, Cindy, and Bradley to memorize it too. And for God's sake don't write it down and stick it on the exterior of the phone. That's a security no-no!" Louis said, then stood indicating their meeting was over.

10

During the time Mark and Anne had been in their hour-long meeting with her dad, Cindy had raided the kitchen and prepared sandwiches and iced tea for everyone. When Cal finished eating, he checked his watch, then borrowed Louis Loveman's house phone to file a return flight plan. "If we want a smooth ride home, we need to get going before the afternoon thermals kick in," Camarada explained to the group.

Returning from the study, Loveman, Mark, and Anne approached the table where the others had eaten … including Samson, who still went politely from chair to chair, begging for scraps.

When the shepherd spotted Loveman approaching, he promptly sat and ceased his begging. "Sampson, I see my daughter and her friends are spoiling you rotten!" Loveman exclaimed, then laughed as he joined the others at the table.

"Dad, I hope you guys had a productive meeting," Cindy said.

"I think so," Louis replied, accepting the sandwich Cindy handed him on a plate. "But when strangers are present, I've told 'Jon' and 'Kristin' to continue to use their WITSEC names, and not break that habit just yet. They'll explain that to all of you if they haven't already. We've established a way they, or Cindy, or Cal, or Brad can securely communicate with me. I gave them a satphone. I won't rehash the whole discussion we had in my study, but I've given them permission to fill you guys in on all the details we discussed. Those details, however, are to be shared *only* among us present at this table. *No exceptions!*" Louis added. His brief penetrating authoritative stare at each member present told Mark's mind one thing: *This guy means exactly what he says.*

* * *

For the next hour, Cal again drove the Suburban that returned them to the Walden-Jackson County Airport. Ten minutes later they were back in the air, heading southward for Camarada Aviation's airfield in Tucson.

When they reached their cruising altitude, Cal made an announcement: "It may get a little bumpy going back. The cumulous clouds are showing some vertical development, and some are becoming cumulonimbus, which tells me we should expect some thermals."

Cal had been right. Thirty minutes later, the Cessna began to bounce around like a toy as the pilot tried to avoid the spots he felt would have the most marked thermal activity. Anne soon developed a tinge of nausea, and had broken out in a cold sweat. *Hot flash* crossed her mind.

Mark noted Anne's developing distress, and asked Cal where the "barf bags" were. Cal calmly replied, "Under the seat. I'm hunting the smoothest air I can find."

Anne's retching caused Cal to briefly turn his head. He was relieved to see she had gotten the bag out in time. Reaching across the aisle, Mark tried to comfort her as best he could, while remaining buckled in himself. He placed a comforting hand on her forehead. *She's got a significant fever … neither airsickness alone nor hot flashes can do that,* he thought.

Thirty minutes later, the clouds dissipated and the air became quite smooth. Bradley was sitting in the copilots seat, and Cal was now in his "instructor mode," calmly explaining the airplane's instruments and controls to Bradley.

Anne now appeared more embarrassed than ill. Mark again felt her forehead. *She's still hot,* he thought. She next had a shaking chill that lasted several minutes. *Need to get her checked by a doctor as soon as we get back to Tucson,* Mark thought.

Cindy was sitting in the seat in front of Anne and had heard or seen what had transpired. "Jon, I think we need to get Kristin checked by a doctor when we get back home. I know you're a doctor, but—"

"I'm a surgeon, Mark finished. "And whatever her problem is, I don't think it's surgical. Besides, it's an unwritten rule: Doctor's don't treat their own family."

"We have a great hospital just a few blocks from our apartment in Tucson," Cindy said. "It's University Medical Center, or UMC, as we call it. It's a private, nonprofit hospital located at the Arizona Health Sciences Center, and it's affiliated with the medical school there."

* * *

Whatever was ailing Anne was getting progressively worse in a hurry. By the time they'd gotten to Brad and Cindy's apartment, Anne was having another chill, and she said she was having difficulty breathing. She said that every muscle in her body ached. Ten minutes later she was in the ER at UMC. Dr. William Baxter, the Chief Medical Resident in the ER, was examining Anne in the presence of Mark, Cindy, and an ER nurse. After listening to her chest with his stethoscope, he frowned. "I don't like what I hear. Her lungs are very congested. I want a stat chest x-ray and some blood gasses," he said to the ER nurse.

Mark first identified himself as Dr. Jon Traer, a retired surgeon. "Dr. Baxter, Mary Kristin is my wife and she's a retired nurse. In professional terms could you please tell us what you think is going on?"

"I'm not sure, but I think your wife has had either a large pulmonary embolus or has an acute viral pulmonary infection. Why don't you guys meet me in x-ray on the second floor. Wait for me in the little x-ray waiting area where they have their vending machines. We're going to start her on five liters of oxygen by nasal canula, then open an IV line. Then I'm going to draw some routine venous blood, plus arterial blood for blood gasses before they take her up. I'll meet you in x-ray in just a few minutes."

Mark kissed Anne on the forehead, then quickly departed for the second floor. Cindy and Brad accompanied him. Ten long minutes later Dr. Baxter appeared holding x-rays in his hand. "Let's step into a viewing room."

They did. Mark was shocked at what he saw. "My wife has a severe interstitial pneumonia. That's my diagnosis as a surgeon."

"Unfortunately, sometimes you surgeons get a medical diagnosis exactly right! This is the worst interstitial pneumonia I've ever seen!" Dr. Baxter said, alarm in his voice.

Cindy chimed in. "Dr. Baxter, I'm not a doctor, but I'm a grad student at UA doing research on hantavirus. Have you considered Sin Nombre, a.k.a. hantavirus, in your differential diagnosis?"

"Frankly, I had not. That's a pretty rare disorder. Irrespective of cause, what is now life threatening is her level of arterial oxygenation. The oximeter clipped to her finger indicates it's only 75 percent. As you may know anything below 88 percent is quite dangerous!"

"Oh my God! She needs to be on a *ventilator* stat, Dr. Baxter!" Cindy yelled.

Mark felt too frightened for words, but not thoughts: *Dear God, please don't let it end this way. At least give me a chance to say goodbye.*

"Young lady, I've already called the ICU and they are setting up a vent room stat, Miss 'Whoever You Are!'" Baxter yelled back, a tinge of anger in his voice.

"Sorry I yelled, Doctor. I'm Miss Cindy Loveman. I just want to be sure everything that can be done, is being done."

"Sorry I raised my voice," Dr. Baxter said, a tone of apology now in his speech. "It's been a long shift and this gal is really sick. You said you are studying hanta at UA?"

"Yes," Cindy replied. "I'm a grad student in microbiology, specifically in virology. Doctor, if hanta is in your differential diagnosis, and if your lab here can't run the antibody tests, we can do it in our lab at UA. We are set up to run both IgM and IgG. We use ELISA, or enzyme-linked immunoabsorbent assay for hanta. In fact, I can personally run the test myself and have the results for you in an hour or so. All I need is two milliliters of her blood."

Dr. Baxter reached into the pocket of his white coat. He withdrew a labeled five milliliter vial of blood, and handed it to Cindy. "I was going to have this sent to a reference lab for ELISA, as well as other tests. You take this sample. I can draw another. But right now, I'm gonna scoot up to ICU and be sure she's squared away on the ventilator. It's on the third floor. I'll see you there."

"When can I see her?" Mark finally managed to ask, as Baxter headed for an elevator.

"It'll probably be about half an hour. I'm gonna put her in an isolation room until we're positive of what we are dealing with here. We've got to get her sedated, and intubated. She won't be able to talk, but you can see her soon," Baxter promised as the stainless-steel elevator doors closed slowly, leaving Mark with two consuming emotions: *fear* and *isolation.*

"Brad," Cindy demanded, "let me have our car keys. I'm going to scoot over to the lab and start running the tests on Mary Kristin's blood. You stay here with Jon and keep him company. I should be back in an hour."

Neither of the men said anything. But Mark thought: *Cindy Loveman, all 100 pounds of her, is certainly a take-charge kind of person ... a trait that seems to be a chip off the old Louis Loveman block. But why are her eyes so blue, and her dad's such a dark brown? Wonder what color her mom's eyes were?*

* * *

Brad and Mark made small talk after they'd gotten coffee from a vending machine and moved to the ICU waiting area on the third floor. Mark approached the ICU reception desk, and identified himself as Dr. Jon Traer. "My wife, Mary Kristin, is supposed to be coming up here. Is she here yet?"

"Yes. She's in Room 10, Doctor. Dr. Baxter is with her right now and they are getting her situated on a ventilator. I'm sorry, but you can't see her until Dr. Baxter gives me the OK. Just stay here in the waiting area. I'm sure her doctor will be with you shortly."

Dr. Baxter soon appeared in the ICU waiting area, a haggard look on his face. He spoke immediately to Mark. "She's been intubated without incident, and is now on the ventilator. We've got her sedated using an IV morphine drip, and she's not fighting the ventilator. Her oxygen sat is up to 88 percent. Her heart rate has stabilized at a little over 120. She still has an elevated temp at 102.4 degrees. They are going to put her on a cooling pad. I've also put in a central line. Her CVP is acceptable. Until we learn more, I'm treating her as an ARDS, or as an adult respiratory distress syndrome patient. A pulmonologist and an infectious disease doctor will be seeing her soon."

"Can I see her now?" Mark asked, a quaver in his voice.

"Yes. Very briefly," Dr. Baxter replied. "You'll have to slip on some contamination gear. I'm considering her infectious until proven otherwise. I'll go back there with you."

Before slipping on a mask, gown, and gloves, Mark removed an old Saint Christopher medal he'd carried in his wallet for years. Both he and Anne considered that medal their "good luck charm," and a substitute for the formal religion neither had.

During many years of surgical practice, Mark had spent hours in ICUs before. Still, he was not prepared for what he saw: The love of his life now lay unconscious amid multiple wires and tubes. To him the beeping and hissing medical technology surrounding his wife were all familiar sights and sounds. *But this is so different now ... it's my wife on the other end of this technology! God, how terrified must the visitors have felt when they visited my own ICU patients?*

With Dr. Baxter at his side, Mark lightly touched Anne's right cheek with his gloved hand. Her eyelids fluttered a moment, then she opened the beautiful hazel eyes that had always captured his heart. "Honey, I brought someone to see you," he whispered. He held up the Saint Christopher, hoping she could recognize it through the morphine haze. Though the ventilator tube prevented her from speaking, she managed a smile that was distorted by the tape securing her tube to her lips and cheek. She then lapsed back into unconsciousness.

"I think we better go now," Dr. Baxter said. "The pulmonology and ID docs will be here any moment to do their consults."

Reluctantly, Mark stepped out of her room and shed his contamination wear into a special container marked with a biohazard symbol. Dr. Baxter did likewise, and they went to the ICU waiting area to find Bradley and Cindy eagerly waiting there.

Cindy immediately sprang up and handed Dr. Baxter a slip of paper. "Doctor, both her hantavirus-specific IgM and IgG are positive! It's definitely hanta, specifically Sin Nombre strain. There's no doubt in my mind she's got HPS."

11

The ICU waiting area was devoid of other visitors when the infectious disease (ID) doctor and pulmonologist arrived simultaneously. Dr. Baxter immediately jumped up and approached the ID doctor. "Dr. Schroder, take a look at this! I didn't have this information when I put in my request for a consultation. Please put this report in the patient's chart when you check her."

"Wow! How'd you get this done so fast?" the ID consultant physician asked.

"You can thank this young lady right here, Miss Cindy Loveman. She's a grad student at UA working with hanta. She kindly ran it in her own lab on campus."

"Is her lab certified?" the ID doctor asked with a skeptical tone.

"Definitely!" Cindy shot back. "In fact we're a certified *reference lab* when it comes to hanta. Verify my results all you want, Doctor, but there is no doubt in my mind. Your patient definitely has hantavirus pulmonary syndrome, or HPS. I realize I'm not a doctor, but when it comes to hanta I know exactly what I'm talking about! I'll also bet her hematocrit is elevated, her CBC shows a depressed platelet count, an elevated white cell count with a left shift, and her peripheral blood smear will show the presence of immuoblasts if you look for them."

Both consulting doctors seemed quite taken aback by this tiny, yet quite beautiful and spirited little woman. She spoke forcefully and seemed to know as much about an obscure disease as they did. Bradley smiled. So did Mark, for the first time since seeing Anne.

"How far away from the hospital do you guys live?" Dr. Baxter asked.

"We're less than five minutes away," Cindy replied for everyone. She searched her pocket book and found an old business card. She drew an "X" on the face of the card, then scribbled a number on the back and handed it to Dr. Baxter. "That's a cell number where we can be reached."

"Good," Baxter replied. "I suggest all of you go home and rest. If you're right about this being hanta, I'm sure you know all we can do is give her supportive care and hope her own immune system whips this thing. We're going to do all that can be done, and I'll call you immediately if there is any significant change."

* * *

As Bradley drove the VW back to their Tucson apartment, Mark had the feeling he was abandoning the most treasured thing in his life … Anne, his wife of 30 years. *I hope she saw Saint Christopher,* he kept thinking, over and over.

At the apartment, even though their friendships had just formed, both Cindy and Brad became totally supportive. They acted like lifelong friends. Now dark outside, Cindy and Brad insisted they fix a light meal before returning to the hospital. Mark really didn't feel like eating, but consumed a few saltines and some vegetable soup.

Mark sighed. "Cindy, tell me the truth. What do you think her chances are?"

"Better than most with HPS," Cindy replied. "Overall the disease carries a 50 percent mortality rate. But that mortality rate includes the very young and the elderly. It also includes a number of patients who did *not* get prompt pulmonary support. The single most important thing is that she was put on a ventilator very early, and they've got her oxygen saturation on the upswing."

"Baxter told me it was up to 88 percent," Mark said.

"If they can get her oxygen saturation in the 90s, we'll know the worst has passed," Cindy explained. "We should know that in the next several hours. I'd also like to recheck her antibody levels tomorrow. I'll try to talk Dr. Baxter into giving me another sample of her blood in the morning. If her IgM and IgG are rising, that's a very good sign her immune system is responding to the challenge. But I'm now wondering exactly *how* and *when* she got exposed to hanta in the first place. Do you have any ideas?"

Sitting at the dining table with Cindy and Brad, Mark stared at Brad's cell phone resting in the middle of the table. He dreaded what the message might be if it rang. Holding his head in his hands, eyes closed, Mark finally answered Cindy's question: "As for *when* she got exposed, it had to be when we were in New Mexico. I've lost track of exactly how many days ago that was, but it was approximately ten days."

"Cindy, that would be a rather short incubation period, wouldn't it?" Brad asked.

"Yes, Brad ... unless the *amount* of the virus she contacted was quite large. The studies I did in college indicated the incubation period can be quite short if a person inhales a large amount of the virus. When I was doing my epidemiological studies on hanta, I recall one patient who got sick within *three days* of exposure. The poor fellow was using an electric leaf blower to clean dust out of a mouse-infested warehouse. And he was wearing no mask for protection."

"But my wife certainly didn't do anything like that!" Mark said. "I still think it has something to do with Dr. Abbas."

"Why so?" Cindy asked.

"When we were at the RV park in Gallup, Dr. Abbas brought a pillowcase inside our camper. It was filled with white-footed deer mice ... or so he claimed that's what they were. He said he needed to keep them cool, and that the AC in his own camper had quit working," Mark explained.

"Just an ordinary pillowcase? Did any of the mice get loose in your camper?" Cindy asked.

"I think it was just an ordinary pillowcase, but he had its open end secured with a zip tie. I don't think any of the mice got out. They weren't inside our camper more than 20 minutes," Mark answered.

"Brad, just how large are the hantavirus particles?" Cindy asked.

"The actual hanta virons I study measure 100 to 270 nanometers in their greatest dimensions," Brad explained. "That's a lot smaller than the weave of the cloth in an ordinary pillowcase. So, viral particles could have easily been left behind, even if none of the mice physically escaped from the pillowcase."

"Where in the camper did Abbas place his mice?" Cindy asked Mark.

"On the carpeted floor next to our dinette table. If fact, it left a little dust on the floor. I don't know if that dust was on the outside of the pillowcase, or if it sifted through the cloth from its interior. Maybe a little of both," Mark added.

"And how did you clean up that dust?" Cindy asked Mark.

"I didn't. My wife did. She used her Dustbuster, and it sucked it right up."

Bradley and Cindy stared at one another for a long moment, each nodding their heads. "I think we may have figured out part of the puzzle. Don't you, Cin?" Brad asked.

"Maybe. We need to get our hands on that Dustbuster, and study it in the lab," Cindy remarked.

"*Cautiously,* get our hands on it," Bradley remarked. "I'll bet the filter inside that Dustbuster won't trap viral particles, not even ones *larger* than hanta's 270 nanometers maximum!"

The ring of Brad's cell phone caused Mark's heart to race. Brad picked it up. "Hold a second. I'll put him on."

Mark placed the phone to his ear:

"Is this Dr. Jon Traer?" Dr. Baxter asked.

"Yes."

"This is Dr. Baxter at MSU. I've got some bad news. We're having a hard time maintaining your wife's oxygen saturation. It's back down to 84 percent. We need your permission to do some minor surgery. We want to put a vascular shunt in her arm, and connect her to an experimental oxygenating device. We've used it several times before in patients with severe pulmonary failure, and with good results."

"I'll come right away. I realize she can't sign the surgical permit in her sedated condition."

"Doctor, I'm gonna break the rules. I'll accept your verbal permission by phone, and have them do it stat. You can sign the paperwork after the fact. I'll be waiting for you in the ICU."

* * *

Mark, Cindy, and Brad arrived at the ICU in record time. Dr. Baxter was pacing the floor and looking at his watch when they arrived. Mark scribbled his signature on a surgical permit he didn't bother to read.

"They're putting the shunt in right now," Dr. Baxter explained. "They're doing it in her ICU room under local anesthesia, but she's got enough morphine aboard she probably wouldn't feel a thing anyway."

"Can I see her?" Mark asked.

"As soon as they've got her connected to the membrane oxygenator. The surgeon is a vascular man, Dr. Dooley. He's our very best," Dr. Baxter added, trying to comfort Mark. "I was supposed to go off shift an hour ago, but I'm not about to leave your wife until I'm satisfied she'll be OK."

"Thanks," was all Mark could think to say. He immediately recalled the numerous times he'd been in Dr. Baxter's position: a time when it was time to pass the baton to another member of a critical care team ... but you couldn't, or wouldn't. You found yourself so personally invested, you just couldn't let that patient go.

"Dr. Baxter," Brad asked, "would you consider using something else that's experimental? Something I've got it in my lab at UA? I'm a molecular biologist, but my main interest is in developing a vaccine for hanta. As you know there is no vaccine yet, but I have a large quantity of anti-hanta hyperimmune globulin in my lab."

Dr. Baxter thought a moment, then said, "I'd rather we confer with Dr. Schroder. He's the ID guy who's consulting on this case. I'll have them page him stat for the ICU."

Five minutes later the bearded bald-headed rotund elderly physician appeared in the ICU. He wore a long white lab jacket. "Hi, I'm Bill Schroder. Somebody need me?"

"Yes," Dr. Baxter replied. "I had them page you. I appreciate your coming so quickly. This gentleman here is a molecular biologist at UA. His name is Bradley—"

"Bradley Buck," Brad interrupted, and extended his hand to the professorial-looking physician. "I have offered Dr. Baxter some hanta-specific hyperimmune globulin I have in my research lab. I think he wanted your thoughts about using it on Kristin."

"I see," said Schroder. "Is it *human* globulin?"

"Yes," Brad answered.

"And how did you acquire it?" Schroder asked.

"By drawing small amounts of blood from every hantavirus survivor I could find in the Southwest. I've collected it over the last three years," Brad answered. "I now have almost 30 milliliters. It's frozen in liquid nitrogen."

"And has it been screened for HIV, AIDS, hepatitis, et cetera?" Schroder asked.

"Certainly!" Brad shot back. "After all, we handle the stuff in the lab, too."

"Let's see what the next few hours bring. Personally I'd require an experimental procedure permit from the family. Even though the risk is probably low, it is still *experimental.* I'm not aware of hyperimmune globulin ever being used in treating an active hantavirus infection."

Dr. Baxter entered the conversation: "Dr. Schroder, since you last saw the patient her oxygen saturation has been falling. It's now in the mid-80s. I've gotten a surgical consult with Dr. Dooley. He is with her now. They're putting in a shunt to connect her to an external membrane oxygenator."

The words were no sooner out of Dr. Baxter's mouth when a tall asthenic man wearing green surgical scrubs stepped from inside the ICU. He smiled broadly, stuck his right thumb in the air, then announced, "Everything went fine. We've got her up to 95 percent!"

Baxter beamed. "Thanks, Dr. Dooley. And this gentleman here is her husband, Dr. Jon Traer. He's a retired surgeon."

"Sir," Dooley said, "your bride is one sick gal. But being a doctor yourself, I'm sure you already realize that. If this new external membrane oxygenator works as well as it has in our similar recent cases of respiratory failure, I think she's got a real shot at recovery." Without further words Dooley shook Mark's hand, and quickly departed the ICU.

Those were the sort of words Mark desperately wanted to hear, but he realized things were still precarious at best. "Can I see her now?" Mark asked Dr. Baxter.

"Sure. I've taken her off isolation since we now know this is hantavirus. We know it's not contagious person-to-person. We are still isolating any of your wife's secretions as possible biohazards, but you won't have to gown this time."

12

Mark followed Dr. Baxter into ICU Room 10. The nurse at Anne's bedside made some notes on her chart, then politely stepped out of the room.

Anne actually had her eyes open now, and Mark could tell by her attempted smile she'd immediately recognized him. He again showed her Saint Christopher. She smiled again, then turned her head and eyes toward the right. Apparently she was trying to get Mark to notice the strange little bucket-sized medical device that stood there on a standard. Blood-filled tubes ran from the device and disappeared beneath a surgical dressing covering her right forearm. A single clear tube from the device connected to an oxygen port on the wall. Using her left index finger Anne traced out a big question mark on the bed's sheet.

"Just nod a 'yes' if you're asking me what that device is," Mark said.

She nodded.

"Well, it's something relatively new. It wasn't in clinical use back when we were in practice. It's something we never had in our surgical ICU where you worked. It's called a membrane oxygenator. They've put a vascular shunt in your forearm, and some of your blood circulates through the device where it gets highly oxygenated, then it's returned to a vein in your arm," Mark explained.

She smiled again, then slowly closed her eyes.

"Let's let her rest now," Dr. Baxter said. "That was a pretty good explanation of a membrane oxygenator. It's great to know she recognized you, and recognized a change in her surroundings well enough to 'ask' a question. The hypoxia she's had certainly does not seem to have affected her brain!"

"I certainly hope not," Mark said. "She's a damn smart woman, but I'd still love her even if her IQ falls to 60."

"I'm comfortable she's stable. As Chief Medical Resident, they allow me to take call from home. I'm less than ten minutes from the hospital, so I'm going home to get a little sleep. I'll meet you back here at 8:00 in the morning, or before then if anything changes."

Mark felt tears coming, so he quickly left her ICU room with Dr. Baxter on his heels.

* * *

Mark, Cindy, and Brad returned to the apartment. Cindy immediately began her pursuit of the "how" regarding Anne's contraction of hantavirus.

"What we really need is that Dustbuster, even if she's emptied it."

"I doubt she did, Cindy. We use a good mat at the door, and track very little dirt into our camper," Mark explained.

"Why don't we go get it tonight?" Cindy asked, anxious to get her hands on what she considered to be a pivotal piece of evidence needed to prove her theory.

"Cin," Brad began, "it's a 20-minute drive out to Camarada's airfield, and 20 minutes back. I don't know how Jon feels, but I don't think we should get that far away from the hospital until we're sure things are stable with Kristin."

"I agree with Brad," Mark said. "Besides, I need to sleep … if I can. And I've got to check in with the Marshals Service at 7:00 in the morning. Maybe we could go get the Dustbuster about midmorning tomorrow."

* * *

Mark was able to sleep, though fitfully so. He kept reaching to the other side of the twin bed hoping to touch Anne, who was not there. Over and over he kept dreaming that Anne had died, then dreamed that he, too, was coming down with symptoms of hantavirus infection. Awake at 6:00 a.m., but not well rested, he showered in the guest bath, one connecting to the guest bedroom. He dressed in the only change of clothes Anne had packed, then called Marshal Salizar promptly at 7:00. The reception was less than cordial:

"And why haven't you gotten the GPS on your camper fixed yet?" Marshal Salizar demanded right off the bat.

"Well, it's like this: Kristin is critically ill and in the hospital at University Medical Center in Tucson. She's in Room 10 of their ICU. It's located on the third floor. If you don't believe me, you can call the hospital. She's admitted under her WITSEC name, Mary Kristin Traer."

"Sorry to hear that. What's the matter with her?" Salizar asked.

Mark wanted to say "None of your damn business," but didn't. "They think she's got a hantavirus infection and pulmonary failure. She's on a ventilator, and getting excellent medical care. I'll get the damn GPS fixed when I've got the time … but right now, that's real low on my list of priorities."

There was a long pause before Salizar spoke. "Uh … I'm sorry. OK? Call me tomorrow at 0700."

Apparently Louis Loveman hasn't gotten word to this jerk-off yet, Mark thought before clicking his satphone off.

Mark entered the kitchen area where Cindy or Bradley had already made coffee. Cindy was cooking pancakes.

"Good morning, Jon," Brad said. "I hope you were able to sleep."

"Just a series of catnaps and bad dreams, but I do feel a little more rested. You didn't get any calls on your cell during the night, did you?" Mark asked.

"No," Bradley explained, "but we did call the ICU earlier this morning. As nonfamily, they wouldn't tell me much other than she's 'stable' and still on their 'critically ill' list. You want to use my cell to call? The direct line to the ICU nurses' station is stored in my phone."

"Sure," Mark said, and promptly used Brad's phone. Dr. Baxter was already there when he called, and a nurse promptly put him on the line:

"This is Dr. Traer, Dr. Baxter. How's my wife this morning?" Mark asked.

"I don't want to sound overly optimistic, but I think we may be over the hump. Her oxygen sat is up to 98 percent, but that's with both the membrane oxygenator and the ventilator assisting. Her breath sounds are a lot better this morning. I just ordered a portable follow-up chest x-ray. I've now got to make rounds on a number of other patients. Think you could meet me at the ICU about 10:00? We could go over her chart, and look at her latest chest film then."

"That would be great! See you at 10:00 … and thanks for all you've done." Mark allowed a broad smile to dominate his face, then spoke to Cindy and Brad: "Might be 'over the hump,' Dr. Baxter said!"

"Great!" Cindy and Brad exclaimed in unison.

"I don't know what I would have done without you two," Mark said. "I feel like we've wrecked the three-day vacation you two had planned. How can I ever pay you guys back?"

"Jon, this really is a vacation from the boring mechanics of dissertation writing," Cindy explained. "I think I can speak for Brad, too. It just happens this is very much a change of pace for us. It's giving us both some hands-on experience with hanta, and motivating us to learn more, especially since Kristin is directly involved. We desperately want her to be a survivor. I know you realize we're not out of the woods yet. When I was doing my epidemiological studies, I learned it sometimes takes quite awhile to wean the patients off the support equipment. I'm not trying to be negative, just realistic. And I still want some of Kristin's blood to see what her antibodies are doing … and I want to examine that Dustbuster."

Small, beautiful, brilliant, tenacious, and a scientist to the core! Mark thought.

Brad poured coffee, and distributed silverware and plates. Cindy served their pancakes and poured orange juice. Over breakfast they quickly established the day's game plan: First, they would go to Cindy's lab at UA to pick up supplies needed to safely retrieve the Dustbuster from the RV. Second, they'd call the hospital and see if Dr. Baxter would issue an order for a tech's drawing of a fresh blood sample from Anne, then leave it at the nurses' station in the ICU. Third, they'd retrieve the Dustbuster, then the blood sample, and take both items to Cindy's lab. Cindy would remain at her lab to begin running the antibody tests; Brad would then drive Mark to the hospital to meet with Dr. Baxter at the ICU by 10:00 a.m.

Mark's head was still spinning when they arrived at Camarada Aviation's hangar. Cindy quickly donned a full biohazard suit that was at least a size too large for her. Mark explained where the Dustbuster was kept in the RV, gave Cindy the RV's door key, and he and Bradley opened the hangar door. In less than five minutes, Cindy exited the RV, locked its door, and walked out of the hangar with the Dustbuster inside a special bag bearing the bright yellow international biohazard symbol. She carefully stripped off the disposable biohazard suit, and did it in a way that her skin never touched an exterior surface of the protective suit. With gloved hands, and both wearing special masks, Brad held open another biohazard bag. Working as a team, they carefully placed Cindy's discarded suit inside it, then their masks and gloves before sealing the bag.

"God, those damn suits are hot!" Cindy said, flipping her pink tank top up and down to fan herself, oblivious to the fact Mark was getting an eyeful.

"Nice looking bra, Cin," Brad said, apparently trying to remind her Mark was present.

"He's a doctor, Brad. He's seen a woman's stuff before! I think I would have died if I'd stayed in that suit another five minutes. It's not like in the lab—where we have air conditioning, and it's kept at a constant 68 degrees!"

Bradley chuckled, then placed the plastic bags in the VW's trunk. They immediately sped off, heading for the hospital. Fortunately the blood sample was waiting for them at the ICU. The next stop was Cindy's lab at UA. When they arrived, she hopped out. Brad popped the trunk and Cindy disappeared inside the lab building carrying the biohazard bags and blood sample with her.

Bradley quickly worked through the VW's manual gears as they sped back to the hospital to meet with Dr. Baxter at 10:00. Before arriving at UMC, Mark could not resist a question: "Does Cindy always move at the speed of light?"

Brad laughed. "Except during sex. That's the only time she slows down to a delightfully slow pace!"

"Same for Kristin," Mark added with a chuckle.

* * *

A few minutes after 10:00, Dr. Baxter appeared in the ICU to review his patient's status in detail. He had her chart and current x-rays in hand. "I assume the blood sample I had them draw earlier has already been picked up, correct?"

"Correct," Brad replied. "Cindy is running it in her lab as we speak. I'm sure she'll phone me as soon as she gets the results." Brad removed his cell from his pocket, quickly checking it to be sure it was turned on.

Dr. Baxter led Mark and Brad to a private consultation room that adjoined the ICU waiting area. With a smile, Dr. Baxter first placed yesterday's film on a view box, then placed the one made an hour ago alongside it.

Mark could not believe his eyes. "Even a surgeon can see the infiltrate has dramatically cleared!"

"Even a molecular biologist can see it!" Brad piped in.

"But here's the important stuff," Dr Baxter said, opening her chart. Just look at the graph of her oxygen saturation since we added the membrane oxygenator. She's staying in the high 90s. Her white blood cell count is returning to normal, her platelet count beginning to rise … all very good signs."

Dr. Baxter was going to say something else, but the chirp of Brad's cell silenced him.

"What's up, Cin?" Brad said, checking his caller ID. "I'll let you tell Dr. Baxter personally. He's sitting right here with us."

Brad passed his cell to Baxter. "That's great! Can you fax me the results so I'll have a hard copy for her chart?" There was a pause. He gave her a fax number, then said, "Thanks, Miss Loveman, I'll tell him."

Dr. Baxter was silent for a moment. He smiled broadly, looking at Mark. "She told me Kristin's IgG and IgM have almost doubled, meaning her immune system is responding *extremely* well! Miss Loveman also said for you guys not to worry about picking her up at the lab. She said she'd walk back to the apartment and start preparing lunch … and for you guys to visit Kristin as long as I'd allow. Sorry, but that's only five minutes!" Dr. Baxter said, then scurried off to talk with another family whose loved one was in the ICU.

13

The ICU visit was brief. Anne had her eyes closed and remained totally unable to communicate. The nurse in attendance assured them she was unresponsive solely because they'd recently increased her sedation to keep her from fighting the ventilator. "Doctor, she's getting stronger by the hour! Her right arm was previously restrained by Dr. Dooley. He did that because it's connected to the membrane oxygenator, and he certainly didn't want to risk any of those tubes getting disconnected. We've now had to restrain her left hand because she'd earlier tried to pull her endotracheal tube out! Her vitals are great, and as you can see, her oxygen sat is 98 percent," the nurse said, pointing to the digital readout from the oximeter. "Moments ago I removed the cooling pad because her temp is now normal, and it has been that way for the last 12 hours."

* * *

Mark and Brad arrived at the apartment where Cindy already had nice chef salads prepared. While eating, it was obvious that Cindy's mind was still in overdrive.

"As soon as we finish eating, why don't we all go to my lab?" Cindy asked. "That Dustbuster is still bugging me."

"No," Brad said, "let's go to *my* lab. I can do electron microscopy on the dust, and you can't do that in *your* lab."

"I know that, Brad! But just save me enough dust so I can attempt to propagate a viral culture from it."

"Can do, my dear," Brad said, then gave her a peck on the cheek.

* * *

They first went to Cindy's lab to get the "bagged" Dustbuster, then walked to Brad's molecular biology lab located in an adjoining building.

"I think it would be best if everyone watched from behind the glass of the lab's observation room," Brad suggested. "That would save time, and everybody won't need to suit up."

"We'll watch your every little move, dear Bradley," Cindy teased, then explained the procedure to Mark: "This observation room is basically for students. It lets them actually observe working in a bio-containment environment before they are ever allowed to actually work in one. While working, Brad will keep the door locked. It's an electronic lock he controls from inside the lab. This box on the wall here in the observation room is an intercom. We can communicate with him even though he's locked in there."

"Similar to the observatory area in a teaching hospital's OR," Mark commented.

Inside the lab on the other side of the glass, Brad wiggled into a biohazard suit, then moved the bag with the Dustbuster to a specialized work area that Cindy said was called a "laminar flow hood." She explained how the hood's air currents were always away from the worker, and then highly filtered and sterilized before that air was ultimately discharged to the exterior of the building.

Brad soon had the Dustbuster disassembled. He placed a portion of the dust in a small glass vile, secured its top and wrote "Cindy" on the label. Still working under the hood, he then placed the vial in a small chamber that contained ethylene oxide gas. "He's doing that to sterilize the *exterior* of the vial," Cindy explained. Brad next prepared standard microscopic slides, then made a special preparation for the electron microscope. He placed those items in the gas chamber and left them there, but removed the vial marked "Cindy." He carefully placed Cindy's vial in doubled Ziploc bags. "The preparation Brad just made for the electron microscope is imbedded in a special resin. It usually takes about a day for that resin to fully cure. You can speed the process by using something like a hairdryer on it, but then the resin surfaces have to be highly polished to remove any irregularities or scratches. So, it'll probably take at least another day to get that sample ready to look at with the EM."

Brad reassembled the Dustbuster, and placed it in a new bag leaving it on the work surface beneath the laminar flow hood. Methodically, he shed his protective gear, stowed it in biohazard containers, and exited the lab carrying only Cindy's specimen inside the Ziplocs. "Well, I'm sure Cindy explained some of what I was doing in there. Any questions?" Brad immediately asked.

"Just two," Mark smiled. "Why the heck did you put that vial for Cindy inside *two* Ziplocs? And will we get our Dustbuster back?"

Cindy and Bradley both broke out in laughter. Brad finally answered: "Sometimes I get clumsy and drop stuff, especially tableware. That's why we have only eight of the original twelve dishes Cindy and I started out with!"

"And the double-bagged vial for Cindy was in case you dropped it and broke it?" Mark teased.

"Yes. The glass vial for Cindy may have live hantavirus *inside* it. It's exterior is now sterile due to its exposure to ethylene oxide gas. And yes, you'll get your Dustbuster back. I'll put it in a larger ethylene oxide chamber tomorrow to completely sterilize it. I'll then do some tests on the filter in that unit. I specifically want to see if hanta-sized particles can pass through it. Might even send Black & Decker the results of my testing!"

"I can envision another product-warning label in the making!" Mark chuckled, soon to be joined by Cindy and Brad's laughter.

The threesome walked to Cindy's lab, where she started a viral culture from the contents of the vial Brad had prepared for her. Mark noted she took essentially the same precautions Brad had taken in his lab. Mark's mind pondered: *God! I'd hate to spend my life working in an environment where so many of the things I handled had lethal potential. But then I've operated on many patients I knew were HIV positive.*

* * *

Back at the apartment, Brad and Mark started with beers, Cindy with iced tea. They were having a roundtable discussion:

"Brad, when will you do your EM studies?" Cindy asked.

"About 48 hours. And when will your cultures tell you if that dust contains viable hantavirus?" Brad asked.

"About that same time frame," Cindy replied. "But here's something that just came to mind. Let's suppose we do find hanta inside the Dustbuster. Wouldn't that mean the *entire* RV interior could be contaminated?"

"I think you're right, Cin," Brad said. "And that would be a very difficult space to decontaminate."

"Unless we gassed it!" Cindy exclaimed.

"Gassed it?" Mark asked.

"Yes. With ethylene oxide, the same stuff Brad used to sterilize the exterior of the small vial of dust he gave to me," Cindy explained.

They next tried to compute the cubic volume of air inside the RV, and from Mark's memory of dimensions, they came up with a good estimated interior air volume. "That's about 2,000 cubic feet," Cindy said, "and it takes about two pounds of ethylene oxide to attain a lethal level in 1,000 cubic feet … so that means we would need about four pounds of the stuff to effectively fumigate his RV."

"Wow!" Brad replied. "That would take more ethylene oxide than we've got in the entire lab! Maybe both our labs combined. I guess I could order that much tomorrow. Might take a day or two to get it here."

They finally decided to wait until they'd proven hantavirus was inside the camper before they did anything so drastic as "gassing" the entire vehicle.

"I think we should update my dad," Cindy said. "Especially about Mary Kristin being in the ICU at UMC with a proven hanta infection. I think we should also tell him what we're doing in our labs to try to document the source of the hantavirus that has made Kristin so critically ill."

Mark spoke up. "I've got the satphone your dad gave me. It's in the bedroom. I'll go get it."

Mark returned a moment later. "Cindy, you wouldn't happen to have a Band-Aid, would you?"

"Sure. Got a whole box of the circular ones. I'll go get you one," Cindy said, and disappeared into their bedroom.

Brad chuckled, then whispered, "Cin gets very visible nipple erections when she wears thin stuff and gets excited, especially in the lab where it's cool. It embarrasses her, so she puts those circular Band-Aids over her nipples under her bra … keeps the guys in the lab from teasing her."

Cindy quickly returned, and handed Mark the Band-Aid. "I didn't ask you why you needed it, but here it is."

"I'm gonna use this one as a marker to put on the satphone your dad gave me when we visited him. That way I can distinguish it from the identical-looking phone issued to me by the U.S. Marshals Service," Mark explained, as he applied the flesh-toned round Band-Aid to the back of the FBI phone Louis Loveman had given them.

Bradley burst out laughing, soon to be followed by Mark. "Bradley! You didn't dare tell Jon why I use these—"

"Yes I did! But earlier today, it was *you* who reminded me Jon was a doctor, and had seen 'ladies' stuff' before! True?"

Cindy blushed, said nothing, then burst out laughing, keeping her arms tightly folded over her chest.

"Let's move on. Call my dad," Cindy finally said.

Mark removed the owner's manual from his pocket and punched in the numbers Louis Loveman had written there. He answered on the third ring.

"Mr. Loveman, it's Jon Traer calling."

"Thanks for identifying yourself, but the last five digits of your phone number are displayed on my phone's LCD. That serves as a caller ID for satphones. So, what do you have to tell me?"

"I hope we're not interrupting your evening meal. A lot has happened since we left your place yesterday."

"I've got plenty of time. Sampson and I have already had our microwaved TV dinners. So shoot."

"First, Kristin is in the hospital at UMC. She's on a ventilator and special oxygenating support equipment. She got a proven hantavirus infection, but I think she may be over the worst."

"Good God!" Louis exclaimed. "Is Cindy OK? What about Brad and yourself?"

"We're all fine, sir. The stuff is not contagious person-to-person. I have possibly been exposed when Abbas brought his mice into our camper, but so far I have no symptoms. I don't think either Bradley or Cindy are at risk. Just me."

"Is Cindy where I can talk to her?"

"She's right here, sir," Mark said.

"You don't need to 'sir' me. 'Louis' is fine. Can you put Cindy on?"

"Yes, Louis. Here she is," Mark said, and passed the satphone to Cindy.

"Hi Daddy! It looks like the stuff has really hit the fan on our end. But I think Jon has told you all we know about Kristin at the moment. But I do have a question. Have the lab guys in Denver analyzed the dust from that envelope Jon and Kristin passed to the FBI?"

"Yes. There was only a very small amount of dust inside the envelope. They've looked at it with an electron microscope. They say it's chock full of particulate organic material compatible with dried fecal matter, and most importantly, viral particles. They are still trying to identify the virus."

"Daddy, I hope your lab guys who looked at the dust in the envelope took precautions and considered it a possible biohazard!"

"They sure did! Treated that dust just like it was anthrax, or worse," Louis assured.

"Could you get the Denver lab to e-mail us digital images they made through their electron microscope? Bradley may be able to identify the virus from the images alone."

"Honey, I'll do what I can. I may have to break some of the Bureau's rules about evidence, but I'll see what I can do. You sure you're OK?" Louis asked.

"Yes, Daddy. Just send the images as an e-mail attachment to us here at the apartment. I'll get Bradley to look at them. Any new news about where Abbas is located?"

"Still in Gainesville, Georgia, messing with some chicken houses he's purchased. We're going to try to get an undercover detail to keep an eye on what he is doing there."

"Keep us informed, Dad." Cindy said.

"Tell Jon to keep the satphone I gave him charged and turned on … and do it as close to 24/7 as possible. And tell him I think his next encounter with Marshal Salizar will be a little different."

"OK, Dad. Love ya. Bye."

14

Before ending their whirlwind day, Bradley kindly offered to drive Mark to the ICU for the day's final check on Anne. They were not disappointed. The doctors had decreased her sedation again. Her eyes were open. She tried to smile the moment she saw Mark and Bradley enter her room.

"She's doing great!" the nurse said. "We've cut way back on the oxygen flow to the membrane oxygenator, and she's still maintaining a 98 percent saturation. Dr. Baxter and her pulmonologist both saw her about 30 minutes ago. They want to begin weaning her off the ventilator tomorrow morning."

Mark removed Saint Christopher from his wallet, then turned to the nurse. "You wouldn't happen to have a piece of string a couple of feet long, would you?"

"No, Doctor, I don't have any string … but I think I know what you want to do. I can lend you the chain for my crucifix. Would that help?"

Without words, the cute young Hispanic nurse unbuttoned the top button of her uniform, and fished out a Christian cross buried deep in her ample cleavage. *It's still warm,* Mark thought as he removed the nurse's cross, then threaded his Saint Christopher medal onto the silver chain. He returned the crucifix to the nurse, then began fastening the borrowed chain around Anne's neck. Mark bent over and placed his mouth close to Anne's ear to speak. "Honey, I love you. I hope you can hear me and understand. You and Saint Christopher keep on fighting this thing. I'll see you in the morning." *Oh God, how I want to kiss her,* he thought as he finally got the chain's clasp closed, then tears tried to form in his eyes.

"Doctor, I think you'd better leave now. Her pulse just jumped to 120, but it's normal sinus rhythm. It's just the excitement of seeing you."

* * *

On the drive back to the apartment, Bradley spoke: "Jon, I normally don't talk this way with other men. But what you did with that Saint Christopher was … well, it was just plain *sweet,* for lack of a better guy-term."

"Brad, that medal has a long history with Kristin and myself. It was jokingly given to me by a Jew about 30 years ago. He gave it to me right after we married. For both of us, that medal has served as our good luck piece, our faith, whatever you want to call it. Kristin and I aren't active churchgoers, but we both believe that medal has given us faith and guidance when faced with tough times and difficult decisions we've had to address during our lives together."

"I still can't think of another word … other than *sweet!*" Bradley said, as he parked the VW at the apartment.

When Mark and Bradley entered the apartment, Brad spotted a note on the counter. "I've crashed. Love, C."

Brad chuckled as he read her short note. "That means *two* things: 'Not tonight,' and 'I'm really tired.' Want a beer before we call it a day?" Brad asked.

Mark checked his watch: midnight. "Sure. But just one for me. I'm quite tired myself, and I don't think I'll have any trouble sleeping. And I want to be sober enough that a beeping satphone would wake me up right away. And you have your cell that Dr. Baxter might call. Also, I've got to check in with Marshal Salizar at 7:00 in the morning. I have a travel alarm. I'll set it in the guest bedroom. So, you guys sleep in, just get up when you'd normally wake up."

Brad popped the caps on two longneck Dos Equis and handed one to Mark. They sat on stools facing each other at the granite-topped island in the kitchen area.

Mark took a sip of his beer, then spoke. "Ya know, that's one thing the Mexicans do well. Make beer."

"These are the last two beers in the house. Remind me to buy some more tomorrow," Brad said.

"No!" Mark replied. "*I'll* buy. As it is, I already feel like an absolute and total moocher! Free accommodations and meals here in Tucson, thanks to you and Cindy. Free place to store my RV, and a free plane ride and ground travel to meet Cindy's dad in Boulder … all thanks to Cal Camarada. And free high-tech lab tests in UA's research labs, thanks to you and Cindy."

"Jon, the only payment Cindy and I want is to see Kristin get well. If Kristin recovers, and I'm almost positive she will, my payment would be to have her periodically donate blood in my lab so I can harvest her hanta-specific antibodies."

"I feel positive she'd want to do that. But that Cal Camarada probably spent hundreds of dollars flying us to Boulder. I feel I should at least offer to pay him for the fuel!"

"Only if you want to insult him. Cal's a funny guy, Jon. He's a self-made multimillionaire, possibly a billionaire for all I know. But he doesn't flaunt his wealth. He derives great personal pleasure by helping others. His wealth may still show in the 'toys' he owns, like his Cessna 310, and that $50,000 Porsche Boxster he drives. What's not obvious is his anonymous donations to UA. For a fact, I've learned he secretly donated well over five million to the biology department at UA. That was last year alone! Cindy and I both would like to be rich, but know we'll probably never get that way by doing what we're planning to do with our lives. Though academic grants cover the bulk of our expenses, we've both decided we'd never mention to Cal our need for a little extra money while we're in grad school. He'd insist on helping us out. So, Cindy will probably do work in the university bookstore, and I'll probably again work at the convenience center for the Gallup RV park next summer."

"How did you two come to know Cal?" Mark asked.

"It's like this: Cal Camarada and Louis Loveman were buds in the Air Force back during the Korean War. Both were very young fighter pilots, flying F-86 Sabre jets. Cal told me it was the first time U.S. jet aircraft entered into battle, and on a routine basis they bested Soviet-built MiG-15s. Apparently Cal was considered the 'Ace' in their squadron, but on one sortie Cal made a mistake and was about to get hammered by a MiG. Louis somehow intervened, shot the MiG down, but got his own plane badly damaged in the process. Louis limped back to base but survived the crash landing he made upon his arrival. Over the years Cal has been forever grateful to Louis. When the war ended, and they got out, Louis went through some special training, then to work with the FBI. Cal flew corporate jets for awhile, then crop dusters for a big cotton-growing consortium in Texas. He bought more and more crop dusters, and eventually had a dozen of them. He started his own flight training school for 'duster pilots' here in Tucson. Not satisfied with that success, Cal also started another business: He bought and sold aircraft parts for older jets and vintage aircraft, like the old DC-3s and World War II birds collectors and aviation clubs were restoring. He actually took me to Davis-Monthan Air Force Base here in Tucson, what he called the 'aircraft boneyard.' Truly impressive! They got thousands upon thousands of old planes there.

Cal says the government chose this area because its low humidity and desert-like conditions were perfect for preservation."

"Sounds to me like everything Cal touches turns to gold!" Mark replied.

"True," Brad said. "He's made all the money he'll ever need. He's slowing down now, and enjoying the fruits of his many years of hard work. I don't think he's flying the dusters himself anymore, just leases trained pilots and planes to the big agricultural folks, mainly in Texas and Mississippi. He founded Camarada Aviation, Inc., the umbrella corporation for all his business ventures. But I think he's now dismantling that corporation, but will keep his airfield and flight training school here in Tucson. So, basically we know Cal because he's one of Louis Loveman's closest friends. Louis knows I want to learn to fly, and as my future father-in-law, he told me he does not want his daughter married to *any* pilot ... unless that pilot was trained by Cal Camarada!"

"So, Louis has utmost faith in Cal, who is obviously a good pilot, and is truly self-made, as you explained earlier," Mark replied. "But what about Louis?"

"I don't know much about the structure of the FBI, but Louis hung with it. He came up through the ranks, so to speak. I know he's now well beyond the FBI's normal mandatory retirement age, but through some special dispensation—something to do about 'national security'—they've begged him to continue working with the Bureau. He's now some Special Senior Field Agent for the Denver Field Office, and oversees part of their counterterrorism investigations. That's all I can tell you," Brad said, and took the last sip of his beer.

"Your dad was with the CIA, right?" Mark questioned.

"Yes, and still is. He's nearing retirement age, though. I remember when I was a kid, Dad was almost never home for any period of time. He spent a lot of time in foreign countries, and still does. He told our family virtually nothing about his work, always telling us it was 'classified information.' So, I grew up with a father I really didn't know ... and still don't," Brad said.

"I didn't know my dad well, either," Mark admitted. "He was a senior partner in a large CPA firm in Atlanta. A true workaholic, who spent little time at home. He died of a massive heart attack when he was only 63. I guess he was trying to get rich like Cal. Who knows? But you say Cal and Louis have stayed in contact over the years, right?" Mark asked.

"Yes," Brad said, "but I have no idea what they discuss. Something about airplanes and old times in Korea, I'd guess. Whenever Louis comes to Tucson, he stays with Cal in his condo. Cal's definitely a very eligible bachelor who has multiple girlfriends. I suspect, but can't prove, and would never mention it to Cindy, but I think Cal probably fixes Louis up with female companionship during his visits here. I also know Cal takes Louis flying whenever they visit, but that's about the extent of my knowledge regarding their friendship."

Mark yawned and took a deep breath. "Brad, I don't know about you but I need to call it a day." Mark took the last swallow of his beer. He checked his watch: 12:45.

"I need to call it a day, too. I'll wake you if Dr. Baxter gives us a call on my cell. Sleep well," Brad said in parting.

* * *

The buzzing of his travel alarm at 6:00 a.m. reminded Mark where he was. He'd had a dreamless sound sleep. He quickly showered, and dressed in the same clothes he wore yesterday. His full short facial beard needed a trimming, but he decided to put that off a day or two. Promptly at 7:00 he called Salizar using the satphone that did not have a Band-Aid stuck to its back. The marshal answered on the first ring:

"Good morning, Jon. How's Kristin?" Salizar immediately asked.

"As of late yesterday, she's doing a lot better," Mark replied.

"Great to hear that!" Salizar exclaimed. "And, I've been thinking. I know you're going through a bad time right now, and I think we can stop the daily call-in. Just call to let me know how Kristin's doing, or if you change your location. And there's really no rush on getting the GPS on your camper fixed. Just do it when you can."

"What about getting us out of WITSEC? Any progress?" Mark asked.

"Yes. You both still want to go back to your original names, Dr. Marcus Milton Telfair, M.D. and Mrs. Anne Hunt Telfair, R.N., right?"

"Correct, including the professional titles," Mark confirmed.

"Good. That means I've got almost everything done except for current photos. I'll need them for your U.S. passports and driver's licenses. I assume you and Kristin want Georgia drivers' licenses again. Right?"

"Correct," Mark replied.

"To complete everything all I need are current full-facial photos of both you and Kristin. They need to be two-by-two inches, chin to crown, high-resolution, and on a monochromic light blue background. It's probably best if you go to any place that routinely does passport photos. I think even Wal-Mart does 'em now. Can you get that done for me?"

"As soon as Kristin's off the ventilator and well enough to leave the hospital. I don't know exactly when that'll be," Mark explained.

"Well, please do it as soon as her condition permits. I'll arrange for a Marshals Service courier to pick up the new photos after they're made. The courier can also have you sign the petition for change of name. Just let me know when they're done. When I get your new photos, it'll take me only a couple of hours to finalize your new identity documents. I can arrange for another courier to personally deliver your new ones. He'll pick up all the old ones and the satphone we've issued. We'll also need you to return the GPS on the roof of your camper. You'll have to sign a few additional things as well, but the Marshals Service courier can take care of all that. Bottom line, I'll have everything ready for you two to get out of WITSEC within 24 hours of your request to do so. All you have to do is tell me you are ready and exactly where to find you."

"So, you're telling me it'll be *our* call. We can get out when *we* say *we* want out!"

"That's it in a nutshell," Salizar responded. "And give Kristin my very best wishes for a speedy recovery," the marshal said, then clicked off.

Standing in the guest bedroom in a daze, and still holding the Marshals Service satphone, his mind filled with thoughts: *I would not have believed I was talking to the same jerk-me-around Marshal Salizar if his voice were not so familiar over the phone! His attitude's now totally changed ... polite and accommodating beyond all belief. I wish I could have heard exactly what Louis Loveman must have said to some of the higher-ups in the U.S. Marshals Service ... and I wonder what Salizar's boss must have said to him!*

15

At times it seemed touch and go over the five days it took to wean Anne off the ventilator. But finally she was flying on her own. Her oxygen saturation was 99 percent, unassisted, and she was breathing room air. Dr. Dooley, the vascular surgeon who had placed the shunt in her right arm, finally agreed to remove it. Anne was now permitted to walk in the hall following her transfer to a regular hospital room on the fifth floor.

Today, Brad and Cindy had remained in the apartment, each working on their dissertations. Mark had taken a brisk 10-minute walk to the hospital to visit Anne. She wore an undistorted smile when Mark entered her room.

"Little Man, that was a close one, wasn't it?" she asked, her voice still a little husky from the endotracheal tube she'd had while on the ventilator.

"It sure was a close call! I think that's the most frightened I've ever been in my entire life," Mark admitted.

"It's funny, though. I never really felt 'frightened,' only worried I might die without being able to tell you how much I love you, and how much I've enjoyed being married to you. For days I lived in that morphine fog that took all the fear and pain away. Some of it was actually pleasant, especially when I imagined having great sex with you. I can surely see why people can get addicted to that stuff! Did I do anything stupid to embarrass you while they had me so drugged up?"

Critically ill, and she worries if she embarrassed me? Mark's mind questioned. That did it. He broke down in tears he'd wanted to shed for days. Anne stood by her hospital bed, and wrapped her arms around him. She loosened her embrace just enough to show him the Saint Christopher hanging around her neck on a borrowed chain. "Mark, I think this is a great hospital with great doctors, but I think we need to give this little guy some credit, too," she said, pointing to the Saint Christopher medal.

"Agreed." Mark said, drying his eyes on her hospital gown. "You actually remember me putting it around your neck?"

"Yes. Foggy, but it's one of the few things I'm positive was not a morphine-dream."

Now composed, Mark had a question: "Has Dr. Baxter made rounds yet?"

"Yes."

"And when did he say you can be discharged?" Mark asked.

"In 24 hours, if my oxygen saturation stays in the mid-90s. For the next couple of weeks he said he wants me to have only *very light* physical activity. So, I guess that means no sex for us. We've never been able to 'screw lightly.' But when Dr. Baxter gives me the OK, I see a marathon catch-up session coming!"

"Honey, just having you alive with a sharp mind is all I need to keep me happy for now. I was so worried that the periods of low oxygen saturation you experienced might have damaged your brain … but they haven't. I'll be content just to have you with me at night, where I can reach over and touch you, feel your warmth, or just listen to your breathing."

"Dr. Baxter also said he wanted me to remain in the Tucson area for outpatient follow-up visits. 'At least for a couple of weeks,' he said. I told him we lived in a motorhome, and had no immediate plans to leave the area."

"Anne, our motorhome is exactly where we left it. It's still in Cal Camarada's hangar. Our RV itself is fine, but we can't actually live in it for at least another few days, or so Brad says. And I feel like we're keeping Cindy and Brad from their dissertation writings. I feel like we should leave their apartment as soon as we practically can. So much has happened while you were sedated, and parts of it I'll need Bradley and Cindy to explain. The most important thing is that you *are* recovering. Let's plan a roundtable discussion with Cindy and Brad after you get out tomorrow."

"I'll look forward to learning what happened during the days I was unconscious. I have so many questions I hardly know where to begin."

"Then don't! Save them for when we're all together," Mark said, just as someone lightly knocked on the door to Anne's room.

Mark opened it. The ICU nurse who'd offered her crucifix chain poked her head in the door and smiled. "Remember me? I'm Maria Sanchez. I'm on break from my nursing shift down on the third-floor ICU. Is it OK if I come in to see Kristin?"

"Certainly!" Mark and Anne replied in unison.

"Well, I have a gift for you," the cute Hispanic nurse said, reaching into the pocket of her uniform, and removing a small gift-wrapped box.

Anne eagerly opened the package. It contained a silver chain. Anne wore a look of puzzlement; Mark's face indicated he might cry at any moment.

"Thank you Maria," Anne said. "I remember him putting the Saint Christopher around my neck when I was still on the ventilator, then wondered how he'd done it. Somehow I remembered we'd lost the chain for that Saint Christopher many years ago. Jon had been carrying it around in his wallet!"

"Well now you have a new chain," Maria smiled. And as we say in my native tongue, Que Dios este contigo siempre … May God be with you always."

The nurse quickly turned to leave.

"Wait, Maria! Let us return your crucifix chain."

They swapped chains, though Maria hadn't really seemed concerned about getting her original one back. The nurse again reached in her pocket, retrieved her crucifix and handed it to Mark. He strung her cross on its original chain and handed it to Anne, who placed it around Maria's neck. After Maria had dropped the cross into her cleavage, she said, "My crucifix will now be even more special to me, and always close to my heart." Without further words, Maria turned and left.

* * *

By midday the following day, Mark and Anne were comfortably situated in the Tucson apartment with Bradley and Cindy. Their hosts seemed to enjoy an excuse to take another day postponing their dissertation writing. The first few hours were spent on essential things, like washing and ironing the few clothes Mark and Anne had with them. Then Anne took a 30-minute shower, and used Clairol to touch up her dark red hair that was beginning to show her gray-blond roots. For the first time in days she applied makeup. "Voilà!" Anne announced to group applause as she made her appearance for their group discussion. Anne noted several legal pads and pencils Cindy had rounded up, and placed at the dining table.

It soon became apparent Cindy was the "organizer" and de facto "moderator" of the meeting. "I've prepared a list of facts and questions, more or less in chronological order," Cindy said. "Let me go over what I have so far. If you think I've left something out, speak up ... especially if it's something Kristin doesn't know because she was unconscious.

"First, there is no doubt Kristin had a hantavirus infection with associated HPS, or hantavirus pulmonary syndrome. Her antibody studies, the hanta cultures I did in my lab, and the electron microscope studies Brad did in his, and the EM images e-mailed from the FBI's forensic lab in Denver, all say 'hanta.' So, we can take 'Do we have the right diagnosis?' off the table as a discussion question.

"Second, *'How* did Kristin acquire the virus?' I think we have very good circumstantial evidence indicating Kristin inhaled a whopping dose of hanta from the air exhausted from the Dustbuster. I'll ask Brad to explain."

Brad stopped doodling on his legal pad. "It's really pretty simple. First, *viable* hantavirus was recovered from the dust inside the vacuum. Cindy's cultures prove the virus in that dust was still alive. Second, using specific-sized test particles of talcum powder, I was able to prove the Dustbuster's filter will not even trap particles as large as 500 nanometers. Hanta never exceeds 270 nanometers in size. Bottom line, there is no way that little vacuum's filter would trap hantavirus. In fact, it's quite effective in putting the virus back into the air exhausted from it. I think that's how Kristin got such a whopping dose. She *inhaled* it!"

Mark raised his hand like a school kid. "Yes, Jon," Cindy responded.

"This may not be important, but while Kristin was using the Dustbuster, I was inside the RV's shower. Do you think I may have avoided getting exposed?"

"Good thought, Jon," Cindy replied. "I think that greatly reduces your chances of a high-level exposure. If you breathed any of the virus-laden air, the amount of virus you might have inhaled may have been so small that your own immune system has already taken care of the problem. I can certainly test you for hanta-specific antibodies, but if you were going to get hanta you should have already developed symptoms by now. It's been well over three weeks since your potential exposure."

Anne entered the conversation: "This really helps me understand what's happened. I'll never be able to thank you enough for saving my life. So thanks, thanks, thanks! But I've got several questions."

"Such as, Kristin?" Cindy asked.

"*Motive!* Why would Abbas single us out as persons to expose to hanta? If he's such a 'brilliant virologist,' as your dad said during our meeting with him, why would he risk exposing himself? The only precautions we saw him use were snake leggings. He indicated they were to protect himself from rattlesnake bites while he was harvesting his traps in the New Mexico desert."

Silence fell around the table. Mark saw that special look in Anne's eyes. She always got it when she was thinking far faster than others. "He's immune! Abbas is immune! That bastard is immune!" Anne loudly blurted.

Cindy checked her notes. "Kristin, that's a brilliant point! It's something I'd never even thought of."

Anne had another question for Cindy. "Since I've apparently survived a severe hanta infection, am I now immune?"

"That is part of a question I address in my dissertation. We are positive hanta survivors acquire what we call 'short-term' immunity. We know it can last up to several years following an active infection, but there is not enough long-term data to tell us exactly how long it lasts. In other words, Anne, we don't know how long your own immune system will keep pumping out those anti-hanta antibodies. To answer your question, you are probably immune for the moment. Hanta is not like smallpox. For example, if a person survives the smallpox virus, they will usually have *life-long* immunity. Fortunately, the example I gave you, smallpox, is essentially eradicated from the planet due to successful immunization programs."

Brad spoke next. "So, do you think Abbas could himself be a survivor of a recent hanta infection? Perhaps he's secretly developed a vaccine and immunized himself, or even periodically injected himself full of hanta-specific immunoglobulins, like the stuff I've got stockpiled in my lab. But those immunoglobulins are very hard to come by in any quantity, and their protection only lasts for a few weeks at most. They last such a short time because they don't actually trick your own immune system into continually reproducing those antibodies the way a true vaccine does. Any of those scenarios could explain his casual handling of the mice. Possibly Jon and Kristin just happened to be at the right place at the wrong time. Maybe his true objective was simply to collect white-footed deer mice, the viral carrier ... and he really didn't give a damn about other folks he might expose in the process!"

Cindy responded, "Brad, I doubt Abbas has developed a vaccine. We all know it's coming, but I doubt Abbas would be stupid enough to keep it a secret. Just his personal financial rewards alone would be enough to make him go public with it. He'd sell his production process to the highest bidder in the pharmaceutical industry. He'd retire a millionaire, possibly billionaire!"

Mark spoke. "I know nothing about the dollar value of a hanta vaccine. But I do know there's one thing that just does not fit. Abbas came to our camper *claiming* the air conditioner in his RV had crapped out, and said his mice would get too hot and die. I think he intentionally crippled the AC in his own camper by removing a fuse. He even lied to us about no fuses being available at the convenience center at the Gallup RV Park where Brad worked. So I think his 'failed AC' was simply a ruse to get inside our camper. It's either that, or he's a 'brilliant virologist' who's an absolute and total klutz when it comes to electrical and mechanical things!"

"Jon, don't write off that last possibility entirely," Cindy replied. "At the lab, I've worked with some truly brilliant virology professors, ones who'd call maintenance to change an ordinary light bulb in a desk lamp. I even had one prof who called maintenance to plug in the power cord to a new centrifuge, claiming he didn't like to get his hands that close to electricity! Yet that same professor had absolutely no qualms about working with Ebola virus, which is a heck of a lot more dangerous than hanta—or the relatively low-voltage electricity we have in labs! I think many of these 'great scientific minds' are dumber than dirt when it comes to trivial everyday things … things we'd all do for ourselves without even a second thought."

"OK, so maybe I am being paranoid about Abbas, but that doesn't change the fact *he* introduced the virus to our camper and that's *where* Kristin acquired it."

"Speaking of your camper," Brad began, "I think we should explain to Kristin why it'll be off limits for about ten more days."

"*Off limits?*" Anne asked.

"Yes," Brad began. "We've fumigated your entire camper with ethylene oxide gas. That will kill any residual hantavirus in your RV. The gas will penetrate into every nook and cranny, even into the interior of cushions, carpet and bedding. We now have your camper 'airing out,' so to speak. Though the gas has no appreciable odor, chronic exposure to even trace amounts can be adverse to human health. All the windows and doors of your RV are open, even its exterior storage bays. But don't worry, it's still secure. We've still got it locked up inside Cal's hangar, but we've got the hangar's exhaust fan running 24/7. I'd also recommend discarding all on-board food, and restocking with fresh supplies. I realize your RV's water storage tank is sealed and below the living area, but I'd recommend draining it, then refilling it with fresh water. I'm confident it'll be safe to use everything again in about ten days."

"Wow!" Anne said. "So much has happened while I was 'sleeping,' so to speak."

"Jon, do those satphones have a speakerphone function?" Cindy asked.

"I've never used that function, but the manual indicates you can use it as a speakerphone," Mark replied.

"This evening when Dad gets back to Boulder from his workday in Denver, I think we should get him on the phone. We should share with him some of what we've just discussed. We need to see if he's learned more about Abbas ... and we need to be positive Abbas is still in Gainesville, Georgia."

16

At 8:00 p.m., the speakerphone call with Louis Loveman began: "Daddy," Cindy said, "we're all sitting around the table here in our apartment. That's me, Bradley, Jon and Kristin. We tried to phone Cal, but he's apparently not at his condo."

"Well, don't worry about Cal. He's probably taking his latest girlfriend out for a night on the town. You can fill him in later."

"Sure, Dad. We'll do that."

"First, my congrats go to Kristin on beating that bad bug she had," Louis commented. "And thanks for keeping me posted about her condition."

"Louis, I think I had a lot of help in that department," Anne reminded. "These kids, sharp doctors, competent nurses, and a great hospital deserve most of the credit!"

"Kristin, are you calling my daughter and Bradley *kids?*" Hell, they're both 28-year-olds!"

"Just speaking in *relative* terms, Louis," Anne replied.

Louis laughed, then said, "Jon, how'd the Marshals Service treat you when you checked in this morning?"

"Couldn't believe it! I don't know exactly what you did, but whatever it was left Marshal Salizar a changed man!" Mark replied.

"It's good to know I still have a little clout with DOJ and their U.S. Marshals Service. Speaking of that Service, I've been thinking. As soon as Salizar arranges delivery of your new supporting identity documents, I see no reason to continue using your WITSEC names. Just go back to your originals."

"Boy, will that ever be a relief!" Anne commented. "We're both sick and tired of using 'fake' names, and constantly afraid we'll slip up. Our main concern is Abbas, though. Any current news on him?"

"Yes," Louis replied. "He's still in Gainesville, Georgia, living in the same motel at night. I now have three young undercover FBI agents there. During the daytime hours they are physically on site where they are working on the chicken houses. They're all Hispanics, and Abbas has hired them as day labor to help him modify the chicken houses. They tell me Abbas may be smart, but he can't do so much as drive a nail with a hammer! So, my undercover guys are actually functioning as his construction workers as well. He's generously compensating them in cash, and they tell me Abbas seems to be very well funded. When materials are delivered to the job site, he pays in cash. I've got a separate off-site detail trying to track the source of his funding. The on-site undercover guys are also taking pictures with their regular cell phones, then e-mailing those images to me at a secure FBI site here in Denver. Using their Bureau-issued satphones, they are also verbally telling me what they actually see at the site."

"And Abbas has no clue?" Brad asked.

"No. Our men there are all bilingual, fluent in both Spanish and English. In fact, they are actually Hispanics who've had past experience in the construction industry before becoming U.S. citizens and joining the Bureau. They talk freely among themselves in front of Abbas, who does not understand the first word of Spanish. They tell me Abbas frequently jabbers on his cell in front of them in a language my undercover guys think is Arabic. What I really need is a *trilingual* undercover guy there … so we can get some idea of what Abbas is saying, and to whom he might be talking. Trilinguals are hard to come by, so I've got another off-site detail working on intercepting his cell phone calls, recording them, and feeding them to one of the Bureau's Arabic translators here in Denver."

"Louis, could you describe to us what they seem to be doing at the chicken houses?" Mark asked.

"I'll do my best. I'd like to send you images from the site, but I'm hesitant to send them through ordinary e-mail. If I come up with some secure way to get images to you, I will.

"This is what has happened so far … at least as I understand it: They've insulated the underside of the metal roof and the interior walls in all three houses. They've removed all the old wood shavings that once covered the original dirt floors, and have poured concrete slabs to serve as floors in all three houses. I think I told you before, but the chicken houses are each approximately 50 feet wide and about 100 feet long. In each house, the floor slabs slope to a long shallow trough in the middle. The trough is centered, or about 25 feet from the long sides. The troughs themselves have enough slope so that they all drain to one end at the rear of the buildings, then drain into a single small septic tank with a metal access lid. At all three of the houses they've also poured small concrete slabs *outside* the buildings. They're squares, about four feet on each side. The undercover guys think those exterior slabs are going to be foundation pads for large AC units that are not yet installed. Today, they said a large number of clear four-by-eight-foot acrylic panels were delivered to the job site, and Abbas has not told them how they are going to be used. Also, today, they received multiple rolls of stainless-steel wire mesh, with the mesh size being about a quarter-inch square. In addition, a large number of two-by-sixes of treated pine were delivered today. Again, our guys have not been told how the new materials are going to be used."

"Sounds to me like they are trying to climate-control the houses, no matter what they are planning to use them for," Mark said.

"Agreed," Cindy said. "They haven't seen any mice, have they?"

"They did mention they discovered a few mouse burrows when they were shoveling out the old wood chips." Louis replied.

"What did the mice look like? Were they brownish with white feet?" Cindy asked.

"No. They told me the few mice they saw were small and silver-gray in color. That's all I know," Louis Loveman replied.

"That doesn't sound like the type of mice Abbas would be interested in," Cindy explained. "He would be interested in deer mice. Specifically, the white-footed deer mouse, which is about four inches long not counting its tail. They are a medium brown in color, except for their bellies and the tops of their feet, which are snow-white in color."

"Daughter, fill me in. Why that particular mouse?" Louis asked.

"Because it can be a natural carrier for the hantavirus. That particular mouse won't get sick from it, just carry it. If the mice don't already carry the virus, all Abbas would have to do is infect just one of them, then keep them penned up together. They'd all soon become carriers. I'm assuming Abbas could have live hantavirus cultures in his possession, and could do that if he wanted to. He could even have stolen hanta cultures from UA when he disappeared from there. Who knows? Anyway, once the mouse is infected, the virus is shed in their poop and urine, and breathing dust contaminated by their feces and urine is how humans usually get the disease … and then get sick as hell like Kristin did! I personally think the mice Abbas brought into the camper were already natural carriers, and I plan to let the folks at the Gallup RV Park know they need to have their mouse population checked again."

Brad butted in: "And *if* they are carriers, you can bet I won't work there again next summer!"

Cindy resumed, barely missing a beat. "Dad, you might want to get a picture of a white-footed deer mouse from the Internet, and get it to your men in the field. Should they see one, tell them they may be in danger of exposure to hantavirus. Tell them to run, and not show up for work again!" Cindy exclaimed.

"I wouldn't intentionally send men into harm's way. They should be checking in with me later this evening, and I'll warn them about the mice. So that's about it for now," Louis Loveman said. "Let's set up another satphone call for about this same time tomorrow evening, say about 8:30. And if you can separate Cal from his latest flame, ask him to be there, too—*alone* of course! That OK?"

In different voices, and almost simultaneously, Louis Loveman heard, "OK," "fine," "sure," and "yes Daddy," then clicked off.

* * *

About 8:25 the following evening, the distinct bark of the Porsche Boxster's tuned exhaust announced Cal Camarada's arrival at the apartment. He was alone. He burst in without knocking. He was carrying a case of cold Dos Equis. "How long is this so-called 'conference call' with Louis going to take?" Cal asked Cindy. "I've got important hot 'obligations' anxiously awaiting at my condo!"

"If she's all that 'hot,' she'll still be there an hour from now. Want a beer, Cal?" Cindy asked.

"Sure, but let's get on with the meeting."

While Mark was making the satphone connection, Cindy and Bradley were making room in their fridge for the beer Cal had delivered. Mark soon had Louis Loveman on the line with the satphone set to speakerphone. At the dining table, Anne, Mark, Cal, Cindy and Brad arranged themselves in chairs surrounding the satphone; it was as if the satphone was some "mysterious god" they were planning to jointly worship.

Cindy began: "Dad, everyone is here, including Cal, who is chomping at the bit to get back to his condo to tend to some serious 'personal business,' he says."

Louis Loveman chuckled. "Young, beautiful, brunette, big boobs, and loaded with libido. Right Cal?"

"Pretty close, except this one is Korean. I've been trying to get her back in the U.S. for years. I gave up on blonds several girlfriends ago!"

"OK, you guys. I get the blond-thing!"

"Cindy, you're the only really smart blond I know," Cal said.

97

"Maybe it's because you're natural platinum. Who knows? I'd grab you up in a heartbeat, but Bradley would kill me!"

"No he wouldn't," Louis shot back. "I'd beat Brad to it!"

"OK, OK! Enough of the guy-talk," Cindy announced. "Dad, what's happened today?"

"Right, Cin. Need to move on, and Sampson is giving me his 'where's my supper' look. So, here's what happened today: First, the clear acrylic panels were installed on the interior of the houses. 'Kind of like Sheetrock over studs in a conventional home's interior wall, but only going to a height of four feet from the concrete floor.' That's what one of my undercover guys told me. And they placed the two-by-sixes directly on top of the concrete floors, 'like floor joists,' another of my men said. They run side to side spanning the 50-foot dimension, their bottom edge being in contact with the concrete, except at the central tough which is about a foot wide. There, the joists 'bridge over' the trough. Abbas told my guys that tomorrow they were going to cover the 'joists' with the stainless-steel mesh."

Cal was doodling on a legal pad as he spoke. "Louis, let me be sure I've got this straight. You've got a concrete floor with a central trough-like drain, then joists, and I assume you mean covering the top edges of those joists with the stainless mesh, somewhat like a carpet."

"That's my understanding. One of my men mentioned Abbas had said the mesh would need to be pulled very tightly across the joists, then nailed down. And they'd have to keep it under tension during the entire installation, so it would be taut, and not sag down between the joists after they'd finished."

"Strange," Bradley commented. "I don't think a *human* could walk on top of the screen without it collapsing. But maybe chickens could! Maybe Abbas is simply building a super-sanitary high-tech chicken house. Instead of periodically recovering the floor with fresh wood chips, you'd just hose the sucker out!"

Everyone laughed.

"Any additional brilliant thoughts, anyone?" Louis asked.

The group again laughed.

When the laughter stopped, there was an abrupt silence. Cal finally spoke: "Louis, we need photographs to study. I think that is the only way we'll ever figure out what this Abbas guy is up to. If you can put your undercover guy's images on a disk, I'll be glad to fly to Denver and pick it up. That way you won't have the security issue created by using the Internet."

"Cal, that's a very generous offer. I'd hate to put you to all that trouble, but I'll think about it. Let's just see what a few more day's worth of information brings," Louis said. "And I need to feed myself and my dog!"

"And I need to go take care of the cute 'pet' I've got waiting in my condo!" Cal added. Moments later, the loud sound of Cal's Boxster peeling out of the apartment parking lot brought smiles to everyone's faces.

Louis laughed. "Even over this satphone I think I just heard Cal make his exit! Anybody else got a comment?" There were no new ideas. Louis signed off by saying, "I'll call you guys back when I know more."

17

About ten days passed with no new word from Louis Loveman. Cindy and Brad had returned to their routines of dissertation writing. A day ago, after profusely thanking Cindy and Brad for their hospitality, Mark and Anne moved out of the apartment, feeling they'd disrupted the young couples' lives and privacy long enough. They'd retrieved their camper from Cal's hangar, and relocated it to the Pima-Swan RV Park in Tucson. The Pima-Swan was within walking distance of Cindy and Brad's apartment, as well as the UMC hospital where Dr. Baxter had an outpatient office.

Anne had already seen Dr. Baxter as an outpatient for two follow-up visits thus far. The present one, her third, was grueling. She spent 15 minutes on a treadmill while Baxter monitored both her EKG and oxygen saturation. Smiling, the doctor said, "Looks like your lungs are now completely normal, Kristin. You're running 100 percent saturation even during heavy exercise. I now see no reason to limit your physical activity any longer. In fact, I'd now encourage regular vigorous physical activity. Let's plan to see you again in two weeks, and we'll do some final follow-up blood work."

Hand in hand, and walking at a brisk pace, the couple left the doctor's office smiling. They now had their camper fully re-provisioned and parked at the Pima-Swan. Upon entering their RV, and without words, they stripped off all their clothes, and raced to their mirrored-ceiling bedroom. Their rambunctious sex lasted for over an hour. "At least hanta didn't destroy my libido!" Anne finally exclaimed.

"I think that forced abstinence jacked mine up! It's been years since I was a three-time man!" Mark said, lying flat on his back, catching his breath.

Anne smiled. "But who's counting?" She slowly assumed a position on all fours, suspending herself over him. She allowed Saint Christopher to dangle in a way she could use it, along with her hard nipples, to tickle and tease his private anatomy. Anne observed his developing erection, and when it became full she climbed aboard, and began a slow rocking and thrusting motion. Her pace slowly increased. His did too. Like an old steam engine leaving the train station they gained speed, and soon moved at a good clip. "God, Anne! I love you. Do it! I'm about to—"

"Become a four-time man!" she screamed as she felt his, then her own telltale involuntary spasms.

* * *

They quickly collapsed in each other's arms for a one-hour nap. When they awoke, they dressed and walked to the nearest photo shop. They waited at the store until they had in hand their passport-type photos made to specifications Marshal Salizar had requested. Leaving that shop, and walking several blocks, they located an electronics store and purchased their first regular cell phone.

They soon developed a routine with their new phone: Either Cindy or Brad, or Mark or Anne, would call to check on one another daily. In their RV, the couple had just finished a late lunch when their new cell phone rang. Anne answered. It was Cindy calling: "Kristin, Dad just called me and said there are some new developments, and he thinks we need to have another conference call this evening. Brad and I think it would be best if you two can come to our apartment. There's a little more room here, and Cal is definitely planning to come."

"What time?" Anne asked.

"Dad said 8:30. Cal's OK with that time. What about you and Jon?"

"That'll work for us. It won't take but ten minutes for Jon and I to walk over."

"Bradley could drive over and pick you guys up."

"Thanks anyway, but I'm taking Dr. Baxter's advice about getting plenty of exercise."

Mark had been listening to Anne's side of her cell phone conversation with Cindy. *Plenty of exercise? I just got a month's worth in our bedroom!* he thought, then burst out laughing.

"What's so funny, Little Man?"

"Just thinking how glad I am to have you back to normal."

* * *

Precisely at 8:30, everyone again gathered around the FBI-issued satphone set on speakerphone mode. Louis Loveman was already on the line.

Cindy began: "Dad, I was getting a little worried because it's been so long since we've heard from you. We're all doing fine here. Kristin seems to have made a full recovery from her hantavirus infection. In fact, Jon and Kristin have moved back into their RV. They have it at the Pima-Swan RV Park. It's only about ten blocks from the apartment. How are you and Sampson doing?"

"We're fine, except there's a collie bitch in heat the next farm over, and Sampson is pissed he has to stay inside his pen! Your mother would be pissed, too. You know how she felt about allowing Sampson to freely roam the farm. 'I don't like to see animals artificially confined,' your mom would have said."

"I can certainly identify with all that!" Cal butted in. "Turned out the lovely Asian brunette bitch in my condo was not in heat today ... I was!"

Louis Loveman laughed, then asked Cal a question. "If you haven't told them about the pictures yet, I'll give you that honor."

"No, I haven't," Cal said reaching into a shirt pocket and extracting a sleeved CD. "I really didn't do much other than drive out to my own airfield late last night. I picked up the CD your men flew in. I haven't looked at it yet, figured we could all look at the same time here in the apartment. You know, more eyes, more thoughts, maybe more answers."

"Well," Louis began, "let's set up another call after you've all studied the images on that disk. Altogether, I think there are about 100 pictures. They'll have a date/time stamp on the images, but I'm not sure all my undercover men had their cell phones set to the same time zone."

"We'll figure it out, Louis," Cal said.

"I've got other important information that's not in the form of images," Louis began. "The money trail leads directly to Saudi Arabia. Dr. Abbas receives regular deliveries of cash, usually in the amount of $200,000. A known member of al-Qaeda makes periodic deliveries of cash to Abbas by coming to his motel room late at night. Abbas is staying in the Three Oaks Motel in Gainesville, a seedy low-end one. His personal car is a used 1998 Honda Accord. We've determined Abbas bought it from a used car lot there in Gainesville, and paid $4,500 cash for it. As a bluff, and after flashing their credentials, our agents approached the motel owner. When my men indicated they knew Abbas was paying his motel bill in *cash,* the owner became extremely cooperative. He apparently feared the FBI would relay the paid-in-cash information to the IRS. The motel owner even allowed the agents access to his room, where they found a Koran, a prayer rug, and several hundred thousand in cash. A small refrigerator in the motel room contained about 100 small unlabeled medical-looking vials. They also observed several boxes of disposable hypodermic syringes on a vanity top in the bathroom. My men did not touch anything inside the refrigerator, fearing they may get contaminated by some bad-assed biologic agent. Also, my guys lifted prints from the motel room that match those from the interior of that envelope Jon and Kristin gave the FBI. They also got some hair they think is from Abbas, and the Denver lab is running DNA now to see if it matches what we got from inside the envelope."

Cal butted in. "Louis, don't you need a search warrant to go into the guy's motel room like that?"

"Technically, yes," Louis replied. "But to get a warrant we'd have to disclose information to some two-bit local judge by telling him exactly what we know about Abbas thus far. And we cannot control how that judge disseminates the information. We realize anything we learned by searching the motel room will be inadmissible in court. And I really don't care. Sometimes you have to break the law to catch people who are going to break the law and possibly put us in danger. I think the motel owner will keep his mouth shut, fearing we'll go to the IRS."

"Daddy, last time we talked, you indicated you were trying to record the cell phone calls Abbas was making and receiving. Any luck?"

"We've had some success at recording him. It seems Abbas speaks in an Arabic dialect that does not translate into English very well. Two things caught our attention, though. First, Abbas is wanting to buy an airplane. Second, he is interested in the number of people that attend sports stadiums in Atlanta, Georgia. 'Olympic Stadium' and 'Turner Field' were both mentioned in one of his calls."

"What type of plane?" Cal asked.

"Don't know, Cal. But we think it is a small one, for just one or two people, the translators think."

"Louis, let me research that. As you know, I've sold all my planes except for my Cessna 310. I know a broker in central Florida who buys and tracks plane sales. If the name 'Kissimmee Aviation Services' comes up, let me know. In fact, he bought all 12 of my crop dusters. I'll give him a call, but I promise not to disclose exactly why I want to know about plane sales. That OK with you?"

"Sure, Cal. Keep me posted, and give your aircraft broker friend a description of Abbas. There are some pretty good candid shots of him on the disk you have."

* * *

Louis indicated he was tired and soon terminated the call on his end. Cal, Anne, Mark, and Cindy all looked at one another. They, too, were tired. Especially Mark and Anne, who'd already had enough 'exercise' for the day, and weren't ready for the mental exercise involved in looking at 100 images. As a group they decided to stop for the evening and begin again at 9:00 in the morning.

18

Mark and Anne walked slowly back to the Pima-Swan using Tucson's well-lit streets and wide sidewalks. They had little concern for their personal safety, but decided they'd carry their pistol should they encounter any future trouble walking after dark. The only rowdy folks they encountered were actually at the Pima-Swan itself: Two adjacent RVs were having a joint barbecue that probably involved more marijuana, beer, or bourbon than cooked meat of any kind.

Entering their camper, Anne reminded Mark to put the FBI-issued satphone on its charger, which reminded Mark he should charge the Marshals Service satphone as well. He needed to call Salizar at seven in the morning and tell him they had changed their location in Tucson, and now had the photos needed for their new identity documents.

"Little Man, thanks for the 'welcome-to-the-world-of-the-living' sex we had earlier today! I bet Bradley and Cindy can't do it as well as we can."

"Anne, they are just kids. They don't have our experience!"

Both briefly laughed, but were sound asleep five minutes later.

* * *

The travel alarm buzzed at 6:00 a.m. Mark left Anne sleeping while he made coffee and showered. At 7:00 sharp, Mark had Salizar on the phone.

"Good morning, Jon. Is Kristin still recovering well?"

"She's completely back to normal. Thanks for asking."

"And I see you got the GPS on your camper fixed. I've got you at latitude 32.2435, longitude 110.8947. That puts you at the Pima-Swan RV Park there in Tucson, at least according to my sat map. That correct?"

"Yes."

"Did you have to replace the whole GPS unit?" Salizar asked

No, we just moved the damn camper out of a steel hangar! Mark

105

thought, then lied: "No, we just had an experienced RV neighbor look at it. Just a loose wire connection up top."

"Glad it's working again. Have you made the photos yet, the ones for your new documents?"

"Yes. Did that yesterday," Mark replied.

"When would be a convenient time for us to have a Marshals Service courier pick them up?"

"How about 6:30 this evening? We've got other plans for most of the day," Mark said, knowing it would take them hours to look at the photos Cal had on disk.

Salizar signed off, indicating he'd have their identity documents ready within 24 hours after receiving the photos.

* * *

Anne finally woke up and showered. After their breakfast, Mark checked his watch: 8:45. He pocketed the satphone Louis Loveman had issued, and because they were running a little late, they rode their bicycles to Brad and Cindy's apartment. Cal's Porsche was already there. When they entered, everything was apparently set up, ready to go. Brad's laptop already had the disk loaded and rested on the center of the dining table. Mark noted the laptop was connected to a small photo printer. Cindy served coffee without asking if anyone wanted it.

Brad touched a single key, and the first image appeared. It showed the three chicken houses pretty much as Louis had described them: metal roofs, weathered wooden board-and-batten sides and a large central door on their 50-foot fronts.

"Can't make much out of that one, except they need to cut the knee-high grass around them," Bradley commented.

Several frames later, it was apparent the vegetation had been mowed. Mark noted a small Ford tractor with attached Bush Hog at one side of the image.

"So that's how they cut the grass," Cal stated. "Wonder if the tractor is rented, or did Abbas pay cash for it, like he does everything else."

The next several images showed the progress while they poured concrete floors for the chicken houses. "HCC, Hall County Concrete Inc., Gainesville, GA," Mark said, reading the company name on the truck that had its chute extended through one of the open chicken house doors. Cindy wrote the company name down on her legal pad.

The next shot was apparently a candid profile shot of Abbas while he was occupied talking on his cell phone. He was dressed in baggy khaki cargo shorts, leather work boots, khaki shirt and a straw hat. He still had his olive complexion and gray ponytail, but no facial hair was apparent in the profile view. "Can you print that one for me?" Cal asked Brad. "I'll get that to my aircraft-dealer friend in Florida."

Several images later, the interior of several chicken houses was seen. The stainless-steel mesh had indeed been pulled tightly over the joists. At the particular photographic angle, it looked like a dull silver carpet without any wrinkles. There were two strips of lumber on top of the mesh that ran diagonally from the front doors to the back corners of each building. They appeared to be two-by-sixes, flat side up.

Everyone was silent for a long moment, pondering what they were seeing. Anne finally came to the rescue. "Yesterday, Brad said he didn't think the mesh would support a human's weight. But what if those boards on top of the mesh are used as 'catwalks.' That way a human could walk front to back in all the houses without actually stepping on the mesh. And whoever is working inside the chicken house could walk on the boards dragging a water hose with them. They could wash the houses out as was suggested yesterday," Anne said, smiling.

Cindy also smiled and twirled her platinum ponytail with an index finger. "Kristin, the periods of low oxygen saturation you had with your hanta infection certainly didn't damage your brain! That's brilliant. I think I now know exactly what Abbas is up to!"

"Well please share it with the rest of us dumb-assed folks!" Cal blurted.

"Cal, I don't know for sure, but what about this as a theory: Suppose Abbas plans to raise hanta-carrying mice in those houses. When they poop or pee it would drop through the mesh to the concrete floor below. He then could, as Brad said, 'hose it out.' It would all collect in those central drains in the concrete slabs, then go into a septic tank or some other collection device. Over time he could collect a massive amount of mouse feces and urine ... all of it contaminated with hantavirus."

Cal burst out laughing. "So you're telling me it's possible Abbas is a 'rat shit farmer!' Must be a really great market for the stuff!"

"Cal, you're not taking me seriously! Is it because I'm blond? Besides, they are not rats! They are *mice*. Specifically, white-footed deer mice," Cindy said, an offended tone and irritation in her voice.

"Sorry if I ticked you off, Cindy," Cal responded apologetically.

"But where are the rats … uh, I mean mice?"

"Well, we know he had a pillowcase full of them inside Jon and Kristin's camper!" Cindy shot back.

"No, we don't know that for a fact. We know Abbas *claimed* that's what he had inside that pillowcase. I rest my case," Cal said.

"Cal, you're so hard to argue with!" Cindy replied. "Let's just look at the rest of the images and see if we can find anything that would tell us where the mice are."

Bradley went to the next image. It showed large AC units sitting on top of the smaller exterior concrete slabs Louis had earlier described. They could read no brand names on the units, but felt sure someone in the heating and air business could identify them by the appearance of their exterior cabinets. Cindy made another note on her legal pad.

The following frame revealed something Mark recognized: a truck-mounted well-drilling rig. It appeared to be directly behind the central house of the three, and was in vertical position, either actively drilling or preparing to drill. "Tapley & Sons Water Well Contractors" was written on the truck's door. Cindy wrote the name down.

Multiple other pictures revealed nothing new except for two things: Shot at a distance, there was a good frontal image of Abbas standing erect with his hands on his hips. Bradley zoomed the image on his laptop. Its quality was far better than expected. "Print that one," Cal requested. The other image of interest appeared to be nothing more than a long flat pasture that had been recently mowed, at least as judged by the windrows of grass still visible on its surface. In the photo, the mowed area appeared to be at least several thousand feet long. Cal studied the image for a few minutes, then said, "I need to get something out of the trunk of my car." Cal returned quickly, carrying a worn leather flight bag. "Outdated aviation charts," Cal explained. He rummaged through the old charts, and finally extracted the one he desired. Easily finding Gainesville, Georgia's major commercial and general aviation airfields, he started searching for little-known "emergency alternates" in the area. Cal knew many of them were now probably defunct, and not listed on current charts. Finally, Cal located what he was looking for. He explained: "Granted, this is an out-of-date chart, but there once was an agricultural strip, probably used by crop dusters. That would be back in the mid 60s. Judging by the shadows in the photos, the long freshly mowed spot we're now looking at has to be laid out northeast to southwest. According to this old chart, the only emergency alternate that would match that compass orientation is listed as 'turf, 3,500 ft., good condition.' I'll bet that's where Abbas has his chicken houses ... at one end of that old runway."

"I think I know a way we can pin down the location quite accurately," Mark said. "If the undercover FBI guys there have satphones, and if they are like the one we're using to communicate with Louis, they will have an 'emergency locate' function. That will allow the FBI to receive the exact GPS coordinates for that phone ... thus the exact location of what you think is an old runway."

Cal smiled. "Jon, I know they don't teach that kind of stuff in med school, but that's some pretty good out-of-the-box thinking!"

Cindy added to the notes on her legal pad.

Mark found himself in thought: *If Marshal Salizar had been using his head, he could have asked me to punch the locate button on my satphone when he thought the GPS on our camper had crapped out. Salizar probably has a limited future with the U.S. Marshals Service, but I hope they don't kick him out until Anne and I get our new identity documents!*

* * *

A couple of hours later, they had looked at all the images. No new ideas, and no signs of mice anywhere. Cindy exhaled and looked discouraged. She desperately wanted to prove her theory that Abbas was a "rat shit farmer," as Cal had called him. She finally spoke. "I know Dad's at work in Denver, but I think we should call him there now."

Mark removed the satphone from his pocket, and dialed the 15-digit number he now had memorized. When Louis Loveman answered, Mark passed the phone to Cindy.

"Hi, Daddy. We've all just spent a couple of hours looking at the images on the disk your guys delivered to Cal. We noticed a number of things that may give us a better idea of exactly what Abbas is up to. If you have time, I'll read off a list of things that caught our attention. Maybe you could get your on-site undercover guys to investigate them further."

Louis apparently listened with utmost patience as Cindy scanned her notes and, for 30 minutes, rattled off the group's various observations and thoughts. After a very long pause, Cindy finally said, "We'll call you back then, Dad. Bye, Love ya." She clicked off.

All eyes were on Cindy. "Well?" Cal asked.

"Number one, he is going to relay our thoughts to his undercover guys on the site. He wants us to call him in Boulder by satphone in four days. He said make it 9:00 p.m. Second, he wants Cal to look into anything that has to do with airplanes, and wants the rest of us *not* to go poking around trying to answer our questions! He was very adamant about that, so I guess that means we're all sidelined—except for Cal."

19

Immediately following the meeting at Cindy and Brad's apartment, Mark and Anne rode their bikes back to their camper and secured them to the rear of the vehicle with lockable cables. Anne fixed a light lunch. They ate slowly, took a nap, then had some one-time-man sex followed by another light nap. A gentle knocking on the camper door awakened them from their second nap. Mark quickly dressed and went to the door. A clean-cut young man in a dark suit and tie stood outside the camper door. "I'm John Bostwick with the U.S. Marshals Service." The man presented his credentials, then said, I'm looking for Mr. Jon Wayne Traer and his wife, a Mrs. Mary Kristin Traer. I'm here to pick up some items requested by U.S. Marshal Clinton Salizar. Am I at the correct location?"

"Yes, you're at the right place. I'm Jon Traer."

"I've been instructed to pick up photos. Do you have them?"

"Yes. Please give me a moment to get them for you," Mark said, and disappeared inside the RV.

Mark made a brief search of the camper and could not find the photos. Fighting panic, he consulted Anne, who was still in bed. "Honey, relax! They are in an envelope inside my purse," she quickly explained.

Mark retrieved them and apologized to the marshal for the delay, then handed him the unsealed envelope. Marshal Bostwick removed the pictures, compared them to the man he was now looking at. "I'm sorry, but I'll need to see Mrs. Mary Kristin Traer in person also."

"Just a moment, Marshal. She's in bed, but I'll get her to come to the door."

Anne quickly slipped on a bathrobe, and stuck her head out the camper door. Marshal Bostwick again compared the picture with the person before him. "I thank you. Everything seems to be in order. Will you still be at this same location for a couple of days?"

"We don't plan on moving anytime soon. If we do change our location we will notify Marshal Salizar."

"Thank you," Marshal Bostwick replied, and promptly returned to his idling black Crown Vic, then slowly drove away.

Mark immediately returned to the bedroom where Anne was dressing. Mark said, "I think we should call Salizar and tell him the pictures have been picked up."

"Probably a good idea, Little Man. Ya know, we'd have been prepared to greet that courier marshal on time if we hadn't had sex and naps."

"Well, tough shit! I must admit he was exactly on time," Mark said, glancing at his watch to discover it was now 6:40.

Anne sighed. "And I don't know about you, but I think we need to make a definite decision about us getting out of WITSEC. Louis Loveman doesn't seem to think it's important anymore. I don't think it's important anymore."

"And I don't think it's important anymore," Mark said. "I'll call Salizar right now, before we change our minds!"

* * *

Mark talked to Salizar for over 30 minutes. Anne only listened to bits and snatches of Mark's words. When she heard Mark say, "Yes, we both want out as soon as possible," she quit listening altogether.

"Well, that certainly went smoothly with Salizar," Mark commented, after finishing what might well be his next to last conversation with the man.

"Any special instructions from Salizar?" Anne asked, as she peeled carrots at the galley sink.

"A few. He said he'd have our new documents delivered within 48 hours, and to contact him in 24 about the exact time of delivery. Delivery would again be by a courier from the Marshals Service. He said be sure we have all the old documents ready to turn in. Also, we've got to turn in the satphone and its accessories, and the GPS unit off the roof of the RV. Also, he wants the current vehicle tag we have on our camper."

"Mark, *we* bought the tag on this camper! Not the Marshals Service."

"I brought up that point with Salizar. He said the current tag links to our WITSEC names, and it's better if we go with an entirely new license plate. I told him to make it a Georgia plate, and he said that would be no problem."

"*Georgia!* How good that sounds, Little Man. I sure hope we'll end up back on the Georgia coast … before our lifetimes run out."

❖ ❖ ❖

Two days later, Mark and Anne were surprised everything went as planned. The same U.S. Marshal delivered their new identity documents. They turned in all their old documents and equipment without a snag. They signed multiple documents using their original names; they'd been using WITSEC names so long, at first it seemed quite awkward, yet comforting, to sign their true names again. Mark applied the new Georgia tag to their RV and wore a smile the whole time he was doing it. They used their new cell phone to call Cindy and Brad to give them the good news about their official change-of-name. Cindy, though not exactly a "party animal," suggested they should all get together at the apartment and have a "name-change party." They did. Mark and Anne quickly got tipsy on martinis, Brad the same way on Dos Equis. Cal also quickly consumed several beers. He seemed totally unaffected by alcohol, but stated "I wouldn't even fly my own ass anywhere." Even Cindy broke one of her own rules: She drank a whole beer all by herself. Brad and Cal ended up carrying her to the bedroom shortly before she passed out.

When they were sure Cindy was OK, Cal and Bradley returned to the living room. "I'm afraid our self-appointed leader is 'gone' for the evening," Brad announced, embarrassment obvious in his voice and face.

Cal smiled and said, "Well screw our leader! I'm speaking metaphorically, of course. Bradley, that's your job. The evening is still young, and we don't have to call her dad until nine o'clock tomorrow night, right?"

"That's my recollection," Mark said to Cal. "So what do we do in the meantime? You guys wanna practice calling me Mark Telfair? Want to practice calling 'Kristin' Mrs. Anne Telfair? Keep it straight now. Anne's the taller one with hazel eyes, short red hair and big boobs; I'm the short little guy with brown eyes, graying brown hair and a short beard."

"I think we've got it: Mark, Anne, Mark, Anne, Mark, Anne," Cal chanted, opening himself another beer. "But how do you spell the last name? T-e-l-f-a-r-e? Or T-e-l-f-a-i-r?"

"It's T-e-l-f-a-*i*-r," Mark said, knowing Cal was now making fun of him.

"I think we've got that part down, Cal," Bradley said. "So what have you been doing about the airplane stuff? You know Louis Loveman grounded the rest of us, at least as far as doing any poking around on our own goes."

"I'm sure Louis realized my part would be easy. He knows full well aircraft registrations are held on a federal level. He probably wanted to free his men for more complicated tasks. Louis knows anyone with a computer can do searches by tail number, which is the same as their federal registration number. Planes are also listed by manufacturer's serial number, which is the equivalent of a VIN for automobiles. You can also do a search to find lists of aircraft registered to any given owner."

"So what have you found out so far?" Mark asked.

"I've phoned my friend at Kissimmee Aviation Services in Florida. He's the guy who bought all 12 of my dusters when I was getting out of that part of my aviation business. He has now sold all of them, except three. He told me he has had a phone inquiry from a Dr. Al Abbas who has made a $9,000 deposit on one of the remaining three dusters. The deposit was made by wire transfer to Kissimmee Aviation Services' bank account. Abbas has not even seen the aircraft, but said he would pay the balance in cash when he personally picked the plane up in about a month."

"Doesn't that seem odd? Abbas, who can't drive a nail, or change an electrical fuse, somehow knows how to fly a plane?" Mark asked.

"Agreed," Cal commented. "Abbas may take a pilot with him when he picks up the plane. All the dusters I had were Piper PA-25 Pawnees, all trainers with tandem seating. The rear seat is initially for the student, but you could actually fly my PA-25s from either seat. I'd let the student take the front seat only when I knew they were ready. I ordered them that way because I was doing agricultural flight instruction at the time."

"Cal, how will we be sure it is Abbas who picks up the plane? Did you send your friend in Florida those two pictures of Abbas I printed?" Brad asked.

"Not the originals. I faxed both the frontal and profile images to him. I've still got the originals you printed for me the other night when we were looking at all the images on the disk. I've still got that disk in a safe at my condo."

Anne said, "This is all interesting, Cal. But I know virtually nothing about crop dusters or how they work. Could you give me a quick overview?"

"Sure, Anne. Crop dusters are simply agricultural aircraft used for aerial application of herbicides, pesticides, fungicides, or even liquid fertilizer. You can even modify them to distribute certain seeds. The type I had were all Piper's Pawnee PA-25, with a low wing and single Lycoming 235 horsepower engine. The frames are steel and they are covered with fabric, which resists the corrosive effects of some of the ag chemicals better than aluminum skins. The steel frames are specifically designed with pilot safety in mind. The cockpit enclosures are like the 'cage' NASCAR has designed to protect their drivers. They are not big planes. Their wingspan is only a shade over 36 feet. They are not fast either. The ones I had could fly only a little over 100 miles per hour, and had a range of only 300 miles on one tank of gas."

"Cal, I appreciate your explanation thus far, but what I really want to know is how do they spray their stuff out?" Anne asked.

"I was afraid you'd ask that, so I'll keep it as simple as possible. First, you've got the chemical tank that contains whatever you are spraying. That tank is located directly forward of the pilot's instrument panel. Next is the gas tank, then the firewall and engine compartment. The chemical tank holds about 120 gallons of liquid. Little wind-driven turbines power the pumps that deliver the chemicals from the tank to spray bars. Spray bars are long tubes, located beneath both the right and left wings. Each spray bar is about 15 feet long, and has multiple spray nozzles spaced at intervals along its length. When the pilot flips a toggle switch in the cockpit, that opens a solenoid valve that allows the chemical to enter the spray bars under pump pressure, and it exits as a mist through the nozzles."

"Thanks, Cal," Anne replied. "I think I get the idea, but I'm not sure I know what a 'solenoid' is."

Cal scratched his buzz-cut white hair and rubbed his neat little white mustache. He cleared his throat. "Anne, I'm sure you know what a water valve is, like at the kitchen sink."

Anne nodded.

Cal continued: "Just imagine, if you will, that a magnetic force opens that kitchen sink valve instead of a human hand. Suppose that kitchen sink valve had some kind of 'internal spring,' so it would automatically shut itself off if you didn't continually hold it open with your hand. A solenoid is simply an electromagnetic device that supplies the force needed to open the valve, and overpowers the solenoid's spring that keeps that valve normally closed."

"I think I've got it now, Cal! So the pilot flips a switch in the cockpit that sends electricity to the solenoid, which then opens the normally off valve. Right?"

"You got it, Anne!" Cal beamed.

"Me too!" Bradley piped up.

Cal focused his intense blue eyes on Brad's that were equally blue. "Son, you're gonna have to learn a helluva lot more than that when I teach you to fly!"

"Cal, I have no intention of learning to fly," Anne said. "But I do have one more question, if you've got the time."

"Shoot!" Cal said. "I'm going to rack here on the sofa tonight anyway. I'm probably over the legal limit and my Porsche is a cop-magnet ... and flight instructors don't need any DUIs on their record. So ask away, Anne."

"I think we have enough pieces of the puzzle to at least consider Abbas may be intending to do something horrific with a crop duster. My question is this: If you wanted to distribute mouse feces, and therefore hantavirus with a crop duster, could it be done?"

Cal opened another beer before he replied. He looked at Bradley, and said "We're getting low, so I'll bring another case of Dos Equis tomorrow."

"Cal, that's not necessary!" Brad replied. "A case of beer would normally last here for months. Cindy normally doesn't drink alcohol at all. And you just witnessed what a single beer did to her!"

"I'm not thinking about little Cindy. I'm thinking about the rest of us. And we've got that conference call with Louis Loveman coming up tomorrow night," Cal explained.

"Cal," Anne said, "you never did answer my question about possibly using a crop duster to distribute hantavirus."

"I know," Cal said, slipping his shoes off and reclining on the sofa. And I won't. At least not tonight ... because I'll have to do it all over again tomorrow night when we talk to Louis."

20

At one o'clock in the morning Mark and Anne unsteadily walked Tucson's deserted streets back to their camper parked at the Pima-Swan. It was cool and both wore light jackets. Neither seemed concerned because Mark had their little .38 in his jacket's pocket. They had carried their own premade martinis in a two-quart thermos when they'd earlier walked to Brad and Cindy's apartment for their official "name-change" celebration. When departing the party, they'd decided to leave the now-empty thermos behind, rather than risk dropping and breaking it on the way home. They'd also left behind Cal, who was comfortably snoring on the sofa. Brad, possibly the soberest of the group, had apparently joined his passed-out girlfriend in the bedroom they shared.

"Mark, we did lock their apartment door when we left, didn't we?" Anne asked.

"I personally remember doing it," Mark answered. "But I think booze should be off limits when we talk to Louis Loveman."

"Agreed. Nobody left the stove on, did they?" Anne asked, her mind full of questions even when tipsy.

"No. It was off. We never turned it on for any reason. All we did was drink and talk, drink and talk! But I'll tell you one very important thing we absolutely need to do tomorrow."

"What?"

"We need to go to UMC, and take our identity documents with us. We need to get them to put our real names on all your medical records and our insurance papers. As it stands now, their records probably all have our WITSEC names on them," Mark said, dreading a day of paperwork, and worrying about problems getting the insurance companies to cover their six-figure hospital bill. "And we owe Dr. Baxter the courtesy of explaining our name changes."

"Crap! I hadn't thought about all that," Anne admitted. "I'm a lot of trouble, aren't I?" Anne asked.

"No, it's not *you*, Anne. It was *WITSEC* that created the trouble! But just your being well is worth every bit of it," Mark said, and kissed her.

Now about 50 yards from their RV, Anne asked another question: "Little Man, you don't think we're getting in over our heads again, do you?"

"Over our heads? Like what?"

"Like we did on the coast in Georgia. Like when we were spying on those drug smugglers there. That's what caused us to get involved in WITSEC. We just got out of their darn program, and I sure don't want to go back there again!"

Mark paused at their camper while fumbling in his pockets for the RV's door key. He finally found it, then replied, "Louis did say he'd place us in 'informant status' with the FBI, whatever that is. I think we should ask him more details when we're completely sober. I sure don't want us to do anything that would put us back in something like WITSEC again."

They entered the RV. Without preliminaries, other than a good night kiss, both went straight to bed … to sleep.

* * *

They slept soundly and naturally awoke midmorning. Each nursed mild hangovers. Coffee, a tall glass of V-8 juice apiece, plus a full breakfast and Tylenol chased the residual overindulgence cobwebs away. Following breakfast Anne called Medical Records at UMC and made an appointment for one o'clock that day to deal with the name-change issue. Before going to Medical Records, they had the operator page Dr. Baxter, and arranged a private meeting with him. In that meeting they fully explained why his patient's name was being changed on all her medical records. Those activities alone killed most of the rest of their day. Had UMC not had a very efficient Medical Records Department and business office, the process could have taken forever. Mentally, Mark retracted many of his negative thoughts he'd had about U.S. Marshal Clinton Salizar; at least he'd gotten their names changed with their insurance carriers.

* * *

Weary from their day of paperwork, but relieved insurance was going to cover Anne's hospitalization cost, they returned to their camper. Upon entering, Mark made a totally off-the-wall statement: "Ya know, I keep wondering why they put those clear acrylic sheets on the interior walls of the chicken houses?"

118

"Maybe to protect the insulation they put on the interior walls." Anne suggested.

Mark mused a moment. "You mean like to keep chickens from pecking at it?"

"Or like keeping mice from chewing it up?" Anne asked.

"Or like keeping mice from *climbing* the walls. I remember the mice we had in the college labs at Emory were all kept in aquarium-like acrylic cages about 36 inches high, and they were *completely open* at the top. That way we could reach in and pick them up for tests or inspection. We never had any of them get out on their own. They can't jump very high, and could not climb the slick surface of the acrylic walls."

"Little Man, I think you just figured out something that supports Cindy's theory about the chicken houses actually being for mice, not chickens."

Mark smiled. "Don't let me forget to mention that during our conference call this evening."

* * *

As planned, their conference call with Louis Loveman began precisely at 9:00 p.m. They'd mutually agreed: no booze. Everything was set up as before. At the dining table they all gathered around the satphone and Brad's laptop. Cal even brought the disk, just in case they wanted to look at any of the images a second time. Cindy seemed to have survived her single-beer pass-out, and was mentally as sharp as ever. She was again in control, wasting no time getting down to business:

"Daddy, what did you find out about the Ford tractor and Bush Hog we noticed in the pictures?"

"About what we expected," Louis replied. "Abbas paid cash for the equipment. It was bought at a local dealer there in Gainesville. The total cost was a little over $5,000, and the salesman said Abbas didn't try to haggle over the price. The dealer offered a short-term lease or a rental, but Abbas declined, saying he had a small pasture he wanted to 'keep mowed year-round.'"

"What did you find out about the heating and air stuff?" Cindy asked.

"Three Rheem ten-ton heat pumps capable of keeping the houses at almost any temperature Abbas desires year-round. Their cost, including installation, came to a little over $15,000, again paid in cash."

"What did the Hall County Concrete Company have to say?" Cindy asked.

"They remembered Abbas well," Louis said. "The company's owner said Abbas just showed up at the concrete plant driving a fairly new Honda Accord. He immediately stated he needed 200 yards of concrete. Abbas even specified the mix, one that had low alkalinity, and said he wanted it delivered right away. Abbas paid $12,000 cash in advance, and told the concrete man he had his own concrete finishers waiting at the job site. Of course the 'concrete finishers' were actually my three Hispanic undercover guys. Boy did they bitch, piss, and moan! One of my men said, 'This backbreaking undercover stuff ain't worth the extra pay!' Anyway, they got it done and Abbas seemed satisfied."

"Now what about the water well drill rig?" Cindy asked, checking off items on her legal pad notes.

"Now that is something strange we're still trying to figure out. Tapley & Sons, the water well contractors, indicated they tried to discourage Abbas from drilling a well in the first place. They reminded him that the Hall County Water System already had a six-inch main that ran in the right of way directly in front of his property. Being honest, the well drillers told Abbas it would be a heck of a lot cheaper for him to connect to the county system. Apparently, Abbas was concerned that the county water system was chlorinated, and would make his chickens sick. The well contractors even told Abbas a number of other chicken farmers used chlorinated county water without experiencing any problems with their birds. Nonetheless, as Abbas insisted, they drilled him a $4,500 well. Again, he paid cash. Any ideas why Abbas wanted his own well?" Louis asked.

Cindy immediately answered. "Dad, municipal water systems are all chlorinated to a standard level of two to three parts per million. That is done primarily to quickly kill any waterborne bacteria. If hantaviruses are also exposed to that same level of chlorination they, too, will be killed. It just takes a little longer exposure time. Maybe about an hour."

"So, Cin, you're telling me Abbas doesn't want municipal water on site because it would kill the hantavirus?" Louis asked.

"That's how I see it, Dad. Others here—well at least *Cal*—have considered me a little batty when I suggested Abbas is planning on raising hantavirus-carrying mice, not chickens. Cal would call it my 'rat shit farmer' theory!"

Louis Loveman chuckled. "Sounds just like something that crazy old flyboy would say. Cal is there, isn't he?"

"Yes, and he's listening to your every word," Cindy said.

Cal immediately replied to Louis: "All six feet of him is present and accounted for, sir. And by way of apology to your daughter, she may have a point. As bits and pieces of this are coming together, I'll give her credit for thinking ahead of the pack. I now think her theory concerning Abbas has credibility."

"What changed your mind, Cal?" Louis asked.

"Several things. I've phoned my good friend, Ben Hunter. He owns and runs Kissimmee Aviation Services. A man who identified himself as Dr. Al Abbas contacted him by phone, and subsequently made a $9,000 deposit on a crop duster. The deposit was made by wire transfer, and Abbas said he'd personally pay the balance in cash in a month. That's when he's supposed to pick up the plane. 'On or about 28 August,' Ben said. The tail number of the duster Abbas made a deposit on just happens to be one of my old birds, and was among those I sold to Ben when I got out of that business. And that duster was in top functional condition with a current airworthiness certificate."

"Cal, you didn't tell Ben Hunter *why* you were making inquiries, did you?" Louis asked.

"Hell no! I just told him I needed information, and not to ask me why. Ben is no dummy, though. I personally know, in times past, he has refused sales to persons he felt may be wanting to use planes for some nefarious purpose. I know for a fact he has previously contacted the FBI when he thinks something is suspicious," Cal explained.

"Cal, your friend, Ben Hunter, did call the FBI about 30 minutes after receiving the call from Abbas. So, your call to Hunter just confirms what we already knew. We could legally block the sale of the plane to Abbas, but I think we should let it go a little further. We need to get an overview of this whole scenario, and identify the others who might be involved in it. On the other hand, we can't let it go so far that Abbas actually executes some act of terrorism."

"Louis, I consider you an old and dear friend. You asked me to look into the airplane thing. I did. Now I feel like a useless piece of shit!"

"Understandably you are pissed, Cal. But what if your buddy, Ben, had *not* called us? What if he had not been one of the good guys? Please think about that before you stay mad at me."

"OK, OK, OK! Sorry I'm wearing my feelings on my shoulder," Cal replied.

Anne finally spoke: "Louis, this is Anne."

"I recognize your voice, and congratulations to you and Mark on getting out of WITSEC. I'll keep your new names straight, I promise. Both DOJ and the Marshals Service had given me a heads-up. So, for me, it's Mark and Anne Telfair from now on."

Anne continued: "Thanks, Louis. It's great to hear our old names. But last night I asked Cal how a crop duster could be used to distribute hantavirus. He never did answer me, claiming he'd have to explain it all over again tonight for you. So, maybe he can do it right now."

"Cal," Louis said, "are you going to answer Anne's question? Keep it simple enough that I'll be able to understand it, too."

Cal started: "First, I'd think, the virus-laden poop would have to be suspended in a liquid. If Cindy is right about chlorinated water killing the virus, they'd probably have to use water from the unchlorinated well Abbas had drilled. My assumption is they'd use that same water to wash out the mouse feces, then collect it at the low ends of the central drains in the concrete floors, or from some receptacle they drain into. Because the washout would probably produce a sludge, they'd need to dilute it with more unchlorinated water. Dusters can't pump sludge. It would then have to be highly filtered. Any particulates larger than ten-thousandths of an inch will clog the spray nozzles. Uneaten food, fur, particles of concrete, et cetera, would all have to be filtered out. On a duster, there is a disposable inline filter between the chemical tank and the pumps, but that filter can easily clog if you don't carefully prefilter stuff before it goes into the plane's chemical tank."

"That seems pretty complicated," Louis commented. "Do you think they could do all that at the chicken houses?"

Cindy responded: "It's a lot simpler than you think, Dad. I'm talking about the collection, dilution, and filtration process. What I don't see is how they can do that outside a bio-laboratory setting without infecting themselves. Anne had earlier concluded Abbas is immune to hanta. Brad thinks Abbas could be periodically injecting himself with hanta-specific immunoglobulin, even though it is quite hard to come by. Brad's been collecting blood from hanta survivors for three years, and he has only about 30 milliliters frozen in his lab at UA."

Mark spoke: "Brad, Anne should be a good immunoglobulin donor."

"If she'll agree, she can come to my lab tomorrow," Brad said.

"Anything for the cause," Anne replied. "Brad, you name the time, I'll be there."

"Louis," Mark said, "I feel like so much excess baggage here, but I think I've figured out one little thing about the chicken houses: the acrylic panels. This may be trivial, but I think those panels present such a slick surface that it would prevent rodents from climbing the walls, and finding some escape route, like beneath the eaves of the roof."

"Mark," Louis said, "I don't think that is 'trivial' information. It's just one more observation that tells us Abbas is *not* using his chicken houses to raise chickens!"

"Dad, have we covered everything?" Cindy asked, checking her notes, yawning.

"Yes, I think so … except for one thing. I did get my undercover men to use the 'locate' function on their satphones. I now have GPS coordinates for various areas on the property Abbas owns. Unfortunately, I left my notes at the office in Denver. I'll call Mark and Anne on satphone early tomorrow as soon as I get to the office. They can share the numbers with the rest of you guys. Using those coordinates you should be able to bring up civilian satellite images on your personal computers there in Tucson. Of course our guys will be looking also, but using higher-resolution military-type satellites."

"Daddy, I know you're tired, especially after the long day at work and the drive to Boulder. I still think you should get a condo for your workweek in Denver."

"Thanks for the daughterly advice … again. But what about Sampson? Your mother would turn over in her grave if she knew I penned our dog up in a condo during the week … assuming I could even find one in Denver that allowed large pets. 'Artificial confinement,' she'd have called it," Louis said, then signed off.

21

The Telfairs slept well in their RV despite the amount of information that had been crammed into their brains during last night's satphone conversation with Louis Loveman. At 9:00 a.m. they heard the distinct beeping of the FBI-issued satphone. Mark answered it. Anne was still doing cleanup from breakfast.

"Mark Telfair, here."

"Good morning from Denver!" Louis said. "Here are the GPS coordinates I promised you guys last night."

Louis quickly rattled them off, and Mark scrambled to write them down. The first pair of latitude/longitude numbers located the centermost chicken house. The next coordinates consisted of a pair for the beginning of the suspected grass runway, another pair for its opposite end. A fourth and fifth coordinate pair defined the sides of the runway about halfway down the runway length. Mark repeated the numbers to Louis to be positive he had transcribed them correctly.

"I'll get these to the others. Cal will probably be the most interested. He can see if they match the location of an old 'emergency alternate' airfield he found on some of his outdated aviation charts."

"Thanks, Mark," Louis said. "I've now got to—"

"I hate to interrupt you, Louis, but have you've got a minute?"

"Sure, a short one."

"Louis, Anne and I are both very concerned about this so-called 'informant status' you mentioned when we first met you in Boulder. Neither of us wants to ever go through another experience like WITSEC."

"Rest easy, Mark. Tell Anne to relax, too. My word to you is as good as any notarized legal document. Just ask Cal, he'll tell you. You and Anne will *not* be put back in the position you experienced while in WITSEC. You, Anne, Cal, Brad and Cindy are *all* 'informants.' I had to put all of your names in 'informant status,' because I had to list your legal names as 'informers' in order to issue you a secure FBI satphone. Though I initially issued that phone to you and Anne, any of you on the list can use it. So, basically, you guys are all simply my noncriminal 'snitches.' I just need your observations and thoughts. The combination of you guys—you, Anne, Cindy, Brad, and Cal—represent specialized skills in unique areas. That's something most of our average FBI agents don't have. You are all 'off the record,' and you'll never get a subpoena to appear in any court of law. End of story!"

"Thanks Louis. That'll certainly put both Anne and myself at ease. On your FBI records, did you change the names for myself and Anne?"

"Already done. You're Dr. Marcus Milton Telfair, M.D. and Anne is Mrs. Anne Hunt Telfair, R.N. Sound about right?

"Perfect!" Mark said, smiling.

"Mark, sorry but I've got to cut this short. I've got some other Bureau fires to put out. Just be sure to get those numbers to Cal, OK?"

Louis clicked off, but Mark stood like a statue, holding the satphone and smiling.

"Mark, are you gonna tell me what that call was all about ... or are you just going to stand there grinning like a monkey?"

"Anne, you ever had sex with a monkey?"

"I'm not into bestiality, Little Man. Just watching us in the mirrored ceiling is my comfortable limit for kinky. So exactly what was that call all about?"

"Louis Loveman first gave me multiple latitude/longitude numbers for the chicken farm area, then personally assured me our 'informant status' would never result in us getting into another WITSEC-like situation. He even said we'd never get a subpoena to appear in any court of law. We're simply educated snitches working at a distance from any danger. Does that make you happy, Anne?"

Anne smiled broadly. "Little Monkey, bring your big banana with you ... I'll answer your question in our bedroom!"

* * *

A customary postcoital nap followed. When they awoke, Anne used their regular cell phone to call Bradley. He answered, and indicated he was presently working in his lab at UA.

"Brad, is now a good time for me to come to your lab to donate some blood?"

"I'm in the middle of running some timed tests right now, Anne. Could you come about an hour from now?" Brad asked, then thanked her for her offer to donate.

"See you then," Anne said. "Mark and I will just walk over. We think we remember how to get there."

After getting dressed, Mark and Anne began slowly walking hand in hand from Pima-Swan to the UA campus. After troubling several different students for directions, they again spotted the four-story molecular biology building. While walking on the campus grounds, both felt they were ambling along in a "time capsule," one created back during their own college years, his at Emory in Atlanta, hers at Georgia State.

"You know, Mark, this sure brings back memories, but I don't think we ever looked as young as these kids do today!"

"Anne, we need to remember we're mostly among 18- to 21-year-olds. And other than the way they dress now, do you notice what really seems odd?"

"*Odd?* Like what?"

"Hardly anybody is carrying *books* anymore! Most of them seem to have laptops now!"

"Face it, Little Man, we're just having a hard time adjusting to our age and admitting it's the 21st century," Anne remarked, as they entered the building, then boarded an elevator for the molecular biology building's third floor.

"Step right into my parlor," Brad said when the Telfairs entered his lab. "'Count Dracula' will be with you momentarily!"

"You're a mess, Brad!" Anne replied, laughing. "I hope I'll have plenty of hanta-specific antibodies for you."

"I'm first going to do a quick finger stick. Just need a drop of your blood to do a fluorescent antibody screening test I've recently developed."

Brad did her finger stick, then applied a drop of Anne's blood to a standard glass microscope slide. He spread the drop of blood into a thin film that quickly air-dried. With an eyedropper he applied another clear solution to the dried blood film. Brad slipped the slide beneath a regular binocular microscope. Brad beamed when he quickly looked at the slide. "Wow!" he exclaimed. "Anne you're loaded! If you can spare me a whole unit of your blood, I think I can harvest about 60 milliliters of antibodies. That's *twice* what I've harvested over the last three years! And I had to draw much smaller amounts of blood from about 25 different hanta survivors to get it."

Brad had Anne stretch out on a table in the lab. He applied a rubber tube tourniquet to her left upper arm, prepped the front of her elbow with Betadine, then expertly did a vein puncture with an 18 gauge needle connected to standard tubing and blood collection bag like those used by the Red Cross. Brad smiled as he watched the 450 milliliter bag slowly fill to capacity. Brad removed the tourniquet, withdrew the needle, and applied a pressure dressing. He quickly labeled the warm bag of blood, and promptly placed it in a refrigerator. From the fridge, he removed a half-quart bottle of orange-colored Gatorade.

"Here, Anne. Drink as much of this as you can. It might keep you from pulling a 'Cindy,' like she did the other night following her single beer."

The Telfairs chuckled, but soon got into a technical discussion with Bradley.

"Bradley, why don't other labs use the fluorescent antibody test you just used?" Anne asked, now sitting on the edge of the table.

"Because they don't have it, and it's still experimental. I need to be sure it won't give false negatives or positives. I'd appreciate your not mentioning that test to anyone in another lab. If I accumulate enough data to prove my self-developed test is highly reliable, I may attempt to market the process. Could make me rich, but that could be years down the road."

Anne took a couple of swallows of her Gatorade.

Mark had a question. "Brad, I thought you were primarily interested in developing a hanta vaccine."

"I am. But part of the process is to understand the molecular structures of the antibodies the human immune system naturally develops when challenged with live hantavirus. That's what I will harvest from Anne's blood, the natural anti-hanta antibodies. Also, we need to understand the molecular structure of the virus itself. We need to define what part of the molecular structure of hantavirus causes hanta pulmonary syndrome, and which part stimulates the human immune system to begin its own antibody production. That's what we need to find. Something that will stimulate antibody production, yet not give the patient a hanta infection."

Anne took the final sip of her Gatorade, then said, "If you find I'm 'loaded' with antibodies, as your experimental test indicates, when can I donate another unit of blood to your cause?"

"Anytime your numbers are OK. I first called Dr. Baxter to get his approval. He said your recent numbers are fine for a donation. My guidelines are the same as those used by the American Red Cross. As medical folks, I'm sure you already know your hematocrit value must be at least 38 percent, and your hemoglobin level must be 12.5 grams or higher. Has Dr. Baxter dismissed you yet?"

"No, he hasn't. He wants to see me again in a couple of weeks."

"I'm sure he'll check that again at your next visit with him. If you're 38 percent and 12.5, or higher, let me know. We'll do this again if we can. Are you and Mark still planning on hanging around Tucson for awhile?"

"You bet! At least until I'm dismissed by Dr. Baxter. And this is the place that saved my life … and I'm now so intrigued by this thing with Dr. Abbas I'm not about to leave unless Mark wants to."

"We have no travel plans," Mark replied. "I've also gotten addicted to figuring Abbas out. But let me ask you a question that may be stupid."

"Ask," Brad said. "The dumber the question the better I can answer them!"

"OK, I'll ask. You know I've been trained as a surgeon, Anne as a surgical nurse. We didn't get much training about the research areas you and Cindy deal with. But here's my question: Why not inject patients who've been exposed to hanta with hanta-specific antibodies? Why go to the trouble of developing a vaccine?"

"Mark, that's actually two questions. To answer the first one, the vast majority of patients have no idea—not even a clue—they've been exposed to hanta … until they become critically ill. That is exactly what happened to Anne! To answer your second question, that's why we need a vaccine. If we had one, people could be immunized and be protected before they ever get exposed."

"It really was a stupid question," Mark admitted. "Brad let me ask you this: If someone has an active hanta infection, giving them hanta-specific antibodies should kill the virus, right?"

"I feel almost positive that it would. I think giving a hanta-infected patient hanta-specific antibodies could stop the infection very quickly."

"Then why isn't it used to treat known hanta-infected patients?" Mark asked.

"Mark, I'm sure you recall us sitting in the ICU at UMC when I offered my entire collection of hanta-specific hyperimmune globulin to the doctors treating Anne. The infectious disease consultant, a Dr. Schroder as I recall, indicated he felt we needed some kind of 'experimental procedure' permit and suggested we wait."

"Wait for what! For her to die!" Mark said, his voice raised, face flushed.

"Mark, I understand your anger. There is also the issue with the FDA."

"FDA?"

"Yes. 'Big Brother.' If the doctors had used my hyperimmune globulin, and Anne survived, there'd probably be no problem. If she had died, you can bet the doctors could lose their licenses for 'human experimentation' and using a substance the FDA has not approved."

Anne spoke: "Mark, are you watching the time. We need to get some numbers to Cal, remember?"

"Sorry, Anne," Brad said. "Even though you're at the center of this conversation we've neglected you. Want some more Gatorade?"

"I'm feeling fine. You guys finish," Anne said.

"Brad, have you tested your hyperimmune globulin in animals infected with hanta?" Mark asked.

Brad scratched his head, then spoke. "Therein lies the problem. We do not have an ideal test animal to use in the lab. All mice, including most rodents, are out of the question. Even most canines and felines, too. Sure, we can infect those animals with hanta, but they either don't get sick from it, or in many cases they simply become 'carriers,' like the white-footed mice almost always do. The real test animals we need are *primates.* And if we used chimps or monkeys, or whatever, you can bet the animal rights folks at PETA would clobber the university!"

"Brad, I've another stupid question: Why don't you intentionally infect one group of white-footed deer mice with hanta?"

"You mean just make them *known* carriers?" Brad asked.

"Yes," Mark said. "Then periodically give them some of your hanta-immune globulin. You could follow them over a period of time and see if they *lose* their hanta-carrier status. As a control, compare them to a second group of infected white-footed deer mice that did *not* get the globulin."

"Mark, I forgive you for any dumb questions. That is a fucking brilliant suggestion! It would at least prove my immune globulin can eliminate the virus from a living mammal!"

"OK, you guys," Anne piped in. I'm hungry for lunch, and we need to call Cal about the latitude/longitude numbers Louis gave us earlier today."

"Anne, sorry your donor session took so long. I really need to get back to some timed experiments, but maybe we could all meet at the apartment this evening. Say, about eight o'clock. And before

I forget it, here's your Dustbuster. I guarantee it's hanta-free." Brad said, reaching inside a lab cabinet and handing it to her.

22

Walking hand in hand back through the UA campus toward Pima-Swan, Mark felt like a dork. College kids were staring and snickering at this "elderly couple," one with a bandage on her left arm, the other a short bearded guy carrying a Dustbuster. Mark and Anne both broke out laughing.

"Bet they think we are stoned!" Anne said.

"We might fit in better if we were!" Mark said, avoiding eye contact, wishing he had a jacket to hide the Dustbuster beneath.

"Boy, you sure got Bradley excited with your suggestion," Anne remarked.

"You mean about using mice to see if he could reverse hanta-carrier status?"

"Yeah. Bradley even used the f-word. 'Fucking brilliant,' he said. I don't think I've ever heard him curse a single time before."

"Me neither," Mark confirmed. "I'll just be glad when we get off campus and these kids quit staring!"

* * *

Back at the camper, Anne began preparing lunch. Using his cell, Mark called Cal.

"Hey, boss," Mark said, "I've got a bunch of latitude/longitude numbers Louis called in to me earlier this morning by satphone. You want the numbers now?"

"No. Not now. Not over a cell. I can come to your camper and get them," Cal suggested.

"Are you in any big hurry to get them?" Mark asked.

"No big rush, but certainly by later today."

"Cal, we just left Bradley's lab. Anne donated some of her blood so he could harvest her anti-hanta antibodies. At the lab, Brad told us he wants all of us to meet at 8:00 at his apartment tonight. That work for you?"

"Swell. I'll be there, and I'll have both old and current aviation charts in hand."

"See you then," Mark said, and clicked his cell off.

"Little Man, lunch is ready," Anne announced.

Mark and Anne sat at the dinette in their RV eating lunch. Upon finishing, Anne had her elbows resting on its Formica top. Mark observed, then commented, "I think you can take off that bandage Brad put on. I think the needle track should be clotted by now. We can stick a regular Band-Aid on it. I'll go get one."

Moments later, Mark returned with an assortment of Band-Aids. He removed Brad's bandage. The puncture wound was barely visible, so he selected a circular Band-Aid about three-quarters of an inch in diameter. He gently applied the circular flesh-toned bandage to the puncture site on the front side of Anne's left elbow, then inexplicably burst out laughing.

"What's so funny, Mark?"

"Well it's just … it's …" Mark could not finish the sentence.

"Just ask Cindy," Mark finally got out. "She might tell you."

To change the subject, Mark asked Anne to show him the surgical scars on her right forearm. She rotated her right arm so Mark could both see and feel the scars. "That darn Dr. Dooley did a plastic closure after he removed the tubes for the membrane oxygenator! When these scars mature, they are going to be very hard to find. I know good surgical work when I see it."

"So do I, Mark. But I'm not a vain person. I haven't even given those scars a second thought. What matters to me is that I am *alive* … thanks to a team of people here in Tucson. What if I'd gotten sick somewhere else? What if there had been no Dr. Baxter, who immediately recognized the urgency of getting me on a ventilator? What if there'd been no Dr. Dooley, the vascular surgeon who pushed to get me on an experimental oxygenating device? What if there had been no competent hospital, one with a staff well versed in managing patients on a ventilator? What if there had been no Cindy and Brad to do lab work, and take us under their wing?"

"Anne, you have a way of summarizing. It's a gift I don't have." Mark stood, leaned across the dinette, and gave her a kiss on the forehead. "What if I had to live the rest of my life without you? That's a 'what if' I hope I never have to face."

Anne smiled and had tears in her eyes. "For me that would be my most feared 'what if' … living without you." Anne dried her eyes on a napkin, then laughed. "Now tell me about the darn Band-Aids!"

* * *

Cal's Porsche Boxster was already parked at the apartment in a visitor's space when Mark and Anne arrived on foot at 8:00. The VW was not in its assigned spot. When they entered the apartment, Cal had his aviation charts spread out on the dining table, intently studying them. Cindy was in the kitchen making tea, coffee, and snack hors d'oeuvres. Brad was not present. Cindy quickly explained his absence. "Brad is running a little late. He called earlier and said Anne's blood was the 'mother lode' of antibodies he hoped to find. He should be here by 8:30," she said.

Without preamble, Cal looked at Mark over his reading glasses. "Let's double check the latitude/longitude numbers Louis gave you earlier today."

"Right here," Mark answered, handing Cal the note where he'd originally written them down.

Cal made no reply, just studied the numbers and the charts. He remained silent for a full ten minutes as he scrutinized them. Finally he announced, "It's exactly the same. That emergency strip listed on the old chart matches the coordinates from Louis. That sod field is no longer listed on the current charts. What we now need to do is get on a computer, punch in these coordinates, and see what a satellite view of the area looks like." Cal raised his voice. "Cindy, where is your computer?"

"Bradley took it to the lab with him this morning," Cindy replied from the kitchen.

"Shit," Cal muttered under his breath. "I'll run over to my condo and get one of mine," Cal said, as he headed for the door. "Bradley gets so focused when he's in his lab, it might be midnight before he comes home!"

The next sound was that of Cal's Boxster as he rapidly departed. Two minutes later Mark heard Brad's VW arrive. Brad popped in the door, carrying his laptop, and wearing a big smile. "Thanks to Anne, I've got 90 more milliliters of antibodies! Triple what I previously had! But where is Cal?"

Cindy explained. "You know Cal. He got impatient when told we did not have a computer available, so he raced off to his condo to get one!"

"I'm sorry I was just a tad late. Fifteen minutes, to be exact," Brad said, embarrassed, checking his watch.

Moments later, Cal burst in carrying not one but *two* laptops.

"Shit," Cal muttered again, upon seeing Brad with his laptop in hand. "Better to have too much than too little. At least my Boxster got a little workout, and I think a certain Tucson cop has found out you can't catch one with a Crown Vic. Anyway, let's get to work."

In minutes they had all three laptops booted and situated atop Cal's aviation charts that covered the table. Soon they had three different websites that offered civilian satellite imagery. Of course none would offer the resolution that the FBI could access, but they found one site was almost real-time, with its images being refreshed every 24 hours. They elected to concentrate on that particular website, and Cal quickly tapped in the latitude/longitude coordinate pairs.

Without benefit of prior aerial images, they were all surprised how accurately their minds had drawn mental images of the chicken farm as it would appear from above. About 100 yards from a paved Hall County road, the 50-foot fronts of the three chicken houses all paralleled the road. The concrete pad and a small storage tank for the water well pump were easily discerned directly behind the center house; the heat pumps appeared as little squares at the side of each house. Beginning about 50 yards northeast of the houses, the sod runway was readily visible. Looking at the satellite image on his laptop, and studying the aviation charts, Cal made some quick calculations, then announced his conclusion: "That runway is a little over 3,500 feet in length, and uniformly it's 75 yards in width. Heck, I could even land and takeoff there with my Cessna 310 if I practice my soft-field landings."

"Uh … soft-field?" Mark questioned.

"Yeah. Sod. Compacted sand, a beach. Makes almost any surface a runway."

"Cal, certainly you are not suggesting you are planning on flying there!" Mark exclaimed.

"Hell no! Not unless Louis specifically wants me to go there for some reason," Cal added. "Sometime I'll explain why I owe Louis any favor he may ever want … but not tonight."

I bet it's because Louis saved Cal's ass during a dogfight with MiGs, Mark thought, but remained silent.

Anne, Brad, and Cindy were paying attention, though drinking coffee and nibbling on Cindy's hors d'oeuvres. Anne spoke up after studying the laptop screens. "Have you guys noticed what looks like a big truck parked in the woods? I guess that would be on the northwest side of the runway, down close to its end. And what about that big shiny square thing down at that same end of the runway?"

Cal used onscreen controls provided by the website. He navigated to the two items Anne had noticed, then zoomed. "Anne," Cal began, "that truck is an 18-wheeler, with its tractor still attached. The trailer I think is refrigerated, or at least has that capability. See the square thing sticking off the front of the trailer? I think that is a refrigeration unit. And notice how they cleared no more space than needed to back the rig into the woods. If you look closely, you can see the 18-wheeler's tracks on the mowed runway grass. That would mean it was put there very recently. And, it's quite concealed there. Some tree branches even arch over the rig. You couldn't possibly see it from the road and it would be very hard to spot from the air, unless you knew exactly where it was."

"What about the large silver square thing at the end of the runway … the thing Anne spotted?" Cindy asked.

"I honestly don't know," Cal admitted. "It could be a pole barn, a shed … or even a hangar. We need to talk to Louis."

Now 9:00, Mark set his satphone to speakerphone, then dialed Louis, having some reservation because it was late:

"Mark Telfair here, Louis. I apologize for calling this late. The five of us here in Tucson have used the coordinates to look at satellite images. Everything seems to fit, except for two things: First, we can't figure out why an 18-wheeler is parked perpendicular to one side of the runway. It's actually concealed in the woods about 100 feet off the northwest side of the runway. Second, there appears to be a square structure of some sort at that same far end of the runway."

"I can answer your second question. The square you're seeing on satellite is a 40-foot by 38-foot pole barn with a flat metal roof and no sides. It was built by my undercover guys, and the only explanation they got from Abbas was that it was a 'farm equipment shed.' Even though the metal roof is galvanized, my men were told they would be painting the roof some shade of green tomorrow. What you can't see on satellite are two fuel tanks beneath that shed. My guys say one tank is labeled '110 octane avgas,' the other '87 octane unleaded.' The tanks are each about 500 gallons in size and were delivered and installed by a fuel wholesaler in Gainesville. My undercover men are checking that wholesaler out. My guys also said both tanks were filled by a tanker truck shortly after they were delivered to the shed. Even with the two fuel tanks, and the tractor and Bush Hog, they think there is still enough space left beneath the shed for a small airplane."

"Well, what about the 18-wheeler truck?" Cindy asked.

135

"That remains a mystery. All my men did was clear a space in the woods for it. They were told that a large truck would soon be parking there. They were given no details, and were told if they got caught snooping around the truck they would be fired on the spot! They are trying to figure some way to use their cell phones to get pictures of the truck's exterior, maybe a tag number, or USDOT information. Needless to say, we need to find some clever way to determine what's inside that truck ... and do it without my undercover guys getting caught and run off the job."

"Dad," Cindy said, "I think I can tell you exactly what's inside that truck—essentially all the missing pieces!"

"Missing? Like what, Cin?"

"Like his stock of white-footed deer mice, and the equipment needed to dilute and filter their fecal sludge to make it ready for use in a crop duster."

Louis Loveman audibly exhaled. "I hope you are wrong, Cin. Abbas may be closer to executing his plan than we think. If I asked my men to go inside that trailer, I could be asking them to expose themselves to hantavirus. In good conscience, I cannot do that. Let's all think about it and get back together tomorrow evening about 8:00. Be ready to unload your thoughts on me then," Louis said, then clicked off.

23

They all realized Louis Loveman was their 'official leader,' and he'd obviously just signed off for the day ... but they could not shut down their own minds. The evening was still young. Their self-appointed 'local leader,' Cindy, spoke: "I don't care if it is nine o'clock. I'll stay up the rest of the night. I'm going to keep thinking until I figure out a way to prove Abbas is raising mice for the sole purpose of accumulating hantavirus on a massive scale. Brad, you can go to bed if you want, and the rest of you guys can go home if you like. But I'm going to keep thinking tonight until my brain gives out."

Cal stood, went to the fridge and opened himself a beer before speaking to Cindy. "Madame Leader, I'll stay and think along with you until the beer runs out ... provided, of course, I can use your couch again if needed. And you have to agree to be the official note taker for all our thoughts. OK?"

Cindy asked if anyone wanted to leave. Everyone wanted to stay.

"I have a suggestion," Cindy began. "Why don't we begin by looking at four major categories of issues: the airplane, the truck and its contents, risk of hantavirus infection to Dad's undercover men, and, most importantly, figure some way to *stop* Abbas dead in his tracks if he tries to execute his plan. I realize these categories may overlap, but we can always add more issues as we think of them."

"Cindy, under your 'airplane category,' why not figure some way to delay delivery of the plane to Abbas?" Mark asked.

"Better yet, go ahead and let the duster get delivered on time, then figure some way to cripple the plane, or its spraying function," Brad added. "That would possibly allow Louis to nab the pilot and others involved in the plot."

Cal smiled. "Delaying delivery of the duster, as Mark suggested, would only make Abbas suspicious, and he may decide to abort the purchase altogether. I think I know Louis well enough to say he wants to let this thing run right up to the wire, then kill the operation. As Brad suggested, that would allow catching a larger number of the bad guys. There is no way Abbas could pull this thing off acting alone."

"Cal, what about my suggestion of crippling the plane and its spraying function?" Brad asked.

"Brad, that idea has merit. It's something I would probably have to rig up myself. I could fly to Kissimee and see my friend, Ben Hunter. I'm sure he'd give me a few moments alone with the plane Abbas plans to buy. I could rig it so that if the pilot flips the switch to start spraying, it would kill the engine. Of course my 'unapproved modification' would mean the airworthiness certificate is worthless, and I can see where that could get Ben Hunter in trouble with the FAA."

Mark thought a moment then spoke. "Invalid airworthiness certificate aside, the pilot could possibly crash! Maybe into a populated area, with a tank full of hantavirus-laden liquid. I don't like that idea, Cal. And besides, suppose you yourself had just bought a used crop duster. Wouldn't you want to personally test its spray function? Maybe do a test flight with nothing but pure water in the chemical tank?"

Cal exhaled, was silent a moment, then spoke. "I think you guys got me on that one. Sure, I'd test it with plain water before I put other stuff in the tank for an actual spray run. My idea was to rewire the cockpit's spray switch. Rig it so that when the pilot turned it 'on' it would ground out the hot wires going to the Lycoming's twin magnetos. That would instantly kill the entire ignition system. If I were flying the duster, I think I'd quickly figure out I couldn't spray and keep the engine running at the same time. I'd probably return the spray switch to its 'off' position, restart the engine, then try to fly my ass to some emergency landing spot."

Cindy, who'd been taking notes, said "What about leaving the plane untampered with? Just figure some way to neutralize the hantavirus solution before it gets sprayed out."

"Like how?" Cal asked.

"Like put something in the plane's chemical tank that would kill hantavirus," Cindy explained. "Maybe chlorine bleach. Put it in there even before they filled it with the hantavirus solution."

"There are two problems with that," Cal responded. "First, Abbas or the pilot might smell the chlorine while loading the tank, and they'd know something was amiss. Second, you'd need an accomplice on the ground when they were loading the chemical tank … someone who could put chlorine in there when Abbas or the pilot weren't looking, and do it just before they took off for an actual spray run."

"I've got another idea," Mark said. "Cal, do you remember your elaborate explanation of how a crop duster spray system works? Remember telling us there is a disposable filter between the chemical tank and the pumps that feed solution to the spray bars? Well, how big is that filter?"

Cal smiled. "I think I see where you're going. The filter housing is a stainless-steel tube about a foot long. It's about four inches in diameter. When I said the filter is 'disposable,' I was referring to a disposable paper-like cartridge *inside* the stainless filter housing. Are you thinking what I'm now thinking?"

"Cal, I never know what you are thinking!" Mark replied. "But here is my thought: If the paper-like cartridge was removed, and you packed the steel filter housing full of chlorine tablets, I think they'd slowly dissolve as liquid flowed over them, yet leave no particles that would clog the spray nozzles."

"Brilliant!" Cal exclaimed. "But I think we can make one improvement on your idea. I know you have no idea what a duster's filter element actually looks like. It is an accordion-like paper cylinder very similar to the air filter for a car. Fluid flow across the filter is from its outside to its inside hollow core. It should be possible to pack the chlorine tablets in the external pleats of the filter element, and still replace the element in its normal position inside the steel filter housing. That would cover all bases. No alteration would be obvious unless you actually took the filter apart. No suspicious odor in the chemical tank. The duster's spray would function fine if they decide to do a test flight using plain water. And if they don't filter the hantavirus solution as well as they should, the filter would still catch any particles that could clog spray nozzles. If one of the chlorine tablets fragments as it dissolves, the filter would still catch those fragments as well."

Bradley, who'd been quiet for awhile, had a question. "Cal, you don't suppose you have one of those filter elements on hand, do you?"

"I can do better than that, Brad. I've got half a hangar full of spare parts at my airfield. I can bring a complete filter unit to you ... housing, disposable core, and all. What have you got in mind?"

"Just some tests. I want to pack the filter element with chlorine tablets, let water run through it, and see how much chlorination we've got in the water that exits. We'd need several parts per million. Exactly how much, Cindy?" Brad asked.

Cindy ceased taking notes long enough to answer Brad's question. "We know when hanta is exposed to two to three parts per million it is killed in about an hour. I'd say we need 5 to 10 parts per million, just to be on the safe side. That would kill it instantly. I've got some hanta cultures going in my lab, and I'll lend you some if you want to do some testing."

"Then it's settled," Cal said. "I'll get Brad a complete duster filter to play with, Cindy will get him some live hanta to experiment with ... but where do we get the chlorine tablets?"

"Would you believe Wal-Mart? In their section where they have their swimming pool supplies," Anne said. "I've noticed those tablets there before."

Everyone laughed, and when it died out Cindy said "I think we've about talked the airplane stuff to death. Though we've reached a tentative solution, I think we should move on to the truck."

"How about if we have someone steal the truck," Mark immediately suggested. We could have it driven to some site where they can use those things like they are beginning to use at seaports to inspect containers."

"It's called millimeter wave or backscatter x-ray," Cal explained. "I think we'll soon see that technology used at airports to inspect luggage and passengers. I've read of squabbles about its use on humans, because the images undress you. In other words, it causes your clothes to disappear!"

"Wow!" Cindy and Anne said in unison, each hugging their chests.

"Come on, guys! Let's get practical. Cal, how big are these scanners?" Cindy asked.

"For trucks they are huge," Cal said, holding his hands as far apart as possible. "Trucks with trailers, or those hauling containers, must physically drive through the scanner. Moving a scanner to the truck site on the chicken farm is not an option. I know scanners are powered by electricity, but I have no knowledge of the required voltage, and that could be a problem on site. I think the best option is to see if we can get Louis to have his undercover men take thermal images of the trailer. That may tell us if there is something warm-blooded inside ... like the mice you are so desperately looking for, Cindy."

"Cal, I'm sure you know mice are warm-blooded mammals. Their body temperature varies widely with the species. Common healthy well-fed mice would average about 100 degrees. If poorly fed, they become torpid, a sort of semi-hibernation, and their temperature can drop down to lower levels."

"Other than stealing the truck, and thermal imaging, that leaves us with what?" Cal asked.

"Maybe some kind of listening device," Brad suggested. "I know if I have a large colony of mice in a pen, there'll be occasional flourishes of activity, squeaking, et cetera. Fighting over food or sex, I've always figured. But the sound is quite distinctive."

"OK," Cal said, "we're down to stealing the truck, on-site thermal imaging, and on-site listening device. What's left?"

"Inspection by a human," Anne said.

"And possible risk of hantavirus exposure," Cindy added. "So that comes to the next point. Only one of us in this room is probably immune to hanta, and that person is you, Anne."

Anne stood. "Oh no you don't, Cindy! Don't you even *think* about asking me to look inside that truck! *Probably immune* is not good enough for me. I damn near died from that hantavirus shit, and I may not be so lucky a second time. You can call me a chickenshit all you want, but my ass is not getting anywhere near that truck!" Anne said emphatically, face flushing, tears approaching.

She's really upset to be cussing like that! Mark thought.

Cindy immediately detected Anne's fear and anger. She got up from her chair, moved to Anne, and put her small arms around Anne's neck. "Anne, I do apologize if I've upset you. I wasn't implying I wanted *you* to personally look inside that trailer. I was simply making a statement of probable fact. According to Brad's studies, your present anti-hanta antibody levels should make you immune. That's all I was trying to say," Cindy said, her electric blue eyes focused on Anne's hazel ones that were now filling with tears. Tenderly, Cindy handed Anne a linen napkin to use as a handkerchief. "We still friends?" Cindy asked, as Anne dried her eyes, nodding a "yes."

"I think it's time for a beer break!" Cal said. "Anybody else want one?"

Mark and Brad nodded an affirmative; Cindy and Anne shook their heads indicating "no."

Anne soon settled down completely and apologized to the group. "Sorry to have interrupted the serious discussion. I think we were talking about immunity."

"Brad, that's your department," Cindy said, picking up her legal pad again.

"Immune globulin is all I have to offer. Fortunately, thanks to Anne, I probably have more hanta-specific immune globulin than anyone else in the world. It works best if given IV, and would probably have to be given every three of four weeks to maintain the blood level of antibodies needed to protect you from hanta. As an additional precaution, I'd recommend wearing gloves and a good viral-filtering mask for anyone entering the truck's trailer. Also, a shower with a good decontaminating solution when they got out of the trailer would be a good idea. Of course this is all predicated on there actually being hanta-infected mice inside the trailer … and that's something we do not know for a fact at this point."

"Why don't we wait until we next talk with Dad?" Cindy said. "I also had 'stop Abbas' if he tried to implement his plan on my list. But I don't think we know enough yet to figure out how to do that."

"I agree," Cal said. "Until we figure out his *whole* plan, it's hard to know exactly where to kill it."

"If it's agreeable to everyone, I'll call Dad at his office in Denver in the morning. I won't give him any specific details over the phone, but I'll try to establish a time for us to make another satphone call to him. Unless it's an emergency, I know he prefers we call him in Boulder in the evenings. Cal, do you think you can get Bradley that filter, like early in the morning?"

"Yeah, I can do that. As soon as there's daylight. I've had the power company shut off the electricity to the hangar where the parts are stored. There's a ground fault in the underground wiring that serves that particular one, and I haven't gotten it repaired yet. Or at least I haven't found an electrical contractor that can do it without cutting up my concrete runway! Anyway, I can find the crop duster filter a lot quicker in daylight than by flashlight. In the morning I'll drive it over to Brad's lab, and give him the filter so he can run his tests. I'll even zip by Wal-Mart and pick up some chlorine tablets for him."

Now approaching 3:00 a.m., Bradley insisted he drive Mark and Anne back to the Pima-Swan. They didn't argue with Brad. They were exhausted.

The Telfairs promptly went to bed. Before going to sleep, Anne said, "Little Man, I hope I didn't embarrass you when I got so upset with Cindy and cried in front of everybody."

"No, you didn't embarrass me. Not at all. Even if you'd volunteered to enter the trailer, I would have stopped you. I'd have physically restrained you if necessary. I certainly don't mind assisting law enforcement, but in the process, I'll never allow them to put us in harm's way again. We made that mistake once with the drug smugglers. We don't need to repeat that mistake. And I really don't think Cindy was implying *you* should be the one to go inside the trailer. I think she was honestly commenting on your status of immunity."

Considering the late hour, they settled for a quick goodnight kiss, and promptly fell asleep.

142

24

At 10:00 a.m. the Telfairs' cell phone rang in their camper. They were sound asleep. Their cell's repeated rings first awoke Mark, who reluctantly answered it. It was Cindy: "I called Dad, and he's good for a phone meeting this evening at 8:00. Will that work for you guys?"

"I'm sure it will, but we're not good for an all-nighter like we almost pulled last night."

"I realize you older folks need your sleep. Dad does, too. He's 67, you know. But there are exceptions, like Cal. I have no idea where he gets his energy, or how he gets along on so little sleep. And he's 68, a year older than my dad!"

"Cindy, thanks for making me feel so much better about my aging. But tell me, when is Cal going to get the stuff Brad needs for his filter experiments?"

"It's already done. That darn Cal woke me up here at our apartment … at 6:30! He was banging on the door, and smiling when he handed me one of those filter things for a crop duster. He also had a ten-pound bag of one-inch-diameter chlorine tablets. He felt sure that size tablet would fit inside the filter. He'd apparently first gone to his hangar at daybreak to get the filter, then to Wal-Mart to get the chlorine. He said Wal-Mart had the 'good business sense to stay open all night.' He did have a problem with the Wal-Mart's cashier, though. Seems her scanner wouldn't read the price of the tablets. Cal gave her two 50-dollar bills, his business card, said 'keep the change,' then walked out of the store. He said he next went by the lab at 6:20. He discovered Brad was not there yet, so he came to the apartment. Cal then had the audacity to tell me, 'If you youngsters really want to get ahead in this world, there is absolutely no excuse for *anyone* sleeping past 5:00 a.m.!'"

Mark chuckled, while thinking: *I don't think I've ever met a go-getter quite like Cal Camarada!*

"So, where is Bradley now?" Mark asked.

"He's at his lab, working. Got there about 9:30."

"You think he'll have the results by this evening?"

"I think so. It's actually a simple test. So, I guess I'll see you and Anne this evening," Cindy said, and signed off.

* * *

That evening at 8:00, Cindy called the meeting to order. "OK, Guys, let's keep it short and to the point tonight. I've made no hors d'oeuvres, only coffee and tea … and we're out of beer. So let's get dad on the line."

Mark was already dialing the satphone as Cindy spoke.

"Hi, Louis. It's me, Mark. We're all here and you are on speakerphone. Cindy wants to keep this meeting short, because we all stayed up late last night kicking around possibilities."

"Fine with me. I'm beat, too. Stayed up most of the rest of last night talking with my undercover guys. Abbas had driven to town yesterday to get them some more olive drab paint for the roof of the shed they've built. They are also going to paint the 18-wheeler's roof and the tractor's cab the same color. Abbas has told them he wants to run electricity and a small water line to the shed, as well as to the spot where the truck is parked."

"So, they are trying to camouflage it from aerial view," Cal said. "They make several patterns of camouflage cloth and netting that would be far more effective than paint!"

"I know, Cal," Louis replied. "Like some of the stuff we pulled over our planes and choppers while we were in the Air Force in Korea. I'm simply reporting what my men do and observe, then report to me.

"While Abbas was in town getting the paint, they looked the truck over fairly closely. Odometer has only 2,100 miles on it. All 18 tires show virtually no wear. The tractor is a Kenworth, and they think it's brand new. They got the VIN for the tractor, and I've got some men working on its origin. The doors to the cab were not locked, but there was no key inside the cab."

"What about the trailer?" Brad asked. "What is it made of?"

"My guys think the outer skin is aluminum. 'Looks new,' they say. It's a Fruehauf brand, approximately 45 feet long. There are no tags on the trailer, or tractor, but they got some of the manufacturer's numbers off the trailer. I've got some men working on the origin of the trailer, too. The trailer has a refrigeration unit mounted to its front end. They think the refrigeration unit is diesel, and thermostatically controlled. They think the Kenworth's saddle tanks are close to full, at least as best they could judge by tapping on the tanks. The fill caps for the diesel tanks are locked, so they couldn't take a direct look at the fuel level."

"Louis, could someone with the proper key drive the 18-wheeler away?" Mark asked.

"That would be driving away with a lot of evidence. But I think I've got that possibility covered. I've sent my men several spike strips. They have inserted them in front of the truck's front wheels and drive wheels. They've concealed the spikes with the thick pine straw and leaves that naturally cover the ground where the truck is located."

"What about the door to get inside the trailer?" Anne asked.

"It's at the rear of the trailer, a roll-up type, apparently aluminum. It is secured with a large Master padlock, but my guys got a manufacturer's serial number off the lock. I'm going to personally call Master Lock about getting us a key. One of my men is pretty good at picking locks, but that takes time. They were afraid Abbas would return from town and catch them in the act. They spotted two gray hairs that had been stuck to the trailer's rear door. The other end of the hairs are stuck to the bed of the trailer. They are secured with some light grease, maybe Vaseline. If the hairs are disturbed, Abbas would certainly know someone had entered the trailer door. Pretty sharp observation on the part of my men, I'd say."

Cindy ceased scribbling on her legal pad and spoke up. "Dad, we all had a very long discussion here last night. My basic concern relates to the mice. If we have no mice, Abbas is less of an urgent concern. We are trying to find some way to determine if Abbas is in the process of constructing a 'rolling lab,' so to speak. I'm talking about the18-wheeler's trailer becoming his lab. He's got to have a climate-controlled place to keep his breeder stock of mice that are probably infected with hanta. He's also got to have some place to dilute and filter the mouse fecal soup we think they'll collect from the modified chicken houses. In other words, he's got to have a place to get the stuff ready to put into a crop duster's chemical tank. I think his next step would be to put some of his breeders in the modified chicken houses, then go into mass production. To determine if we have mice inside the trailer, Cal suggested the use of thermal imaging. That would possibly allow us to determine if any warm-blooded creatures are inside the trailer. We know mice have a body temperature that averages about 100 degrees. Do you think thermal imaging would work through the aluminum skin of the trailer?"

"Cin, I honestly don't know. If the trailer is refrigerated it may also be very well insulated. I'll promptly get a thermal-imaging camera to my undercover guys there in Gainesville. As of late yesterday afternoon, my men told me there are no mice inside the modified chicken houses. Though lockable, Abbas presently does not keep the doors to those houses locked. As for mice inside the trailer, we'll certainly give thermal imaging a try," Louis said.

"And what about listening devices?" Brad asked. "I suggested that last night."

"Listening for *what?*" Louis asked, amusement in his voice.

"Mice! Inside the trailer, Louis. Mice intermittently make definite squeaking sounds. I hear them all the time in my lab," Brad explained. "I'm being serious here."

Louis chuckled. "I can also get listening equipment to my men. We use audio bugs all the time. Using simple pocket-sized receivers, my men can listen as well as record any sounds inside that trailer. The actual transmitting bugs are quite small, not much bigger than a dime. They are powered by a battery about the same size as those used in a digital watch, and can stay hot for several weeks. They are stuck on with a special adhesive, and my men will know the best location to place them. If the chance presents itself, I might get them to stick one inside the car Abbas drives. In fact, a GPS on his car might prove useful, and I'll get a GPS unit to my men also. Of course I might have to enlist Bradley as our 'mouse audio expert' ... to interpret what we pick up with the listening devices for the trailer!"

When the laughter died, Cal spoke up. "Louis, don't worry about the crop duster. I think we've figured a way to allow the duster to fly and spray normally ... but what's sprayed out will be sterile. It involves a modification of the filter for the stuff that gets sprayed out. It's a little involved, and Bradley is running some more tests. When we're positive, I'll explain in more detail. I won't bother you with the specifics now, as I don't want to keep you up beyond your bedtime!"

"You're a year older than me, you old fart!" Louis bellowed.

"I know ... thanks to you, Louis. More later," Cal said, a hint of tears in his eyes.

After a pause, Louis said, "I do have one bit of information I've not relayed to you folks in Tucson. Al Abbas will probably have two accomplices: One is a Muslim named Abdul Aleem, the other is Abdus Salaam, who we assume is Muslim also. One of the two is a pilot. We don't know which one yet. If that's all for this evening, I'll sign off now, then feed Sampson and myself, and get my beauty rest!"

Shit! If the alphabet did not have the letter "A" Muslims would

146

not have names, Mark thought.

"OK," Cindy said, "thanks for keeping it short for my dad. We now need to hear what Bradley spent his day doing. Bradley?"

"Well, I first want to thank Cal for getting all the stuff together. I actually had to call maintenance to get a strap wrench to unscrew the end caps of the filter's cylindrical housing. The actual internal filter element was exactly as Cal had described it last night. I wedged about 50 of the one-inch chlorine tablets into the external pleats of the filter. With a little effort I was able to stuff the chlorine-laden element back inside the metal housing, then get the end caps screwed back on and tightened. The inflow and outflow connections on the caps are three-eights of an inch. I found some tubing in the lab that would fit those connections, then ran tap water through the unit for a few minutes. I then checked the chlorine level in the outflow water. It was an unbelievable 25 parts per million!"

"Brad, were you using municipal water? How long did you let it flow?" Cindy asked.

"Yes, Cindy, I was using municipal water that we know already contains two to three parts per million. I tried the same test using pure distilled lab water, and the outflow was slightly reduced to 22 parts per million. I went back to municipal water and let it run for over three hours in the lab. Back up to 25 parts per million."

"So what's your bottom line here, Brad?" Cindy asked.

"The idea will work! I left it running for the evening in the lab. I'll check the outflow chlorine concentration in the morning. The only problem I see is that you can *smell* the chlorine in the outflow water, at least you can at 25 parts per million. Not overpowering, like sniffing a bleach bottle, but you can definitely detect it with your nose."

"So, we know 50 tablets in the filter will chlorinate at 25 parts per million for at least three hours, possibly longer," Cindy summarized.

Cal butted in. "What we need here is a level of chlorine we know will kill hantavirus, but will be difficult to detect by a human's sense of smell."

"I can run the tests again tomorrow, and reduce the number of tablets I put in the filter. Maybe cut the number of tablets in half, and see what we get," Brad stated.

"Sounds good to me, Brad. The girl that sold me the chlorine tablets at Wal-Mart, left me a message on my business phone. Said her name was Sonya Smith, and to call her if I needed any more chlorine. I looked on the Internet. Seems the actual retail price for the ten pounds of chlorine tablets is only $18.99!"

"Cal, Cindy already told me you paid 100 bucks for the ten-pound bag. Three-quarters of that bag is still left. Don't buy any more from 'Sonya.' I've got all I need to complete the testing," Brad advised.

"Brad, if 'Sonya' were a 'looker,' I may completely ignore that advice. She's got a very cute face, and great boobs. She's got a tattoo on her neck that says 'Let's Get Naked,' but I just can't get fired up about a gal whose ass is a mile wide!"

"OK, boys!" Cindy said. "End of meeting. I think we *all* need some sleep, including Cal ... even if *he* does not know it!"

25

Brad and Cindy drove to the University of Arizona campus the next morning. They arrived about 9:00. After parking their VW, they began walking to their respective labs. "I think Cal would be pissed as all get out if he knew we started working this late in the morning!" Cindy commented.

"As much as I like and respect Cal, he can be a bit overpowering at times," Brad said. "But I must admit he gets things done. Want to meet me for lunch at the cafeteria today? I'm taking my lunch break about 1:30. That should be after the main student rush."

"Sure. I'll meet you outside on the cafeteria steps," Cindy said. "Think you'll have your chlorine experiments finished by then?"

"Should be done," Brad replied. He gave Cindy a peck on the cheek, then turned into the molecular building; she continued walking another 50 yards to the microbiology building.

Entering his lab on the third floor, Brad could smell chlorine. Not overpowering, but definite. He'd left the filter connected to municipal water, allowing it to run through the filter overnight, the outflow draining into a lab sink. A quick check of the chlorine levels in the filter's outflow water indicated it was still 25 parts per million. He turned the water off, disassembled the filter, and noted the chlorine tablets were only slightly smaller in size. He removed all the old tablets and flushed them down the toilet. Brad thoroughly rinsed the filter's element in distilled water. He then reassembled the unit using new tablets, but with half as many as before. Again, he started letting municipal water flow through the filter.

Over the next three hours he checked chlorine levels every 30 minutes. It stabilized at 13 parts per million, and the odor was much less noticeable. He called Cindy in her lab. "I'm going to bring you a flask of water that is chlorinated to 13 parts per million. Could you see what it does to your hanta cultures?"

"Sure, honey. Meet you half way," Cindy replied.

They met on the sidewalk between their respective buildings. Brad gave her a sealed one-liter flask of water. Cindy smiled, turned, then paused and turned again. "Brad, I just figured it out … you rat fink! Since I'll be the one messing with live hanta, I'm the one who has to get into a biohazard suit. That's a pain in the ass!"

"I'll make it up to you tonight. Seems we might have the apartment all to ourselves … for a change. See you for lunch at 1:30."

"Promises, promises, promises!" Cindy muttered, then smiled as she walked away carrying the one-liter flask that looked huge in her small hands.

* * *

Mark and Anne were having a leisurely time, sleeping late in their Fleetwood Discovery motorhome. Except for an occasional rare rowdy customer, the Pima-Swan was delightfully tranquil. Mark had gotten up early and had fixed Anne a surprise omelet breakfast. Anne only pretended to sleep; she'd heard Mark's rattling of cookware in the galley, and she didn't want to spoil his surprise. When he had it all prepared, he delivered it to her in bed on a tray.

"Here you are Madam! I'm at your service, here," Mark said, loudly enough to 'awaken' her with his fake British accent.

"Oh!" Anne exclaimed, upon opening her eyes. "That's so sweet of you, my darling Little Man. But *Madam?* That sounds like you're talking to the gal that runs a whorehouse."

"That's right! Our own little personal two-people whorehouse. We've been the only customers for over 30 years, and we're not hurting for business. You know how it's done, Anne."

"I feel confident that I do … but I learned it all from my personal instructor!" she exclaimed, then took a large bite of her omelet. When she'd swallowed it, she said, "Delicious! What a nice surprise. You should cook more often."

"I think that can be arranged," Mark said.

"You do know you were my very first all-the-way man, don't you?"

"I know that. The thought ran through my head when you were so critically ill on the ventilator. Before we married, you knew I'd had other women, but you didn't know what it was like with another man. If you had died, you would never have had that option. What worried me the most, I think, was that I would not have a chance to tell you goodbye. Let me tell you while we're both living and well: If I die before you, when the time is right, take all that love you have and share it with another very lucky man. Granted, I'm married to you … but I do not *own* you. When and if that time comes, take your time in choosing, but please don't let it go to waste."

"Little Man, this conversation is really not necessary. The subject is fairly maudlin, and I guess it should be making me sad … but it's making me horny instead. I feel exactly the same way you do. Should I die before you, don't let your love go to waste … but don't you *dare* give it to some big-assed bimbo at Wal-Mart like Cal was talking about last night! In my morphine-dreams, I dreamed of sex with you … and only you. I did dream that Dr. Baxter made some sexual advances, ones I rebuffed," Anne admitted. She then took a bite of her toast, a sip of coffee, and a swallow of her orange juice. She paused. "Mark, I'm going to say something that sounds vulgar: Let's don't fuck with perfect … until we have to!"

"Anne, to stay 'perfect' we have to practice, right?"

"Little Man, how about setting this breakfast tray aside. That way we can 'practice' without spilling the rest of my coffee and OJ!"

* * *

After 'practice' and a nap, they dressed and rode their bicycles for about an hour. Conversation was limited while riding. They explored all the lanes at Pima-Swan, then ventured to some of Tucson's streets that had designated lanes for bicycles.

"Ready for lunch yet?" Anne finally asked.

"You bet! After our 'practice' this morning, I'd forgotten all about the omelet I'd cooked for myself. I left it in the galley … still in the pan. I'm sure it's stone cold by now. Might make a great sandwich, though."

"Honey, do you think we need to be quite that frugal? I realize we've lost the subsistence funds we were getting through WITSEC."

"Yeah, Anne, but that was about $2,000 per month!"

"But our IRA is still doing well. At least the Marshals Service got that put back in our real names when we departed WITSEC."

"True," Mark admitted.

"And you can start drawing your Social Security in a couple of years," Anne reminded.

"If it's still there! Our financial guy seems to think the program is headed for 'going broke,' as he put it."

"Let's quit worrying about money, and concentrate on lunch," Anne said, as they secured their bikes to the back of their RV. "Since you cooked breakfast, I'll do lunch. Maybe then we can have a long discussion about this whole deal with Dr. Abbas."

* * *

Anne prepared a meatloaf and put it in their galley oven to bake for an hour. Mashed potatoes and green beans were prepared as sides, along with iced tea, nice salads and egg custards for their desserts.

Their discussion about the "Abbas situation" actually began while they were eating:

"Little Man, when I was so sick with those periods of low oxygen saturation, they may have affected my brain. I just don't seem to be able to put the big picture together. I have more questions than answers."

"Such as?" Mark asked.

"Why should we even be involved with the FBI at all?"

"Well, I can certainly see giving them that envelope Abbas had handled. Apparently the FBI did recover some valuable evidence from it."

"Mark, that's not what I'm talking about. That made sense, even though I didn't like your signing their chain of custody stuff. I think any good American citizen who cares about their country would do that. What I'm talking about is all these many satphone calls to Louis Loveman. Surely the FBI has some folks that have even more information about Abbas than we do."

Mark took a bite of his meatloaf and began chewing. "This is really great, honey."

"Thanks for the compliment about my cooking, but are you *listening* to me?"

"Sure, Anne. I think the FBI's problem is the same one you have … getting the 'big picture,' as you called it."

"So why involve a bunch or amateur citizens to help them put it together?" Anne asked, then took a spoonful of her mashed potatoes.

Mark ate some of his green beans before he answered her question. "Anne, I think what you have missed is that you have not thought about the so-called 'amateur citizens' involved. You and I are experienced medical folks, right? Cindy is a microbiologist thoroughly familiar with hantavirus. Brad is big time into molecular biology, and familiar with hantavirus. Cal is an accomplished pilot, quite knowledgeable about aviation in general, and especially about crop dusters. Together we represent a massive amount of formal education and experience. I wouldn't exactly classify our little group of folks here in Tucson as 'amateur citizens.' Collectively, I think our little group has one big advantage the agents in the FBI don't have: Our backgrounds and experience make it easier for us to think outside the box."

Anne sighed. "When I think 'outside the box,' as you say, I come up with a million scenarios, all frightening to me. I think the FBI already has enough on Abbas to arrest him—for rape and kidnapping if nothing else! That would at least get him out of the picture."

"Anne, as Cal has already pointed out, they want to let Abbas run right up to the edge of his planned bad deed, then nail him and all his accomplices."

"Mark, that brinksmanship scares the crap out of me! What if they fail to stop him in time?"

"That's the FBI's call, not ours. Besides, if the chlorine in the filter works, the spray would be harmless."

Anne paused. She got up from the RV's dinette table, and quickly returned with their chilled desserts. After a spoonful of egg custard, she spoke. "Mark, let me share one of my scenarios with you. What if Abbas is planning *multiple* attacks? What if he discovers the virus-killing filter in his plane and has it replaced with a regular filter? Abbas certainly has been constructing what Cal would call a 'rat shit farm.' Just the apparent size of the operation there in Gainesville tells me he could be producing enough hantavirus for *multiple* attacks. He may even be close enough to metropolitan Atlanta to easily strike there ... and there's gotta be several million people there by now! He could even be supplying *other* terrorists in other countries with quantities of his virus-laden soup. I can't help it, but I get the feeling Abbas is setting up for a long-term operation there in Gainesville. He won't need to have but a single unfoiled attack and he'd create a huge disaster!"

"Anne, you do think ahead. I have no idea why it appears Abbas seems to have chosen hantavirus as a biologic weapon. I think I would have chosen some bad-assed virus that has close to a 100 percent mortality rate, yet it seems he has chosen one that has a 50 percent mortality. Remind me to ask Cindy why she thinks Abbas seems to have chosen hantavirus. Your close call certainly makes me share your apprehension, especially after you damn near died from hanta."

"If it were not for the fact that I was drugged while on the ventilator, I think I would have been scared shitless."

"Relax, if you can," Mark said. "Let's look at the reality of the situation. So far, this is all *theory* on our part. There's no crop duster there in Gainesville, yet. We haven't even proven mice are on his farm. We have assumed the chicken houses will be used to raise hanta-infected mice, then collect their feces and urine as a source for hantavirus. I know Cindy will stay involved because of her dad and her loyalty to him. Brad will stay involved because of his academic curiosity and his loyalty to Cindy. Cal will stay involved because of his strong friendship and sense of indebtedness to Louis. We, on the other hand, do *not* have to stay involved unless we choose to do so. Geographically, Gainesville is about 1,500 miles away from our current location, so we're isolated from Abbas. We know we don't need to fear another WITSEC-like situation. Our home is completely mobile, and we can move at any time. But I think we should stay involved at least a little longer."

"Me, too, Little Man. Just promise me we'll haul ass if we need to."

26

The next morning, Mark called Cindy at her lab using his cell phone. He had asked her if she had time to answer a few questions about hantavirus, but indicated he didn't want to discuss it over a civilian cell. Cindy had said 11:00 a.m. would be a good time to meet him at her lab.

Mark and Anne ate breakfast in their RV, washed some clothes at the convenience center at Pima-Swan, then slowly walked to the UA campus. The campus grounds were almost vacant.

"Must be between classes," Mark commented. "But at least this time I don't look like a dork carrying a Dustbuster!"

"But you're *my* dork, Little Man. If some of these young coeds could see you without your clothes, they'd probably forget all about 'dork,'" Anne said just as they entered the microbiology building.

Entering the lab, they immediately spotted Cindy. She wore a crisp white lab coat, one that looked perfectly tailored for her small size. The plainness of the lab attire only accentuated the natural beauty of her blue eyes, platinum hair, and flawless skin. Smiling, she ushered them to a private room in the lab she identified as her "office."

"Could I interest you in some coffee or hot tea?" Cindy asked.

Mark and Anne both shook their heads, indicating "no."

"We don't want to take more of your time than necessary," Mark explained. "Yesterday, Anne and I had a long discussion about this whole scenario regarding Abbas. Anne's main question seemed to be why in the heck would the FBI even want to involve civilians in their case?"

Cindy chuckled. "The answer to that question is quite simple: The FBI does an excellent job at locating individual pieces of a complex puzzle. But when it comes to putting the pieces together, they are sometimes a flop. My own dad is a perfect example. If I asked him to take a farm tractor apart, he'd do it with precision and efficiency. Just don't ask him to put it back together again! Part of the problem is the sheer size of the FBI, and sometimes communications among its various divisions leaves something to be desired."

"That's pretty much the conclusion I reached," Mark explained. "He wants you, me, Anne, Brad, and Cal to put it together for them."

"Exactly! And the neat thing is we don't have to do any work in the field. We're pretty much isolated from the dangers of actually working on site with the bad guys. In fact, the biggest danger, especially for myself and Brad, is working with live hanta in our labs here in Tucson. But we follow biohazard safety rules to the letter, and that makes our personal risk quite miniscule."

"Thanks for your thoughts, Cindy," Anne said. "During our discussion yesterday, Mark brought up an interesting question: Why would Abbas choose hantavirus, as opposed to other really bad organisms that carry an even higher mortality rate?"

"I think his choice of using hantavirus was brilliant. Why? Because it's so easy to obtain, easy to propagate in mice, carries significant mortality, yet doesn't require highly extraordinary precautions for those who work with it in a lab. Granted, hantavirus still carries a 50 percent mortality across the board, less if you're quickly diagnosed, and lucky enough to get prompt supportive treatment on a ventilator."

"So, Abbas has elected to use an easy-to-get virus," Mark responded.

"Yes. Abbas could have chosen viruses like Ebola or Marburg, which are usually 90 percent fatal even with ideal treatment. It would be almost impossible for Abbas to get his hands on those really bad bugs without raising a bunch of red flags. Fortunately, in nature, Ebola and Marburg are largely confined to central areas in Africa. Only a few very highly secured labs, such as our CDC in Atlanta, or Fort Detrick in Maryland, have those viruses on hand for study. Either of those viruses can cause a fatal hemorrhagic fever and multiple organ system failure in humans. They are also *readily transmissible* human-to-human. Their use by a terrorist very well could mean starting an unintentional global pandemic, one that might end up killing a number of the bioterrorists along with us good guys. As you already know, hanta is not contagious person-to-person, so a pandemic would not occur with hanta. The terrorists could, however, simply spread it globally in some controlled manner as they saw fit."

"Well, why not just distribute a bunch of hanta-infected mice, and not fool with crop dusters and other artificial means of spreading it?" Mark asked.

"Doctor," Cindy replied, "there are a couple of things wrong with doing it that way. First, white-footed deer mice will not naturally reproduce or even survive in all ecosystems. Secondly, highly effective rodent control programs could quickly be made available globally, even to the world's undeveloped countries."

"So," Anne said, "using really vicious viruses, like Ebola and Marburg, would be sort of like starting a nuclear war during the height of the Cold War—mutually assured destruction!"

"Exactly!" Cindy said. "And there is another factor that makes his choice of hanta brilliant: overwhelmed medical facilities."

"*Overwhelmed?* Like how? We've got plenty of hospitals in this country," Mark replied.

"It sure could happen, though!" Cindy responded. "Granted, we've got over 5,000 hospitals here in the U.S., and probably close to a million staff members who work at those hospitals. But let's shrink that down to a smaller geographic area, say to an area the size of the State of Georgia where Abbas is located. Back in 1993, when I was doing my epidemiology work in college, we had that natural hantavirus outbreak at Four Corners here in the Southwest. I researched the hospital statistics for every state in the country. I recall the State of Georgia having well over 100 hospitals, and Florida having about twice that number."

"That's a lot of hospitals to 'overwhelm,'" Mark said, a little defensively.

Cindy twirled her platinum ponytail with a finger. It apparently was a nervous habit she revealed when thinking. The twirling stopped and she spoke: "Doctor, I just don't think you've thought this thing through. Sure, 100 Georgia hospitals is a lot. But what *kind* of hospitals are they? You take the small county hospitals, psychiatric facilities, maternity hospitals, drug rehab facilities, et cetera, out of the mix, you are left with what? Very few hospitals that are acute care facilities, ones well equipped and staffed to handle a large number of *ventilator* patients."

Mark and Anne both blushed. *Dammit, she's right!* Mark thought.

"To make this even more frightening, suppose you have a metropolitan area of one million people. It would certainly have quite a number of hospitals, but probably it will have only a dozen or so hospitals that can manage a significant number of ventilator patients. I can go back to my college papers and give you some hard numbers from 1993. Or you can get on the Internet and get current figures yourself. I think you'll see exactly why I said hantavirus is a brilliant choice."

"I think I see where you are going with this, Cindy," Anne said.

"One pass of a crop duster over a sporting event—football, baseball, NASCAR, you name it—could result in many thousands of people being *simultaneously* infected with hantavirus!"

"You got it, Anne!" Cindy exclaimed. *"Hospitals overwhelmed. Total chaos. Total terror for our country."*

"Cindy, have you discussed this scenario with our government?" Anne asked.

"You bet I have! Especially with my dad, since he's involved with the FBI's Counterterrorism Division, or the 'CTD,' as they call it. I've also expressed my concerns to the CDC in Atlanta. No response there, just an acknowledgment they'd received my data. I've even written to the American Hospital Association. The AHA did send me a thoughtful letter pointing out how difficult it would be to have every hospital equipped to deal with a large number of ventilator patients. I think I've stirred some interest, especially within the FBI. This current investigation of Abbas is the first real action I've seen in trying to investigate a potential attack using hantavirus. Brad and I have both come to the same conclusion: There is simply no way to prevent all attacks using hanta. We both feel *immunization* of the population at risk is the only way we'll ever eliminate the successful use of hantavirus as a biologic weapon. If it will not make the population sick, why use it? After Brad and I marry, that's one reason why we've decided not to have children. Instead, we plan to dedicate our lives to developing a successful anti-hanta vaccine."

"Cindy," Anne said, "I think you're one of the smartest women I've ever met … not to mention one of the most patriotic."

"Ditto that," Mark allowed. "Have you got time for another question?"

Cindy checked her watch. "Sure. I don't have to meet Brad until 1:30 for a lunch here on campus. So what's your question, Mark?"

"You might not recall, but during one of our earlier satphone calls to your dad, he mentioned his undercover guys had seen some 'medical-looking vials' in a refrigerator located in the motel room rented to Abbas. They also saw some syringes on the vanity top inside that same motel room where Abbas stays in Gainesville. Any chance his men could get one of those vials?"

"That question is one for my dad. Last night when talking to me, Brad raised that very same question. He thinks the vials contain hanta-immune globulin, and he desperately wants one of them to examine in his own lab. Brad does not believe Abbas has developed an actual vaccine, but has only the temporary passive protection afforded by periodic self-injections of hanta-immune globulin. Where's the satphone?" Cindy asked.

"In my pocket," Mark replied, handing it to her.

"You dial, Mark. I'm afraid I haven't memorized the number yet," Cindy admitted, blushing.

Mark dialed, and when Louis answered, he passed the satphone to Cindy.

"Hi, Daddy! It's me. No problems here, but I have a question. Do you think you could have your undercover men get us a vial of the stuff Abbas has in the fridge in his motel room in Gainesville?"

"What's the risk to my men?" Louis asked her.

"Virtually none, if they take some precautions."

"Precautions? Like what?"

"Tell them to wear latex gloves and pick up the vial with a cloth dampened in Clorox bleach. Wrap the vial in that same cloth, and promptly put it in a Styrofoam container filled with dry ice. Seal the Styrofoam box with packing tape, so no liquids could leak out of the container. I'll try to talk Cal into flying to Gainesville to pick up the vial if your men can get their hands on it."

"Cin, let me do the talking to Cal. I'm sure he'll do it, but I'd rather talk to him personally. And why is this so important?" Louis asked.

"It may be nothing, Dad. But I think we need to know exactly what those vials contain. Bradley thinks they probably contain hanta-immune globulin ... the same stuff Brad now has in large quantity at his own lab. If Abbas has the same globulin available to him, that's probably how he is working with hanta and not getting infected himself. He may self-inject hanta-immune globulin on a regular basis. It may even tell us how to protect your undercover men, especially if they need to get closer to the virus."

"Cin, that's certainly enough reason for me to make my request to Cal," Louis said. "Keep your satphone on. I'll call you back after I've talked with Cal."

* * *

Mark and Anne accepted Cindy's invitation to join her for lunch with Brad in the cafeteria at UA. They'd eaten about half their lunch when the satphone beeped in Mark's pocket. He immediately answered.

"Mark Telfair, here."

"Mark, it's Louis Loveman. Is Cindy nearby?"

"Yes, sir. Anne, myself, your daughter, and Brad are all sitting at a table in the UA cafeteria. It's almost empty and we're sitting at an isolated table. Here's Cindy," Mark said passing the satphone to her."

"Hi Daddy. Did you reach Cal?"

"Yeah, I finally found him. I had a little trouble convincing his office secretary I needed his location and cell number, but they finally told me. Cal's in Kissimmee, Florida. He's flown down there to have his buddy, Ben Hunter, do some work on his Cessna 310," Loveman explained.

"Dad, what's wrong with Cal's plane? We all flew in it to Boulder not long ago, and it seemed fine then."

"Nothing is 'broken.' Cal's just having some wingtip tanks installed and having new tires put on the plane. He said he would be glad to fly to Gainesville to pick up a vial of the substance Abbas has in his motel refrigerator, provided my undercover guys can get their hands on it. He'd then fly it to Tucson. His plane should be ready to fly again early in the morning. Cal and I will work out the logistics over the phone. He'll probably pick the vial up at an airport in Gainesville, then fly it back to Tucson. I'll let you know when we get it to Tucson. Tell Brad we're counting on him to tell us exactly what the stuff is. Gotta go now. Love ya," Louis said, and clicked off.

"Wow!" Cindy exclaimed. "That Cal really gets around!" She then explained details of her satphone conversation with her father.

Bradley beamed. "I don't know when I've been so anxious to test an unknown substance inside a stolen vial! And I guess I should tell you about the chlorine experiments. Cindy and I finished them late yesterday. It takes only eight parts per million to instantly kill hanta. The modified crop duster filter only needs seven chlorine tablets. I have it prepared, ready to go. If we'd only known Cal was going to Kissimmee, he could have taken it with him to put in that crop duster Abbas is planning to buy. That would have saved a lot of time and avgas."

Wingtip tanks? New tires? Cal is planning something with his plane he is not sharing with the rest of us, Mark thought, but remained silent.

27

At 3:00 a.m. a satphone beeped in Room 127 at the new Hampton Inn located on the Jesse Jewel Parkway in Gainesville, Georgia. Senior Agent Adelio Rivera was the first to be awakened. It was, after all, his satphone that was beeping, and doing so less than two feet from his head on his bedside table. As he began talking to the caller, his fellow agents, Eduardo Alvarez and Enzo Moreno, began awakening. The undercover FBI agents knew it wasn't a cheerful wake-up call from the front desk. They knew the caller was their FBI boss, Louis Loveman. Rivera was about to receive important information, or get a special request to do something.

After listening and talking several minutes, Rivera spoke. "Sure, boss, we can get that done. One of us will call you when we have obtained the item you've requested. We'll have it prepared to be picked up at the airport."

Rivera, the senior agent, had the luxury of sleeping single in a double bed. He had turned on his bedside light when his phone had beeped. The other two agents were now awake, but yawning and sitting on the edge of the double bed they shared.

"Well …?" Eduardo Alvarez asked.

Rivera explained: "Loveman wants us to steal a vial of the stuff that's in the refrigerator in the motel room where Abbas stays. So, one of us is going to have to play sick, and not show up for work with Abbas today."

"You mean that same stuff we were afraid to touch the first time we went into his motel room?" Moreno asked.

"Yes, the same stuff. The stuff we thought might be some bad-assed biologic agent. Loveman seems to think we can now do it safely, if we use precautions." Rivera explained the precautions Loveman had relayed to him.

"So which one of us is going to do it?" Alvarez asked.

"I'll do it," Rivera volunteered. "I'll watch his motel room, and when he leaves for the farm, I'll get a vial of that stuff in his refrigerator. I'm sure the motel owner will let me back in, but if he won't, I'll pick the lock."

"Not so fast, Rivera," Enzo said. "You told us Loveman said to use latex gloves, and handle the vial using a cloth dampened with household bleach. Wrap the vial in that same cloth, then place everything inside a small Styrofoam box filled with dry ice. Seal the box with packing tape, and don't label the package. Are we supposed to call Loveman on his satphone for further instructions after you get the vial?"

"Yes," Rivera replied. "I know that seems complicated, but it's really simple enough. Finding a source for dry ice may be the hardest part. I don't know about you guys, but I'm going back to sleep until we get the wake-up call from the front desk at 6:00."

Without further words, Rivera snapped off the light; all three quickly resumed their sleeping.

* * *

Agent Rivera departed the Hampton Inn at 7:30 using their "good car," and headed to downtown Gainesville. The other two men had headed to the farm using a raggedy 1971 F-150, their transportation being appropriate for their being "poor Hispanic dayworkers."

At 8:00 a.m. Rivera entered a Gainesville pharmacy wearing a suit and tie instead of the ragged work clothes he and the others wore when they went to the farm as "dayworkers." Rivera presented his credentials and the pharmacist quickly produced a six-inch by six-inch empty Styrofoam box used for shipping pharmaceuticals that had to be kept cold in transit. When Rivera inquired about a source for dry ice, the friendly pharmacist at Eckerd directed him to a nearby industrial welding supply. "They'll make it while you watch!" the pharmacist had said.

At Skanks's Welding Supply, a flash of his FBI credentials again worked wonders. In the back of the shop, Rivera watched in amazement as an employee bled off some highly compressed carbon dioxide gas into a quart-sized porous bag of some sort. The bag soon filled with a snow-like blob. "Whatcha gonna put it in?" the welding shop man asked. Rivera made a quick trip to his unmarked Crown Vic bearing Alabama plates. He returned with the empty Styrofoam box he'd gotten from Eckerd's. The "blob" was forcefully packed into the Styrofoam box, and it quickly became a more solid mass. "She'll keep that away for several days, if you keep it out the sun," the Skank's employee advised, then refused the payment Rivera had offered.

Rivera made a quick stop at a 7-Eleven, bought a small bottle of

Clorox, and a package of cotton handkerchiefs. He was positive he had a box of latex gloves in the trunk of the Crown Vic, if he could find it amid the junk left there by previous agents. He now found himself cautiously approaching the Three Oaks Motel. The "Vacancy" sign was on and the Honda Abbas drove was not there. For a third time, a flash of his FBI creds insured full cooperation, this time from the wary motel owner. "You don't have nothing to do with the IRS, do you?"

"I'm a federal officer with the FBI, and I don't have anything to do with the IRS ... provided you let me into the room rented to Al Abbas. Five minutes is all I need. You stay outside, and if you see Abbas coming back, quickly let me know."

The motel owner said nothing, just smiled and quickly used his passkey, then stepped out to the long street to see if he could spot Abbas, should he return unexpectedly.

That part of Rivera's mission was completed in under five minutes. He'd even taken the time to count the remaining identical-looking vials. He thanked the motel owner, who asked no questions about the gloves, Styrofoam box, or bottle of bleach.

"Say, ain't you one of them same fellas that was here awhile back?"

"Yep," Rivera replied, without additional comment.

"If you're still FBI, I'll help you anytime," the owner said in parting.

Back in his Crown Vic, Rivera left the area and made a satphone call to Loveman:

"Agent Rivera here, sir. I've got the vial you wanted. There's a total of 94 similar-looking vials left in his fridge. Maybe he won't miss the one I've got. Tell me where you want it delivered?"

"Lee Gilmer Memorial Airport," Loveman replied, then read off the GPS coordinates for that Gainesville airfield. "You're to give it to a gentleman named Cal Camarada. He's Caucasian, six-feet tall. Has white buzz-cut hair, small white mustache, blue eyes and is tanned. He's 68, but looks younger. Ask to see some ID. A driver's license is OK. He will be flying a twin-engine Cessna 310, tail number N122AZ. Be sure you see the plane with that specific number before you hand over anything."

"I understand, sir," Rivera replied, and jotted down the tail number. "What's his ETA?"

"1600 local time there in Gainesville, plus or minus 15 minutes. I trust you've packaged the vial as instructed."

"I think so, sir. It's wrapped in a handkerchief moistened with bleach, and it's inside a small Styrofoam box filled with dry ice," Rivera explained.

"Did you seal the box?" Loveman asked.

"No. The lid is a snug fit, though."

"Rivera, you've got plenty of time. Get a roll of that clear packing tape and seal the lid so no liquid could leak out. It'll be flying in an unpressurized plane, and liquid containers have a strange way of sometimes leaking under those conditions. If the Styrofoam box will fit, put it inside a one-gallon Ziploc bag as an extra precaution."

"Yes, sir. I can do that. But may I ask what is in that vial?"

"We honestly don't know yet. If you followed instructions when you acquired the vial, you will not have put yourself at risk. We'll let you know what's in it as soon as we know."

"I see," Rivera replied.

"I personally thank you for doing a great job. It will not be on your Bureau record, but will be noted in *my mind* when it's time to talk about promotions. Give my best regards to the rest of the undercover crew there," Loveman said, then clicked off.

* * *

Rivera had little to do for a few hours. He got the package sealed as the boss had required, ate lunch at a place on the Dawsonville Highway called Shane's Rib Shack, and made a dry run to the airport to be sure he knew exactly where to go to meet a small plane. He presented his FBI credentials to a security officer at the small airport and told him he needed to meet a private plane about 4:00 p.m. "No problem, sir," the security officer replied. "I'll be on duty until 6:00. Just find me and I'll escort you to the parking apron. That'll avoid security hassles for you."

Rivera checked his watch. He had about a two-hour wait if Cal Camarada was on time. He went back to his parked car, retrieved the vial package, now also inside a large Ziploc. He crammed it all inside an empty Kentucky Fried Chicken box he found in the trunk of the Crown Vic. *Some agents are a bunch of pigs!* he thought, and entered the terminal carrying the KFC box. He bought a newspaper, and sat in a comfortable seat near a large window that gave him a good view of the airfield. In his mind he debated the direction from which Cal Camarada would arrive. He also wondered how his partners were doing on the Abbas farm. Yesterday they had run over 1,000 feet of electrical wire and three-quarter-inch water line using a small ditching machine. They had at least another 2,000 feet to go until they reached their destination: the shed and 18-wheeler parked at the far end of the runway. He smiled, knowing their day was going to be a lot harder than his.

At 4:15, coming from the south, Rivera spotted a small twin approaching, its gear already down. He watched it land. Soon it was close enough to read the tail number: N122AZ.

Rivera quickly located the security guard, who escorted him to the field.

"Taking the pilot a late lunch?" the guard asked.

Rivera laughed. "No. It's just some FBI evidence that has nothing to do with KFC."

Cal parked his Cessna, and got out. Rivera approached. "Mr. Camarada?"

"Yeah, that's me. Sorry I'm running late. Headwind cut my speed over ground about 15 knots. And I need to pee before I can be civil!"

Camarada rushed inside the terminal and left Rivera standing beside the plane holding what appeared to be a KFC box. *Shit!* Rivera thought. *The boss sure hooks up with strange people.*

Ten minutes later, Cal Camarada returned to his plane. He had a bag of sandwiches and soft drinks he'd purchased inside the terminal. "Sorry I had to rush off. Just wait until you get older and your prostate gets too big. Anyway, I understand you have something for me. I hope it is not Kentucky Fried Chicken, because my doctor has forbidden me to eat that shit."

"Sir, I am agent Adelio Rivera with the FBI," Rivera said, presenting his credentials. "My boss, Agent Louis Loveman, told me to meet you and give you this," Rivera said, but he did not pass the KFC box to Cal Camarada.

"Your boss once saved my life in Korea, and now he's trying to kill me with saturated fat!" Cal exclaimed.

Rivera wore a quizzical look, but quickly explained: "Sir, there is no KFC inside the box. The actual content is some evidence Agent Loveman requested. I will give it to you if you show me your driver's license."

"*Driver's license?* Do I need one to fly a fuckin' plane?"

"No. I just need photo ID. Could I see your license, please? It's Agent Loveman's requirement."

Cal apparently figured he had harassed one of Loveman's agents long enough. He complied, and showed Rivera his Arizona driver's license.

"Thank you, sir. Here is the item Agent Loveman has requested," Rivera said, handing the KFC box to Cal.

Cal immediately opened the box, then sniffed it. "God, that sure smells great! But I don't want that box tempting me by stinking up my plane. You take the box. Just discard it in the terminal. OK?"

"Sure, I'll be glad to do that. But can I ask you a question?"

"What's the question?" Cal responded.

"Why did you stay on your big wheels so long, before you let the little nose wheel touchdown? I watched a lot of small planes land while waiting for you, and you landed quite differently."

"Rivera, I'll have to admit you are a very observant man. I'm just practicing soft-field landings. Someday I may be forced to land in a cow pasture or an agricultural field, or even sand on a beach somewhere. They don't teach this stuff in the FBI, but airplanes have only three positions: in the air flying, on the ground ... or underwater, if you *really* fuck up! There are a lotta places that don't have real paved runways. Understand, now?"

"Yes, I think so. I wish you a good flight to wherever you're going next," Rivera said.

"See ya later," Cal said. "Need to top off with fuel, and fly to Tucson."

28

Some four hours out of Gainesville, Cal was heading due west, and cruising at 180 miles per hour. His present altitude was 12,500 feet. He briefly flipped on the cockpit lights and looked at the Ziploc bag containing the Styrofoam box. It rested in the unoccupied copilot seat to his right. The bag had enlarged slightly, indicating the air inside it had expanded a bit due to the diminished barometric pressure at his present altitude. He turned the bag over, checked it again, then flipped the cockpit lights back off to preserve his night vision. No liquid had leaked from the Styrofoam box. *Good,* he thought.

Somewhere over the middle of Mississippi, he checked his fuel. *This little bitch really eats it!* he thought. Even with the new wingtip tanks he'd had installed in Kissimmee, Florida, he was afraid to shoot for Tucson without a fuel stop. He settled on Denton, Texas, that had a small field he'd used a couple of years ago on a trip to Florida. Though the Denton Airport was a rural low-traffic one with a paved field, he knew he could get quick service there; he also knew he had about eight more hours of flying time before he reached his own airfield in Tucson, Arizona. He paced around his plane while the attendant topped him off with fuel.

"Never seen a landing quite like that before on a hard field. You must be practicing for a soft-field landing. You spent a lot of time on the mains before lettin' the nose down. I thought your landing looked great! What's the secret?" the guy who was doing the fueling asked.

"Practice, practice, practice!" Cal boasted. "Might need to do a soft-field someday. Ya never know."

In 20 minutes, Cal was back in the air, heading for his own private airfield at Camarada Aviation in Tucson. Somewhere over eastern New Mexico, Cal decided to use his cell phone. He called Cindy and Brad at their apartment. Cindy answered:

"Cindy, it's Cal. I'm in the air over New Mexico, heading for my field in Tucson. I'll call again when I get a little closer. Tell Brad I have the vial he wants to examine in his lab. Ask him to be prepared to meet me at my field."

"Cal, I'll tell him *after* you call again. He's asleep right now. He's gonna be so excited he wouldn't be able to go back to sleep!"

Cal laughed. "Tell Brad sleep is for chickenshits. You can sleep all you want after you die! Catch ya later," Cal said, and clicked off.

* * *

At 1:30 a.m. Bradley and Cindy met Cal at his airfield. The package was quickly passed off. Cal made only a brief comment: "If I can fly that sucker around for 14 hours without breaking it, at least you two should be able to drive it to your lab and keep it in one piece." Cal looked exhausted, but quickly got in his Porsche Boxster and sped away without further words.

"Wow! Brad said. "Cal's a man with a lotta action, but few words. I'm sure I won't quit working on it until I know exactly what's in that stuff. How about we stop at a Waffle House and eat a big breakfast before we go to work?"

"Sounds great, 'Big Boy,'" Cindy replied, using her rarely used pet name for him. We can work on it together in your lab. I think we should treat the contents of that box like it is really bad stuff, don't you?"

"Agreed. I'll even volunteer to be the one to get in a biohazard suit and open the box," Brad said. "You can stay in my lab's observation room until I've got the sample ready to look at."

* * *

By daylight, Brad had successfully gotten his hands on the vial stolen from Abbas. He'd been frightened on only a single occasion during the unpacking process. While wearing his protective suit, and working under the laminar flow hood, the top of the Styrofoam box forcefully blew off with an earsplitting *POP*. It did so the instant he'd completely cut the clear packing tape that secured the lid. The lid had flown to the interior top of the hood, and remained stuck there due to the strong vacuum pulling air through a grill at the top of the hood.

Even through the thick glass of the observation room, Cindy had heard the loud *POP*, and saw Brad jump several feet back from the hood. "Honey, are you all right in there?" Cindy asked, using the intercom.

"Yeah. The Styrofoam box was *pressurized*. Sucker kinda

exploded! I think it's because some of the dry ice had melted, and returned to carbon dioxide gas under pressure. Make sense?"

"Yes, I agree. But is the vial still intact?" she asked over the intercom.

"Yeah, looks OK, I think," Brad replied.

He calmed down fully only after being sure the glass vial had not sustained even the smallest of visible cracks. The vial was two inches long with a three-quarter-inch diameter. Though only about half-full, it contained several milliliters of an amber liquid that was slightly viscous. A red rubber stopper retained by a metal band closed one end of the vial. It bore no label, but otherwise resembled the standard small vials used throughout the American pharmaceutical industry. He knew the intended method of removing the liquid contents was to pass a hypodermic needle through the rubber stopper, and draw the liquid out with a medical syringe.

While still in his suit, Brad reached up and pulled the box's Styrofoam lid off the hood's grill. He put the entire box, still containing residual dry ice, into the ethylene oxide chamber. *The chamber is vented to the hood's exhaust, so it shouldn't blow up my ethylene oxide chamber,* he rationalized. He sanitized the exterior of the vial with a strong bleach solution, then removed his protective suit and placed it into a special bin bearing a biohazard symbol.

"Is it clean enough that I can come in there yet?" Cindy asked Brad.

"Yeah, all clear. I'll unlock the door for you," Brad said, pushing a button on the wall.

After an electronic buzzing sound, Cindy entered the lab. She gave Brad a long kiss, stepped back, and said, "I'm proud of you. I think I would have jumped out of my skin if a box had blown up in my face like that!"

"Sure scared the crap out of me! But in just a minute I think we'll know what we've got here," Brad said, donning gloves and then putting on a viral filtration mask.

Cindy put on a similar mask, but not gloves.

Using a medical syringe, Brad carefully withdrew a single drop of the vial's content. He placed that drop on a standard microscope slide, then used another glass slide as a spreading tool to create a thin film of the liquid. The film quickly air-dried and he placed it beneath a regular microscope. He applied a drop of his self-developed fluorescent antibody test solution. Brad held his breath while he peered through the scope. "HOT DAMN! Take a look, Cindy!"

She did. "It's loaded! Just as you had guessed, my Big Man … *anti-hanta antibodies!*"

Brad effortlessly picked Cindy up and swung her around in his arms while kissing her.

"Tell you what I'm gonna do. I'm first gonna make a quick prep for the EM to confirm my test later today, then we're going straight to our apartment and—"

"And you'd better say you're gonna screw my brains out!" Cindy giggled, then kissed him again.

Brad smiled. *God! I wonder what her reaction will be when we finally develop a successful hanta vaccine!*

* * *

At the Pima-Swan, the Telfairs' cell rang inside their RV. Mark answered, noting it was 1:30 in the afternoon. Cindy Loveman was obviously quite wound up:

"Mark, you're just not going to believe this! Very early this morning, Cal flew in with a vial of the stuff Abbas has in his refrigerator in Gainesville! The undercover guys got it to Cal at an airport in Gainesville, and he flew it on to here. Brad has just checked the stuff in his lab. He's almost 1,000 percent certain: The stuff is nothing but hanta-immune globulin, the same stuff he has stockpiled in his lab. It's *not* an anti-hanta vaccine, so it looks like we have guessed right."

"That's great, Cindy! Does your dad know about this yet?"

"No. We haven't told him. We are going to do some electron microscope studies a little later today. After lunch, Brad went back to his lab hoping to speed up the EM study. He wants to be absolutely positive the molecular signature matches that of hanta-immune globulin. Then we'll tell Dad."

"When?" Mark asked.

"About 8:00 tonight at our place. Would that time be good for you and Anne?"

"Cindy, I'm sure that'll be fine. But I've somehow become the 'custodian' of the only satphone our group has. I'll bring it, but we probably shouldn't have had this conversation over a regular cell. We really need to talk to your dad about getting us a couple more satphones. One for you and Brad, another for Cal. That way we can securely talk among ourselves anytime we need to."

"Mark, you've got a point there. Guess I was just too anxious to tell you guys. See you and Anne at 8:00 this evening."

* * *

The satphone conference call to Louis Loveman began a few minutes late; they were awaiting Cal's arrival at Brad and Cindy's Tucson apartment. Upon arrival, Mark noted Cal looked tired, limped a bit, and kept his hands pressed to his low back area.

"Cal, are you all right?" Mark asked.

"Just having problems with my damn back," Cal explained. "Let's move along, and get this meeting over."

Mark set the satphone to speakerphone, dialed, and placed it in the middle of the dining table. Cindy, their self-appointed "leader," was first to speak:

"Hi, Dad, I've got some great news! Brad has verified the content of a vial Abbas had in his motel room. It contains nothing but anti-hanta hyperimmune globulin. It is *not* a hanta vaccine. In all probability, that's how Abbas is protecting himself ... by self-injecting globulin."

"Cin, in your opinion, could my undercover men be protected the same way Abbas is protecting himself?" Louis asked.

Brad spoke: "Let me answer that question. The concentration of hyperimmune globulin in the vial stolen from Abbas is essentially identical to the concentration found in my own lab's supply. Louis, I think your men could be injected with one milliliter about every two weeks, and be completely protected."

Louis paused. "The problem I see is getting my men in Gainesville, Georgia, injected with Bradley's globulin that is presently located in Tucson, Arizona."

Cal butted in: "That's what planes are for ... to move people and stuff quickly over a long distance."

Louis replied, "Cal, you have already flown thousands of miles for us in your personal Cessna 310. I think it's time the Bureau steps up to the plate. Let me send an FBI jet to your private field there in Tucson. If Bradley can spare it, we can pick up some more of that globulin, then fly it on to Gainesville."

"You can have half of what I've got in my lab," Bradley replied. "That should be enough to protect your three undercover men for several months."

"Great! I'll work out the logistics of getting my undercover men in Gainesville injected with it."

"Normally, I'd argue with you, Louis," Cal said. "I'd volunteer to fly the stuff to Gainesville, but I'm going to have to see a doctor about my low back pain."

"I certainly hope it's nothing serious, my friend," Louis said. "Please keep me posted about what your doctor has to say."

Though concerned about Cal, Mark asked Louis a question before he forgot to do so. "Louis, is there any way you can get us two more satphones? There are times when we need to securely communicate among ourselves here in Tucson."

"Consider it done," Louis replied. "I'll have them put two satphones on the same jet I'll send to Tucson to pick up Brad's globulin. Otherwise, I'm afraid I've both bad and good news. The thermal imaging did not work at all. The trailer is insulated too well. The good news is that the audio listening device did work. We've recorded definite episodes of 'squeaking noises' inside the trailer. As an attachment, I'll e-mail that audio to Bradley for his 'listening enjoyment.'"

"So, Dad, it's possible the mice are already on site, at least inside the trailer. Any mice in the chicken houses yet?" Cindy asked.

"No. None. But they now have electricity and water connected to the shed, the 18-wheeler site, as well as all three chicken houses. Today they received a shipment of a number of bags of some type of dry pelletized food. The bag labels indicated it is a balanced nutritional product for rodents. They've also installed a lockable metal gate at the highway. Presumably they did that to keep unwanted vehicles from entering the property."

Anne had been silent but obviously listening intently. "Bottom line, Abbas may be ready to start up his hantavirus factory any day now. The only missing component is the crop duster."

"And the pilot," Cal reminded, slowly standing, wincing in pain, and still holding his lower back. "Louis, if you don't need me further, I'm leaving this meeting and going to my condo for the night ... and to my doctor early tomorrow morning."

"Cal, if it's not too much trouble, and if you feel up to it, check with your buddy regarding the status of that crop duster. I'm talking about the fellow down in Kissimmee, Florida ... Ben Hunter, I think you said his name was. When our FBI plane is in Tucson picking up the anti-hanta globulin, and delivering you guys a couple more satphones, we'll pick up that filter Brad modified for the crop duster. They can then fly on to Gainesville to deliver some of Brad's globulin, then continue on to Kissimmee to deliver the filter. I'll call you with a date and time for our plane's arrival in Kissimmee. Just give your buddy in Florida a heads-up about a visit by an FBI jet. They'll be in a Learjet 60. Can his runway in Kissimmee handle that bird?"

"And more," Cal said. "And I'm sure I can count on Ben Hunter to install the filter before Abbas picks up the crop duster."

"Cal, you're dismissed!" Loveman said, sounding like a drill sergeant over the satphone. "Go home and take care of your back. Take a good stiff drink for me. Just rest, and that goes for the rest of you guys, too. In fact, I'm going to put my old butt in bed very soon. Goodnight folks."

29

Walking hand in hand, the Telfairs ambled along Tucson's well-lit sidewalks toward their camper parked at the Pima-Swan.

"Anne, I don't know about you, but I'm worried about Cal. He's really in pain. And he's probably taken nothing for pain, being the macho guy that he is."

"Do you think you should have at least offered to examine him?" Anne asked.

"Maybe so. But Cal did indicate he's planning to see a doctor early tomorrow. We know they have great doctors here at UMC. Using what we've got on hand in the camper would allow me to do no more than a cursory physical exam. As a starter, Cal really needs to have some lumbar spine x-rays. I hope the problem will all be muscular, and perhaps related to all those long hours he spent sitting in his plane while flying stuff around for Louis."

"I think we should at least give him a call on his cell in the morning," Anne suggested. "Just see if we can help him in any way. We've never been to his condo, have we?"

"No, but it can't be all that far away," Mark replied. "Remember the night Cal impatiently left our meeting at Brad and Cindy's apartment? It was the night we all wanted to look at satellite images. Bradley was a little late returning from his lab and he had their only computer with him. Cal rushed off to solve the problem. He couldn't have been gone more than ten minutes before he returned from his condo with two laptops."

"Yes, I remember," Anne said. "But you need to remember Cal was driving his Porsche, and you know how fast he drives! His condo could be several miles away from Cindy and Brad's apartment."

As soon as they entered the camper, Mark called Cindy using their cell. "I know we just left your place, but do you happen to have a cell number for Cal? I'd like to give him a call and see how he's doing."

Sounding a little out of breath, Cindy rattled off Cal's cell from memory, then said "I think he'd appreciate a call from you, especially since you are a doctor. Maybe you could suggest something to make him feel better until he sees a doctor at UMC in the morning."

"Thanks for his number," Mark said, writing it down. "I'll call him as soon as we hang up."

"Keep us posted about Cal ... but tonight Brad and I will be taking a long refresher course."

"Refresher course? Mark asked her. "Refresher course in what?"

Cindy giggled. "Intercourse 101! We've been so busy doing extra things, we needed to brush up on the basics!"

Mark laughed, then said, "I'll hang up now so you won't be late for class! And I do hope you two were not already 'in class' when I called. Bye."

Anne had been listening to Mark's side of the conversation. "Are Brad and Cindy taking some kind of classes?"

"Yeah. 'Intercourse 101,' and I may have interrupted them."

"Little Man, don't you think it's about time we had some refresher courses, too?"

"Definitely! But let me call Cal first."

Mark immediately dialed Cal's cell. Cal answered on the second ring, but strange background noises caused Mark to ask a question: "Cal, where in the hell are you?"

"I'm sitting in a wheelchair in the ER at UMC. When I left our meeting at the apartment I realized I couldn't make it till morning. I bypassed my condo, and drove straight here. I've already been seen by Dr. Baxter, the same ER resident who evaluated Anne when she was so sick with hantavirus. Baxter has given me a strong pain shot, and they are examining urine and blood samples before I go up to x-ray. The pain shot is beginning to work, and it's probably a helluva lot better than the double scotches I'd planned to drink at my condo!"

"Cal, Anne and I will walk over to UMC right now. Is there anything we can do? Something we can bring for you?"

"Perhaps. Dr. Baxter has already indicated I will be admitted to the hospital. My condo is on autopilot, and will need no attention. But I'd very much appreciate you two taking my Boxster when you leave, and park it in a visitor's spot at Brad and Cindy's apartment. The security at their apartment is far better than that at the hospital's parking lot."

"Consider it done," Mark said. "We'll be there in about 15 minutes. We know our way around the hospital, and we'll find you. Bye."

"And ...?" Anne asked.

"Cal's in the ER at UMC. He is being evaluated by your doctor, Dr. Baxter. Cal is going to be admitted and wants us to take his car from the hospital parking lot and drop it off at Cindy and Brad's."

"Let's get to it!" Anne said.

* * *

When the Telfairs arrived, Cal was no longer in the ER. "He went up to x-ray and Dr. Baxter went with him," a nurse at the desk explained.

In x-ray they quickly spotted Dr. Baxter, who was sitting alongside the radiologist examining Cal's chest and spine films.

"Mind if we look along with you? Mr. Camarada is a friend of ours," Mark explained, as they approached the pair of seated doctors staring at the x-ray view boxes. Dr. Baxter and the radiologist both turned toward Mark and Anne. Dr. Baxter immediately recognized both, and quickly explained to Dr. Mike McGinnis, the radiologist: "Mike, this gal is my miracle patient," Baxter said, pointing to Anne. "She's a retired nurse, and recently had a bad case of hantavirus with full-blown HPS! But I think it was the membrane oxygenator and a ventilator that saved her life."

Impulsively, Anne hugged Dr. Baxter and gave him a quick kiss on the cheek. Both Baxter and Anne blushed horribly. Still red-faced, she said "And this doctor I just kissed, and this hospital are *my* real miracle workers!"

"Wow!" Mike McGinnis said. "Patients certainly don't give that kind of reward to me as their radiologist. But I'm afraid there won't be any such 'miracle' for your friend, your Mr. Cal Camarada, here," the radiologist said, pointing at the lumbar spine films. "It's too far gone."

Mark studied the films. Nausea first gripped him, then sadness competed for first place. Mark saw the several well-defined dense areas in the bones of Cal's lumbar spine. *Cal's got incurable metastatic cancer in his lumbar spine, probably from his prostate,* Mark thought, but felt too shaken to speak.

"Does he know yet?" Anne asked, brushing away a few tears with the backs of her hands.

"No. We'll do a CT-guided needle biopsy of his lumbar spine to confirm, then tell him," Dr. Baxter said. "I'm confident it's from the prostate. I'll get a consultation with one of our very best urologic oncologists. Between radiation, chemo, and hormone therapy, I feel certain they can palliate his pain, slow the progression of the disease, and perhaps buy him a little more quality time."

"What room will he be going to?" Mark asked.

"I think he's on the way up now. They told me Room 525. I've asked them to set up a morphine drip. We'll certainly keep him comfortable while we are determining the extent of his disease. At least his lungs show no gross lesions, right Mike?"

"I see nothing there in the lungs, nor in his ribs at this time. His thoracic spine looks negative as well. We'll do an isotopic bone scan and a full body CT to be positive," the radiologist replied. "And I'd recommend a contrast-enhanced CT of his brain to be sure there is nothing there either."

* * *

Mark and Anne went to the vending machines on the third floor and got large paper cups of black coffee. They sat and quickly drank their coffees, while discussing Cal's plight.

"Cal has everything. Good looks, lots of money, expensive toys, abundant girlfriends … and now what? He won't be able to enjoy any of it," Mark commented.

"I know," Anne said. "As I understand it, Cal would have died in the Korean War, if Louis Loveman hadn't come to his rescue during a dogfight with MiGs. We need to get him to tell us about that sometime. But not now, and I don't think we should tell Cal what we know about his diagnosis."

"I agree. That would be a breach of medical ethics. His attending physician, or consultants chosen by his attending, should be the ones to tell him. I do pity Dr. Baxter. It's a job any physician hates … telling someone they have a fatal condition that cannot be cured."

* * *

The Telfairs took the elevator to the fifth floor, found Room 525 without difficulty, and gently knocked on the door that was partly ajar.

"Come in, especially if you're a good-looking young nurse," Cal boomed.

Mark and Anne entered smiling. "Fifteen minutes, my ass! It took you guys an hour to find me. But at least I've now got a good-looking slightly older nurse in my room," Cal boasted.

Cal was not in his hospital bed. He was sitting in a bedside lounger, his IV pole at his side. "I tell ya, this modern medicine is great stuff!"

Mark glanced at the label on the IV bag, then laughed. "Cal you're getting morphine in your IV. It's not exactly 'modern.' It has been used in this country since the early 1800s."

"Well, why have they kept it such a damn secret? I'd give up scotch if I could get this stuff."

Mark knew they had his morphine drip regulated perfectly. Cal was in no apparent pain, his cognitive functions and speech little impaired. "Cal, if you still want us to take your car to Cindy and Brad's, we're gonna need the keys."

"The keys are in the bedside table," Cal said, pointing. "My cell is in there, too. In fact, moments ago I did use it to call my friend in Kissimmee. He'll get the filter installed in the duster as soon as it arrives there. I used no specific names during the conversation, so my using a regular cell should be OK. God, I wish I could talk to Louis securely and personally. Please tell him about the filter over the satphone. And tell him I still thank him for saving me from sure death in Korea ... and keeping me alive long enough to suffer the infirmities of old age!"

Anne smiled and spoke softly. "Cal, it's obvious you and Louis share a very special bond that runs quite deep. We don't know exactly why you and Louis are so close, but we're glad you have a friend like that."

"This stuff they're giving me for pain makes me want to talk! If you wanna listen, I'll give you two the condensed version."

"Tell us any version you like," Anne replied.

"Well it's like this: I was once the so-called 'Ace' in our squadron, with seven confirmed MiG kills. Louis had only four. I thought I knew it all, and thought the pre-sortie briefings were for the amateurs. I frequently skipped them. Louis attended them all. On the day Louis saved my life, I'd skipped the pre-sortie. That day, the tacticians had explained the recently discovered standard attack methods the North Korean MiG pilots were then using. One part was called 'zoom and sun,' the other part 'hit and run.' The scenario involved four MiG-15s, the standard number of planes in their sorties.

"The day Louis saved me, it started with 'zoom and sun.' We were also a four-plane sortie. The sun was to our backs. We were flying our F-86s in a shallow V-formation at 26,000 when two MiGs, coming from behind us, made a quick pass from above, then pulled almost straight up and flew back toward the sun. Those two were the decoys. Louis, who attended the briefing, knew there would be two more MiGs hiding in the sun, and that pair would be the actual 'hit and run' attackers. Louis was flying off my left wing and promptly broke formation. He quickly positioned his F-86 above my plane, then pulled straight up and headed for the sun. He quickly positioned himself behind a MiG that was coming after me. That's one of the two that had been hiding in the sun. A few bursts from the F-86's 50 cals sawed the tail off the MiG that would have unloaded his 37 millimeter cannon on my unsuspecting ass. You don't take but *one* hit from a MiG's cannon, which shoots an inch-and-a-half round! After Louis shot down that MiG—the one that would have gotten me—he dove vertically down. The second 'hit and run' MiG hiding in the sun tried to follow Louis down, but the 86s could dive much faster than a MiG. I watched from above feeling sure Louis would never pull up, but he finally did. At the very last moment he made an inverted loop, got behind the second MiG and sawed its tail off as well!

"Over the radio, I talked to Louis. To this day I recall exactly what I told him. I said, 'I owe you one. Big time! Thanks.' And I remember exactly what Louis said back: 'That's six for me! Just need one more to catch up with the very best.' I then asked him if he sustained any damage to his F-86. He told me his plane was still flyable, but was leaking hydraulic oil and he'd sustained other major damage to his left wing when he'd hit fragments from MIGs unraveling in front of him. Louis requested I fly cover for him as he limped back to base. He made a successful gear-up crash landing at Suwon. He suffered no life-threatening injuries, but some MiG-15 fragments had penetrated his cockpit, one piece going deeply into his left leg. That's why he still walks with a limp today. Seems the fragment severed a nerve in his leg, and it could not be surgically repaired. And that, my friends, is exactly why I'm forever indebted to Louis Loveman. I just hope they can fix what's wrong with me … and I can enjoy all that 'borrowed time' Louis has given me."

30

Mark and Anne left the fifth floor with heavy hearts. Both knew additional studies might reveal an even more hopeless situation. They easily found Cal's car in the parking lot. Two clean-cut teenaged boys were giving it a thorough inspection.

"Mister, is this your car?" one teen politely asked.

"No, it belongs to a friend of mine who's in the hospital. He just asked me to take it home for him."

"Says 180 on the speedometer. Will she do it?" one of the teens asked.

"It's not my car. I don't know," Mark curtly answered. He and Anne got in and drove off without further words to the teens.

* * *

Mark drove slowly and carefully to Cindy and Brad's apartment. He selected a visitor's parking place that was beneath a nightlight, yet close to the door of the apartment. Mark pocketed the Porsche keys, and they began walking slowly to their camper at Pima-Swan.

"Mark, do you think Cal knows?" Anne asked.

"I think Cal is no dummy. I know he can be brash and egotistical, but he's certainly no dummy. After they complete their testing, I think Cal is the kind of guy who would want to know the entire truth."

"Mark, I know how you handled situations like this when we were in practice in Statesville. If the patient outright asked you, you told them the objective truth; if they didn't ask, you assumed they were not mentally ready to accept the fact they had an incurable fatal disease."

"'Just tell 'em straight out … *if* they're ready to know,' our senior partner, Dr. Holton, would always say."

"Mark, you're in the age range for prostate cancer. When was the last physical you had?"

"It was right before we first went into the WITSEC program. It was a requirement for both of us. Remember? That's also the last time *you* had a complete physical, with a PAP and mammograms. We both need to have colonoscopies. You did have a lot of testing while you were in the hospital with hantavirus, but nothing that screened for common cancers. I think we *both* need to set up routine complete physicals with Dr. Baxter. Agreed?

"Yes ... provided tonight we take 'classes' like Cindy and Brad. We both need to get our minds completely off this depressing stuff, even if it's only for a little while."

* * *

In their camper they held "class" until about 1:00 a.m., then fell into the relaxed dreamless sleep they both needed. When they awoke at eight the next morning, both knew their reprieve from thinking about Cal, Abbas, mice, and crop dusters had been too brief. *Shit,* Mark thought. *I need to call Louis and find out when the FBI jet will be here to pick up the anti-hanta globulin ... and I need to get to Camarada's field to pick up the satphones, and give them the filter to take to Kissimmee.*

"Whatcha thinking about, Little Man," Anne asked, as she poured their coffee.

"It's just all the stuff we've gotta do today."

"Such as ...?" Anne asked.

Mark quickly enumerated the "chores" he had on his mind.

Anne thought about 30 seconds, then said "This is what we need to do: First, we call Louis on the satphone and get an ETA for the FBI's jet coming to Camarada's field here in Tucson. While we've got Louis on the phone, we can give him a status report on Cal's health. Second, we contact Brad and get him to package some of his globulin for its flight to Gainesville. He can hold it in his lab until we know exactly when the FBI plane is coming. We need Brad to put *written* instructions inside the globulin package ... the dose, how often to give it, storage conditions, et cetera. Third, from Brad, we pick up the filter for the crop duster and have it in our hands, ready to go. Fourth, we're gonna need a car to go to Cal's field."

"Anne, after all these years, your mind still amazes me. It would have taken me an hour to sort that out," Mark admitted.

"Yeah, but it would take me half a day to do a simple appendectomy!"

From memory, Mark dialed the 15-digit satphone number for Louis. He answered on the fourth beep:

"Loveman, here."

"Louis, I apologize for calling at this time of day. I realize you are probably driving to Denver for your workday."

"I'm already in Denver and at my office. Whatcha need?"

"I need the ETA for the FBI's jet at Camarada's field."

"Mark, I was just getting ready to call you. It's 2:00 p.m., your local time, today."

"Louis, I think I've got some bad news about Cal. We haven't even told Cindy or Brad yet. He's in the hospital at University Medical Center here in Tucson. The tentative diagnosis is prostate cancer with spread to several bones in his lumbar spine. I'm telling you this in strict confidence, so please don't call Cal and tell him. Let *him* call you. We'll tell Cindy and Brad after his doctors do more tests, and are absolutely certain of the diagnosis."

There was a long pause. Mark heard Louis clear his throat and blow his nose. "Louis, you still there?" Another long pause. "Louis?"

"Ah, shit!" Louis finally exclaimed. "The extra satphones you wanted are already on the plane. Be sure you get one to him in the hospital. Ask him to call me, and give him my satphone number if he doesn't already have it."

"Are you all right, Louis?" Mark asked.

"Hell no! I'm crying and very pissed! Pissed at myself ... for saving his ass to face something far worse than going down in flames in his F-86. I might tell you about it sometime, but not now. I'm too upset. Besides, about ten years ago, I had a close friend here in Boulder who had the same problem. The medical folks did buy him some pain-free time. That lasted only about 18 months. The second 18 months were a pure hell for him. He even begged me to come to his home and shoot him. I just could not bring myself to do it. But I did the best I could ... by lending him my Glock. He did it himself."

"Louis, that was ten years ago. New technologies and medications may make it significantly different for Cal."

"Mark, I realize you are a doctor. I know you're retired, but I still respect your knowledge and experience. In situations like this, I've heard a lot of feel-good bullshit from doctors before. I certainly hope you're right about my buddy Cal having a better shot at it than my friend in Boulder. I'd very much appreciate you keeping me posted with the absolute truth about Cal's condition."

"That's a can-do, Louis. He's having additional tests today, and I'm sure his doctors will share the results with me. In turn, I'll share them with you. I should warn you, though. Cal is on a morphine drip. We visited and talked with him at length last night. He was out of pain, yet carried on a very coherent conversation. If they need to get a little heavy-handed with the morphine to control his pain, he may not make a lot of sense when you talk with him. Last night, he did tell us he'd already talked to his friend in Kissimmee, and the filter will be installed upon its arrival there."

"Thanks, Doctor. I'm sure glad you and Anne agreed to work with us. I can assure you money is not an issue for Cal. Just be sure he gets the very best care money can buy."

"Will do," Mark said. "Let me run now. I need to touch base with Brad to get the filter and the globulin. We're going to ask Brad to include specific instructions regarding the globulin's use and storage. Have you got someone lined up to administer the globulin injections to your undercover men in Gainesville?"

"I certainly got lucky there," Louis replied. "It just so happens my senior undercover guy is a former EMT. He keeps his certification current. That's my Agent Adelio Rivera. If Rivera has a question about the globulin, would you mind if he gave you a satphone call?"

"Louis, you need to understand I do not have an active medical license for Arizona—or any other state, for that matter. When I retired, per my own request, I had my license placed in the 'Inactive Category' by the Georgia State Board of Medical Examiners. I'll help Rivera any way I legally can. If I don't know the answer to a question Rivera may have, I'll find an actively licensed doctor who has the answer. I'm sure you realize the use of anti-hanta immune globulin has not yet been approved by the FDA. That would technically make the use of it illegal."

"Doctor, sometimes in this business you have to say 'screw technicalities.' I'm much more interested in the end result: catching bona fide terrorists … the guys that want to fuck up our peaceful way of life here in the U.S."

"Louis, I need to sign off now so we can get busy, and be sure we have everything ready for your plane once it gets here. We'll check on Cal after we meet the plane, then give you a call. Bye for now."

31

It took a bit of hustle, but they got everything ready for the FBI plane's arrival at 2:00 p.m. To the minute, it was on time.

Mark was a little surprised at how quietly the Learjet 60 had landed. The screech of its tires as it touched down on Cal's concrete runway was the loudest part of the landing. Standing next to Anne, Cindy and Brad, and their VW parked on a gravel taxiway, Mark waived to the plane indicating it should come toward them. The plane stopped midfield, engines quietly idling. They seemed to ignore Mark's "come here" hand gestures altogether. Two men got out of the plane and began slowly walking toward the VW. They seemed to be inspecting the surface of the runway and taxiway as they approached.

Mark began walking toward the two men dressed in dark suits. "Hi, I'm Mark Telfair. Louis Loveman has requested we meet you here."

Both agents stated their names, flashed their credentials, and asked Mark to show some ID. He did, in the form of a Georgia driver's license. Both men nodded, then one of them said, "Sorry to make you walk to the middle of the field. There's just too much loose gravel on the ground near the taxiway. The Lear's intakes look high but they're really not that far off the ground. We don't want to take a chance on sucking loose debris through an engine."

"I understand. I'll walk back to our car and get the stuff we're supposed to give you," Mark replied.

"We'll help you carry it to the plane," one of the agents offered.

"No, I'll get it," Mark said. "The stuff is not big or heavy."

Mark went to the VW and retrieved the foot-square Styrofoam box that Bradley had prepared for the globulin. Mark tucked the box securely under his arm, then picked up the crop duster filter with his free hand. As he approached the FBI men standing beside the Lear, one of them spoke to him: "Stop where you are! Tell us what you've got there."

Mark explained quickly. "This Styrofoam box contains some dry ice and a number of sealed vials containing a human globulin." Mark removed the lid and showed them the contents. "If the box needs to

184

be sealed, we've brought some packing tape with us."

"The Lear is pressurized. It won't need to be sealed airtight. But we'll tape the lid on anyway, just tight enough to be sure the lid stays on. And what's that other thing you've got there?" the agent asked, pointing at the four-inch diameter, foot-long silver cylinder Mark had in his hand.

"This is a modified aircraft filter for a crop duster. It contains a filter element and some chlorine tablets, the kind used to chlorinate residential swimming pools. I'd recommend you leave on the duct tape we've placed over the inlet and outlet of the filter. It's dry inside. Nothing should leak out of it. The Styrofoam box goes to Gainesville, Georgia; the filter goes to Kissimmee, Florida," Mark explained.

"We've gotten very specific instructions from Agent Loveman about what goes to where. And we're supposed to leave two satphones here for you."

One of the agents quickly entered the Lear and returned with two small boxes. "Sign here," the agent said, handing Mark a form he did not read, but signed nonetheless.

Both men returned to the plane. The Lear's engines quickly spooled up as the pilot made a slow 180-degree turn mid-runway. During the turn, when the thrust from the twin jet engines was aimed at the taxiway, everyone covered their eyes to protect them from sand and dust. Mark noted the loose gravel on the taxiway moved about considerably, some of it bouncing high enough to strike Brad's VW. The pilot slowly taxied to the far end of the runway, did another 180, then throttled up and was airborne again by mid-runway.

"Well," Bradley commented, "that certainly went off smoothly ... except for a few minor dings in our VW! Nothing worth fixing, though."

Mark handed Brad one of the satphone boxes. "Open it, and see if the phone's number is inside the front cover of the manual."

Brad quickly opened the box. "It's there, Mark. Apparently written there by Louis himself. We can all exchange satphone numbers later today. I'll drop you guys off at your camper. Cindy and I really need to go to the apartment and get back to writing our dissertations. Otherwise, we may be in grad school forever!"

"Brad, why don't you drop Anne and me off at the hospital. We want to check on Cal," Mark said, without thinking.

"*Hospital!* Cindy said. "I thought Cal went back to his condo to take care of his ailing back. When Brad and I left for our labs this morning, we noticed a Boxster parked in a visitor's spot at the apartment. It looked exactly like Cal's. We even checked the car, to be sure Cal wasn't slumped over in the seat, dead or sleeping or something. But *why* didn't you tell us he is in the hospital!"

Anne calmly explained: "Cindy, last night when Mark called you to get Cal's cell number, he got the impression you two were …"

"Yeah, 'having classes,' I called it," Cindy said, smiling.

"Anyway," Anne said, "when we got to the hospital last night, they had gotten Cal comfortable using a morphine drip. When we left, Cal requested we take his car and park it at the apartment. He's in Room 525. They'd made some x-rays last night, and are going to do a number of other tests today."

"Mark," Cindy demanded, "just how serious is this with my Uncle Cal?"

"I'm not sure," Mark lied. "But what's with this 'Uncle Cal' stuff?"

"He's not really an uncle," Cindy explained. "That's just some of my dad's doings. Cal would come to Boulder quite often to visit with my parents, and with me after I was born. Dad insisted I call him 'Uncle Cal,' and I did up until I was 12 or 13. I quit calling him that when my curious teen friends were trying to figure out the Loveman family tree. Cal is still legally my godfather. Anyway, call us when you check on him today. Depending on how Cal feels, maybe we can all visit him this evening."

* * *

After Brad dropped them off at UMC, the Telfairs went immediately to Room 525. With them they carried the satphone that was going to be specifically for Cal's use. The room was empty. They both hurried to the nurses' station where Mark immediately identified himself as *Doctor* Mark Telfair, inquiring about the 'missing' patient in Room 525.

"Doctor, are you new on the staff here?" the cute young brunette nurse asked.

"No. I'm just checking on a close friend of mine. Dr. Baxter is his primary physician," Mark explained.

"Dr. Telfair, Mr. Camarada had a bone scan plus a total body CT this morning. About an hour ago he went back downstairs for a CT-guided needle biopsy of his fifth lumbar vertebra. They're doing it under local anesthesia. He should be coming back to his room any time now. You want me to page Dr. Baxter?"

"Good idea," Mark said. "Just find out where Dr. Baxter is located,

186

and we'll go there."

Five minutes later, Mark and Anne were in the first-floor pathology lab, where Dr. Baxter and a pathologist were seated. Both doctors were peering through a teaching microscope, one that allowed two viewers to simultaneously look at the same specimen. Mark spoke: "Hello again."

Dr. Baxter turned and said, "Are you guys following me?" Baxter grinned at first, but it quickly melted into a frown. "Doctor, please have a seat. We're just looking at frozen sections of the lumbar spine needle biopsy that was just done on Mr. Camarada. Look through the scope and tell me what you see."

Mark handed the box containing the satphone to Anne, then quickly assumed Dr. Baxter's seat. After 30 seconds of study, Mark said "Crap! It's an adenocarcinoma. And I see what looks like some normal bone on one end of the specimen."

"And you were a *surgeon,* correct?" Baxter asked.

"Mostly GI surgical oncology, and I'd often look at my own patients' biopsies along with our pathologist. I learned a lot that way, but I almost wished I hadn't looked at this one."

"My name is Abe Altman," the pathologist said, extending his hand to Mark. "I'm the senior pathologist on the staff here at UMC. Unfortunately, Doctor, your call is correct. It is an adenocarcinoma. At least 95 percent of prostate cancers are adenocarcinomas. I'm confident the permanent sections will tell us no more than we already know. Do you know if Mr. Camarada had regular examinations?"

Mark frowned. "Probably no more than the FAA-required pilot physicals. Mr. Camarada is a pilot with many years of experience, and he's still quite active in aviation using his own plane. It's gonna kill him if he can never fly again!" Mark said. *No, it's this damn tumor that is going to kill him!* Mark thought, immediately correcting his own spoken words in his mind.

Dr. Baxter spoke up: "When I did his admission history and physical examination, he said he'd had nothing but regular pilot physicals since the end of the Korean War. Flight physicals do check cardiovascular status, visual acuity, color vision, hearing, et cetera. But they certainly are not *complete* physicals. His prostate specific antigen, or PSA, is well over 100. He has moderate prostate enlargement, but I could feel no defined mass when I did a digital rectal exam. I think only annual blood tests and physicals might have prevented it from going this far."

Anne sighed, clutching the box with the satphone to her breast with both hands. "Dr. Baxter, is there *any* good news in the testing he's had today?"

"Yes. The metastatic disease seems to be confined solely to his lumbar spine. His brain, lungs, ribs, thoracic spine and even pelvic lymph nodes are all negative, as judged by the additional scans done today. The lumbar tumor deposits are still relatively small, and I don't think they'll cause his bones to spontaneously fracture there. But they are causing him very substantial pain. It is my guess the urologic oncologist is first going with radiation."

"Thank you, Dr. Baxter," Anne said. "I realize you have told us a lot in confidence, possibly because Dr. Telfair and myself were formally active medical professionals. I assure you we will not discuss your findings and opinions with your patient. Unfortunately, that's your job."

"I know. I know that … and hate that part of my job! I did visit Mr. Camarada during or following most of his studies today. He is getting information about the extent of his disease as we get it," Baxter replied. "He has specifically requested that I tell him *everything*. And I'm sure he will have more questions in the future, Mrs. Telfair."

"Please just call me Anne. And call my husband Mark. You need to realize we're from the South, and a little less formal than you guys out here in the Southwest."

"OK, Anne. The hospital has already sent me a memo about your name change, the one you and Mark had already told me about in private. But please just call me 'Bill,' not William. And I'll share something else with you. Beginning tomorrow, Dr. Bill Baxter will no longer be a Chief Medical Resident. I'll be coming on the staff here at UMC as one of their full-time general internists. My office will be in the professional complex that adjoins the hospital."

"Congratulations! Please let us be among your very first private patients. Mark and I both need complete physicals. I hate to admit it, but It's been four years since we've had one," Anne explained.

Dr. Baxter produced an appointment card from his wallet. "Just call my receptionist in the morning. She'll give you the time and date. Now, can I ask you a question?"

"Sure," Anne replied.

"It's really none of my business, but what's in that box you're so desperately holding to your chest?"

"It's just a gift for Mr. Camarada. Is he back in his room yet?"

"Should be," Baxter said, looking at his watch. "Gotta scoot now … need to make rounds."

* * *

Mark and Anne took the elevator to the fifth floor and immediately went to Cal's room. They found him as they had the evening before, just sitting in the bedside lounger, IV pole at his side. This time he had the TV on, but the sound was muted.

"It's about time you found me!" Cal said. "But I guess I was a lot harder to find today. They've had my ass scattered all over this hospital … picking at this, poking at that, scanning and x-raying everything I own!"

"Well I've brought you a little present that may cheer you up," Anne said, smiling. She handed Cal the box. "It's a secure satphone. Your number is written inside the front cover of the manual. Before we leave, we'll put our number there, as well as the number for Louis. Brad and Cindy now have their own satphone, and we'll get that number to you, too."

Cal quickly opened the box, found the manual, and handed it to Mark. "Go ahead and put your number and the one for Louis in there right now. There's a pen in the bedside drawer where my car keys were. You did get my car moved, didn't you?"

"Yes. We'll hang on to your keys until you are ready to drive it again," Mark said. "We'll come back and visit you this evening, and we'll bring Cindy and Brad with us. That OK?"

"Great! But before you go, I have one small request: Could you dial my satphone, and get Louis Loveman on the line for me? I need to have a very long talk with him … alone, please."

32

"Did you have the feeling Cal was giving us the brush-off as soon as you dialed his satphone for him?" Anne asked, frowning, while they walked down the hall leaving Room 525.

"Well, sorta," Mark replied. "But the man is entitled to have a private conversation with a man who's probably his closest friend on the planet."

"I guess you're right, Little Man. But I still think we need to talk to Loveman. We did promise we'd keep him posted with the medical facts regarding Cal."

"You're right," Mark replied. "Because he's on IV pain meds, we can't be positive of what Cal might have told Loveman. Let's plan to call Louis right after all of us visit Cal this evening. I feel calling right now would not be a good choice. Cal will probably have Loveman's satphone tied up for quite awhile."

* * *

Arriving at the Pima-Swan, Mark used their regular cell to call Cindy and Brad. Both were at the apartment working on their dissertations. They mutually agreed on a satphone call to Louis immediately following their evening visit with Cal at the hospital. Anne prepared a quick supper in the camper, while Mark attended to several routine maintenance items all RV folks have to do, even when their RVs are parked.

The groups' hospital visit to the patient went smoothly. Mark immediately wrote Cindy and Brad's satphone number inside Cal's satphone manual before he forgot to do it. Cal seemed quite relaxed, even mildly euphoric. Possibly it was due to the morphine drip, or was it words exchanged during his phone conversation with Louis? Or perhaps it was a combination of the two? Mark felt unsure.

Upon their entering the room, Cal smiled, then announced: "They are going to start my treatments tomorrow … radiation from some new experimental gadget they've gotten here. They feel confident they can stop my pain that way, and I'll no longer be tied to this damn IV pole, or even require oral drugs that screw with my mind."

"That's great, Uncle Cal!" Cindy exclaimed.

"Young lady, you haven't called me that in years! But come here and give me a hug and a kiss, you beautiful little thing!"

Cindy blushed as she sat on Cal's lap and complied with his request. "Cal, your beard is getting longer, your mustache bigger!"

"I know. I've decided to let nature run its course for a bit."

A nurse bearing a small medication cup entered the room. Cindy hopped off Cal's lap, and the nurse watched as Cal swallowed the two capsules. "Time to sleep, Mr. Camarada," the nurse said. "You've got a busy day ahead of you tomorrow. I think it's time for your visitors to leave, and let you sleep."

* * *

At Brad and Cindy's apartment the hospital visitors all came to the same conclusion: Cal knew his diagnosis. Mark checked his watch: 8:45. He then suggested, "Let's give Louis a call, to give and get the latest scoop."

The foursome sat around the satphone as though it might be some strange deity resting in the middle of the apartment's dining table. Louis answered on the first beep:

"I figured you guys would be calling. Earlier today, I talked with Cal for over two hours. We discussed a lot of personal stuff, and he made a few strange requests that he wanted to keep just between the two of us. I'll honor that request, so I may not answer some of your questions about our discussion."

"Daddy," Cindy chimed in, "did Cal tell you how serious his problem really is?"

"I think so, at least as best he understands it. I'm directing this question to Mark: Can you give me a capsule of the situation with Cal? I know they have him drugged up, and I just want to be sure he got it straight."

"Louis," Mark began, "it's like this: Cal has a common type of prostate cancer called an adenocarcinoma. The primary tumor is still small enough it can't be felt on a rectal exam, but his blood tests show a very high PSA level, one exceeding 100. He has biopsy-proven metastatic prostate cancer in his lumbar spine bones, primarily the fifth lumbar. After a full bone scan and a CT scan today, they can find no additional metastatic tumors in his brain, lungs, ribs, upper spine, or lymph nodes in the pelvic area. Tomorrow they are going to start proton radiation to his prostate, as well as his involved bones."

"What in the hell is a *proton?*" Louis asked.

"I was afraid you'd ask that," Mark replied. "To tell the truth, I don't know much about it. When I was studying physics in college, I recall it being considered a particle that has the same mass as an electron, but has an opposite charge. All I know is that it is now considered superior to other types of radiation. Apparently, UMC is only the second center in the U.S. that has this type of experimental treatment currently available."

"Mark, do you remember I said money is no object?" Louis asked.

"Yes, Louis. I remember."

"Well, just do your best to be sure Cal's getting the best. Your summary of his diagnosis fits well with what Cal told me on his satphone. I'm now personally comfortable he understands the full extent of his problem."

Bradley chimed in: "Louis, allow me to change the subject for a moment. I appreciate the mouse audio you sent by e-mail. There is no question in my mind that those squeaking sounds are mice. So I'm positive there are mice present on site, at least inside the 18-wheeler's trailer. Any other news about the mice?"

"I do apologize," Loveman said. "Cal's illness has sidetracked my thoughts. I've neglected to give you guys an update about what's going on in Gainesville. First, my undercover men have all received their first injections of the anti-hanta globulin, and I do thank Brad for supplying it. Second, out at the farm, there are now colonies of mice in all three of the chicken houses. Also, Abbas has indicated he wants all three of my undercover men to keep working for him. He allows them to go inside the houses to feed and water the mice, but requires them to wear special masks he issues to them. He also requires them to wear latex gloves he also provides. Abbas seems totally unaware my men are already protected against hanta by Brad's immune globulin."

"Dad, how large are the colonies now?" Cindy asked.

"My men have estimated there are about 100 mice in each house. Agent Alvarez says they scurry about so quickly it's impossible to get an accurate count. He told me the mice all run to the far corners of the building when they enter to water or feed them."

"Dad, the gestation period of those mice is only 19 to 21 days. The average litter is 5 to 10 pups. They'll be in knee-deep mouse poop before you know it!"

"Any word on the crop duster? Is it still in Kissimmee?" Mark asked.

"It's still in Kissimmee. During the long conversation I had with Cal earlier today, he gave me a home phone number. It's a landline number for his friend, Ben Hunter, at Kissimmee Aviation Services down there in Florida. I realize that the communication link is not as secure as we'd like, but it's far better than using an ordinary cell phone," Louis explained.

Anne spoke: "Louis, any word on the pilot for the crop duster?"

"Yes. We've confirmed his name. It's Abdul Aleem, a Muslim and Saudi national. He's definitely the pilot. We've learned Abbas himself does not know how to fly. Unfortunately, we Americans trained Aleem right here in the U.S. We did it at a well-known flight school in Deland, Florida, and Aleem is fully qualified to fly Piper's PA-25—the *exact* plane Abbas intends to buy in Kissimmee!"

"Louis, what about the other guy you mentioned awhile back? Didn't you say his name was Abdus Salaam, or something like that?" Anne continued.

"Excellent memory, Anne!" Louis said. "We've established that Salaam is also a Muslim of Saudi citizenship, but his role in this whole scenario is not yet clear. We now know Salaam, like Abbas, does not know how to fly a plane. I personally think Salaam is simply a bodyguard, or some sort of errand boy for Abbas."

"So exactly where are these other two men, this Aleem and Salaam?" Anne asked.

"Our best intelligence indicates they are already here in the U.S. We know they flew into our country on a commercial flight that landed in Atlanta. We think they are planning to soon join Abbas in his room at the Three Oaks Motel in Gainesville," Louis explained.

"How do you know all that, Louis?" curious Anne asked.

"Let's just say that the motel owner has been a godsend. He has again allowed Agent Rivera free access to the motel room whenever Abbas is away at the farm overseeing activities there. Rivera tells me an extra double bed has been placed in the motel room. The Bureau's cyber geeks have given Rivera a miniature transmitting device. It's a 'computer bug,' so to speak. It plugs directly into one of the unused USB ports of the computer Abbas uses in his motel room. Rivera tells me nothing 'sticks out' from the computer that would alert Abbas to its being there. The motel owner has even allowed Rivera to use a vacant adjoining room to set up the receiver for the computer bug. Wirelessly, we've downloaded the entire content of his hard drive, and now monitor his computer on an ongoing basis. We're still monitoring his cell phone calls as well, but Abbas is smart enough not to say anything on his cell that helps us much."

"Wow!" Mark said. "High-tech stuff! And this is all coming together much faster than I'd personally anticipated."

"I feel the same way," Loveman echoed. "And it's quite obvious Abbas and his buddies have been planning this whole thing for quite some time. I think it's time we all wake up here in America ... before something really catastrophic happens. We're facing a very determined and sophisticated enemy, one that wears no uniform, has no formal army, and is driven by an ideology totally foreign to us."

"Agreed," or similar words were simultaneously uttered by all sitting around the satphone.

"I'm gonna sign off now," Louis said. "I'll make a call to Cal's friend in Kissimmee. If he has not yet crippled the crop duster with the virus-killing filter, I think it best the Bureau steps in to block the sale. I'll catch one of you guys tomorrow. Bye."

33

Brad had offered to give them a lift in the VW, but Mark and Anne elected to walk back to their camper. They knew the ten-minute walk would give them some needed exercise. It also gave them private time to discuss what they'd just learned in the meeting.

"Anne, it sounds like they are really coming down to the wire, doesn't it?"

"I agree. At least it's a little too close for comfort. The likelihood of real danger hinges on being sure that the virus-killing filter gets installed in the crop duster *before* Abbas and his pilot pick it up from that guy in Kissimmee."

"Do you recall what date Abbas is supposed to pick up the plane?"

"Cal said the 28th of August," Anne answered, certainty in her voice.

If I had her memory, med school would have been a damn site simpler, Mark immediately thought, then spoke: "When I retired, I sorta quit keeping up with dates," Mark admitted, studying his digital Timex. "But my birthday was on August 14th and yours on the 17th. So that would make the crop duster pick up about two weeks after my birthday."

"Proud of you, Little Man. You remembered them both! And, boy did we ever celebrate them the way we usually do—in bed!" Anne exclaimed, then gave him a kiss on the cheek. "But the plane's pick up, and its relationship to our birthdays, is not what really counts: It's how long from right *now* that matters."

"Well, it's now Saturday the 18th, so that means they could possibly do something in 10 days."

"I don't think so. At least not quite that quickly," Anne said. "When and if the crop duster arrives in Gainesville, and they start harvesting the mouse poop, we'll know they are almost ready to strike."

"At the end of our satphone conference call, Louis indicated he would check with Kissimmee Aviation Services and let us know about the filter. I guess hearing from Louis is the next step," Mark said, as he turned the key in their camper door.

* * *

While patiently waiting in their RV, they had received no word from Louis, not during the night, nor even by noon the next day. Following lunch in the camper, they gave Cal's satphone a call, then Cindy and Brad's. They'd heard nothing either.

Anne said, "If we haven't talked with Louis by early this evening, I think we should call him."

"The way he left it, *he* was supposed to call one of *us*. Maybe he hasn't had time to check, or maybe he has no news yet," Mark replied.

"Well, if we did call Louis, it would only be to satisfy our own curiosity. We're well over 1,500 miles from where the action is: Gainesville, Georgia. It's not like last time we got involved down there on the Georgia coast—that was in our own backyard! We were actually rubbing elbows with the bad guys. This time I'm a lot more relaxed, and enjoying the distance that separates us from them."

* * *

By nine o'clock that night, neither Mark nor Anne could stand it any longer. Still at their camper, Mark made the call to Louis Loveman. Busy. He next made a call to Cal. Also busy. Finally he called Cindy and Brad. Cindy answered:

"Have you heard from my dad yet?" Cindy asked without preamble.

"No. His satphone is busy. So is Cal's," Mark replied. "My guess is they're talking over old times, and your dad has forgotten he was supposed to call one of us."

"Well, Cal is certainly one of us! Let me call the hospital. Bradley and I visited Cal during our lunch break earlier today. He's off the IV morphine, and claims the radiation has already stopped all his pain. He indicated he may even be discharged from the hospital later today. I'll check with the hospital and call you right back, OK?"

"Sure," Mark said, and clicked off.

That would be good news ... if Cindy is right, Mark thought. He quickly explained aloud to Anne: "Cindy answered the satphone she and Brad share, but told me she found the ones for Louis and Cal were still busy. Cindy said when they visited Cal at the hospital at lunch today, he'd indicated he might even be discharged sometime later today. Cindy's now checking with the hospital, and will call me right back."

Mark had barely gotten the words out of his mouth when their satphone beeped.

"Well …?" Mark asked.

"Discharged about 8:30 this evening."

"Discharged to *where?*" Mark asked.

"His condo. Apparently one of his current girlfriends picked him up, and will be bringing him back to the hospital five days a week for his radiation treatments and checkups," Cindy explained.

"Cindy, that's great news about Cal. Otherwise, I guess we just wait for your dad's call," Mark said and clicked off.

Five minutes later the Telfair's satphone rang. Mark answered. The unmistakable voice of Louis Loveman boomed on the other end of the phone: "I guess you think I've fallen off the planet. I've been on my satphone, first with Agent Rivera, briefly, then with Cal for the last couple of hours. Cal didn't sound drugged up and is very upbeat about the effectiveness of the radiation treatment he's receiving. He's very downbeat about the world situation in general, especially the threat he feels Muslim terrorists present to our way of life we enjoy here in the U.S. I tried to assure Cal the Bureau shares his concerns, and so do many other federal agencies, especially our CIA. He thinks we need to form a 'Department of Homeland Security,' or at least some kind of 'superagency' that would improve and coordinate intelligence gathering and sharing. Cal thinks lack of *timely sharing* of information is one of our weakest links when dealing with terrorism. Well that, and our 'stupid insistence on political correctness,' he said."

"Louis, you must be about talked out for the day."

"I am. But I was not about to go to bed without calling one of you guys."

"I'll understand if you make it short tonight. So, shoot," Mark replied.

"First," Louis began, "the crop duster is still in Kissimmee. Ben Hunter said he has installed the chlorine-laced filter in the plane and has given it a test flight using only pure water in the chemical tank. He told me it sprays perfectly."

"What about the date the plane is supposed to be picked up? Has that changed?" Mark asked.

"No. It's still 28 August. Abbas is paying the balance due, some $19,000, in cash. Using information we've gotten out of the computer Abbas has in his motel room, we've also learned Abbas, Aleem, and

Salaam all plan to drive together to Kissimmee. They will use the Honda Al Abbas has. On the return trip, Aleem will be the pilot, and Abbas the single passenger. Those two will fly in the plane back to the farm in Gainesville. Salaam will simply drive the car back to the motel in Gainesville."

"Sneaky bastards, aren't they?" Mark asked.

"Yes. And we were hoping to catch a larger group of them while they try to execute their plan. It seems this is just a three-man 'sleeper cell' or an 'al-Qaeda sleeper,' as we call them. But the computer records we have will eventually enable the Bureau to track down a much larger number of those who've secretly supported them, especially their financing."

"Any indication they are preparing the virus stuff yet?"

"Perhaps, or getting close. Agent Rivera told me Abbas has purchased a 200-gallon agricultural tank. It's a plastic job that's mounted on a trailer that can be pulled by that Ford tractor we already know is there. Earlier today, Rivera told me Abbas brought several items to the farm with him: a 12-volt battery, a battery charger, a large 12-volt marine bilge pump, plus several garden hoses."

"Louis, you don't have to be a rocket scientist to figure out what they are going to do with that stuff. They're going to wash out the mouse houses, pump the washdown water into the agricultural tank, then take it somewhere to filter and refine. My bet is the facilities to do that are inside the 18-wheeler's trailer."

"I think you've hit the nail on the head, Mark. That's exactly what we figured on our end, too."

"Have any of your undercover men actually gotten inside the 18-wheeler's trailer yet?"

"No. But I finally got the padlock keys I requested from Master Lock. Recall I earlier told you my men had gotten the manufacturer's serial number off the lock that secures the trailer's rear door. Well, it took ten days, but I've finally gotten the keys to Rivera. Agent Rivera and my other guys may give it a shot tomorrow night. It'll be a new moon, and plenty dark. I think that's all the new information I have."

"Louis, I know you've had a long day on the phone. I won't keep you any longer. Be assured I'll relay this new information to our group here in Tucson. Get a good night's sleep. Bye," Mark said, then clicked off.

It took Mark about ten minutes to bring Anne up to date regarding his just-finished conversation with Louis Loveman. Another ten minutes informed Cindy and Brad of the latest. As a group, they decided they should all go to Cal's condo and give him the latest as well.

Five minutes later, Cindy and Brad picked up the Telfairs at their camper. Another five minutes placed them at Cal's upscale condo. Cindy lead the way through the well-lit ground-level parking beneath the condos. *Nothing but BMW, Jaguar, Mercedes, Corvette, and assorted upscales here,* Mark thought as they approached the elevator. Silently, the foursome entered the elevator. Cindy deftly punched the button for the third floor. "It's been quite awhile, but I've been here once before. I came to see Dad while he was visiting Cal. I do hope Cal has someone staying with him," Cindy remarked as the elevator stopped at the third floor and opened silently. "If I remember correctly, Cal's is 302. There are only two condos on each floor. So, if 302 doesn't work, we'll try 301."

Cindy pressed the button beside the door of 302. After a full minute's pause, a very attractive Asian woman appearing to be in her mid-40s cautiously opened the door. She was dressed in an expensive-looking fluffy white terry bathrobe that bore burgundy embroidered initials "CC." The thick robe did little to conceal the ample breast anatomy beneath. *Surgically enhanced … Asians aren't naturally built like that!* Mark immediately thought. The white towel that wrapped her head indicated she'd obviously just gotten out of a shower or bath. Her bare feet, with beautifully manicured red toenails, sank deeply into the condo's plush burnt sienna carpet.

Smiling and speaking with no accent, the woman asked "May I ask who is calling?"

"Please tell Mr. Camarada it is Miss Cindy Loveman and her friends. This *is* Mr. Camarada's condo, isn't it?"

"Yes, that is correct. I will tell him you are here." She gently closed the door in their faces. They all heard the sentinel *click* that told them the door was again locked. Standing outside the door, the visitors blankly stared at one another, each wondering if they were going to be denied access to the condo. About 30 seconds later, the terry-clad woman reopened the door. She smiled, then said "Please come in! I am Shima Kye, Cal's friend. I am … uh … 'assisting' him while he recovers from his illness. He is in bed right now, but he's wide awake and wants to see you in his bedroom. I will lead the way."

Shima quickly escorted the visitors to Cal's bedroom, then she politely retreated across the hall to a second room; presumably, it was a second bedroom with its own bath. Cal quickly swung his bare feet off the side of his queen-sized bed and sat there in his black satin robe, one that contrasted sharply with the red silk sheets that covered the bed. "Great to see you folks! But what took you so damn long? I've been out of the hospital for several hours."

"Uncle Cal, you may be a great pilot but communication is not one of your best skills. I even had to call the darn hospital to find out you'd been dismissed!" Cindy shot back.

"Sorry, Cin. I guess I forgot to call you, and that makes me a lousy godfather. But lately I've been thinking about so many things ... mainly about my own health, and especially about this stuff Al Abbas wants to pull off."

"Well, let us bring you up to speed," Cindy said. "Mark got off the phone with my dad about an hour ago. Apparently your friend in Florida has the virus-killing filter installed in the plane. At the farm they are now setting up to produce the viral solution, and the crop duster will probably be on the farm by the 28th of August. I think they could be ready to attempt to do their dirty deeds in a week."

Cal had no immediate response. He gathered up several of the many silk-covered pillows, and stuffed them against the headboard of his heavy wrought iron bed. Cal reclined into the pillows before speaking: "I think the four of you have done all that can be done at this point. I'm still thinking about anything I could do that would bring this threat to a just end. My medical condition makes it unlikely I'll have much to contribute ... but I'll keep on thinking."

34

Before leaving Cal in his bed, he'd indicated he had no pain, but was going to take some sleeping pills … "To turn my mind off," he'd explained. He pressed a button on the wireless intercom at his bedside, and spoke to Shima: "My guests will be leaving my bedroom now. If they'd like to see it, please show them around the condo before they leave. After that, please come back to my room, and stay with me until I fall asleep."

"It will be my pleasure, Mr. Camarada," Shima replied over the intercom. "Don't fall asleep too soon."

Moments later, Shima appeared. She'd quickly dressed in a beautiful knee-length silk kimono. The kimono's black floral pattern appeared to be hand-painted on its scarlet background. A single wide gold sash cinched the garment at the waist, accentuating her alluring figure. Her small feet were still bare, her shining black hair now pulled back in a loose Geisha-style bun. "Would you care to see Mr. Camarada's condo?" Shima asked, smiling.

Shima's "tour" took ten minutes. Mark Telfair had seen opulence a few times before while living in Atlanta, but he'd never seen such simplicity and tasteful masculinity crammed into a living space no larger than 2,500 square feet. Anne walked around with her mouth open at times, her eyes and mind taking in every detail that Shima showed to them. Brad and Cindy uttered an occasional "Wow!" Otherwise, they both looked bored.

Following the tour, the foursome quickly departed the condo. Bradley dropped the Telfairs off at Pima-Swan, then he and Cindy returned to their apartment to continue working on their dissertations.

Without discussion, Mark and Anne showered, then prepared for bed. Nude and reclining in bed, Anne finally spoke: "Well …?"

"Well what?" Mark responded.

"What do you think about Cal … and his condo … and Shima?"

"Anne, I think that's really several different questions. As far as Cal goes, I think he has accepted his illness. Understandably, he's depressed. I think he realizes that life as he'd been living it is now over for him. He seems to have accepted he won't be able to make much of a contribution, at least as far as justice for Al Abbas goes. I think that's pretty much a done deal anyway. In fact, I don't know much of anything *any* of us can do that will help Louis further."

"And what do you think his relationship with Shima is?"

"Sex and live-in companionship would be my guess," Mark replied. "It could be more than that, but who knows? It's really none of our business."

"So what about his condo?" Anne asked.

"It's impressive, but pretty much what I'd visualized in my mind … at least for a wealthy bachelor like Cal."

"I don't have any experience with so-called 'bachelor pads,' so I don't have any basis for comparison. First, the place is immaculately clean and uncluttered. The whole décor exudes testosterone, or maleness. The massive brown leather sofa in the great room says 'man.' So does the huge granite and oak coffee table. The hallway with accent-lighted original aviation art says the same thing … plus expensive! Did you notice each piece was signed by the artist?"

"Frankly, I looked mostly at the paintings themselves. But I do have to admit it was striking artwork, especially when it came to MiGs and F-86s. Did you notice one of the F-86 paintings was also signed by Louis Loveman, in addition to the artist?"

"No. I guess I was too busy taking in other stuff," Anne admitted. "Such as?"

"Such as the kitchen with a commercial gas cooking surface, stainless-clad appliances, granite countertops, even a special fridge for wine tucked beneath the counter. Things like that. I also noticed that every light in the condo has a dimmer switch, one that allows mood-lighting on demand, plus there were candles scattered at strategic locations throughout, especially around that hot tub with all sorts of different jets. Though she didn't say, I presume that was Shima's bathroom. That bathroom even had a bidet!"

"I've seen bidets before. Some of my Atlanta friends jokingly call them 'cooter washers.' I'll have to admit they might be better than the warm washrags most folks use."

Anne giggled, and gave Mark one of her special looks.

Mark had reclined in bed wearing only fresh Jockey shorts. Anne slowly reached over and began lightly rubbing Mark's inner thigh, but continued talking. "Did you notice what was missing, Little Man?"

"No. Not much, though," Mark replied. "Cal even has healthy live plants."

"Mark, the place was missing *photographs!* I saw only a single photograph in his entire condo. That photo was one in well-preserved color, and the only people in it were Cal and Louis. I saw it in Cal's office. It was framed and standing on his desk. It was a picture of a very young, smiling Louis Loveman with jet-black hair, dressed in a flight suit. Both were standing right next to what I assume was an American fighter jet. Also in a flight suit, and standing beside Louis, was a very young smiling Cal Camarada, who had his arm draped over Lovemen's shoulder. As a youngster, Cal's hair was platinum, not white as it is today, but his eyes were just as blue as they are today. It was signed by Louis, and there was some handwritten message I could not read, except for one word: 'Ace.'"

Anne moved her gentle rubbing to the bulge that was beginning to form inside Mark's Jockey shorts. "You better stop that, or we'll never finish this discussion," Mark said, smiling, yet not resisting the least.

"We're almost through talking," Anne replied, and continued gently teasing him with her fingertips. "Did you notice the books Cal had on the shelves in his office?"

"Mostly flight manuals, but I did notice Hemingway's *Old Man and the Sea,* and Twain's *Huckleberry Finn."*

"So you missed the *Kama Sutra?"* Anne asked.

"No, I saw it. But it's a book you and I could have written. Of course we'd need to hire someone to do the illustrations of the positions. But there's really not a thing in it we haven't already tried."

"I know," Anne said. "I think every nurse at Grady read the entire book at some point during her training." Smiling and assisting Mark with the removal of his shorts she said, "At least our little 'bachelor's pad' has a mirrored ceiling ... and Cal's doesn't have that!"

"Nor does it have a beautiful woman like you inside it," Mark said, before giving her a long deep kiss, and pushing his shorts off their bed with his foot.

* * *

Following their extended lovemaking, both slept like contented puppies after a large meal. If they'd had dreams, neither recalled them. The beeping satphone finally caused Mark to get out of bed to answer it. It was Louis Loveman calling:

"Damn! I was beginning to think you guys were taking a vacation. It's 9:30 and I had to let it beep ten times!"

"We stayed up late catching up on conjugal things," Mark honestly replied. "So what's new on your end?"

"Agent Rivera and the other undercover guys got inside the 18-wheeler's trailer last night. After their visit, they carefully replaced the strands of hair Abbas had placed to tell him if anyone entered. It seems Abbas has taken a car trip to Florida, taking both Aleem and Salaam with him. My UCs have apparently gained his complete trust."

"Your *UCs?*"

"My undercover guys," Louis quickly clarified. "My guys are now running the farm while Abbas is gone. Abbas told them they were going to Florida to pick up some equipment, and while he was away he wanted them to feed and water the mice, and groom the pasture, filling in any potholes they may find. He also had them place a pair of strobe lights at the southwest extent of what we think is their runway. As best I understand it from Rivera, those strobes can be activated from the cockpit of a plane by using a certain radio frequency."

"Louis, we all know what that means. He's gone to pick up the crop duster. But you never did tell me what your men found inside the trailer."

"Exactly what we had expected, with one exception. There is the rather elaborate centrifuge and filtration system we'd expected, a system we think could quickly get the mouse-house washings ready to put into the crop duster's tank. My men also found three empty cages inside the trailer. Apparently that's where Abbas kept his breeding stock of mice until the chicken houses were ready for them. What we didn't expect, however, was living quarters."

"*Living quarters?* Like what?" Mark asked.

"Like they had the trailer's interior partitioned to create a living space: three wall-mounted bunks, small stove, microwave, fridge, chemical toilet, running water, small sink ...everything set up like a small RV."

"Louis, we'd already figured Abbas intended to make this a long-term operation. I think this tells us he'll soon be moving out of the motel in Gainesville, and actually living on site with his two buddies."

"I agree, Mark. We hope he moves the computer we've 'bugged' to the trailer. My men have already installed another receiver for the bug in the frame of the trailer. Hopefully, we can continue to monitor his computer's hard drive if he moves that computer with him. They've also planted some new audio bugs inside the living space."

"Sounds like you've got the bases covered, Louis. I guess all we can do now is wait."

"Have you talked to Cal lately?" Louis asked.

"All of us here visited Cal at his condo last night. Quite a place! Cal says he's now out of pain, but I have a strange feeling something is still bugging him badly. A woman is staying with him. Her name is Shima, an attractive Asian."

"What is the woman's family name?" Louis asked.

"She introduced herself as 'Shima Kye,'" Mark said.

"She may be from the same South Korean Kye family that had their several homes and businesses accidentally destroyed. Fortunately, none of them were seriously injured on the ground. It was simply collateral structural damage during a bombing run that went slightly off target. Though Cal wasn't flying that night, it was still planes from *our* squadron that did it. Cal always felt quite guilty about that, and for years has sent the Kye family money to assist in rebuilding their postwar lives."

"All I know is last night he told us he was going to take some sleeping pills to 'turn off his mind,' as he put it."

"Mark, Cal and I have had extensive personal conversations over the satphone. Please don't ask me for details, because I promised Cal portions of our conversations were personal and totally confidential. I'm sure Cal is having trouble 'turning his mind off,' and he's apparently admitted that openly. I may have trouble with my own mind before this is all over. Just don't judge me badly if Cal might do something totally unpredictable. And don't share my concerns about Cal with the others. That's just between you and me."

"I understand, sir," Mark said. "I'll only tell the others about Abbas and his buddies going to Florida … that, and the new findings inside the 18-wheeler's trailer."

"I'll keep you posted when the crop duster arrives. Agent Rivera has promised to call me as soon as it gets there. So, it's bye for now. Give my best to Anne and the others."

* * *

It took Mark about half an hour to bring Anne up to date regarding the developments at the farm in Gainesville. He did not disclose that Louis had admitted he and Cal had had extensive "private" conversations. Nor did he tell her that Louis seemed to have some reservations about the predictability of Cal's future actions.

35

A few minutes past noon, Aleem, Salaam, and Al Abbas arrived at Kissimmee Aviation Services in Florida. Salaam had liked the "feel" of the inconspicuous Honda Accord, the car Abbas had provided. He constantly had to resist the temptation to drive it faster. He never exceeded the posted speed limits, and frequently scanned the Honda's rearview mirror, looking for highway patrolmen.

Without incident, Salaam had driven the entire 500 miles, mainly because Al Abbas had ordered him to be the sole driver. Salaam knew why Abbas had chosen him; of the three, he had the most experience driving on U.S. highways. Salaam didn't seem the least fatigued after driving the entire distance with only one brief stop for gas. More importantly, Salaam had the best counterfeit driver's license, and his passport and work visa were the very best of counterfeits produced by the North Koreans. The Glock 17 he carried in a shoulder holster beneath his casual jacket created minimal visible bulge, yet gave him confidence should things suddenly turn bad.

"Good driving," Abbas had commented to Salaam, upon their arrival at Kissimmee. "I assume our Mr. Ben Hunter would be in that building over there," Abbas said, pointing to a small metal building with a sign on it: "Kissimmee Aviation Services—Office."

Abbas got out of the Honda and walked to the building. Aleem and Salaam followed. Salaam carried a battered black attaché, and had buttoned his jacket to conceal the fact he was armed. Abbas knocked on the door of the building. Moments later, the door opened. There stood a blue-eyed six-foot man with short black hair. He wore dark blue coveralls. "Ben" was embroidered below a more elaborate logo that sported a pair of silver aviator's wings stitched into the fabric.

"Hi. I'm Dr. Al Abbas. I trust you are Mr. Ben Hunter, correct?" Abbas asked.

"You got 'em. That's me," Ben said extending his hand to Abbas. "You must be the guy who's made a deposit on one of my dusters."

"Yes. It was a $9,000 deposit by electronic transfer. I want to see the plane, and have my pilot give it a test flight," Abbas said, pointing to Aleem. "I want to do that before I give you the $19,000 balance and complete the sale. I have brought the balance in cash," Abbas said, pointing to the attaché Salaam held at his side.

"Sounds fair enough," Ben Hunter said. "I'll have one of my employees bring it to the taxiway here in front of the office." Ben pulled a cell from his coveralls, and punched a button on speed dial. "Mike, if you can stop what you are doing, could you bring that PA-25 we've got in hangar 11 to the office? It should be ready to go. I flew it myself several days ago. But double check."

Ten minutes later the bright yellow PA-25 appeared on the taxiway. It looked brand new, and had obviously been well cared for. When the plane stopped and its driver got out, Aleem approached the plane, smiling. He did several walk-arounds, then said "I'd like to put some plain water in the chemical tank. I want to test the spray."

"There should be about 20 gallons of pure water left in the chemical tank," Ben said. "I personally tested the spray when I flew it. I'll put more water in it if you want, but what's already in it should be enough to give it a good test."

"Twenty gallons will be fine," Aleem said. "In which direction is it safe for me to fly? I know you have a commercial airport nearby, and I don't want to enter their approach and departure corridors."

"Just stay south of my main runway here, and you'll be out of the way of the big boys going to or from Kissimmee Municipal. Also keep an eye out for the little general aviation guys that use my field, and look for the two 225-foot cell towers that are about five miles south of my main strip here. I suggest you test the spray function right over my own runway. Stay as low as you safely can. Some folks get uptight when they see stuff coming out of an ag plane. Seems they assume it's some horrible poison that will make them sick, and they phone in complaints."

"I assume you want to see my license, before I take off with your plane," Aleem said to Hunter.

"Yes. For liability reasons. I'm the owner of this field, and presently the owner of the plane."

Aleem quickly produced his wallet and removed his genuine agricultural pilot's license. Ben Hunter quickly inspected it, then said, "As a form of photo ID, could I see your driver's license?" Aleem produced a counterfeit Georgia driver's license that passed Hunter's inspection.

"Looks fine. Do your preflight and go," Ben said to Aleem.

A few minutes later Aleem had climbed aboard, started the engine, and taxied to the east end of Ben Hunter's runway. There, he turned the plane around. Minutes later Aleem had skillfully taken off by mid-runway, and slowly banked south. He disappeared from sight a few moments, then reappeared at the runway's western end, and leveled out about 15 feet above the paved runway. The white fog streaming out of the PA-25's twin spray bar nozzles was uniform. A light breeze out of the north caused the fog to drift to the runway's southern side, but it quickly dissipated as it settled on grass at the runway's edge. Aleem repeated the maneuver, and on his third approach from the west he skillfully landed. He got out of the plane, and began walking slowly toward Abbas and Salaam, who were now casually standing beside the parked Honda.

Ben Hunter had quickly stepped into his office, indicating he needed to process the paperwork required by the sale. Ben made a quick call to Louis Loveman in Denver. "The men are here to pick up the plane. Do you want the sale to go through?"

"Yes," Louis replied. "I recognize your voice. But let's have no additional words on this unsecured line."

"I understand. Bye," Ben Hunter said, then clicked off.

Al Abbas began knocking on the office door. Ben let him in, along with Salaam and Aleem. "Well, what do you think of that little baby?" Ben asked, grinning, and shuffling papers on his desktop.

Aleem was all smiles. "She looks, flies, and sprays like new! I recommend to Dr. Abbas that he complete the sale."

"Great! But I need to see some money," Ben said.

Abbas nodded to Salaam. "Show him."

Salaam quickly placed the attaché on Ben Hunter's desk and popped it open. Ben quickly counted 19 bundles of 20s, $1,000 in each bundle. "Seems to all be here. I need your signature on the papers, along with my own. That will make you the legal owner of PA-25, tail number N347AZ. Here is the current Certificate of Registration for that number. I'm sure you know a change of the plane's ownership means you can change that number if you want to, but you'll have to do that through the FAA. Here is the Certificate of Airworthiness, and it is current. I'm also giving you Piper's manual, as well as an aircraft mechanic's shop manual for that plane. The plane also has a very good GPS, and here's the manual for that instrument. If anything ever needs repair or certification work, we can do it all right here at Kissimmee Aviation Services. You can also take it to any aircraft service that is certified to work on this particular plane."

"Don't worry, Mr. Ben Hunter," Abbas said. "I'm sure Aleem will help me take very good care of it. It has been my pleasure to do business with you. I do have one request. We would like to top off with gas before we leave."

"No problem. It was full before Mr. Aleem took it up for a spin. No charge for the extra gas. Just remember your safe range is only 300 miles, so plan your return trip accordingly. There is a current set of Southeastern charts in the door pocket."

Salaam got behind the wheel of the Honda and began driving away, heading back to Gainesville, Georgia. Aleem and Abbas boarded the plane and sat tandem. Aleem sat up front in the pilot's seat; Abbas sat in the rear in the seat that would normally be occupied by a flight instructor. Obviously Abbas had never been in a small plane before. Aleem turned in his seat to give Abbas instructions on how to fasten his harness, then said, "Don't mess with the stick between your knees, and keep your feet off the pedals. Here, put on this headset," Aleem ordered, passing it over his shoulder to Abbas. "That way you can hear what I say while we are flying."

In five minutes they were 1,500 feet off the ground. Abbas was already having the time of his life. "Praise Allah! This is fantastic! Someday I want you to teach me how to do this on my own. I want to fly all the way up to Paradise!"

"Dr. Abbas, I do not have the patience of Allah. I suggest you do as I have done: Take a flight school course. That should be available near Gainesville, where we are going."

* * *

The weather for flying a light plane was perfect. Their first fuel stop occurred in Valdosta, Georgia, a second one in Macon, Georgia. Aleem chose small uncontrolled general aviation fields, ones where a crop duster would not seem out of place and attract unnecessary attention. As dusk approached, Aleem spoke: "We have only 50 more miles. You told me you have strobes that mark the runway. You also said they can be activated by radio frequency. Do you have the frequency?"

"Yes, of course! Here it is," Abbas said, reaching inside his jacket. He passed a note forward to Aleem.

"We still have fairly good light, plus I have GPS," Aleem commented. "At five miles out, I will try the radio frequency."

Descending from 5,100 to 2,500 feet about five miles from the runway, Aleem activated the radio frequency Abbas had given him.

Like magic, two blue strobes could be seen pulsing at the grass strip's southwest end. With skill Aleem headed straight for them, and made a perfect soft-field landing, touching down 200 feet beyond the strobes.

As the crop duster slowly taxied toward the shed at the northeast end of the field, Agent Rivera quickly crouched behind a 500 gallon fuel tank. Using his satphone he made a call to Louis Loveman: "The eagle has landed, with Abbas aboard. We don't know where Salaam is, but we assume he is still driving the Honda back to Gainesville. More later when we check that out. Bye, sir."

Louis attempted no return comment, sensing that Agent Rivera was trying to avoid having Abbas catch him while chatting on a strange-looking phone. Rivera pocketed his phone, then came out of his 'hiding place' and joined the other undercover men who were slowly walking to the spot where the plane had stopped.

Aleem first, then Abbas exited the plane. Now standing on the grass-covered ground, Abbas wrapped his arms around Aleem, repeatedly slapped him on the back, then said, "I thank Allah for your great skills! I, too, will one day have those same skills."

"Welcome back, Dr. Abbas," Rivera said, extending his hand as he approached Abbas. "We have taken good care of your farm while you've been away. The mice have been fed and watered for the day. I heard the plane coming, and I could see the strobe lights we installed seemed to work fine. If there is nothing more we can do for you this evening, we will return to Gainesville for the night."

"That will be fine, Rivera. But I expect all of you back here tomorrow morning by seven o'clock. But before you leave, please help us push the plane beneath the shed. I don't want to leave my new 'baby' unprotected. Don't worry, I will have plenty of work for all of you tomorrow. Then, I will also pay you for the work you've done while I've been away."

With Aleem indicating the "safe areas" to push upon the plane, it was quickly turned around, and rolled beneath the shed so it faced the runway. "Just need to tie it down now," Aleem said.

"Why?" Abbas asked. "It can't go anywhere without the motor running, can it?"

"If we have no wind, as we have right now, it would be fine. But what if we have a bad storm with strong winds? Later, I will explain how to have your men make tie-downs and wheel chocks. We must do that to insure the safety of your plane between uses."

* * *

Agents Rivera, Moreno, and Alvarez walked to their ragged Ford pickup and immediately began the short drive to their room at the Hampton Inn in Gainesville.

"Wonder what Abbas has in mind for our work tomorrow?" Rivera asked, while driving.

"Beats me. Probably collecting mouse shit!" Alvarez said. "Guess we'll all find out at seven in the morning."

36

Reaching the Hampton Inn at dark, the three undercover FBI agents entered their ground-floor room. They mutually decided to eat at the Hampton's own restaurant. They showered, then dressed in casual clothes before seating themselves in a secluded area of the restaurant. Ordering beers along with their evening meal of pizza, they began a discussion:

"Ya know," Rivera said, "that Abbas is an odd dude. I mean, like, how does he know how to put all this shit together? I know he's supposed to be brilliant, but he does not know jackshit about actually building all the stuff we have done for him. It's like he knows exactly *what* to do, yet doesn't know *how* to do it himself. At least not using his *own* hands."

Agent Moreno drained his mug of draft and placed it on the table before speaking. "I think Abbas is getting a lot of technical advice from someone we don't even know about yet. Probably it's coming out of Saudi Arabia. I'll bet it's coming in over the computer he has in his room at his motel. Agent Loveman has told us he's not getting any important information over his cell. It's his computer. That's my guess."

Agent Alvarez put in his two cents: "Look, the guy is a freaking Ph.D., for God's sake. He's a virologist that was teaching microbiology at the University of Arizona. True, he's not a carpenter, plumber, or an electrician. I think he's here simply to get the microbiology part right. He's just preparing the virus inside the truck's trailer, and probably doing that all by himself. But then he gets some dumbasses, like us, to do the physical work."

"Where do you think Abbas and Aleem are right now?" Agent Moreno asked.

"My bet is they are both counting on staying inside the trailer at the farm tonight," Alvarez answered.

"And what about Salaam?" Agent Moreno asked.

Rivera answered: "My bet he's still driving back from Kissimmee. After we eat, maybe one of us should check the Three Oaks Motel."

Their pizzas were soon served. Their conversation slowed, but didn't stop.

"So who's gonna volunteer to check the motel?" Rivera asked, chewing a large bite of pizza.

"Rivera, it's not polite to talk with your mouth full," Moreno advised.

"Look. I'm the senior agent here, and the EMT who gives you your globulin shots. That does not make you my mother. And remember: I have the option of giving you your next globulin shot with the dullest and biggest needle I can find. I'll just volunteer to check the Three Oaks myself!" Rivera shot back.

"OK, boss," Moreno replied, a hint of apology in his voice. "But what's your guess about what Abbas wants us to do tomorrow?"

"I have no fuckin' clue. You guys have another beer and speculate. I'm gonna have one more slice of pizza, then I'm haulin' ass for Three Oaks. You guys can catch the tip for the waitress, and leave the 6:00 a.m. wake-up call at the front desk."

* * *

Agent Rivera drove past the Three Oaks. Salaam had yet to arrive, or at least the Honda that belonged to Abbas was not there. In his head, Rivera tried computing the driving time from Kissimmee to Gainesville. As the crow flies, he knew the distance was a little over 430 miles. *He should be here any moment now,* Rivera thought, glancing at his watch. *It's a longer distance by road. How much longer? Accident? Mechanical trouble with the car? Stopped to eat?* Thoughts were still crossing his mind, as the Honda Accord turned into the motel and parked directly in front of the room rented to Al Abbas. The area was poorly lit but Rivera was confident the man who got out of the car was none other than Abdus Salaam.

A quarter-mile away, Rivera parked and slouched in the seat of his unmarked Crown Vic. Reaching into the glove compartment, Rivera removed night-vision binoculars. He trained them on the door Salaam had entered. He waited, then waited some more.

Ten minutes later, Rivera's patience rewarded him. Salaam began loading the trunk of the Honda. Among the many items Salaam loaded, Rivera positively identified only a couple of items: *a desktop computer and a small satellite dish.* Salaam quickly left the motel, and headed east. He actually passed Rivera's parked Crown Vic without slowing the least. When Salaam's tail lights could no longer be seen, Rivera pursued. He mainly wanted to be sure Salaam was going to the farm. He needed to be positive before he called his boss, Louis Loveman.

Having caught up with Salaam, and following at an inconspicuous distance, Rivera smiled when he saw the Honda signaling for a turn into the farm. In the headlights of the Honda, he could see Salaam fiddling with the lock on the metal gate. Not slowing, Rivera passed by and continued on down the highway. *That's it. Time to call Loveman,* Rivera thought.

FBI Agent Louis Loveman answered his satphone on the fourth beep. "Loveman, here."

"Sir, Agent Rivera reporting. Salaam is now back from Kissimmee, and has taken several items from the Three Oaks Motel. He's transported them to the farm. I'm positive one of the items is a desktop computer. The other item appears to be a small satellite dish of some kind."

"Rivera, are you positive it's the *same* computer you put the transmitting bug in?"

"No, but when I've previously been in the motel room Abbas uses, there was only a *single* desktop computer present."

"I sure hope it's the same one. That was the only way we were getting up-to-date information about any future schedule Abbas may have. The satellite dish is probably to allow his computer to access the Internet from a remote location, like at the farm."

"Sir, our receiver for the computer bug is still in the adjoining room at Three Oaks. I assume you want me to retrieve that item."

"Yes, by all means," Louis replied. "My main concerns now are two: First, I hope Abbas reconnects the same computer without discovering the bug. Second, I've got to figure some way to get the information out of that second receiver you planted in the truck's frame. Somehow, we need to get that information into your personal laptop so you can upload it to the secure FBI site. That is, we'll just do it as we were doing it before."

"I'll defer the logistics to the geeks the Bureau has," Rivera commented. "The Hampton has Internet connections in all rooms, so using my laptop won't be a problem. Just keep me posted."

"Are you where you can answer your satphone if it beeps?"

"Yes, sir."

"Let me call you right back. I need to talk to my geeks. Catch you in a few," Loveman said, then clicked off.

Agent Rivera was driving slowly back to Gainesville. Ten minutes passed. No call from Loveman. Some 15 minutes later his satphone beeped just as he was pulling into the Hampton Inn.

"Problem solved, Rivera," Louis said. "One of my computer guys said 'That's a piece of cake. I can build what you need in two hours, max.' I'll see that you have the device in your hands sometime tomorrow. I'll send it by FedEx overnight to the Hampton."

"How does it work and how big is it?" Rivera asked.

"That's two questions. 'How it works?' is above my pay grade. The geek told me it's no larger than a Band-Aid box, and easily concealed on your person."

"How close do I have to be to the transmitting computer bug? Will it receive a signal through metal?" Rivera asked.

"That also is two questions," Loveman reminded Rivera. "You'd have to be within 100 yards of the transmitting computer bug. My geek said the thin aluminum covering the 18-wheeler's trailer will not block the bug's outgoing signal. If the steel in the truck's frame where you planted the second computer-bug receiver is one-eighth-inch thick, or more, that receiver probably won't work anyway. My geek's idea was to have the computer bug transmit directly to the small box he's gonna build for us tonight. You'd simply turn the device on, conceal it on your person, and position yourself less than 100 yards from the trailer. He said he'd include written instructions on how to retrieve data the new device captures, and upload it into your personal laptop. Then it's all downhill from there ... just like we were doing before. You simply forward the information to our secure site."

"I have no idea what we'll be doing, or exactly where Abbas will have us working the next couple of days. It may take more than a day to get close to the trailer, at least without making Abbas suspicious. I'll do the very best I can, sir."

"I'm sure you will, Rivera. You always do. That does not go unnoticed. Just call me when you've got data in your laptop ready for upload to our secure site."

"I'll tell the other guys where we stand."

"Thanks," Loveman said, then signed off.

* * *

When Rivera returned to the Hampton Inn, he found both Alvarez and Moreno had returned to their room and were still speculating about the work they'd do for Abbas tomorrow.

"Quit worrying about tomorrow's work. Let me bring you guys up to speed about Salaam," Rivera announced. He then spent 15 minutes telling his fellow agents the latest. "So, when the device Loveman is having his geek make arrives here, any one of us who has an excuse to get close to the trailer will carry the device. Understood?"

Alvarez and Moreno said nothing, but nodded an affirmative.

* * *

The agents spent an uneventful night at the Hampton Inn. Exactly at seven the next morning they arrived at the farm to find the gate locked. They parked their old truck on the right of way for the highway and considered walking through the thick underbrush that flanked the locked gate.

"Best we wait here," Rivera said. "I don't want to do anything that could cause Abbas to fire us ... like being late for work, or bypassing the gate without his permission. If he's on the property, and outside the trailer, he might be able to see that we are parked here and on time."

At 8:15, arriving from the highway, Salaam drove up in the Honda.

"Sorry you are locked out," Salaam said. "Dr. Abbas had me go into town early this morning to pick up some items for today's work. I had to wait for the Home Depot to open in Gainesville. I now have everything you will need in the trunk of the car. I will unlock the gate for you. Drive your truck directly to the shed where the airplane is parked. I will follow you there after I relock the gate."

When the agents reached the shed, Abbas and Aleem were standing beneath the shed beside the plane. Aleem again supervised pushing the plane out of the hangar so that it was in the early morning sun. "We must wait until the plane's skin feels dry and slightly warm to touch. Then we can begin the painting process," Aleem explained to Abbas.

"*Painting?*" Agent Rivera asked.

"Yes," Abbas replied. "I've decided I want my plane to be entirely black. But while the plane's surface is warming, maybe we can do those tie-down things. You did get what I need for that?" Abbas asked Salaam.

Salaam said nothing, just walked to the Honda and removed two mobile home anchors from the trunk. Rivera and his men screwed the auger-like anchors into the soil beneath the shed, placing them exactly where Aleem indicated they needed to be. Aleem also had them fashion wheel chocks, using scrap lumber left over from the chicken house floor modifications.

By 10:00 a.m., Aleem deemed the plane's surface was warm enough to begin painting. He had them first wipe down the plane's exterior surfaces with Home Depot's equivalent of Fantastik, a household cleaner. After carefully placing blue masking tape on the entire Plexiglas canopy and lenses of the plane's various lights, the painting process began. Salaam had bought 48 cans of Krylon flat-black spray, a product commonly used on barbeque grills.

"You want us to paint over the black tail numbers?" Rivera asked.

"I want you to paint *everything* that is not already covered with masking tape. I can remember the tail number!" Abbas barked.

"OK, you're the boss," Rivera said, and kept on spraying, while thinking: *God, what an absolute and total nutcase! This plane had an impeccable yellow paint job, and this screwball is wanting us to fuck it up.*

After the paint dried fully, they pushed the plane back beneath the shed. Aleem used nylon rope to secure the tie-down points beneath the duster's wings to the eyes of the mobile home anchors screwed into the soil.

Now getting dark at the end of their long workday on the farm, the undercover men were all tired. Abbas approached Agent Rivera and began counting cash by flashlight. "Here, Rivera. This is the money for your men. I've included yesterday's pay as well. I expect all of you back at seven in the morning. Do not be late for work."

37

Upon arrival at the Hampton, Agent Rivera alone went to the front desk and inquired about a FedEx delivery. None had been made for him. *The concierge behind the desk is looking at me very strangely,* Rivera thought.

Rivera quickly went to their room to join his companion agents. Rivera soon understood the strange look he'd just gotten at the desk. He found Agent Alvarez critically studying his own appearance in the bathroom mirror. In good light, both their faces looked like those of a coal miner after a day's work. *Damn overspray from all those cans of black paint,* Rivera thought.

Upon seeing Rivera, Alvarez spoke: "Shit, boss! You look as bad as I do. I've even got black boogers." Alvarez was repeatedly blowing his nose into a Kleenex, and giving the expelled mucous a thorough "clinical inspection" in the bathroom's bright light. "That paint better not have fucked up my lungs," Alvarez muttered. "At least Abbas should have given us a mask to wear. You know, like the ones he makes us wear when we go inside the chicken houses."

"I'm not sure Abbas gives a damn about our personal health. If he did, he would have insisted on giving us globulin injections, like he probably does for himself and his own men. It's obvious he does not know we are already doing that to protect ourselves from the virus. After he has his operation up and running, I think Abbas figures we're totally 'expendable.' So where is Agent Moreno? Does he look as bad as we do?" Rivera asked.

"Worse. He's walking to the 7-Eleven down the street. He's bringing back some rubbing alcohol. He wants to see if it will take this paint off our skin."

* * *

Several showers using plenty of soap and hot water worked better than the rubbing alcohol Moreno had acquired. They all discovered they had "black boogers," and went through a full box of Kleenex and two rolls of toilet paper before they finally figured their noses were clean. Fortunately, none of the agents experienced ill effects from their several hours of inhaling Krylon spray paint.

Dressed in clean casual clothes, the agents returned to the Hampton's sparsely occupied restaurant. They began eating and talking.

"Think we should let Loveman know Abbas has painted the plane?" Moreno asked.

"Definitely," Rivera answered. "After we finish our meal, I'll call Agent Loveman. The way the plane is painted now, nobody could read the numbers, and I'm sure that's gotta be against some FAA regulation."

"Why paint it black?" Agent Alvarez asked. "Is he planning on using it at night? That would make it harder to spot, wouldn't it?"

"I think that's something for Loveman to ponder. I'll put the satphone on speaker when I call him. That way you guys can hear exactly what the boss has to say," Rivera explained.

A man in a red jacket approached the table where the agents were seated. "I do apologize for interrupting your dining experience here at the Hampton Inn, but I'm looking for a Mr. Rivera. Is he among you gentlemen seated at this table?"

"I'm Adelio Rivera," Agent Rivera said, standing cautiously. Why do you need to know that?"

"A gentleman from FedEx is waiting at the front desk. He has a small package for you, but says it requires your signature to deliver it."

Rivera followed the red-jacketed Hampton employee to the front desk where he quickly signed the FedEx form, and was handed the package by a FedEx employee who departed on the run.

Rivera returned to the table. "I think we got it, fellas. The geek-box Loveman promised. We'll check it out after we finish our meal."

* * *

Finished eating, and now back in their room, Rivera made his satphone call to Agent Louis Loveman.

Rivera explained quickly without preamble. "First, something strange happened today. Abbas had us paint the entire plane flat black by using multiple cans of spray paint from Home Depot. We masked the cockpit canopy, marker lights, and landing lights. Otherwise, the entire once-yellow plane is now the same color as a barbeque grill! Go figure. He even had us paint over the so-called tail numbers, that

N347AZ that was on the plane in black. Second, the device your geek made has arrived. Abbas wants us to work tomorrow, so we'll try to get close enough to see if we can receive anything from his computer."

"Interesting," Louis said. "I think he's about ready to launch his plan. Getting information out of his computer is now top priority. I think that's the only way we'll know his schedule, if indeed he has one. Don't put yourselves in danger, or get caught getting the information. I'm assuming all my geek's stuff is going to work, and I want to talk to some of my other assets we've got working on this with us. I'll call you back about this same time tomorrow," Loveman said, then abruptly signed off.

* * *

From his Denver office, Louis Loveman made a satphone call to the secure phone issued to Cindy and her boyfriend, Brad. Cindy answered in their Tucson apartment:

"Hi Daddy! Haven't heard from you in a few days. I promise I was planning on calling you this evening when you got back to Boulder. What's up?"

"Not sure, Cin. Let me give you the basics, then talk it over with your friends in Tucson. All of them if possible. Cal, Anne, Mark, and Brad. One of my undercover guys called yesterday and said Abbas now has the crop duster located at the farm in Gainesville. Today Abbas had my men paint the entire plane flat black. They painted over the tail numbers, so they can't be read. We think Abbas and his buddies have moved to living quarters located inside the 18-wheeler's trailer, and we think he took the computer he had in the motel to the trailer with him. My men have an untested geek-made receiver, one we hope will capture signals from that bug we planted in the computer Abbas has."

"Dad, I'll spread the word. I've made notes about what you just said. It may be late tonight, but we'll definitely call you back. Love ya. Bye."

* * *

It took Cindy about an hour to arrange a meeting for 8:00 p.m. at the Tucson apartment. Cal did not answer his cell or regular phone. He didn't answer his satphone either. *Strange,* she thought, with a flicker of concern. She finally decided to go ahead with a group meeting anyway, even without Cal.

At eight, Cindy, Brad, and the Telfairs settled around the apartment's dining table. "I can't find Cal," Cindy immediately explained. "No answer on *any* of his phones."

"Did you leave a message?" Anne asked.

"None of his phones have that option," Cindy explained.

"Kinda odd for a guy who probably has every gadget known to man," Mark commented.

Brad scratched his head. "Maybe we should check with the hospital. Maybe he's had some complication from his radiation treatments. We know he's not driving anywhere because his Boxster is still parked in front of our apartment."

"I'll call the hospital," Cindy volunteered. And she did, only to discover Cal was not an inpatient there.

"I guess the only remaining option is to check his condo," Anne said.

"Mark, why don't you and I run over to his condo?" Brad suggested. "We'll leave the girls behind in case Cal calls here for some reason."

* * *

Ten minutes later, Brad and Mark were at Cal's condo knocking on the door. No answer. Not even the attractive Asian, Shima Kye, appeared.

"Let's try his next-door neighbor," Mark suggested.

Brad boldly knocked on the door of 301. A man in his 40s answered the door. He was wearing a bathrobe and bedroom slippers. "Sorry to disturb you, sir, but we are looking for a Mr. Cal Camarada who lives next-door in 302. We can't get him to answer his phone or come to the door. Do you know if he's OK?" Bradley asked.

"I know he's been sick, but says he now feels fine. He's away for just a couple of days. He asked me to collect his newspapers and mail until he gets back. I think he took his girlfriend with him. Have you guys ever met his current girlfriend?"

"Uh … yes," Mark said, smiling.

"I bet she's one fine piece of ass! At least Cal could have left her here for me to enjoy while he's away!" the man at the door of 301 exclaimed.

"Did he say where they were going?" Mark asked.

"No. And if I had Shima with me, I wouldn't give a damn where we went … as long as it had an industrial-strength bed. You guys should see her in our swimming pool here at the condo. Her bikini doesn't even have enough cloth to make a decent handkerchief!"

"Thanks for the information," Brad finally said, before the guy could say more about Shima. "Just tell him Dr. Mark Telfair and Mr. Bradley Buck called while he was away."

* * *

Mark and Brad quickly returned to the apartment and explained Cal's absence. Mark spoke: "We got this information from the guy in 301. Cal's away for a couple of days, apparently with Shima. We don't know where they went, but maybe Cal at least took his satphone with him."

Cindy again tried Cal's satphone, but got no answer. "Well, at least we tried to include him," Cindy finally sighed. "Let me tell you about the conversation I had with my dad just a few hours ago. I promised I'd call him back after we talked here. First, the crop duster is now at the farm. Second, they've changed the color of the plane. It's painted black and the tail numbers are painted over, and they can't be read. Third, Abbas, Aleem, and Salaam are now probably all living in the 18-wheeler's trailer at night. Fourth, they apparently took the bugged computer with them to the trailer. Fifth, Dad says the undercover agents now have a device that should wirelessly collect all the data in the computer Abbas has," Cindy explained, reading from notes she had earlier taken while talking with her dad.

A thick fog of silence enveloped the group. Each member was thinking, their eyes closed in concentration. What could this new information mean? How could it be used to anticipate the next move Abbas would make? How soon would it be?

Anne finally broke the silence. "Cindy, no offense to your dad regarding his 'new' information, but we really haven't learned diddly squat! At least nothing that's really new. We already know *what* he's gonna do … like spray his virus-laden stuff on a *bunch* of people. The real question is *where* is that bunch of people he's gonna spray? We know the plane has a range of only 300 miles, so where would you go to find a large number of people, and safely return to the farm? Those people would have to be somewhere *outside*, right?"

Mark and Brad remained silent, both feeling like mental midgets.

"Anne, you're absolutely right!" Cindy said. "If I were Abbas, and *not* knowing the stuff I sprayed was harmless, I'd pick some large outdoor sporting event. I'd get them all sprayed before they knew what was happening. And, like me, Abbas certainly knows the most surefire way to infect someone with hanta is for them to actually *inhale* the virus. So that would rule out a covered stadium or gymnasium or an auditorium. And that leaves what? What's usually got lots of people together outside?" Cindy asked.

Anne smiled. "NASCAR events, baseball games, most football games, maybe a rock festival … stuff like that. And it has to be within the plane's flying range from Gainesville. I think we better get on your computer and check the schedules for outdoor sporting events! And do that *before* we call your dad back."

38

Two hours later, a fog of disappointment still lingered in the Tucson apartment. Regarding major upcoming outdoor sporting events near Gainesville, the foursome felt they had exhausted all information available on the Internet. Brad finally snapped his laptop shut, and said, "You guys can keep on looking if you want. I'm gonna quit and have a beer!"

"I think I've had enough of this guessing game, too," Mark chimed in. "Atlanta Motor Speedway would probably be the easiest target, but the speedway doesn't even have anything like a big NASCAR event scheduled soon. I'm sure that would attract thousands upon thousands! I realize the noise of a racetrack would mean the crop duster could arrive on site, and be virtually unheard. I doubt a single NASCAR fan would even notice it until it started spraying. We couldn't even find a rock festival scheduled within the plane's range. Sure, there's umpteen high-school football, softball, and soccer stuff scheduled, but they won't attract a really large group of people."

Cindy toyed with her platinum ponytail using a single finger. Those who knew her well recognized it as a habitual gesture she made when thinking deeply. "Ya know, if that filter Brad modified functions—and it certainly should—this whole discussion becomes academic. I think the worst that could happen is that the plane could crash into a populated area, killing some folks on the ground."

"Suppose the crop duster's chemical tank ruptured in a crash. What would that do, Cindy?" Mark asked.

"Depends," Cindy answered, still twirling her hair.

"On what?" Mark asked.

"*Fire*. If the plane caught fire in the crash, the virus would probably be killed. Cal told us the fuel and chemical tanks were right next to each other," Cindy replied. "Unprotected emergency people working the crash site could be in danger, especially if there was no fire."

"What if Abbas crashed into a freshwater reservoir, say like Lake Sidney Lanier, or Lake Allatoona, which supply almost all of Atlanta's water?" Mark asked.

"Mark, when I was in college, and doing my epidemiology studies on hantavirus, I learned a good bit about municipal water systems. They pretty much all function the same way no matter which municipality they serve. Before that water is delivered to Atlanta, it is cultured at multiple points for disease-causing organisms. It is tested for hundreds of toxic chemicals, and the results of the tests are continuously monitored by professionals. Immediately before delivery, it is filtered, and treated with ozone or chlorine to insure it is sterile. If any viable hantavirus should ever get into Atlanta's reservoir lakes, it would be massively diluted by the time Atlanta's water-treatment facilities go to work on it. I think infecting people by ingesting hanta-contaminated water is a nonissue," Cindy explained.

"How far is it from Gainesville to Atlanta ... as the crow flies?" Anne asked.

Brad rebooted his laptop. A few minutes later, he answered Anne's question:

"Wow! It's only 55 air miles. That's much closer than I thought. So, that's about 110 miles roundtrip, well within the plane's capability."

"Humor me, Bradley," Anne said. "I know none of us in this room are sports fans, but look up 'Turner Field' and the 'Atlanta Braves.' That's one schedule we didn't look at because we thought it was probably out of the plane's range."

Moments later, Brad again said, "Wow!"

"*Wow* what?" Anne asked.

"Would you believe they've got three upcoming games at Turner Field? The Atlanta Braves vs. the Chicago Cubs. The first in the series will be tomorrow evening, August 31st. They'll play again the following nights, on September 1st and 2nd. Notes about the stadium say it holds over 50,000 people, and all three games are sold out!"

"Cindy, I think it's time we call your dad," Anne remarked.

* * *

Instead of the laptop, they now all eyed the satphone in the middle of the dining table. Mark wondered why they all intently stared at the phone, as if doing so would allow them to hear Cindy's dad more clearly.

Cindy soon had her father on the phone. "Dad, I kept my promise about calling you back. We've all discussed the new information you gave me earlier today. But there's one new thing that worries me on our end. We cannot locate Cal! He's not back in the hospital. He's not at his condo. We can't get him to answer any of his phones, including his satphone."

"Louis, it's me, Mark."

"I recognize your voice. Go ahead."

"Brad and I drove over to Cal's condo earlier this evening. We talked to his next-door neighbor, who indicated Cal and his current girlfriend, Shima, were away for a couple of days. That struck me as odd."

Louis first chuckled, then said, "Don't let *anything* Cal does strike you as 'odd.' He called *me* by satphone less than an hour ago. He didn't tell me where he was, and I didn't ask. We discussed some very personal matters, and I promised not to share our conversation with others. I won't break that promise. Trust me, Cal is OK. He's just making the mental readjustments needed to accept his current medical situation. I can assure you he is not going to answer any of his phones, so don't even try to contact him. He'll call one of us, but only when he's ready to communicate."

"Dad, that still sounds totally weird. Remember, you said 'trust me,' and I will. Anyway, we've all talked it over, except for Cal, of course. We think Abbas might use some outdoor sporting event as his target. There's a series of baseball games at Turner Field in Atlanta. They'll begin tomorrow evening. We think that is one of many possible targets, but that's still guesswork on our part. It was Anne's idea to look up the Turner Field schedule."

"Cin, let me pass your groups' thoughts to my undercover guys in Gainesville. Sometime tomorrow, I hope they will find a way to get the receiver for the computer bug close enough to read the computer we think Abbas has inside the trailer."

* * *

The following morning at the Hampton Inn, Rivera gave himself and his men a "booster shot" of hanta-immune globulin. "I know I am giving our shots a little early, but I think Abbas will have at least one of us messing with that mouse shit before the day is over," Rivera explained, then pocketed the geek-made device Louis Loveman had FedX deliver to the Hampton.

Upon arrival at the farm, Abbas announced he had only a half-day's work for them. He wanted the crop duster filled to capacity with aviation fuel. Aleem would hold the fuel nozzle, while Agent Moreno slowly hand-cranked the mechanical pump mounted atop the 500 gallon tank of avgas, a special formulation of gasoline for piston-driven aircraft. The tractor's air cleaner was cleaned, its oil changed by Alvarez. Abbas instructed Alvarez to start mowing as soon as the dew on the grass had evaporated. Salaam stood silently by, doing nothing other than keeping an eye on the "dayworkers," who occasionally spoke among themselves in Spanish. Salaam, apparently tired of listening to a language he did not understand, slowly ambled off into the woods.

Rivera thought: *Alvarez will soon be on the tractor mowing. But it really does not need mowing again so soon. Why is Abbas doing this? Is he crazy? Alvarez will have to make many passes by the 18-wheeler backed into the woods. At times he will be less than 50 yards from the trailer. This is my chance to pass the device to Alvarez and have him make many passes close to the truck.*

Rivera motioned a cautious "come here" to Alvarez, and made his request in Spanish: "Alvarez, por favor, ven aqui un momento antes de montarte en el tractor," he whispered, as he passed off the computer bug receiver to Alvarez.

"Yo entiendo lo que quieres que yo haga, y hare tantas pasadas posibles cerca del camion," Alvarez whispered back, indicating he understood exactly what Rivera wanted him to do.

Dr. Al Abbas suddenly appeared. Rivera now worried Abbas might have *seen* him pass the device off to Alvarez, but remained certain Abbas had not heard or understood the whispered words they exchanged in Spanish. Abbas immediately began talking to Rivera about a totally unrelated matter, leaving Rivera confident his passage of the device to Alvarez had not been observed either.

"Rivera," Abbas began, "I know you're the boss of the other Hispanic workers. I'm talking about Moreno and Alvarez. After Alvarez finishes cutting the grass, I want the Bush Hog disconnected from the tractor. Connect the tractor to the 200-gallon tank I have on wheels, and one of you drive it to the houses where the mice are. I want all three of you there. The mouse houses need a good washing out. I will be there to show you how to collect the wash water and transfer it to the 200-gallon tank. That will complete your work for today, but since all of you have been such good workers, I will pay all of you for a full day."

"Will you be needing us in the future?" Rivera asked.

"No. You and your workers have finally gotten everything where we can manage the farm on our own."

227

* * *

Alvarez finished cutting the grass a little before noon. He disconnected the Bush Hog from the tractor, and attached the trailer-mounted plastic agricultural tank. Behind the tractor, Rivera and Moreno both sat on the trailer's frame alongside the empty plastic tank. Alvarez slowly towed them down the middle of the grass runway, as he headed for the mouse houses.

Abbas got in his Honda, passed the men on the tractor, and beat them to the mouse houses by several minutes. When the undercover men caught up with him, Abbas issued latex gloves, masks, and garden hoses from the trunk of his car. He carefully instructed them regarding the wash-down process. It took over an hour to wash all the mouse feces and urine into the central septic tank that collected drainage from all three houses. The work was a messy process. The putrid ammonia smell was almost overpowering. Even when breathing air filtered by the special masks Abbas had provided, the stench was still horrific. *The Bureau doesn't pay me enough to do this kinda shit!* Rivera kept thinking, and felt certain his fellow agents were having similar thoughts.

The brown stinking muck that accumulated in the septic tank was transferred to the 200-gallon tank on the trailer behind the tractor. The battery-powered marine bilge pump labored and slurped with the transfer of foul liquid having the consistency of pancake batter. But it had worked.

Abbas seemed pleased with himself, and dismissed his "dayworkers." He even complimented them: "Thank you for a job well done. Here is your regular pay for a full day, even though you worked only a half-day," Abbas said, handing each agent a crisp 50-dollar bill. He then handed Rivera a 100-dollar bill, and said, "As a bonus, divide this among your men as you see fit. I have no more work for you. Do not come back here, or tell others to come here seeking work. Do not disclose any facts about work you have done for me. If you do, I'll notify the authorities about suspected illegal workers being here. Are we clear on that point?"

"Quite clear, sir," Rivera said, suppressing a smile. The agents walked to their old truck, departing without further words.

* * *

As the agents drove back to Gainesville's Hampton Inn, the conversation was lively.

"Alvarez, I thought Abbas might have seen me pass the receiving device to you," Rivera said. "But I don't think he did. He just kept on talking."

"If he did, he certainly didn't act like it," Alvarez confirmed. "He even smiled, and gave us a bonus. I was worried that Abbas might have noticed that I *twice* mowed the side of the runway where the 18-wheeler's trailer is hidden in the woods. That kept the device near the trailer much more often."

"I don't think he noticed that double-mow job. He would have said something if he had," Rivera remarked.

Moreno, the junior agent, finally spoke: "When we get back to our motel, I hope we find the device captured the information inside the computer Abbas has. And if I never see another fucking mouse in my entire life, or smell their shit, I'll be one happy Mexican! Never again, I hope."

The agents were chuckling as they pulled into the Hampton, each claiming dibs on the first shower.

"Senior agents go first," Rivera reminded them.

39

After Rivera showered, he placed his dirty clothes in a large black trash bag. He'd "borrowed" the bag from the unattended cleaning lady's cart that was conveniently parked outside the adjoining motel room. "I want all you guys to put your clothes in this same bag. I need to ask Agent Loveman about what we should do with these clothes. Might have some of that virus on them. Might be evidence."

Moreno, last to shower, finally spoke: "Boy, is it good to be clean again! That horrible smell—that mouse-shit smell—is still in the clothes we used," Moreno commented, stuffing his own work clothes into the plastic bag before sealing it.

Agent Rivera had busied himself trying to upload any information the geek-box may have captured. He had his personal laptop physically connected to the geek-box using nothing but a single USB cable. Moments later he smiled, then said, "Wow! The thing worked! There is a whole bunch of writing, but the text is Arabic, I think. The only thing I can read are numbers, which are like ones we use in English. I'm gonna call the boss," Rivera announced, referring to Louis Loveman.

Their boss answered his satphone on the first ring.

"Loveman, here."

"Rivera, sir. I've got information in my laptop ready to upload to the Bureau's secure site. What text I can see appears to be Arabic. There is a number sequence mentioned: 33.7353 followed by a forward slash, then 84.3894. I think they may be latitude and longitude numbers."

"Good work, Rivera. I'll put some of our translators on it right away. Give me 30 minutes and I'll call you right back. Please stand by."

"OK, sir," Rivera replied.

* * *

It only seemed "forever," but Rivera's phone finally beeped. Without delay, Loveman spoke excitedly. "Rivera, those numbers are indeed latitude and longitude … and they are *exactly* where Turner Field is located in Atlanta, Georgia. What a fine piece of work you guys have done on this one! There's a Braves vs. Cubs game there tonight, and my men here are trying to determine the exact time the game will start. Do you think Abbas has everything ready for a 'go' tonight?"

"I don't know, sir. The plane is ready. It's been topped off with fuel. We mowed the landing strip again today. We washed out the mouse houses, all three of them. We loaded the washings into a tank mounted on a trailer, then Abbas dismissed us. He indicated he had no further work for us. Essentially, he inferred he would contact the Immigration and Naturalization Service if we told others of possible work there, or if we gave details about anything we did while we worked for him."

"So, you think it boils down to Abbas getting the mouse-crap solution ready to put in the crop duster?"

"That's the way I read it, sir. But I don't know how long it takes Abbas to prepare the stuff for spraying."

"Rivera, please standby again. I'll call you back in a few," Loveman said, and clicked off.

* * *

"I think it's decision time for our boss," Rivera announced to his fellow agents. "I think he's trying to decide on busting them right now, or letting them go ahead with what should be a harmless spray job. That's if that filter in the plane does what it's supposed to do. I'd hate to be in Loveman's shoes right now. About making the decision, I mean."

Alvarez was going to say something, but the beeping satphone stopped him. Rivera answered it. Louis Loveman spoke excitedly: "I've talked with a microbiologist, who just happens to be my daughter. She says it should take less than an hour to prepare the fecal soup for spraying. They'd first centrifuge it to separate solids from liquids, then pass the liquid through a filter that would not trap the hantavirus particles, but would trap any particles that could clog the plane's spray nozzles. Then it's simply a matter of putting the filtered liquid into the chemical tank of the plane. The only thing that seems critical is not letting the temperature of the solution exceed 140 degrees during processing. She said exceeding that temperature could possibly kill the virus."

"What about the Arabic text I uploaded to the site?" Rivera asked.

"My translators tell me they are planning a first attempt about the fourth inning in the game tonight. They know it is sold out, and about 50,000 fans should be there."

"Why not bust them now? Do it before they leave Gainesville in the plane?" Rivera asked.

"I've given that a lot of thought," Lovemen replied. "There's three of you undercover guys, and three of them. The odds of a successful bust without one of you guys getting hurt is slim. On the other hand, you guys are probably better armed than they are. Have you seen any guns?"

"No," Rivera replied. "But I think Salaam is carrying a pistol in a shoulder holster beneath his jacket. At least he has a bulge in the right place. When we went inside the trailer, we found no arms or ammo. Their sleeping quarters aside, all we found inside was the equipment to prepare the stuff for the plane's chemical tank."

"Rivera, there's another angle to consider. As it stands now, the only solid case for nailing Abbas is the rape and kidnapping of a coed at the university where he taught virology. He even transported her across a state line and raped her. Those charges are quite serious in themselves, but I want him because he is a *terrorist*. We have a good case against him for stealing some laboratory equipment and viral cultures from the University of Arizona, but that's piddling stuff. Since Abbas is the legal owner of the plane, flying it without visible tail numbers is another charge, but still a relatively minor charge. If we can only add *attempted* bioterrorism to those charges, I think that will be the final nail in his coffin. Also, anyone who assisted Abbas will be easier to prosecute."

"So, you want him to *attempt*? Is that it, sir?"

"Yes, in a nutshell. Stay put at the Hampton Inn. Order room service if you guys are hungry. Just stay where you are, and keep your satphones on. Be sure your dark field dress and weapons are ready. I want your creds on your person. Continue to standby," Loveman said, before breaking the connection.

Rivera immediately turned to his men. "Guys, I think it's gonna hit the fan tonight. Or at least Loveman is willing to let them attempt to pull it off. Nobody leaves this room until we hear from Loveman. Get your dark field dress and weapons ready. Carry your creds. All satphones on," Rivera demanded, then used the house phone to order a large pizza sent to their room.

"I didn't hear you ask him what to do with that bag of stinking clothes we have," Moreno reminded.

"Shit!" Rivera muttered, slapping his forehead with his own palm. "I forgot, Moreno. You go put them in the trunk of our Crown Vic. I know we've been ordered not to leave this room, but go do it right now! I'll take blame for ordering you to break Loveman's orders. But be quick about it! OK? And be sure our car will start, and check its fuel level. Be sure to lock it up."

* * *

At the farm in Gainesville, the black crop duster's 120-gallon chemical tank had been filled to capacity with the processed virus-laden liquid. The plane had been pushed about 50 feet out of the shed, heading it down the grass runway. Aleem, Abbas, and Salaam slowly went to their knees, and soon bowed together on the ground, facing Mecca. After prayers, they checked their watches: 8:30. Aleem did his preflight, then announced, "It is time to fly." Abbas, then Aleem, boarded the crop duster. Before Aleem started the plane's engine, Abbas gave Salaam specific orders: "Return to the trailer, and remain inside to monitor the computer. Salaam, as you know, Abdul Qadeer is our most holy leader in Saudi Arabia. Send him a message that our mission here has begun! Allah willing, we will return in less than two hours, and we'll personally tell him of the results."

"Allah be with you!" Salaam exclaimed, just as Aleem started the duster's engine. Salaam watched as an essentially invisible plane headed through darkness toward the blue strobes flashing at the far end of the grass field. Without moonlight, or lights on the plane, only the direction of the engine's sound told Salaam they had at least taken off successfully. He waited until he could no longer hear the distinctive drone of the crop duster's engine, then slowly walked to the trailer. He removed his jacket and shoulder holster containing his Glock 17. He placed his pistol on top of the microwave, drank a glass of milk, then turned on the computer to send a "mission started" message to Abdul Qadeer.

* * *

Flying at 1,500 feet and maintaining 90 miles per hour airspeed, Aleem first identified I-85 as a good initial visual aid to follow on the ground. He knew that would lead him to I-75, which ran very close to the west side of the stadium in Atlanta. But he was not foolish enough to follow those highways alone; he would use the GPS coordinates received over their computer. They would put him directly on target. Over Northeast Atlanta, the bright lights of the city could not be missed. The brilliant stadium lights at Turner Field clearly stood out like a shining star among the ground clutter of dimmer lights. Once he had cleared the tall buildings north of the stadium, he swooped down to 500 feet, and slowed his airspeed to 80 miles per hour. Aleem could now clearly see the interior of the bowl-shaped baseball field which had *no* empty seats. *So many infidels packed in one place! Allah is with us!* he briefly thought, but immediately redirected his full attention to flying the plane.

The Cubs and Braves were now in the bottom of their fourth inning. The plane descended and Aleem entered the stadium over its north end. He cleared the large scoreboard located there by only a few feet at most. Over centerfield he immediately started spraying. The amber-colored vapor looked like an off-colored steam, one that glowed fluorescent in the bright stadium lights. The mist trailed behind the plane in the still night air, slowly sinking toward the field and stands. Over home plate he abruptly banked the crop duster and throttled up to make not one, but two, circular passes at 25 feet over the packed stadium seats. During his second pass, he noticed the fans had all panicked, and were trampling one another as they scrambled for the aisles. By the second pass, all players had run from the ball diamond, apparently using field-level exits beneath the stadium seats; the fans were still struggling to find a way to escape the foul-smelling fog that was settling upon them.

Abbas, sitting behind Aleem, uttered his first words of elation to his pilot. "Allah has guided your gifted hands! I can't wait to send the message to Abdul Qadeer. He will be so filled with praise for us."

"Dr. Abbas, our mission is not yet completed. We must successfully return to land in a small dark field. I have landed there only once before, and had the advantage of twilight. I will relax only after we land."

* * *

Salaam had taken his departing orders from Abbas seriously. He constantly watched their website, their major link of communication. Abdul Qadeer had quickly acknowledged the message about the mission's beginning: "Congratulations to all who have participated in 'Mouse Hunter,'" Abdul Qadeer had replied, using the code name he had personally chosen for the operation.

Salaam took his eyes off the screen to pour himself another glass of milk. When he returned to the monitor, a flashing message from Abdul Qadeer appeared in Arabic text:

ATTENTION MOUSE HUNTER! THE AMERICAN FBI IS FULLY AWARE OF THE OPERATION. THEY ARE PLANNING A RAID ON THE GAINESVILLE FARM EARLY IN THE MORNING. WHEN THE CROP DUSTER RETURNS TONIGHT, ALL THREE OF YOU ARE TO REMAIN ON SITE. I AM SENDING A LARGER PLANE TO RESCUE THE THREE OF YOU. IT WILL BE THERE BY MIDNIGHT, LOCAL TIME. IT WILL TAKE YOU TO A SAFE PLACE. DESTROY THE COMPUTER BEFORE YOU LEAVE. MAY ALLAH BE WITH ALL OF YOU. —ABDUL QADEER.

Salaam blinked rapidly as he reread the message. Panic struck him. He had no way to notify Aleem and Abbas, who should be on their way back by now. Flashlight in hand, he stepped into the darkness outside the trailer to listen. He cupped an ear with his hand, and finally he heard the unmistakable distant drone of the crop duster's engine. The runway's blue strobes began flashing, and the engine sounds quickly grew louder. Completely unlit itself, the little black plane landed moments later. The runway strobes immediately went out. Pilot Aleem skillfully taxied to a perfect stop in front of the shed.

40

"Come! Come now. We have trouble!" Salaam exclaimed, as Aleem and Abbas clambered down from the plane. "Quick, come to the trailer. Look at the computer. We have a most urgent message from Abdul Qadeer!" Salaam yelled, motioning toward the trailer with his flashlight.

Inside the trailer all three men now stared at the monitor. Abbas first read the message silently, then aloud. "How could this be! I bet it is those dayworkers. I knew they were too smart to be dumb Mexicans. They have turned us in ... and now I don't know where they are! We have no way to get revenge."

"The two of us could escape right now," Aleem said, smiling and looking at Abbas. "The plane has room for two. We have gas. I have charts for the entire Southeastern U.S. You could let Salaam escape in your car."

"Not on your life!" Salaam said, retrieving his Glock from atop the microwave, and sticking it in his waistband. "We all leave together, or *none* of us will leave here alive!"

"I agree," Abbas said. "The message from Abdul Qadeer says to 'remain on site.' And if we break the Holy One's order, we will only be in deeper trouble. Salaam, you would not have to kill us, or yourself. Abdul Qadeer would see that it is done! I suggest we *all* wait for the larger plane as ordered ... and we should immediately burn the computer!"

* * *

At the Lee Gilmer Memorial Airport in Gainesville, Cal Camarada kissed a tearful Shima Kye goodbye, then tarried just long enough to see her board a commuter flight bound for Atlanta, to meet her connecting flight to Tucson, Arizona.

Cal walked briskly to general aviation, then went to the specific hanger that was supposed to house his Cessna 310. His friend in Kissimmee, Ben Hunter, had not let him down. An attendant helped

Cal pull the plane to the concrete apron, and gladly accepted the $20 tip offered. His quick preflight indicated his plane was filled with fuel and ready to fly. The cold engines were a little sluggish in starting, but quickly evened out as they warmed.

In ten minutes Cal was at 9,000 feet east of Gainesville, and in a holding pattern over the darkness of the chicken farm. By satphone, Cal called Louis Loveman. "Yo, Louis. It's me, Cal. I'm just holding over the farm at 9,000. What's next?"

"Pick up the bad guys at the chicken farm," Louis replied. "It's very important that you tell them you were sent there by *Abdul Qadeer*. My geeks hacked their computer, and sent them a false message, one they think came directly from Qadeer himself. He's the head of their central leadership in Saudi Arabia. They think the FBI is going to raid the farm in the morning. The false message told them Abdul Qadeer has arranged to extract them by air tonight, well before the FBI's so-called raid in the morning. They have no idea you'll instead be flying them to our interrogation and detention center in Kentucky, the one we discussed earlier on the satphone."

"You clever bastard!" Cal exclaimed.

"You comfortable landing on grass in Gainesville at night?"

"I'd be more comfortable at a controlled field, like they have at the Kentucky detention center, but I've got the coordinates, and a great GPS. I'll make a couple of low passes over the grass strip, and maybe someone on the ground will get the idea to turn on some lights at the approach ends of the runway. That's all I need, but I could probably do it by GPS alone."

"I know my undercover guys installed some blue strobes at the southwestern end of the runway. They are activated by a radio signal sent from the duster's cockpit," Louis explained.

"I'm going down now to buzz them a time or two. Keep your phone on, Louis," Cal said, then rested his own satphone in the empty copilot's seat.

At 450 feet, Cal flew directly over the GPS points he had. After the third low-altitude pass, Aleem smiled. "That sounds like a twin to me. Let me go outside to the crop duster and turn on the radio-controlled blue strobes. That will mark that end of the field. Then I can turn on the lights the crop duster has. That will mark the other end. I know about flying. Our rescue pilot is simply hunting the ends of the runway!"

Cal picked up the satphone resting in the seat to his right. "Louis, at least they are not entirely brain dead. Got blue strobes at the southwest approach, and there's a dark little plane lit like a Christmas tree at the other end. I'm going in. Uh … Abdul Qadeer's the name of the guy … the guy who sent me, right?"

"Roger, Abdul Qadeer," Loveman confirmed. "And their code name for the operation is 'Mouse Hunter.'"

Cal made a perfect landing. He didn't even turn on his landing lights until all the plane's wheels touched the ground. *Would be just like those bastards to leave a tractor or some piece of shit parked in the runway!* he thought, trying to remember the last time he'd landed on grass. He slowly taxied toward the crop duster in front of the shed, and turned the Cessna 310 around, but left the engines idling.

The three men had gathered on the plane's left side. Cal opened his cockpit window and yelled down to them. "Abdul Qadeer has sent me to pick you up. Everyone from Mouse Hunter please come aboard quickly!"

Al Abbas was first to scramble aboard. He immediately sat in the copilot seat. "I am sitting on something that is uncomfortable," Abbas complained, and removed Cal's satphone, which remained turned on. "I hope I did not damage your instrument," Abbas said, and casually passed the satphone to Cal. With equal casualness, Cal dropped the phone into his shirt pocket.

Aleem assumed a seat behind Abbas. Salaam climbed aboard, but in his effort to do so, his Glock slipped from his waistband, bounced off a wing and fell to the ground. "I'm sorry, sir," Salaam said, "but I've dropped my gun. I need to get back out and get it."

"Where Abdul Qadeer has requested I take you, you'll have no need for a gun. We are leaving now!" Cal said, and throttled up. Five minutes later, and 1,500 feet up, Cal banked to the left. He could still see the flashing blue strobes as well as the lights on the crop duster. He watched those lights out of the corner of his eye, using them as easy reference points. Cal slipped the satphone from his pocket and spoke loudly into it: "This is Cal Camarada. Please forward this message to Abdul Qadeer. All men from Mouse Hunter have been successfully picked up. I repeat, *all men from Mouse Hunter have been picked up.* We are now heading to the arranged safe meeting place. Camarada, clear."

"So, you have direct communication to our central leadership?" Abbas asked.

"Yes, I have very direct communication," Cal replied, smiling.

"Why are you now turning back toward the field?" Aleem questioned over the twin-engine's noise.

"Because I am going to God's Heaven ... and you, gentlemen, are all going to Allah's Paradise. Relax ... your virgins will want you well rested!"

Flying at full throttle, Cal dove straight toward the crop duster parked in front of the shed. He then leveled out flying only a few feet above the grass. Only Aleem seemed to realize what was happening, but found himself so paralyzed by fear he could do nothing; he could not make himself reach forward to grab the yoke and make the Cessna 310 pull up. At 195 miles an hour, and six feet off the ground, the 310 first struck the duster, then the other items beneath the shed. A gigantic fireball erupted as the Cessna's wingtip fuel tanks impacted the stationary fuel tanks beneath the shed. Cal's plane actually exited the backside of the remaining shed structure, then traveled several yards into the woods, where trees ruptured the 310's larger remaining internal tanks. Their leaking fuel immediately burst into additional flames coalescing with those of the massive inferno immediately behind.

* * *

In Boulder, Colorado, tears ran down the face of Louis Loveman. He was sitting at the desk in his study at his farm, still clutching his satphone in disbelief. He didn't hear every word over the phone, but he'd certainly heard enough to know exactly what had happened. His German shepherd, Sampson, sensed his master's distress. Still holding the satphone, Louis reclined on the sofa in his study. Sampson climbed aboard the sofa (normally not allowed!) and began licking Loveman's salty tears. "God, why? Why did Cal have to do it that way?" Louis asked his dog, as if he expected his canine companion to answer the questions for him. Cal's final words played over and over in his mind: *Because I am going to God's Heaven ... and you, gentlemen, are all going to Allah's Paradise. Relax ... your virgins will want you well rested!*

* * *

Knowing that within the FAA, the Office of Aircraft Accident Investigation (AAI) is the principal organization which investigates aviation accidents, Louis Loveman began making a series of calls. He first called AAI, then Agent Rivera, to tell his undercover men what had happened and to continue their standby at Hampton Inn. The call he dreaded the most was calling his daughter, Cindy, and the others located in Tucson.

He first reached Cindy, who was at the apartment taking a "TV break" from working on her dissertation. "Brad's at the lab working late, Dad. I'm glad you called. I was about to call you. Have you seen the TV news? KGUN? It's our Channel 9 here, probably your ABC in Boulder. They have breaking news about two planes that just crashed in a rural area of Gainesville, Georgia. Have you heard from Cal?"

"Honey, I'm afraid so. Cal apparently had the three terrorists aboard his plane. All are probably dead … including Cal. The FAA will be investigating, but there's little doubt in my mind that one of the planes was Cal's, and I'm almost positive he had Abbas, Salaam, and Aleem aboard with him when he crashed."

Cindy first burst into tears, then managed to say "No more Uncle Cal. No godfather." Cindy's sobbing slowly stopped. She hadn't lost it altogether. Her scientific mind kicked in. "The mice, Dad! The mice! Who is guarding the mouse houses? If they escape, this could change the whole dynamic regarding hantavirus infections acquired directly from the local environment there in Gainesville."

"Fortunately, my undercover men are all safe. When it happened, they were away from the scene, waiting on standby at the Gainesville Hampton. I'll send them to the farm immediately and have them guard the mouse houses. I know we all need to talk further. Call Brad, Dr. Telfair, and his wife, Anne. Set up a speakerphone call where we can all talk. I'm sorry to rush off, leaving you with such bad news, but I've got a bunch of calls to make within the Bureau. I love you, Cin. Call when you have set up a conference call."

* * *

Cindy quickly set up a conference call to begin at noon in the apartment. She notified her dad, who had arrived at the Denver Field Office. She gave up on working on her dissertation. She watched several TV stations but kept coming back to Channel 9, which seemed to have the best coverage. The news of the Gainesville crash soon became overshadowed by more "breaking news" coming from Turner Field in Atlanta.

Don Herrington, the morning newscaster for Tucson's KGUN, began: "Last night in Atlanta, in what may have been a prank, a crop duster pilot halted the first game between the Braves and Cubs at Turner Field. It happened at the bottom of the fourth inning. An unnamed source has mentioned possible terrorism, but we have no official confirmation to support that claim. The CDC is actively looking into the matter. From droplets of spray accumulated on rooftop skylights, CDC scientists have collected enough of the sprayed liquid to examine in their laboratories. Area hospitals are still completely overrun by patients fearing they have been poisoned by the liquid the crop duster sprayed on them. Three fatalities are known to have occurred when fans at Turner Field panicked, and were trampled to death by other fans. An additional death of a fan is thought to be due to a heart attack, but we have no official word from the Office of the Medical Examiner. Authorities have yet to release any names of those who died. Spokespersons for area hospitals indicate many more were injured during the stampede to exit the stadium. The total number of injured is expected to be in the hundreds. Stay tuned. After a brief commercial break, our reporter, Sally Moran will have a live interview at Turner Field with a witness who actually saw the plane fly into the stadium."

Cindy waited through a breakfast cereal commercial, one that promised lower cholesterol and better colon health. Another commercial for a prescription medication for arthritis followed, and listed more side effects (including death) than benefits. *You'd have to be crazy to take that stuff,* she thought, just as the live TV interview with Homer Smith began:

Reporter: "I'm Sally Moran, reporting for Tucson's KGUN. I'm here at Atlanta's Turner Field. I have with me Mr. Homer Smith, who lives in Atlanta. He and his family attended the Braves game last night. Exactly where were you seated, Homer?"

Homer: "We was a settin' directly behind home plate, four rows up," Homer said, pointing from their standing position at the pitcher's mound. The KGUN camera man quickly panned to the empty stadium seats behind home plate. Knowing he was off-camera, Homer quickly popped a prune-sized wad of Red Man into his mouth, adjusted something in his crotch, and turned the bill of his ball cap so it pointed forward. The KGUN camera returned to Homer and the reporter.

Reporter: "And when did you first realize something was wrong?"

Homer: "I didn't, at first. I thought it was some kinda joke. 'At plane was black as smut all over, an' ain't got the first number on it. No lights on it neither. I been in the Air Force awhile back, an' I know planes is gotta have numbers. And they's required to have lights, if they's a flyin' at night."

Reporter: "So that's what caught your attention first? A black plane with no numbers or lights?"

Homer: "Reckon so, but what caught my attention—big time!—was when he started sprayin'. It smelled just like pure … well, don't reckon I can say that on TV, but it smelled like a cross 'tween a road-killed skunk an' a outhouse what needed a heap of lime. Terrible smell!"

Reporter: "Which direction did the plane come from?"

Homer: "From north. Popped up right behind th' big scoreboard sign back behind second base, you know. His wheels musta missed hittin' the top of th' sign by inches. But then I seen that son of … don't reckon I can say that on TV, but that sucker really knowed how to fly that duster. He made two circles 'bout 25 foot over the stands, sprayin' all of us real good, you know. Then he hauled … is 'butt' OK to say on TV?"

Reporter: "I think so Homer. Are you feeling any ill effects from the spray?"

Homer: "Well, I throwed up when I got home last night. So did the wife and kids. First I thought it was 'em ballpark hotdogs, but now I ain't so sure. Maybe we're all gonna be fine, now that we finally got th' stink off us. I sure hope they catch the fella what done it."

Reporter: "Thank you Mr. Smith. KGUN appreciates you taking the time to explain to our viewers what you saw firsthand here at Turner Field. I hope you develop no ill effects."

41

From the Tucson apartment, the conference call to Louis Loveman originated promptly at noon. Brad, Cindy, and the Telfairs were all in somber moods. On the phone, Louis sounded absolutely exhausted, yet his mind seemed sharp as he fielded and asked questions.

Cindy had the first question. "Dad, are they still sure it was Cal's plane?"

"Yes," Louis answered. "They are also sure the other plane was an unoccupied Piper PA-25. There were four occupants in Cal's Cessna. All are charred beyond recognition. A medical examiner is on the scene, and the bodies are going to be moved to the ME's facility in Atlanta to attempt to get a positive identification."

"Did any of the mouse houses get damaged?" Brad asked.

"No. They are at least 3,500 feet away. All of them are way down at the other end of the field. My undercover guys are now closely guarding those houses," Louis explained.

"Who's feeding and watering the mice?" Mark asked. "And how were they feeding them before, without any of them getting out?"

"No one is feeding or watering them now. Before, my men would simply kick the bottom of the doors before opening them. This caused the mice inside to scatter to the far ends of the houses and pile up in the corners. While all the mice were at the other end of house, they'd quickly slide in a shallow pan of food and place a tray filled with well water. Rivera has told me neither he nor his men have ever seen a single mouse escape during feeding and watering. I've instructed my men to see that the mouse house doors now remain locked at all times," Louis said. "But I do have a question, one possibly best answered by Cindy or Brad. What is the best way to *exterminate* all the mice without taking a chance by opening doors?"

Cindy immediately spoke up: "Stop feeding them their regular food. Begin feeding them some poison, like warfarin."

"*Warfarin?* What the hell is that?" Louis immediately asked.

"Dad, it's the same thing as Coumadin, a blood thinner that is used in humans to help prevent unwanted blood clots."

"Is that stuff safe for my men to handle?" Louis asked.

"Yes," Cindy replied. "Those mice have a very small body mass. They weigh only about three-quarters of an ounce. Even a small amount of warfarin is a very massive overdose for them. It causes them to bleed internally, go into shock, and die. The commercial rodent poisons contain only very small amounts of warfarin. Your men would have to intentionally eat a bunch of it to put them in danger."

"I see," Loveman replied. "Where can we get the stuff, this warfarin?"

"Almost any hardware store, or a place like Home Depot will have it. Trade name is d-Con, best I remember. Comes in pellets, about the size of a BB. The stuff is dirt cheap. I'd have them get several pounds of it, then put about a pound in each house. I agree it's not wise to open the doors under any circumstances."

"Anybody have any suggestions about getting the warfarin inside the houses without the risk of opening the doors?" Louis asked.

Mark, who'd largely been silent thus far, spoke up. "Louis, I assume the houses all have a metal roof, right?"

"Correct."

"Why not have your men punch a small hole in the roof? Then drop the warfarin through the hole? They could even stick the snout of a funnel through the hole, then pour the stuff in directly from bags or boxes, however it comes packaged. We know Abbas had them put acrylic panels on the interior walls to prevent the mice from climbing them. A small hole in the roof certainly would not create a possible route for escape."

"There's a problem with that," Cindy chimed in. "The pellets are small, and might fall through the mesh floor to the concrete floor below. Then the mice couldn't get to the warfarin at all. I know you can buy the stuff prepackaged in small boxes about twice the size of a book of matches. Don't worry. The mice will instinctively chew through the small boxes, because it smells like there's 'food' inside them."

"Good thinking, Mark and Cindy," Louis said. "We'll do it that way. Just make a hole in the roof that's big enough to drop the small boxes through, then maybe seal that hole back up as an extra precaution."

"Not so fast!" Bradley commented. "I'm confident a few pounds of warfarin would kill them all. Might take several days for all of them to die. But then what? We've got a huge number of *dead* hanta-infected mice ... and we have no data on how long the hantavirus remains viable in a dead mouse. We think the virus can live for several years in their dried fecal droppings. I'd personally feel more comfortable if the mouse houses were all burned to the ground *after* we're sure the infected mice are all dead."

"Another good point," Louis commented.

"So, Dad," Cindy said, "it sounds like the scene is fairly secure."

"I think so. The Hall County Sheriff's Department is guarding the road into the place, as well as the perimeter around the crash site. The FAA has closed the airspace over the entire farm. This was done to keep the news choppers from disturbing the scene with downwash from their rotors. Fortunately, there has been no wind. If the wind had been blowing, several adjoining properties could have been endangered by fire. Local fire departments are still dealing with a few hotspots at the perimeter of the burn, but essentially the fire is completely under control."

"Have they found any evidence of foul play at the scene?" Brad asked. "I mean like blood or weapons, stuff like that?"

"No blood," Louis said. "The only thing they've found thus far is a gun that was on the ground. It was out on the grass runway about 150 feet from the shed. It's a Glock 17. The magazine was full, and they don't think it has been fired, at least not close to the time of the crash. That gun was considered evidence, and it's going to our lab for analysis. Might get some prints, who knows? I doubt we'll learn much."

"What happened to the 18-wheeler's trailer? The place where the bad guys were staying at night, and preparing the stuff to put into their crop duster?" Anne asked.

"All of that remains pretty much intact. The truck is about 150 feet from where the shed was. The paint on the cab of the truck is blistered, the windshield glass warped from the intense heat, but the interior of the insulated trailer seems fine. Fortunately, the truck's diesel tanks didn't burst and contribute to the fire. The computer they had inside the trailer is missing, but the guys from AAI have found a pile of ashes they think are the remains of that computer. We're gonna let our geeks have a go at the remains, but I doubt they'll be able to recover any information."

Cindy began twirling her platinum ponytail. "Uh, Dad. Did any of the AAI guys actually go inside the trailer? We think it is possible Abbas had his breeder stock of mice inside that trailer, or at least he did at one time. Remember?"

"Excellent point, Cin. I'll talk with AAI, and find out who the guys were. I'm assuming you think they should be given some of Brad's anti-hanta globlulin?"

"Right. And do it promptly! I know the risk of the AAI guys acquiring hanta is small, but remember the terrorists who were living inside the trailer had probably been pre-protected by anti-hanta globulin regularly administered to them by Abbas. I'm not worried about those who worked with the remains of the aircraft. Those sites would have been sterilized by the intense fire."

"Excellent point again, Cindy. I'll start putting together a list of personnel who actually entered the trailer," Louis said.

Anne didn't seem to be her usual outspoken self, but Mark sensed she was thinking a mile a minute. She finally spoke: "Louis, more and more pieces seem to be fitting together, but several things puzzle me about this whole scenario."

"Like what?" Louis asked.

"Like how did the terrorists all end up getting into Cal's plane? Were they forced to board the plane at gunpoint? Were they somehow tricked? Were they alive before the crash, or had they been killed and then put inside the plane?"

The long pause before Loveman's response to Anne's questions told everyone the same thing: The words in his answer were being carefully chosen.

Louis began: "Anne, I cannot lie to you. I won't lie to Cindy and Brad, nor to Mark. All I'm going to say is that the terrorists were all alive and voluntarily boarded Cal's plane. I realize that doesn't fully answer your questions, but to explain it fully I would have to break a solemn promise I made to Cal. The promise was not to share with others certain things we discussed by satphone shortly prior to his death."

* * *

The satphone call soon ended. Mark and Anne elected to walk back to their RV. The afternoon was surprisingly cool, the pace of their walking a slow amble at best.

"Little Man," Anne said, "I have a strange feeling there's still a lot we don't know about Cal Camarada and Louis Loveman."

"Like what?"

"Like their private conversations on their satphones. I think Louis has been truthful with us, but he's openly admitted there are certain things he will not reveal."

Mark chuckled. "Anne, you're all woman. You're also all the woman I'll ever want, but you're curious as a darn cat! Granted, Louis and Cal may have some secrets. They have a right to have secrets, just like you and I do."

"Yeah, but most of our secrets take place in the bedroom. The variety of sexual things we like and do to each other remains there."

"As it should," Mark said, turning the key in their RV's door.

"What if I said I want to do some of those things right now?"

"I'd say you've just read my mind."

* * *

Their 'mindreading' covered several chapters in the *Kama Sutra*, plus a few things that were not in any book either had ever read. Only the mirrored ceiling in their bedroom had captured their "secrets." Both knew that mirror would never talk. Completely relaxed, and with the sadness over Cal's death waning, they both entered a deep sleep that lasted several hours. They awoke hungry.

"I'm so relaxed, I don't feel like cooking," Anne said.

"Me neither. What about Chinese? There's a Chinese restaurant about two blocks from here. Wanna give it a try?" Mark asked.

"Are you asking me out on a date?" Anne teased.

"You bet! Any woman who's as good as you are at the Lotus position deserves a night out of the kitchen!" Mark exclaimed.

"Any man that can last as long as you do during my Lotus deserves to choose the restaurant!" Anne shot back.

"*Any man?* I thought I was your first. You've tried it on other men?" Mark asked, a tinge of jealousy in his voice.

"No. Never. I've previously told you, Little Man! You were my very first all-the-way guy. I just don't want to mess with perfect."

"Me neither! Let go eat," Mark said, smiling so broadly it raised his ears.

"Let's check our e-mail before we go to the restaurant," Anne said. There was only a single message, one they wished they hadn't read:

```
Dear Mark and Anne,

Please forgive me for departing without giving
you two wonderful people a proper goodbye.
Being medical professionals, you were fully
aware of my condition prior to death. That
```

doesn't make it any easier for me to admit that I truly loved you both. I'd place my feelings toward you two right up there with my love for my country, its freedom, and those who are fighting for it. In case you're wondering, I placed this message in the Drafts folder of my computer at the condo. I instructed Shima Kye to send it after my death had been confirmed.

Forever yours, forever an American,

— Cal

PS: By U.S. mail, you and Anne will receive a token of my appreciation for your friendship. It may be several months in reaching you. Be sure to leave a forwarding address with Cindy and Brad.

"Shit," Mark and Anne muttered simultaneously. They hugged and cried until they ran out of tears. The thought of Chinese food now nauseated them both. Their wonderful lovemaking session had been completely overshadowed by a single e-mail message. Both knew it was going to take much longer than they had thought to get over Cal's death.

Mark finally spoke: "Anne, I think it's time we move our RV."

"Agreed," Anne said. "I think we've done all we can do here. Maybe some distance will help us forget this entire episode."

"Would you feel comfortable going back to the Georgia coast?" Mark asked.

"Yes! As long as we don't have to go through Gainesville, Georgia. I know in a few years we'll probably both have trouble remembering stuff. Right now, all I want to do is *forget stuff!*" Anne exclaimed, amid a new flood of tears.

42

Their night in the RV was restless—a jumble of bad dreams separated only by periods of brief catnapping.

"I wonder if Cindy and Brad received a similar goodbye e-mail from Cal?" Anne asked, at 3:00 a.m.

"I'd hate to call them this late. Just because we can't sleep, certainly doesn't mean they can't," Mark replied.

"How long will it take you to have our camper ready to travel, Little Man?" Anne asked.

"Couple of days. Our tires are beginning to show some dry rot. Even though they've got a safe amount of tread left, I don't want to do a long-haul without a new set of tires ... and I can't just up and leave without saying goodbye to the special folks we have met here in Tucson."

"Neither can I," Anne admitted. "Especially without the goodbyes and thanks to those who saved my life. And next week we've both got our follow-up appointments with Dr. Baxter. He's supposed to review all the lab tests and x-rays he did with our complete physicals. He said he'd also give us copies of our medical records, ones that have our real names on them. And I'd promised Brad I'd donate another unit of blood to replenish his lab's supply of anti-hanta globulin ... that's if Dr. Baxter feels my hemoglobin level will permit me to donate again so soon."

"So, you still want to go back to Georgia?" Mark asked, knowing women have a propensity for changes of mind, though Anne rarely did that.

"Yeah, back to Georgia. Definitely! But not just *any* place in Georgia. I'd like to go back to exactly where we were living when we first retired."

"That means you are talking about Dunham Point, where we built our initial retirement home. Anne, you know we've sold that home, and I'd bet it's not for resale again."

"I don't care, as long as it's somewhere in or near Dunham Point. And I really don't care if it's exactly the same house, or if it's one similar to it. If we can afford to, we can keep our RV and park it in our yard, or even build a special garage for it. But I also want a *real* home ... one *without* wheels! I want something fixed to the ground next to the marsh or the river there in Dunham. My brain just won't let me forget the natural beauty, the wildlife, and that special scent of salt that is created only by the environment there. I've totally gotten over my fear of the Sinaloa Cartel. But if we end up with a real home there, you've gotta *promise* me one thing, Little Man," Anne said.

"Like what? Like we can occasionally go outside to the RV to have sex beneath its mirrored ceiling?"

Anne smiled, then gave him a playful slap. "No silly! We promise ourselves that we'll never let ourselves become involved in solving drug-smuggling crimes again. Never! But I'd still enjoy an occasional fling in our camper!"

"Anne, I can certainly live with that promise. About the drug smuggling, I mean. But what if we discovered some possible local terroristic activity? Are we just supposed to sit on our butts and keep our mouths shut? Just ignore it?"

"Mark, get serious! *Terroristic activity?* Out in the middle of nowhere? Down in rural coastal McIntosh County, Georgia?"

"You're probably right, Anne. The probability of terrorists being there is essentially nil. But neither of us ever thought we'd encounter drug smuggling in McIntosh County. But we did. And because of that, we had to sacrifice our original retirement home in Dunham Point, and several years of our lives ... while we lost our identities in federal witness protection—that darn WITSEC program! But have you ever thought about *real* sacrifice?" Mark asked.

"*Real?* Like how?" she asked.

"Like Cal and Louis putting their lives on the line every time they flew their combat missions in their F-86s in Korea. Like how a large number of folks in *our* generation were never touched by the real sacrifices ... like during World War I, the Great Depression, World War II, the Korean War, and some of us not even by that war in Vietnam. I think Cal had his priorities right in his goodbye e-mail: 'love of country, love of freedom, love of those who fight for it,' or something very close to that. Anne, should I observe it, I could *never* promise to ignore some potential terroristic threat against our country!"

"Me neither, Little Man. So, let's just avoid the drug smugglers."

"Let's try to get a little sleep ... and dream about Georgia before we call Cindy and Brad," Mark said, yawning, as they finally nodded off in each other's arms.

250

* * *

Still in their camper at a little after 10:00 a.m. the next morning, the Telfairs called Cindy and Brad's apartment. Cindy answered, and sounded like she was coming down with a cold.

"Cindy, are you catching a cold?" Mark asked.

"No. I've been crying … trying to get over an e-mail that Cal had Shima Kye send here. Obviously it was written before his death, and I guess I really let his message get to me emotionally. Over the years, it's something I've wondered about, but kept shoving to the back of my mind."

"What in the message upset you, Cindy?" Mark asked.

There was a long pause before Cindy replied. "Mark, I'm not trying to be coy or secretive. It's sort of a personal thing about me, my mom, my dad, and Cal. I don't want to get into it and start crying all over again. I've just got too much work left to do on my dissertation to lose control of my emotions again."

"I understand completely," Mark replied. "Anne and I had a tearful reaction to the e-mail message Cal sent to us. He simply apologized for not giving us a 'proper goodbye,' and said that he loved us both."

"Thanks for your understanding, Mark. Maybe I'll one day feel comfortable sharing it with you and Anne."

"Have you talked to Louis recently?" Mark asked.

"Yes. Emotionally, Dad's a wreck. He's even taken several days of sick leave, something he hasn't done in all the years he's been with the FBI. He also received an e-mail from Cal, one written before his death and subsequently sent by Shima Kye. In fact, Dad even read the entire e-mail to me over the phone. It really didn't say much, other than a long letter would be sent to him at the proper time, whatever that 'proper time' may be."

"Speaking of 'proper times,' and I'm not sure if now is the right time, but I want to let you know how much we've appreciated your and Brad's hospitality and assistance with the successful treatment of Anne's hantavirus infection. Especially, we appreciate the friendship through it all. I just wanted to let you guys know that, before we leave Tucson."

"Leave? Like when?"

"Cindy, it's a decision Anne and I made last night. Realistically, we'll probably be on the road heading for Georgia in a week or so. Before we leave, be sure to tell Bradley that Anne will donate some more blood, if her hemoglobin level will permit it. We'll see you guys

251

in person before we get going again."

"Promise?" Cindy asked.

"Promise," Mark confirmed, and clicked off.

* * *

Mark relayed his phone conversation with Cindy to Anne, who had yet to get out of bed. Both still felt quite depressed about Cal's death, but Anne much more so than Mark.

"Anne, we can't just mope around here all day inside the camper. Let's go shopping for some tires, and fill up with diesel."

"OK, you're right. Just *thinking* about all the things we need to do won't get them done. After we get the new tires and fuel, I'll start working on our computer. I'll pick out a good interstate-avoiding route back to Georgia. Want to plan on it taking us about four days to get there?"

"Sounds good. That will keep us to a little under 500 miles a day. Try to find an acceptable RV park in Georgia, one on the coast. We can stay there while we're looking for our permanent place," Mark suggested.

"Mark, I haven't changed my mind about our permanent place. It's still Dunham Point. I'll try to find a fairly nice RV park that is close to Dunham, and we'll just take potluck for the overnight stops before we get there."

"Attagirl," Mark said, extending his hand to pull Anne out of bed. He was trying to sound and act more cheerful than he actually felt. "And be thinking of something nice we can do for Cindy and Brad. Maybe fix them a nice meal and serve it right here in our camper. A little going-away party, so to speak. They've never visited us socially inside our camper before, and they might enjoy being with us here at least one time before we leave."

* * *

It took six hours to find the best local buy for their RV tires, but Mark complained more about the cost of the 50 gallons of diesel (at $1.51 a gallon) than he did about the $600 they'd just spent on six new tires. He didn't complain at all about the cost of the frozen lobster tails they'd purchased at a nearby seafood market.

While driving back to Pima-Swan, Mark said "One day we're not going to be able to afford to drive this RV very much."

"One day we won't care!" Anne shot back. "I hope we live long enough to be happy with walkers or wheelchairs. Let's just enjoy what we've got while we can. I'm still looking forward to our new little house without wheels, and we'll just take it from there."

She's getting out of her depression caused by Cal's death, Mark thought.

* * *

The next morning at 9:15, they had their final follow-up visit with Dr. Baxter. They held their breath as he detailed the results of test after test. "Bottom line, I have to give you both a clean bill of health," Baxter finally said, smiling. "If you want to stick around the office for about 15 minutes, I'll have them make you a copy of your name-corrected medical records. Please take them with you when you leave," he said. "Not many doctors have hanta survivors. I do hope your friends at UA who are working on hanta end up developing a vaccine. And I'm very sorry your friend, Cal Camarada, is really beyond further treatment."

"You do know he *died,* don't you?" Anne asked.

"What! No kidding! He died? I'm shocked that it happened so quickly. He must have hemorrhaged into one of those metastatic brain tumors," Dr. Baxter said, a total look of surprise stamped on his face.

"Plane crash," Mark quickly explained.

"I'm sorry to hear that, and even more sorry there were no good treatment options left for him. Not even here at UMC, or anywhere else for that matter. As a guest, I attended the UMC conference we held here about Mr. Camarada's case. After listening to all options, he declined further treatment except radiation. I didn't say so at the time, but I think he made the right decision. With known brain tumors, and multiple tumor deposits in multiple bones, I'm surprised he could pass a flight medical. Was anyone else in the plane with him?"

"We don't know all the details yet," Anne said, then impulsively gave Dr. Baxter a kiss on the cheek.

"You're still my miracle patient! Stay in touch," Baxter said, blushing.

* * *

Two days later, inside the Telfairs' camper at Pima-Swan, Cindy and Brad had joined them for a final evening meal together. Cindy quickly dubbed it "The Last Supper." Anne had prepared a lobster bisque to die for. Cindy raved about Anne's meal and wanted details of the recipe she had used. "Got it off the Internet yesterday," Anne finally admitted, then gave Cindy the website where she'd found it.

Cindy initially abstained from the white wine Anne had chosen for the meal, but as the conversation continued, Cindy finally accepted a two-ounce shot glass as being the limit of wine her small body could handle. Even though she sipped it, as others were doing with the standard wine glasses, Cindy got tipsy, and began speaking emotionally:

"When you guys pull out of here, please don't let this be the end of our friendship. *Please,*" Cindy said dabbing at tears. "Our focus on research has gotten us both branded as 'eggheads,' but neither of us care. I've told you earlier, Brad and I are dedicating our lives to developing a vaccine for hantavirus. We may never accomplish that objective. We'll marry, but don't plan to have children. In a way, I guess I'll be friendless after you guys leave."

"Don't talk that way, Cindy!" Mark said, echoing similar words spoken by Anne.

"But you don't understand! I haven't even told Brad yet," Cindy said, tears now a flood. Still seated at the camper dinette, Brad tenderly put his arm around her and pulled her to his shoulder to cry upon.

Mark and Anne looked at one another. It seemed their intended jovial farewell party had just crashed. Anne reached across the narrow table and held Cindy's hand before softly speaking. "Cindy, when you and Brad befriended us, Mark and I were going through some very bad times. We didn't have any friends either, because our whole identity had become a lie. We had no friends we could confide in. Are you pregnant? Are you in some witness protection? Is there something we don't know about?"

Cindy sat upright and dried her eyes with a napkin. "I'm not pregnant, Anne. I wouldn't have drunk even that tiny bit of wine if I were. Neither Brad nor I are in some witness protection thing. Our legal and only names are, and always have been, Cynthia Gayle Loveman and Bradley Burrows Buck."

"Then what is it?" Anne tenderly asked.

"My *father* has just died," Cindy softly whispered, and she began to tremble as her fresh flood of tears came.

"What! You're kidding us! *Louis* has died?" Anne asked.

"No. It's Cal!" Cindy said.

EPILOGUE

The Telfairs' four-day RV trip back to Georgia was uneventful. Somehow lingering sadness over Cal's death made the trip seem much longer. Before leaving Tucson, and using their laptop computer, Anne had found a one-star RV park located at Shellman Bluff in McIntosh County, Georgia. From that park, when looking north across the Julienton River and its marsh, they could now actually see Dunham Point. Subsequently they bought property in Dunham, and would soon contract with a builder for the construction of their second retirement home there. The elation over getting back to the coast was marred by the tragic events of 9/11; it happened only a few days after their arrival on the Georgia coast. Sitting in their camper and watching TV coverage of the Twin Towers going down caused them to mutually agree: They'd both help stop terrorism if any opportunity ever presented them with a chance to rid their country of this scourge. Little did they know, in three months, Anne would go to their mailbox at their just-finished Dunham Point home. She'd open a letter from some attorney's office in Tucson. Inside she would find a check for 225,000 dollars. With tears in her eyes, she'd yell to Mark: "Little Man, we now have no mortgage ... and we can keep the camper! And we can buy us a boat!"

Back in Tucson, Cindy and Brad soon completed their dissertations, then quite successfully defended them before the UA Research Committee. After receiving their Ph.D. degrees they married, with Louis giving the bride away at a small wedding held at the Loveman farm in Boulder, Colorado. Both Cindy and Brad declined extremely lucrative job offers made by several large pharmaceutical companies interested in developing vaccines. Instead, they accepted much lower-paying jobs in the workforce at the CDC in Atlanta, Georgia. At the CDC they continued their very basic hantavirus research that would ultimately make a hantavirus vaccine possible. A very unexpected event had suddenly created a financial independence for them. This allowed them to abandon their goals of becoming wealthy through their high-tech work. They simply remained the pure research scientists they both were at heart.

Louis Loveman continued working with the FBI's Counterterrorism Division for another six months. As expected, he and his superiors were subjected to a rigorous internal investigation within the Bureau. Neither Louis nor his superiors were found guilty of any wrongdoing regarding the deaths of Cal Camarada and the three terrorists killed in the plane crash.

Though Loveman was satisfied the "hantavirus factory" in Gainesville, Georgia had been successfully shut down, he harbored another concern, one he never shared with the "Tucson civilian group" assisting him. When Louis had learned that anti-hanta immune globulin could afford temporary protection against hantavirus, a question loomed large in his mind: *Exactly where and how was Dr. Al Abbas acquiring his own supply of protective hanta-immune globulin?* With assistance from the CIA, the Bureau soon learned human hanta-immune globulin was being manufactured in Syria by a rather sophisticated al-Qaeda cell, then smuggled into the U.S. to supply Dr. Abbas. In Syria, the cell was intentionally infecting innocent local victims, the vast majority quickly dying due to lack of supportive treatment facilities. But those Syrians who survived their hanta infection were later murdered, and their total blood volume recovered to harvest the precious anti-hanta globulin their immune systems had produced while successfully fighting their illness. Exactly *how* that Syrian cell's activities were terminated remains "classified."

Feeling the threat of using hantavirus for bioterrorism inside the U.S. had been put on hold, and knowing that he'd now given the Bureau the best of his remaining years, Louis voluntarily retired from the FBI a few months later. He then moved to Tucson (along with his dog, Sampson), and lived with Shima Kye in Cal's condo. Louis even bought a Cessna 310, and began flying again. His relationship with Shima started as a platonic one, their mutual mourning over Cal's death binding them together emotionally. This eventually changed to a romantic relationship, leading to their marriage several years later.

So exactly what had caused Louis, Cindy, and Brad to redirect their lives? Most of the answers lie in a letter Louis Loveman had eventually received. It had been personally delivered to him by the attorney managing the final settlement of Cal Camarada's estate:

30 August 2001

Dear Louis,

If you are reading this it will be because

I am dead. It's going to be a long letter, so fix yourself a double scotch, kick back in your favorite recliner at the farm, and begin reading. Give Sampson a pat or two on the head for me.

I realize the line between "brave" and "stupid" is often blurred. Some could call what I did "suicide." I'll give you the facts and you can draw your own conclusion. After an extensive examination of the crash site, FAA investigators will probably reach their own conclusion. My best guess is they will decide it was "pilot error," a pilot landing at night who mistook the terminus of an uncontrolled rural runway for its beginning. I readily admit that would hurt my ego a bit, but I won't be around to give a damn about what the FAA finally decides.

Initially, I'd prefer that you, and you alone, read this letter. Under no circumstances do I want Kissimmee Aviation Services drawn into this mess. Specifically, I do not want Ben Hunter's name even mentioned. Lie about it if you have to. At my own request and personal expense, Ben flew commercial to Tucson. He picked up my 310 in Tucson at my airfield, then flew it to Gainesville. He got it squared away in a general aviation hangar at Gainesville's Lee Gilmer Memorial Airport. He had all tanks topped off with fuel as I'd requested. Ben then flew commercial back home to Kissimmee. I did not talk to Ben after he moved my 310, and he never asked me why I wanted my plane moved from Tucson to Gainesville. He knew absolutely nothing of my intended plan. Also, I'd disclosed nothing we'd discussed during our many long and private conversations over the satphone. I do appreciate you helping me accomplish my objective, even though you did so without full foreknowledge of my objective.

Preserve this letter only if it might be

important to your legal defense. Otherwise, destroy it. Let the FAA come to their conclusion, you come to yours. I simply want you to know the absolute and complete truth surrounding my death.

I am writing this a bit earlier than I'd originally planned. Let me try to explain why. In terms of follow-up care, I did everything the doctors at UMC had requested of me. That included agreeing to a number of follow-up scans they had planned. My back pain was completely relieved by their initial radiation treatments, ones I never fully completed. Even my blood tests had indicated my PSA levels were returning to near normal.

The last week in August I began having headaches, a rarity for me. They prescribed an oral medication that completely relieved the headaches. In my opinion, I felt I was as alert and physically capable as ever. Because of the headaches, my doctors insisted that I have repeat scans immediately, rather than wait for the routine ones they'd scheduled some three months away. I complied with their recommendations. They discovered I have several small tumor deposits deep inside my brain. They were in an area that couldn't be successfully cured by surgery, nor with anything else currently available anywhere. They told me no matter what was done, my mental function and motor skills would begin to deteriorate within a short period of time, probably in less than a month or two at most. My doctors had also found a number of small tumor deposits in my upper spine and several ribs, but they were creating no pain for me at the time.

Upon my receiving news that my prostate cancer had spread much more widely than originally detected, they suggested I attend an hour-long joint consultation with all of UMC's oncology doctors involved in my care. As a non-oncologist, and as a courtesy to me, even Dr. Baxter attended the conference. Options discussed ranged from "be very aggressive" to "do nothing." Dr. Earl Winger was my primary urologic oncologist. He flat out stated that I could not be cured with any treatments currently available anywhere on the planet. He was quite candid, and told me the side effects of "aggressive treatments" would be substantial. He openly said, "Chemo, additional radiation, hormonal therapy, and experimental immunotherapy will only delay the inevitable for possibly a year or two at most." Dr. Winger also said, "You'll never be able to fly again." That, my friend, is when I decided to "do nothing," except take oral medication for headaches when and if needed. That is why I'm writing this now, while I'm physically capable of it, while I know I can still fly, and my mind is still clear.

Louis, I realize what I have elected to do could destroy your career with the FBI. I realize my actions could conceivably compromise your planned and well-earned FBI retirement income, not to mention the other benefits that go along with it. That said, I see no way you would ever be criminally implicated in actions that were purely my own doing. My thoughts about my final actions were certainly unknown to you before I actually took those actions. Through our satphone conversations, I knew you thought I would be flying the terrorists to the FBI's Fayette County Detention Center (FCDC) in Kentucky. I knew that was something you had arranged with full approval from your superiors within the FBI. If you can accept a postmortem apology for my deception, I would be most grateful.

While I am seeking apology for deceptions, that brings up the subject of your daughter, Cindy. I know both you and I were a little on the "wild side" when we were young single studs first out of the Air Force. When it came to "scoring" with new girlfriends, you were always the "Ace." I knew you weren't impotent, and could "get it up." You just didn't know your semen had an extremely low count of sperm cells. You didn't know you were shooting mostly blanks! Boy, did you ever waste a lot of money on condoms while we were in Korea, as well as during your early nonmilitary life thereafter! In fact, you didn't even realize there was a fertility issue until well after your marriage to Gayle. When repeated attempts at conception left you and Gayle childless, the doctors determined you were essentially sterile. Apparently this was due to a case of childhood mumps that attacked not only your salivary glands, but your testicles' ability to produce an adequate number of sperm cells.

I clearly recall how upset you and Gayle were when doctors gave you two the bad news. For several years, fertility specialists tried concentrating your own sperm cells from a number of your own ejaculations, then used the "concentrate" to artificially inseminate Gayle. Multiple attempts failed. But the three of us agreed to do something about it. I was to become the accessory sperm donor, and Gayle was to be artificially inseminated with a mixture of semen from both of us. I also clearly remember Gayle's discouragement and her growing aversion to "artificial anything." She didn't even like artificial Christmas trees, artificial sweeteners and flavors, or even animals artificially confined by a fence! That is when we decided to try some "threesomes." And we did, a number of times. I'll have to admit Gayle was one of the most beautiful and unselfish women I've ever had sex with. I don't know any other woman so unselfish she'd agree to what we did. She did it just to give your marriage the child you both wanted. Despite Gayle's natural platinum hair, and beautiful blue eyes, I could not bring myself to have sex with your wife without your being present. I simply couldn't do that behind your back. I'll admit I was tempted, but I never did it. You were always there in bed with us, and when it was your "turn," you had orgasms just like we did. When Gayle finally announced she was pregnant with Cindy, I think I was just as excited as you were! And when that damn brain cancer took Gayle away, I think I was just as heartbroken as you were.

But this is what concerns me now. Cindy is certainly no dummy. She's possibly already figured it out, and had said nothing to either of us. As you know, before my own hair turned white, it was platinum. My eye color is the same as Cindy's. Before I died, mainly for my own peace of mind, I called in a number of "favors" from several of my doctor friends I'd earlier taught to fly. I now openly admit to you I had a little medical and genetic "snooping" discretely done. As you probably know from your military records, you have type O blood. Gayle also had type O, platinum hair and blue eyes, all recessive genetic traits. If both parents have type O blood, irrespective of their hair and eye color, they can only have children with type O. From my own Air Force records, I know my own blood type is A. I learned Cindy's blood type is A. That can mean only one thing: I am indeed her biologic father … but I want you to always be her "Daddy." I was quite content to have been Cindy's "Uncle Cal" and godfather all those years.

Feeling I wanted to communicate with Cindy one final time, I did ask Shima Kye to send an e-mail I'd composed to Cindy. I'd written it shortly before I died. In that e-mail, I openly admitted "I love you just like I would my own daughter." That was probably a very poor choice of words on my part, but there is no way I can take those words back now. So, if Cindy hasn't already figured it out, I'd prefer you leave it that way, unless, in your judgment, there is a very good reason to tell Cindy the truth. To my knowledge, the Camarada family genetic line harbors no "hereditary goblins" that could pose a predictable future health issue for Cindy.

I realize it's pitiful repayment for the many good years you've given me by saving my life while we were dogfighting MiGs in Korea. First, you were my very dearest friend. Secondly, you know I never married, and I have no living family, only a series of girlfriends most of whom were still more interested in my money than any meaningful long-term relationship. Shima Kye is the one and only exception among my numerous girlfriends. I truly loved that woman. I'd loved her since I first dated her while you and I were stationed in Korea, and she was a young teenager living near our base.

Several weeks ago, I finally got Shima back in the U.S. permanently. I'd earlier sent her a letter asking her to marry me. She'd accepted my proposal. But when she arrived here, I think I was the one who began to fully realize just how vast our age difference actually was, and I'm afraid I was the one who developed second thoughts. And now, as you know, I had grave health issues. I finally decided it just would not be fair to have her marry a dying man, no matter how great our love for each other.

Presently being of sound mind, I've decided to make you the major heir of my estate. Even I do not know its exact value, but it's in the vicinity of 800-million dollars. Of course state and federal governments will get their chunk of that, but you'll still be left a multimillionaire. At an appropriate time

262

following confirmation of my death, my attorney will contact you with the details of my will. He will also personally deliver this letter to you. In my will, you, or a bank of your choice, will direct a hefty trust fund account for your daughter, Cindy. Bradley will get my Porsche Boxster plus a smaller trust fund, and he'll never have to do menial work at RV parks to help with graduate school expenses. Shima will get my condo and a trust with sufficient funds to allow her to live there indefinitely, provided she chooses to do so. A several million dollar donation will be made to Tucson's University Medical Center. You will receive the vast bulk of the residual, so you'll still be a triple-digit multimillionaire. You can retire from the FBI any time you like. Please, buy a good plane and start flying again! I'd have left you my Cessna 310, but I had to trash it to accomplish a little off-brand justice. I'd like to think I've saved the taxpayers millions in detention costs and legal fees for terrorists. I do apologize if I've unintentionally created any legal hassles for you, but you'll have more than adequate funds for the very best of legal counsel.

Louis, I may be sticking my nose where it doesn't belong. It may be like a preacher preaching to the choir, or me telling you how to fly an F-86. I'm assuming you're going to stay on with the FBI's Counterterrorism Division, at least for a little while longer, and that you may have enough clout to change some thinking within the upper levels of our government.

For that reason, I'd like to tell you I think terrorism is the single biggest threat to our country—bigger than any natural disaster, or the alleged threat of global warming, or Earth getting hit by an asteroid. As I said, I

think our biggest threat is terrorism. I think
that mainly because of the way we're dealing
with it. It's al-Qaeda and the radical Sunni
Muslim movement calling for global jihad. I
worry more about that combination of occult
enemies than I ever did about those you and I
were fighting in Korea. I worry more about al-
Qaeda than I did back during times when our
country was dealing with the USSR during the
Cold War. At least back then, we knew exactly
where we stood. We knew exactly who we were
fighting. But not now. This al-Qaeda is a whole
different story. It operates as an enemy
without uniforms. It operates as a
multinational stateless army. Its central
leadership, if indeed there is one, is probably
scattered in Afghanistan, and only God knows
where else. Despite their lack of uniforms,
these "Jihad Soldiers" are easy to profile.
Currently, we consider "profiling" to be
"politically incorrect." That's like saying,
"Go fight them, but you can't use the single
most effective tool we have for identifying the
enemy!" They know they cannot beat us
militarily, so they have to fight dirty. When
we were in Korea, we knew the MiGs would always
have large numbers painted on the nose, and one
or more big red stars aft. Our 86s were marked
all to hell and back, even with the letters
"USAF" half-a-wing wide! Still, I didn't like
the MiG bastards, but at least they weren't
chickenshits. They'd say, "Here I am! Come and
get me if you can!"

Louis, I don't know if you believe in
premonitions or not. In fact, I don't know if
I believed in them myself. When I was first
admitted to UMC, and they were giving me IV
morphine, I kept dreaming that all hell was
soon going to break loose. I'm talking about
some major terroristic event right here in the
U.S. I realize the plan Dr. Al Abbas had for

bioterrorism using hantavirus and a crop duster could have been quite significant. It could have killed many thousands, not to mention the devastating effect it would have had on the American psyche. That's when I decided to stop Abbas myself—permanently!

After radiation controlled my pain, and I was off all drugs, I still kept having that same uneasy feeling—that same premonition—something really bad is about to happen in our country. To me, it was no longer just a dream induced by drugs. Over and over I kept thinking it will involve airplanes. Those thoughts didn't surprise me because airplanes have essentially been my whole life. But then I questioned myself: If I really wanted to do something terroristic, exactly how would I do it? I finally decided I'd take some additional flight training and learn how to fly one of the "big boys," maybe a 767. I'd then hijack a commercial jet loaded with 25,000 gallons of fuel for an international flight. Then, I'd intentionally crash it into some major U.S. city's high-population buildings, or maybe even into the nation's capital building itself. Maybe I went paranoid or schizophrenic on you, but I honestly think this could easily be done.

Unfortunately, some of our flight schools are not as conscientious as they should be about selecting the students they train. For example, that Abdul Aleem, the crop duster pilot for Al Abbas, should never have been allowed to train in any U.S. flight school. At least I hope I have guaranteed Aleem will never fly another terror mission. I realize the FBI probably doesn't take advice from dead folks, so I'm asking you to personally be sure your men keep a close eye on our U.S. flight schools—especially the backgrounds and motives of people who attend those schools.

As a final request (as specified in my will)

I'd like my ashes taken to Gainesville, Georgia for their final resting place. Just scatter them at my 310's crash site. Before I died, just realizing I could take three terrorists out with me gave me goose bumps! I sincerely hope they get the 72 virgins they expected. I've already gotten more than my share of them while living. My only regrets are that I've left behind the very best friend any wartime pilot could ever have had, plus a very beautiful young woman with half my DNA, and an Asian woman I truly loved.

Unfortunately, I felt I had to destroy my perfectly good airplane in the process of departing this world with a clear conscience.

Forever grateful — Cal